BETTING ON YOU

**Also by
Lynn Painter**

Better Than the Movies
The Do-Over

BETTING ON YOU

LYNN PAINTER

SIMON & SCHUSTER

First published in Great Britain in 2024 by Simon & Schuster UK Ltd

First published in the USA in 2023 by Simon & Schuster Books for Young Readers, an
imprint of Simon & Schuster Children's Publishing Division,
1230 Avenue of the Americas, New York, New York 10020

3 5 7 9 10 8 6 4 2

Simon & Schuster UK Ltd
1st Floor, 222 Gray's Inn Road
London WC1X 8H

Simon & Schuster: Celebrating 100 Years of Publishing in 2024

www.simonandschuster.co.uk
www.simonandschuster.com.au
www.simonandschuster.co.in

Simon & Schuster Australia, Sydney
Simon & Schuster India, New Delhi

A CIP catalogue record for this book is available from the British Library.

PB ISBN 978-1-3985-3647-0
eBook ISBN 978-1-3985-3646-3
eAudio ISBN 978-1-3985-3645-6

Printed and Bound in the UK using
100% Renewable Electricity at CPI Group (UK) Ltd

MIX
Paper | Supporting
responsible forestry
FSC® C171272

This book is dedicated to the late Nora Ephron—
the greatest rom-com writer of all time and
the queen mother of autumnal comfort movies.

And to the readers who create playlists,
aesthetic boards, and full-on edits—everyone should be
so lucky as to connect with stories in such an immersive way.

CHAPTER ONE

THREE YEARS AGO

Bailey

The first time I met Charlie was at the airport in Fairbanks.

My dad had just said goodbye, so I was swallowing down heavy emotion as I left behind life as I knew it and prepared to fly to Nebraska, where my mother and I would now be living since my parents had officially separated. I lifted my chin and attempted to channel *maturity* as I traversed the airport with my rolling pink carry-on, but every blink of my eyes held back a weighted homesickness for the place and the memories I was leaving behind.

It was when I got stuck in a long line of people waiting to go through security, sandwiched between strangers and stressing over whether or not my braces were going to set off the metal detector, that we made contact.

The line started moving, but I couldn't take a step because the two people in front of me were kissing. Hard-core. As if their mouths were fused together and they were desperately trying to pull them apart by turning their heads from side to side.

Or else they were eating each other's faces off.

I cleared my throat.

Nothing.

I cleared my throat again.

Which made the guy open his eyes—I could only see one eye—and look directly at me. *While still kissing the girl.* As if that wasn't weird enough, he said *to me* while his lips were still attached to hers, *"Oh my God—what?"*

Which sounded like *omiguhdwhruut.*

And then The Eye closed and they were full-on kissing again.

"Excuse me," I said through gritted teeth, my emotional anxiety replaced by irritation, "but the line. The line is moving."

The Eye opened again and the dude glared at me. He lifted his mouth and said something to his girlfriend that prompted them to actually move forward. *Finally.* I heard his girlfriend chirp about how much she was going to miss him, and I could see by his profile that he was kind of half smiling and not saying anything as they stumbled forward, hand in hand.

But I couldn't get past the fact that they looked like they were my age.

What?

I was going into my freshman year. Of high school. People my age didn't make out in public; they couldn't even drive yet. People my age didn't have the audacity to totally *get after it* in the airport security line, where they could get in trouble.

So who *were* these obnoxious PDA renegades?

The girl stepped out of line and waved to the guy, probably relieved to finally be getting oxygen. After making it through security and reorganizing my things, I checked the time on my phone. I wanted to be right next to the door when the Jetway opened, so it was imperative that I get there as quickly as possible. I went around the face-eating jackass as he looked down at his phone, and I walked as fast as I could toward the departure gate.

It wasn't until I took a seat *right* next to the check-in counter, where I couldn't miss any pertinent announcements and would be guaranteed a spot at the very front of the line, that I was finally able to calm my nerves.

I scrolled through my phone, checked the airline's app for updates, then put on my headphones and cued up the freshly curated *Bailey's Airplane Playlist*. But as I sat back and watched the other travelers milling about the terminal, I couldn't help but wonder how many of *them* were being forced to go somewhere they didn't want to go and start a new life they had no interest in beginning.

If I were a betting person, I'd say zero.

I had to be the only person in that entire airport who was going on what was the polar opposite of a trip. I had a ticket to my own transplantation, and it sucked. I dwelled on this for the entirety of the hour wait, especially when Adorable Family of Four plopped down across from me, looking like poster children for the Disney resorts as they bounced around with palpable travel enthusiasm.

The sight of their familial bliss made me want to snuggle with the tiny scrap of blankie I still slept with (even though no

3

one knew) and cry just a little.

So to say I was tightly wound by the time we lined up to board would be an understatement. I was first in line—*hell yes*—but buzzing with my *own* brand of palpable energy. My gurgling turmoil saw Adorable Family's enthusiasm and raised the pot by a hundred.

"Hey, you."

I looked to my left, and there was the face-eating jackass from security, smiling at me as if we were friends.

"I looked everywhere for you, babe."

I glanced behind me at the rest of the boarding line, because he couldn't possibly be talking to me. But when I turned back around, he was actually moving marginally closer, forcing me to take a step over so he could stand beside me. He nudged my shoulder with his and winked.

What in the actual hell? *Was he high?*

"What are you doing?" I whispered, clutching the strap of my carry-on bag as I tried scooting away from him while still maintaining my First in Line status. He was wearing a hoodie that said *Mr. Nothing*, with baggy shorts, and he didn't have a single thing in his hands. No carry-on, no book, no coat; what kind of person traveled like that?

He moved even closer, so his face was about an inch from mine, and said under his breath, "Relax, Glasses. I just don't want to wait in that line, so I'm making it look like we're together."

"But." I looked at him and wondered who Mr. Nothing actually was. He was obviously my age-ish and a generally attractive human. He had thick, dark, careless hair and a nice mouth. But his

4

nerve was just too huge for a normal boy. "That's not fair."

He raised an eyebrow.

"Everyone else has to wait in line," I said, trying not to sound like a child screaming *It's not fair* while kind of wanting to throw elbows. "If you didn't want to wait, you should've gotten here earlier."

"Like you?" he asked, his tone thick with sarcasm.

I pushed up my glasses. "Yes, like me."

Why is this total stranger messing with me? Was this karma for daydreaming about Adorable Family being stranded at the airport? Karma was supposed to be a cat, dammit, not *this*.

He tilted his head to the side and looked at me. "I bet you used to be a hall monitor."

"Excuse me?" It was obvious he meant it in an insulting way, and I was torn between wanting to punch him in the face and wanting to sobbingly beg him to leave me alone. I glanced behind us again, and the man next in line was smirking, clearly eavesdropping. I turned back to Mr. Nothing and whispered, "Not that it's any of your business, but everyone had to take a turn at my school."

"Sure they did."

Sure they did? I made a noise, sort of a growl mixed with a groan, before fleetingly wondering if punching a fellow passenger was a federal offense.

"Are you . . . Do you not believe me?" I asked through gritted teeth. "About *hall* monitoring?"

He smirked. "It's not that I don't believe you; it's that we both know you would've signed up whether it was mandatory or not."

How would he know that? He wasn't wrong, but it pissed me off that he behaved as if he knew me, when our relationship spanned five awful minutes. I was squinting and my nose was scrunched up like something smelled bad, but it was physically impossible to unsquinch it. I managed to bite out, "Whatever."

He stopped talking but didn't move; he just stayed put, right where he was. We both stood there, side by side, staring in front of us in silence. *Why isn't he moving? He's not going to stay here, is he??* After another long minute of non-speak, I couldn't take it and very nearly shouted the words "Why are you still here?"

He seemed confused by my question. "What?"

I pointed my thumb over my shoulder, and he said, "Oh my God, you were serious about that? You're going to make me go to the back?"

I breathed in through my nose. "*I'm* not making you. It's the way things work."

"Oh, well, if it's the way things work . . ." He looked at me like I was an idiot.

The airline employee who'd been standing beside the door grabbed the speaker and began announcing our flight. I gave Mr. Nothing another pointed look, the patented *WTF are you doing* look, punctuated with bug eyes, which made him shake his head and step out of line.

He looked at the guy behind me and said, "It's the way things work; don't worry about it."

And even though I refused to turn around and watch him, I heard him mutter "It's the way things work" no less than five times as he made his way to the back of the line.

Whyyyyyyy? Why was this smug, sarcastic jerk even part of my experience? *He's ruining flying for me,* I thought as I scanned my boarding pass and started down the Jetway, which was ironic when flying was the *only* thing I didn't hate about the day.

My first time flying alone was the one teensy-tiny thing that I'd been excited about, and Assbag Zero seemed determined to destroy that.

I didn't relax until we were boarded, my bag was stowed in the overhead compartment, I'd texted both my parents, and I was seated next to the window. People were still getting settled, but I'd made it. I'd been stressed all day, but now—ahhh. I closed my eyes and felt like I could finally exhale.

Until.

"What are the odds that we'd be seat neighbors?"

I opened my eyes, and there was Mr. Nothing, standing in the aisle, his mouth hard as he looked just as happy to see me as I was to see him.

CHAPTER TWO

Charlie

As if my day wasn't shitty enough, my seat was right next to Little Miss The-Line-Is-Moving.

Wonderful.

She gazed up at me with big eyes and blinked fast, like she was shocked to see me, but she looked like one of those uptight girls who was *always* shocked when life wasn't perfect. She crossed her arms over her chest and said, "One in a hundred and seventy-five, I would guess."

For some reason, she made me want to mockingly repeat her words in a high-pitched voice. *One in a hundred and seventy-five, I would guess.* I looked longingly at the rows behind ours, stretching toward the back of the plane, and wondered if anyone would be interested in swapping seats.

Also—*of course* that girl knew the number of seats in the plane. The second I sat down, the phone in my hoodie pouch buzzed. I knew it was my mom, and I also knew that if I didn't respond, she would keep sending messages.

I pulled it out and looked at the display.

Mom: Did you make it on time?

I leaned back a little in the cramped seat, way too fucking tall for flying.

I hated flying.

I replied: **Yes.**

I buckled my seat belt, but before I could even let out a sigh, my phone buzzed again. **Mom: Did your dad go in with you, or just drop you at the door?**

I reached into my pocket, needing a TUM already. After I popped two into my mouth, I ignored her question (because no good could come of the answer—*dropped me at the door because parking was too expensive*) and texted: **Nana Marie said to tell you hi.**

I knew that would stop the texts.

My mother and my grandmother had always been close, but as soon as my parents decided to divorce, that was history. Now my mom referred to her as "the old battle-axe," and Nana Marie called my mother "that woman."

Mature adults, right?

I rested my head on the back of the seat and tried to wrap my mind around the fact that summer was over. It seemed like *days* ago that I'd been pumped to fly to Alaska and spend the summer with my dad's family, but now here I was, leaving them (and Grace) behind, flying back to life with my mom and her new boyfriend.

I was too damn old to feel this fucking homesick, especially when the plane hadn't even taken off yet.

I felt a dull ache between my ribs as I pictured Grace, and I swear to God I could still smell the fruity mousse she used in her hair. My brain took off on an unwelcome montage that captured a summer full of Grace's laughter, and I gritted my teeth.

Fuck *me*.

I put the phone back in my pocket, even though all I wanted to do was get lost in one of our mindless exchanges.

But there was no point in texting Grace. Like, ever again. Because relationships failed on a daily basis when people lived in the same fucking house. Relationships were doomed to fail *period*.

So the mere notion of a long-distance one? Total joke.

The only good that could come from staying in contact with Grace was that I might finally be depressed enough to take up songwriting or flirt with drinking.

Walking away—no, flying away—was absolutely the way to go.

One of the flight attendants started on the safety checklist, and I glanced over at Hall Monitor. She was attractive, but the braces and poofy hair weren't doing her any favors. Her arms were still crossed, and she was listening so intently that I half expected her to pull out a binder and start taking notes.

Yeah, it was time to mess with her.

Messing with her in the boarding line had actually taken my mind off Grace for a few minutes, so perhaps it was karma that had assigned her uptight ass to the seat beside me. I'd been good all summer, so maybe karma knew I needed a distraction.

Maybe karma was a girl in glasses.

CHAPTER THREE

Bailey

"How much do you think she gets paid?"

"Shh." I tried tuning out Mr. Nothing so I could hear the flight attendant's emergency instructions.

"Oh, come on—you're not actually listening to this, are you?"

I refused to look at him. "Please be quiet."

"Everybody knows that if the shit goes down, we're dead." His voice was deep and rumbly as he murmured, "They go through these motions to give passengers a false sense of hope, but the reality is that if the plane crashes, our bodies are going to be splattered for miles."

"Good Lord." I did look at him then, because there was something seriously wrong with Mr. Nothing. "What is your problem?"

He shrugged. "I don't have a problem—I'm just a realist. I see things for what they really are. You, on the other hand—you probably believe this shit. You probably think that if the plane hits the ocean at Mach five, that inflatable seat is going to save your ass, right?"

I pushed my glasses up my nose and wished he'd stop talking about crashing. I wasn't scared, but it also didn't make a bit of sense to me how an object as heavy as a plane could stay in the sky. "It could."

He gave his head a slow shake, as if I were the world's biggest fool. "Oh my God, you are precious. You're like a sweet baby child who believes everything her mommy tells her."

"I am *not* precious!"

"Are too."

Why couldn't I have been seated beside a mature businessman or Visor Man in front of me, who was already asleep? Hell, the screaming baby squalling somewhere in the back would've been a better choice.

"No, I'm not," I said, irritated by how whiny I sounded but unable to stop myself. But this guy was really pissing me off. "And just because you say shocking things like *Oh, this plane could crash* doesn't make you edgy or any more of a realist than I am."

"Oh yeah?" He turned a little in his seat, so he was facing me, and he pointed to my carry-on. "I bet you put all of your liquids in a baggie before you hit security, right?"

"Um, that's actually the law," I said, unwilling to let the guy think he was hot shit, "so that doesn't mean a thing."

"It's not the law; it's just a stupid rule that isn't going to do dick to save us from a terrorist attack."

"So you don't follow the rule?"

"Nope."

Bullshit, I thought. No way did this guy—a minor, like me—disregard the laws of the skies. He was full of crap for sure. I humored him, though, and asked, "Then how do you transport your liquids?"

"However I want." He gave a half shrug and looked utterly relaxed as he lied, and I was jealous of his confidence. Even if the guy was a compulsive liar, I wished I were that comfortable in my skin. He said, "Sometimes I put a few in my carry-on if I have one, sometimes I pack the full-sized bottles in my checked bag, and today I even stuck a shampoo in my pocket just for fun."

"You did not," I said, unable to let that one go.

He pulled a trial-sized Suave from the pocket of his shorts. "Did too."

"No *way.*" To my horror, a laugh gurgled out of me. I raised my hand to my mouth, quick to cover any evidence that Mr. Nothing was the teensiest bit amusing. "Why do you do these things?"

Damn my curiosity.

"Because it feels good to know I'm besting them."

"Which *them* are you besting, exactly?" I asked, absolutely torn between amusement and annoyance. "The security people? The terrorists? The Man?"

"Yes."

I rolled my eyes and pulled my book out of my purse, desperately hoping he'd take the hint and do anything other than talk to me. It worked until takeoff, but once we were in the air, he turned toward me in his seat and said, "So."

I flipped my book over onto my lap. "We don't have to talk, y'know."

"But I can't turn on my phone yet, so I'm bored."

"You could sleep."

"I'd rather talk." He gave me a closed-mouth smile that confirmed he was *trying* to be irritating. "So how long have your parents been divorced?"

I almost gasped, but I caught myself. *How does he know they're separating?*

And why did the finality of the word "divorced" still make my stomach hurt?

I looked down at the cut-up red heart on the cover of the book. "What makes you think my parents are divorced?"

"Come on, Glasses—it's textbook," he said, drumming his fingers on the armrest as he spoke. "The only kids who fly alone are custody kids. Fly to see the parent you don't live with, fly back from a visit, fly to see the grandparents of the parent you no longer live with . . ."

I swallowed and rubbed my eyebrow, wanting to tell him to shut up because I didn't like the picture he was painting. *Would* I become some sort of "custody kid," racking up frequent-flier miles while getting to know flight attendants on a first-name basis? It'd never occurred to me that I'd have to do this whole sad solo flight more than once after everything was finalized.

God, I still wasn't ready to talk about it, to use the d-word in regards to my parents.

Especially not with Mr. Nothing. I asked, "Does that mean yours are? Divorced?"

He gave me meaningful eye contact then, a look that was almost conversational as our eyes held, and it made me think he might actually be something more than a jackass. But just like that, the look slammed shut and the smart-ass was back. "Oh yeah. They officially divorced six months ago, and this is the third time I've flown solo since then."

I didn't want to be part of the custody kids club; I didn't even want to know it existed. I wanted my life to be normal again, not some surreal version that had me alone on a ten-hour flight, sitting next to a cynical teen divorce expert, when I should be at home in my childhood bedroom.

"Still in denial, huh?" He looked at me like I really *was* a precious gullible child, and he said, "I remember that. You think if you don't identify with your new role, maybe it won't stick. Like if you click your heels together and say, 'There's no place like home,' you might somehow trick the universe into missing the change and resetting your life back to normal, right?"

I felt a hot burn in my stomach as he said that, a radiating heat as he perfectly described my emotions. I cleared my throat and said, "You don't know anything about me. I'm sure it sucks being a 'custody' kid, and I'm truly sorry. Now can I please read my book?"

He shrugged and said, "I'm not stopping you."

I started reading, but it wasn't really the escape I was hoping for because I kept glancing over to make sure he wasn't going to start talking again. I knew it was coming—I wasn't lucky enough to be left alone—and that made it impossible to relax. Especially when he was sitting ramrod-straight in his seat, looking ready to pounce, and his thumbs were tapping on the armrests like he couldn't sit still.

My eyes ran over the words on the page, which were good but apparently not good enough for me to forget about Mr. Nothing and the "new" life that awaited me when we landed. I was working so hard at comprehending what I was reading that I gasped in surprise when the flight attendant stopped at my aisle to see if I wanted a drink.

"And for you, hon?"

"Oh. Could I please have half Coke, half Diet Coke, mixed together in a cup? With no ice, please?"

I could feel Mr. Nothing's head swivel toward me.

The attendant looked irritated, like it was ridiculous that a kid was asking her for something. She said, "You have to pick one or the other. You can't have both."

"I, um, I don't actually want both, really." I gave her what I hoped was a polite smile. "See, since you're pouring the sodas for the passengers instead of just handing out cans, the remaining halves won't get wasted. So I'd like you to just pour a little of each into mine, instead of just one. It will still be the same amount of liquid, just comprising two components."

I glanced at Mr. Nothing, and he was smiling, his attention fully on me. His eyes were twinkling, like he was watching his favorite TV show, and I could tell he was holding back a thousand sarcastic comments.

The attendant gave me my halfsy pop, and I thanked her. I could tell I wasn't welcome. I took a sip and was swallowing when he said, "Now I see it. You're a labor-intensive kind of girl."

"What? What do you mean?"

"Labor-intensive." He looked like he had me entirely figured out, like he'd solved the puzzle. "A girl who requires a lot of work. You want a drink, but you want two different kinds mixed together. And no ice."

"That's just how I like it," I said, trying to sound breezy and *not* defensive as he went into full-on know-it-all mode.

"Sure." He crossed his arms over his chest and said, "But labor-intensive is your way."

"No, it's not," I said, a little too loudly as I lost the battle with my patience.

"Sure it is. You have to stand in the front of the boarding line an hour before takeoff because you need a window seat. You excel at hall monitoring. I bet when they pass out dinner later, yours will be just a little bit different than everyone else's, right?"

I blinked and didn't want to respond.

He grinned. "I'm right—I see it on your face. Vegetarian?"

I sighed and wished for a time machine so I could go back and *not* engage with Mr. Nothing in the security line. "I requested a vegetarian meal, yes."

He looked genuinely happy for the first time since we'd met, and said, "*Of course* you're a vegetarian."

"I'm not a vegetarian," I said, absolutely *thrilled* by his wrongness.

He lowered his dark brows. "Then why did you order the vegetarian meal?"

I tucked my hair behind my ears, raised my chin, and said, "Because I find airline meat to be questionable."

That earned me another arrogant half smile. He said, "See? Labor-intensive."

"Shh."

I lifted my book and tried reading, but I took in only two sentences before Mr. Nothing said, "Want to know how it ends?"

"What?"

"Your book."

I glanced at him over my glasses. "You've read *this*?"

He shrugged. "Basically."

I wanted to call bullshit, but instead I just said, "How is that an answer?"

He swirled the soda around in his glass. "I read the summary and then I read the last three chapters."

Of course you did. Annoyance slid through me as I said, "Why would you do that?"

He lifted the cup to his mouth. "I wanted to know if the alcoholic guy dies at the end, and once I knew the answer, I didn't want to read any more."

"Oh my God." I seriously didn't know where Mr. Nothing got all that nerve, but it was irritating as hell. He was like the polar opposite of the "manic pixie dream girl" in a movie. Instead of being used by writers to bring a character out of their comfort zone, Mr. Nothing was being used by the universe to piss me off and make me grumpier than I already was. "Why would you ruin it for me? Who does that?"

"What? I didn't tell you anything."

"Yes, you did." I took another sip of my soda, annoyed by his spoiler, and said, "If he didn't die, you would've kept reading."

"How do you know? Maybe I like death and didn't want to read a book with a happy ending."

"That actually wouldn't surprise me," I said, absolutely meaning it. If anyone were to find enjoyment in a death book with an unhappy ending, it'd be Mr. Nothing. He seemed to get off on going against the grain.

"So read on," he said, giving a chin nod to my book.

I bristled. "I will."

I pretended to read for a few minutes while my brain had a tiny freak-out over Mr. Nothing. He was like the cherry on top of my dumpster-life sundae, and it was absurdly on-brand that I would be subjected to him on the very flight that was taking me to my unwanted new life.

I was thrilled when he got up to go to the restroom. I put on headphones so that when he came back, I couldn't hear his ridiculous observations anymore.

It was brilliant.

He seemed to be immersed in his phone once he got back, and I managed a few hours of silent reading before the attendants brought out dinner and the words "Your vegetable lasagna is here" punched me in the earholes.

I yanked my headphones off and away from him, looked up, and grabbed the tray from the attendant. "Thank you."

I waited for a snarky comment from the seat to my left, and when it didn't come, I took a bite of the lasagna and looked at him. He was texting, his attention hyperfocused on his phone, and I could see from the contact picture that it was his girlfriend.

I couldn't imagine anyone wanting to date him. Even though he was relatively attractive, he dripped with cynical sarcasm. Which made me curious about her. What was the girl like who loved Mr. Nothing? She was pretty—what I'd seen of her—but her taste was obviously questionable.

Before I could stop myself, I asked him, "Does she live in Alaska?"

He looked up from his phone, and a wrinkle formed between his eyebrows. "Who?"

I pointed my fork at the screen. "Your girlfriend."

He gave me side-eye and set his phone next to the food on his tray. "If you must know, Miss Nosy, she does. She's a Fairbanks girl."

"Oh." I felt bad for him—a little—because leaving someone you love behind felt like utter shit.

"But she's not my girlfriend." He cut into his chicken, took a bite, and moaned—while staring directly into my eyes like a sociopath—"Oh my God, this questionable meat is so delicious!"

I just sighed.

He grinned, pleased with himself, and said, "I live in Nebraska and spent the summer in Alaska with my cousins. I hung out with her a lot, but I'm not really into the long-distance thing."

I swallowed and pictured him kissing the face off Fairbanks Girl. "Does she know that?"

He shrugged and said, "She will."

What a jerk. The poor girl had probably cried all the way home, devastated to see him go, while he shrugged and said, *She will.* I took another bite and couldn't stop myself from saying, "Are you at least going to tell her?"

That made one of his dark eyebrows go up. "What are you—worried about her or something?"

It was my turn to shrug, even though I kind of wanted to rage in Fairbank Girl's stead. "I just think leaving her hanging is a garbage thing to do."

"Really." He picked up his soda and took a long drink before asking, "What would *you* do?"

I wiped my mouth with my napkin. "Well, um, I'd be forthright, for starters. I'd tell her—"

"Did you just say 'forthright'?" He grinned like I was hilarious as he set his plastic cup on the tray. "Who says that? I mean, my grandma probably does, but no one under the age of—"

"Forget it," I interrupted, amazed that the annoyance I felt for this boy kept cranking up to newer and more intense levels.

"Oh, come on. Please continue." He reined in his smile, but his eyes were still twinkling. "I'm sorry."

"No, you're not."

"I am, I swear. Please—tell me what you'd do. I really want to know."

"Nope."

"Pleeeease?"

I rubbed the back of my neck. "Fine. I would tell her what you said about not wanting to do the long-distance thing, but I'd say it nicely enough where we could still be friends. After all, you'll probably go back to your cousins' house again someday, right?"

"Sure," he said, leaning back so he could reach into the

pocket of his jeans and pull out a . . . *TUM?*

Is that a TUM? What was he, a sixty-year-old grandfather of five? And he was making fun of me for seeming "old."

He popped it into his mouth while I asked him, "So wouldn't it be nice if you could be her friend when you fly into Fairbanks, instead of the jerk who broke her heart?"

His mouth went up a little—only on one side—and his eyes narrowed. He stared at me for a long moment, chewing the antacid tablet, and then he said, "Guys and girls can't be friends."

And he said it as if it was a definitive, indisputable fact.

Which it wasn't. I had guy friends (sort of), and I knew plenty of other girls who did too. I wondered if he was just one of those guys who liked having controversial opinions.

"Yes, they can," I said, narrowing my eyes and waiting for him to argue.

"Nope," he said. Like it was scientific data instead of his own antiquated opinion.

"Yep, actually," I said, setting my napkin on top of the piece of flavorless lasagna, unwilling to let his ludicrous statement stand. "I have guy friends."

He gave his head a shake. "No, you don't."

"Yes, I do," I said, defensively and through gritted teeth, because who was he to act like he knew what kind of friends I had? I cleared my throat and added, "A lot of them, actually."

"You do not." He took another bite of his chicken, and took the time to chew and swallow before calmly adding, "You have guys that you know. They're probably nice to you. But they will never be legitimate friends to you—period. That's impossible."

I thought about this for a half second before saying, "Okay—I don't for a millisecond agree or even consider the non-merits of what you're saying, but why on earth do you believe this utter nonsense?"

"I heard it first in a movie. Ever seen *When Harry Met Sally*?"

"No," I said, but I had a vivid memory of my parents watching it on DVD. My dad loved it, but I remembered my mom saying it was boring and a little too "talkie," whatever that meant.

"It's this movie that my mom loved," he said, looking like he, too, was in the middle of a memory. "So I was forced as a kid to watch it with her like a hundred times. The dude in the movie—Harry—says men and women can't be friends, and it's always stuck with me because he's totally right."

"No, he's—"

"Take you, for example," he continued, as if I hadn't spoken. "You're a relatively attractive human female, so biologically, the human males want to score with you. If they're single and hanging out with you, they actually want to be getting down with you."

"Oh my God!" I said, half-surprised he'd called me "relatively attractive" when he seemed irritated by my existence, and half-outraged by the absurdity of his words. "You are so wrong. Not all guys are Neanderthals."

"No, I'm a guy—trust me on this." He lowered his voice and said, "I mean, I've already pictured every relatively attractive human female on this flight naked two or three times, and we aren't even close to landing."

"Oh.My.God." My mouth dropped open and I couldn't bring myself to close it. Was he seriously that big a pervert?

23

Also—did guys really do that?

"And before you say, *But my friend Jeff is in a happy relationship and we hang all the time*," he said, plucking the straw wrapper from his tray and folding it into tiny triangles, "know that little Jeffy will slowly unfriend you because his girlfriend will be pissed if he doesn't. She'll wonder why he needs you when he's got her. And truthfully, part of him probably *does* want you too, so he'll either make a move on you and totally screw the pooch, or he'll save you for his spank bank and remain true to his girl. Either way it will always *be* there, making friendship a complete impossibility."

My mouth was still hanging wide open, the same as if he'd just confessed to murdering his parents. I stared at his self-satisfied grin and couldn't believe he'd *ever* had a girlfriend.

"And the bottom line is that none of it really matters anyway." His voice was sure as he dropped the paper and said, "Relationships are doomed to fail. The odds are greater that you'll be diagnosed with a deadly illness than live happily ever after with the love of your life."

"You might be the biggest cynic I've ever met," I said, hating that a tiny part of me worried he was right about relationships being doomed to fail.

"I'm a realist." He looked very matter-of-fact as he pointed to my tray and said, "Are you going to eat your garlic bread?"

"Take it," I muttered, praying a good tailwind would push us toward Nebraska a little faster.

I couldn't wait for the flight to be over so I would never have to see Mr. Nothing again.

CHAPTER FOUR

ONE YEAR AGO

Bailey

The next time I saw Charlie was at a movie theater. I was there with Zack, my boyfriend, and we'd just paid for our tickets when we heard clapping from the lobby area by concessions.

"Want to check it out?" Zack looked at his phone and said, "We've still got five minutes before the movie starts."

"Sure." I smiled at his handsome face, and he grabbed my hand, leading me toward the fray. I was head over heels for Zack, the cute and oh-so-smart debate captain. He was everything I wasn't—confident, charming, extroverted—and he technically could've led me into fire, and I probably would have followed.

"It's a promposal." Zack pointed just to the left of the popcorn stand, where someone had hung a fake movie poster. Instead of a title, it said "PROM?" Across the top there was a picture of a dude with a hilarious questioning expression on his face.

It was charming and clever, and just as I narrowed my eyes

and thought, *That guy looks really familiar*, I saw the couple. They were standing in front of the poster, smiling as a movie theater employee took their picture. The girl was petite, blond, and pretty, and the guy was tall, dark, and kind of jacked.

Oh my God—Mr. Nothing!

The guy from the airport was *right there*, at *my* suburban movie theater. What in the actual hell?

"Cool idea," Zack said about the promposal, and I nodded and came back to myself.

"Supercute," I muttered, flustered, and at that moment Mr. Nothing's eyes connected with mine, and my stomach dropped to the floor. We shared total eye contact for a second before I looked away and said *way too enthusiastically* to Zack, "We'd better go."

I wasn't exactly sure why, but I didn't want to have to share conversation with Mr. Nothing *and* Zack; it seemed like too much.

Which made no sense. The dude was just a stranger that I'd sat beside on a long flight. There was no reason whatsoever that I should be anxious about running into him.

Still, I was.

I very nearly dragged Zack into the theater, and chose seats that were far away from everyone else. We were seeing a revival of *The Good and the Best*, my all-time favorite movie, but once it started, I found I just couldn't get into it.

Seeing Mr. Nothing left me . . . unsettled.

Maybe it was his tie-in to the shitty time in my life when my parents fell out of love, we moved to a strange place, and my dad stopped caring about me. I still couldn't listen to the Taylor Swift album that'd been popular at the time, because it made me cry.

Every. Single. Time.

Hell, the day of that flight, just before I'd slid into line behind Mr. Nothing, I'd cried my eyes out in the airport bathroom.

No wonder the sight of him was accompanied by a general sense of dread.

"Are you hungry?" Zack whispered. "I'm going to go get popcorn."

"No," I said, glancing at him and thinking he was even hot in the dark. It was still surreal that we were together, if I was being honest. Not that I didn't believe in my own self-worth, but we were two very different people from two very different leagues.

Most of my friends—except the three who went to my school—were fellow book nerds that I'd never actually met in real life. Aside from the content we created and shared on our social channels, I shared my deepest secrets with them and felt like they knew me better than anyone else in the world.

But our friendships were remote.

Zack, on the other hand, seemingly knew everyone at our school and appeared to *enjoy* socializing with them. On a daily basis.

Weird, right?

"I'll do it," I whispered, "because I don't want you to miss anything."

"You sure?" he asked, his eyes on the big screen.

"Definitely—I've seen this a hundred times."

Honestly, I was happy for the escape from the depressing memories that Mr. Nothing had kicked up. I scooted past Zack and exited the theater, and the lobby was quiet except for the concession line, which was three people deep. I took my spot, and was there a mere two minutes before I heard, "Boo."

No, no, no, no.

I braced myself before turning around and looking at Mr. Nothing. He was definitely taller and more mannish than he'd been on the flight, but that *I know everything about you* look in his eyes hadn't changed at all. I felt a weight on my chest as he looked at me, and I knew there was no escaping the reunion.

I tucked my hair behind my ears and plastered a fake smile onto my face. "Hey. How *are* you?"

He said, "Great," the exact second I said, "Congrats on the prom yes, by the way."

We shared the awkward we-both-spoke-at-the-same-time chuckle, and he said, "Thanks. Although to be honest, it was a slam dunk. We've been together for over a year."

I laughed.

He looked at me in confusion.

I stopped laughing and said, "Wait. You're serious?"

"Yeah." He did a little shoulder-shrug motion—God, I remembered his propensity for careless shrugging like we'd *just* been on the plane together—and said, "Our anniversary was last month."

I laughed again; I couldn't help it. *Was* he serious?

"What's funny?" He looked like he genuinely didn't understand.

"It's just . . . I don't know . . . It's just so *hopeful* of you," I explained, remembering his definitive (depressing) opinions on relationships. "On the plane, you told me relationships are pointless and we've got a better chance of being struck with Ebola than finding happily ever after."

The corner of his mouth slid up into a flirtatious smirk, and he gave me a chin nod. "You remembered what I said on the plane, huh?"

"I did," I said, unable to believe that the jerk was taking my remembrance of his idiotic words to be some sort of compliment. "Because it was asinine. Your theories were so *stupid* that it was impossible for me to forget them."

"You've been thinking of me for all these years?" He looked like he absolutely believed that as he tilted his head and said, "That's nice, Glasses."

I gave my head a shake and opened my mouth, but I literally could not think of a response to his arrogance.

And he knew that, because his smirk transformed into a full-on smile of amusement. "And regarding my thoughts on relationships, what can I say? I've evolved."

"Sure you have."

The line moved forward, and I screamed internally for it to move faster and end my torture.

"What about you?" Mr. Nothing's eyes ran all over me before returning to my face. "Is Poofy Hair your boyfriend?"

Don't give him the satisfaction, Bailey. I glanced around before *calmly* saying, "He does *not* have poofy hair."

"I stand corrected," he said, putting his hands into his

29

pockets. "Is Sweater from Baby Gap your boyfriend?"

I rolled my eyes, which was something I rarely did anymore. My mother called it rude, and she was right, but I couldn't hold back when in the presence of Mr. Annoying. I said, "Zack, the guy you saw me with whose sweater fits him just right, by the way, is, in fact, my boyfriend."

"Did you tell him about us?" he asked, his lips turning back into that sarcastic half smile.

"What?" I felt my eyebrows squeeze together in what seemed to be my default response—aside from the eye rolling—to Mr. Nothing. "No. I mean, there is no 'us' to even tell him about."

"You could've told him we're old friends," he suggested. "I'm the friend you flew across the country with."

"I thought you said guys and girls couldn't be friends." I crossed my arms over my chest and felt a wave of satisfaction surge through me as I threw his words back at him.

"What? When did I say that?"

He looked genuinely confused, and I was more than happy to remind him of his ridiculousness. "You told me that on the flight from Fairbanks."

"Wonder why I said that." He barely paused before adding, "Actually, that's pretty accurate. They totally cannot."

"Can I help you?"

I stepped up to the counter and looked at the guy who was waiting for me to order. "Yes. Um, could I please have one small plain popcorn and one small buttered?"

"No problem." He started punching my order into the register.

"Can you please pour them into a large tub?"

"Together . . . ?" The guy looked at me like I was weird, but he was still smiley. "Sure."

I thought I heard a snort from behind me.

"And can you please not shake them up?" My cheeks were warm as I quietly added, "Thank you."

"Labor-intensive," Mr. Nothing muttered, but I refused to look in his direction.

"Can I also get two large Cokes?"

"Of course," the snack attendant said.

And as soon as he stepped over to the popcorn machine, Mr. Nothing nudged my arm with his and said, "You're not getting a halfsy Coke?"

"Not today," I said, even though I *really* wanted one. I knew he'd think he was right about the whole "labor-intensive" thing if I ordered one, so I *had* to deny myself.

"I like your hair, by the way," he said, gesturing to my head.

"Thank you," I replied, shocked that he would say something complimentary to *me*.

"Last time I saw you, it was so . . ." He trailed off, making big eyes while holding his hands out on each side of his head as if to intimate how huge my hair had been.

Of course. There it was.

When I'd met him at the airport, my hair had still been like Mia Thermopolis's at the beginning of *The Princess Diaries*: long, black, frizzy, and out of control. High school had happened, thank God, and now I had a shoulder-length bob that I flat-ironed until it was smooth.

But it was so *him* to remember and mention just how bad it'd been.

"Here you go," said the concession dude, handing over my snacks while I handed over the money. *Finally*. I didn't want to spend another minute talking to Mr. Nothing.

I turned and gave him a smile. "Well, that's me—until next time, I guess."

"Sure."

I walked away, and just as I was about to open the door to the theater with my elbow, I heard, "Hey. Glasses."

I turned around. "Yeah?"

He had a serious expression on his face, his dark eyes lacking the devious twinkle that'd been there every time I'd ever looked at him. He asked me, "How many solo flights have you taken since we met?"

I swallowed and hated him a tiny bit at that moment for reminding me. Mr. Nothing had totally been right; I'd flown to Fairbanks—alone—four times since the split. I was definitely a member of the custody kids now, a club I'd never wanted to join. "Four."

He gave a nod, and it felt like something passed between us before he said, "Later, Glasses."

"Yeah," I said, clearing my throat before muttering under my breath, "God, I hope not."

CHAPTER FIVE

Charlie

I watched her go and wondered what the hell was wrong with me.

She was an uptight weirdo that I'd been stuck with on a flight a couple of years ago, yet for some reason, it'd been good to see her. What was *that* about? She seemed just as high-maintenance as before, just as easy to rattle, yet I was somehow disappointed when she walked away.

I pictured the crinkle of irritation I continuously brought to her forehead and realized that, *shit*—I knew what it was.

She was an open book.

Yes, she was a stranger, but for some reason, when I looked at her, I could just tell what she was thinking. Most of it was annoying and in desperate need of a shake-up, but I liked the lack of a firewall around her thoughts.

Of course, that was probably because my inner circle

LYNN PAINTER

consisted of multiple people who were heavy into mind games. There was my mom, in an eternal battle with herself over *Who to Piss Off—Kids or Boyfriend*; my dad, who no longer battled at all but simply took sides with his new wife no matter what (while spinning his decisions as "good parenting"); my sister, who loved all of these new players in our life but tried to hide it from me because she knew I did *not*.

Add Becca to that—I never had a clue *what* she was thinking—and it made sense why Glasses's open face was so fucking refreshing.

"Can I help you?"

I looked away from the door she'd disappeared through and back at the snack dude.

"Ah, yeah. Two popcorns, please." I paid for the snacks, and as I waited for them, my phone buzzed.

Bec: Do you want to go to Kyle's after this? Apparently he's having people over.

I didn't know how to respond to that.

Did I want to go to Kyle's?

Yes and also *fuck no.*

Kyle was cool and his house was always a good time; on a normal night I'd be all about it. But after the promposal, I kind of wanted to be alone with Bec. It felt like something *big* had happened with us, and I wasn't ready to move on from it.

Fuck. It was embarrassing, how sappy she made me.

It still felt like a trap, like our "us" was going to eventually implode, but God help me, I was happy enough with her to consider the possibility that I might've been wrong.

34

Perhaps all relationships *weren't* doomed to fail.

I grabbed the popcorn and headed for the theater, wondering what Hall Monitor would think about *that* little gem of a thought. She'd raise that stubborn chin and feel like she'd won some sort of point, which would absolutely make me say something about her weird boots just to piss her off.

The boots were actually hot, but I'd rather die than say that to her.

But it didn't matter.

No way was I ever going to see that girl again.

CHAPTER SIX

PRESENT DAY

Bailey

"This is seriously unhealthy."

"I know," I said to Nekesa, swishing my straw in my Frappuccino and staring at the Starbucks entrance from our vantage point in the back of the coffee shop. "But I just have to see."

I wasn't sure why, but I needed to know.

Zack, my ex, used to pick me up every Saturday morning because he said he liked sharing a coffee with me before the day got started. Every single Saturday, no matter what, he whisked me away for Frappuccino and conversation.

It was kind of our thing. Smiles and caffeine in the early morning light.

Just us.

So now that he and Kelsie Kirchner were "official," I wondered if he did the same for her. Deep down, I knew the answer was no, because I truly *did* believe it was exclusive to us as a couple, but something inside me just couldn't let it go.

Which was why Nekesa and I were camped out at the back table at Starbucks.

"I get it," Nekesa said, but I knew she didn't. She was in a perfect relationship with the perfect guy—how could she possibly understand the compulsion to see if one's ex was déjà-vu-ing with their new girlfriend? "But it's been a couple months, Bay. And you're too good for him. Don't you think you should stop dwelling on what Zack is doing?"

"I'm not dwelling on what he's doing," I explained, even though I knew she was probably right. "I'm just curious."

"I should've gotten a sandwich." Nekesa sighed and said, "I'm starving. Why didn't I get a sandwich? They have a glass case full of food, and all I got was a tall Flat White. What the hell was I thinking?"

"I don't know," I said, opening Instagram on my phone. I'd posted a new edit last night, so naturally I had to check notifications every five minutes.

"I should go get—"

"No," I interrupted, setting down my phone and grabbing her arm in a panicked whisper. "If he comes in, I don't want him to see us."

"Why? It's not that weird that we'd be at Starbucks," she said, rolling her eyes and shaking off my hand. "Millions of people go to Starbucks, Bay. Ordering a breakfast sandwich is not remotely suspicious."

"But it is when you're my best friend and this is *our* Starbucks."

"This is *our* Starbucks?" she asked, her dark eyebrows scrunching together. God, she had the best eyebrows.

"Not 'ours' as in yours and mine," I said, "but 'ours' as in *his* and mine."

"Dude." Her eyes narrowed and she said, "Is there anywhere you think of as yours and mine?"

I kept playing with my straw as I thought about it for a minute. With us, it wasn't so much *if* there was a place that was ours but more so which place was the *most* ours. I looked at her and said, "Definitely the dollar store in Springfield."

She snorted. "Holy shit, that is so *ours*. Sour Patch Kids and Cokes."

"Every day that summer," I said, grinning as I remembered our obsession with—

"Remember how we'd just binge episodes of *Big Time Rush* for hours on end?"

"I was just about to say that," I said, laughing. Technically I'd known Nekesa for only a few years, but we'd been inseparable since that first day together in Mr. Peek's gym class, aka Toxic Masculinity 101, where she'd spiked a ball right at Cal Hodge's nose for saying "Looks like Bailey's boobies came in."

I still hate Cal Hodge.

"Ah, the simpler times, before we had cars." Nekesa was chuckling, but then her smile faded away and she said, "Aw shit."

"Aw shit, what?" I asked, still amused. "What is the shit?"

I followed her gaze to the door, and then I knew what the shit was.

Zack and Kelsie were there. *Oh God.* They were holding hands, and his head was bent down a little, so he could hear whatever she was saying. She was smiling and he was smiling, and it felt like my heart was constricting in my chest.

They looked so fucking happy.

My stomach hurt as I watched them walk up to the counter. I couldn't believe it. He really was taking *her* for Saturday morning coffee. It was such a silly little thing, but my throat was tight because I missed him so much.

I missed *us* when we were together.

He put his hand on her lower back, and I could almost feel it on *my* back because that was his go-to gesture whenever we were together.

"Let's go," Nekesa said, nudging my arm with her elbow. "I don't like your face like this."

That got my attention. I looked away from Zack and said, "What?"

She waved her hand in front of my face and said, "You look like a sad puppy when you see him. I think it's my job, as your friend, to remove you from any situation that fucks up your face that way."

I smiled in spite of my heart shattering. "You have no idea how much I love you for that, but can we wait until they go? I'd rather eat curdled milk than have to small-talk with them right now."

"Eat?" She tilted her head and said, "Wouldn't you *drink* curdled milk?"

"You'd drink it if it was mildly curdled, but I was referring to long-forgotten, extra-chunky curds. You'd need a knife and a fork for this shit."

"Of course."

We waited until the happy couple left—*thank God it was a to-go order*—and then we took off. I was walking to her car, trying to shake off the sad and not think about them, when my phone buzzed.

Mom: Was I right?

I rolled my eyes and texted: **Maybe.**

Mom: Gah, I'm sorry. If it makes you feel any better, I called Jimmy Bob Graham's prayer hotline and requested they pray for Zack's bowels to loosen.

I snorted. **You did not.**

Mom: No, I did not, but now I shall.

I opened the passenger door and got into Nekesa's car. Texted: **What are you doing this morning, besides lying about prayer circles?**

Mom: That's it. My only plans are to lie about prayer circles.

Me: We're going to Target and Cane's before work—do you need anything?

Nekesa said as she started the car, "Tell Emily hi."

I added: **Nekesa says hello, Emily.**

Mom: Tell her hi and also that the album she recommended was trash.

"My mom says the album you recommended sucks."

Nekesa scowled at me as she pulled out of the parking lot. "She has terrible taste in music."

I texted my mom: **Nekesa says you suck.**

Mom: Nekesa clearly doesn't know that I used to be the president of the Bobby Vinton fan club.

I buckled my seat belt. **Who's Bobby Vinton?**

Mom: Exactly. Hey—can you grab brownie stuff from the store?

Me: Batter party tonight after I get home?

Mom: I forgot you start the new job today. Don't be afraid to put yourself out there and TALK to other humans. Also, YES DUH ON THE BATTER. You've Got Mail and E. coli—what's better than that?

It would be impossible for me to count just how many weekend nights my mother and I spent watching TV together and jamming food into our faces on that faded beige couch. I hated the divorce for what it did to me and my dad's relationship, but from the day my mom and I moved into our tiny Omaha apartment, it'd just been her and me and the forty-two-inch Samsung.

The perfect team.

I texted back: **Nothing in the world is better than Tom Hanks and salmonella. We're going to the bookstore after we get off but I won't be late.**

Mom: Tom Hanks and the Salmonellas; band name—called it.

"As employees of Planet Funnn, you will be deployed to the intergalactic front lines of happiness. Your out-of-this-world service will be integral to us winning the war on earthly boredom. So let's bounce in the day by starting with our pump-up jump-up! Come on, sunshine troops—keep on jumping till the music stops!"

"Are we sure," Nekesa yelled to me as she bounced, "that we

want to work at a place where people say things like that?"

"Not really." I jumped, springing a little higher with every bounce. The trainer gave me an irritated look from his spot up on the stage platform—yeah, he'd definitely heard us—where he was shouting into a microphone next to the DJ while all one hundred fifty of us trainees jumped across the massive trampoline landscape in our new spacey flight-suit uniforms.

Planet Funnn—sadly, not a misspelling—was a brand-new "mega" hotel that was opening in two weeks. It had a water park, trampoline supercenter, indoor snow dome, ultra-arcade, Tiscotheque (teen disco), movie theater, and karaoke concert hall. There were like twenty other amenities that I'd already forgotten from the job fair Nekesa and I had attended, but basically the place was like a giant landlocked cruise ship.

We'd decided that since we each hated our jobs at the time— she'd been working at Schafer's Market and I'd been working at Noah's Ark Daycare—we would go to the massive job fair, and if we both got hired, that would mean it was fate.

Well, we got hired, along with like a billion other people who were all bouncing alongside us at that very moment.

The staff in charge of the planet seemed to be incredibly boisterous for eight a.m. on a Saturday, wildly enthusiastic, as if they'd shotgunned Red Bulls and snorted lines of Fun Dip before welcoming our group into the fold. I was holding my official opinion until bounce time ended and the actual training began, but my unofficial first impression was that Nekesa and I should sneak out of the place as soon as we were allowed to take our first break.

"Oh my God."

"What?"

"Bay." I glanced over, and Nekesa had a bizarre look on her face, like she was excited and also trying to communicate without speaking as she bounced. She was just under five feet tall and tiny, so she was getting super good air. "Don't look now, but there's a guy on the Jupiter Jumpoline who keeps checking you out."

"And I can't look?" I asked, craning my neck to see the aforementioned Jupiter Boy. "Not that I care."

"Well, I mean, you can *look*," she said, "but not like that. Don't be obvious about it."

"O-*kay*."

"And you *should* care—he's cute."

"He's probably looking at *you*," I said, picturing Zack yet again and feeling the sad return. "Or looking at me and wishing I looked more like Kelsie Kirchner."

"Will you stop with that?" Nekesa said, shooting me a glare that said she was *over* my lovesick whining. "Christ."

And I got it. I'm sure it was *super* annoying to hang out with someone who couldn't get over their ex, especially when Nekesa and her boyfriend were madly in love with each other.

Which was why I was so grateful for Eva and Emma; they didn't mind my whining.

The three of us were *so* the same when it came to guys.

Last night, each of us posted an aesthetic video about the new Emily Henry book. It was a total coincidence, a coincidence that led to an hours-long group text where we commiserated about how much we'd loved the book and how unfair it was that her heroes didn't exist in real life.

With Eva and Em, I didn't feel like I had to *get over* my feelings. They were the friends who allowed me to wallow while also sending me playlists and F1 memes. They were the friends who shared my need to jump wholeheartedly into fictional romances, simply because escaping into the joy of what I *didn't* have was somehow comforting and hopeful.

God, I wished I were in my room right now, rereading that Emily Henry book.

But—ahem—I wasn't.

I glanced out of the corner of my eye in the direction of Jupiter, trying to be discreet as I looked for the dude Nekesa was referring to, but I couldn't stop my loud gasp when I saw him.

It was impossible.

Impossible.

I squinted and craned my neck, but there was no denying the truth.

No, no, no, no, noooooo.

It couldn't be. There was just no. Way.

Mr. Nothing.

CHAPTER SEVEN

Bailey

"Oh my God." I couldn't believe it. Mr. Nothing was bouncing at my new job; what were the odds? *Howwwww is this happening??* I tried to sound casual and like I didn't care as I stared in his direction and whispered, "I know that guy."

"He's hot."

"Is he?" I tilted my head and tried to appraise him as he jumped. He was tall, dark-haired, and broad-shouldered—objectively a handsome human, I supposed—but it was impossible for me to see past his Mr. Nothing face.

I could still hear his deep voice moaning about *questionable meat* on the airplane.

Nekesa tilted her head too, and said, "Totally hot. How do *you* know him?"

I knew what she meant, but it irritated me at the same time that it made total sense. I didn't ever put myself out there and talk to guys, especially not "hot" guys that I didn't know, so the question was valid.

Still, it felt *not great.*

The DJ raised the volume on "Jump Around," but the trainer appeared to be done with the morning invocation. He was drinking coffee and looking down at his phone.

"I sat next to him on a ten-hour flight a few years ago, and he was absolutely obnoxious." I watched as he jumped with an athletic casualness that didn't actually look uncool. "He had all these ridiculous opinions. I remember specifically that he said girls and guys could never truly be friends."

"That's weird," she said, still watching him.

"Right?" He was casually jumping, but I sensed that he was fully aware we were staring at him. I said, "It doesn't matter. He's a total smart-ass who has hated me since I refused to let him cut in the boarding line. Let's—"

"Glasses?" He looked directly at us—at me—and yelled from across the Jump-O-Sphere, "I thought that was you."

Noooooooooooo.

My heart started racing and I wanted to disappear.

He scrambled off the Jumpoline, crossed the crater canyon, and bounced toward us. I managed to mumble something polite like, "Yes, um, it's me. How are you?"

"Fine." He did a little chin nod, his eyes on mine as if trying to see my thoughts. "You?"

I nodded and wondered if that smell—something clean and masculine—was coming from him. "Fine."

Could this be any more awkward?

"I'm going to test out Universal Bounce." Nekesa pointed to the purple section, the adult trampolines with a big bounce-up bar in the center. "I'll be right back."

And she just turned and bounced in the other direction, giving me absolutely no chance to stop her. I clenched my jaw and steeled myself for the impending barrage of the guy's inflammatory rhetoric. I attempted diversion by starting with, "So you're working here too, huh?"

His eyebrows scrunched together, like he was disappointed in me for stating the obvious, as he said, "Yep."

Now he gave me a one-word answer? I would've killed for that on the flight from Alaska. I tried again as I realized I had no idea what his name was. "I'm Bailey, by the way."

Can that be right? It seemed beyond strange that we hadn't exchanged names before, but I couldn't come up with a single, solitary guess of what his was. "Mr. Nothing" just *fit* him, but maybe that's because it's how I'd always referred to him.

Well, in my head. I'd never actually referred to him out loud at all.

"Charlie."

Charlie.

Somehow it suited him.

I tried again for small talk because I just couldn't handle the awkwardness. "So how's the girlfriend? Are you still with prom girl?"

I saw his Adam's apple bob around a big swallow, and his gaze shifted just past my shoulder, like something behind us was in need of his eyes. For a second I thought he wasn't going to respond, but then he said, "No, we broke up."

"Oh. I'm sorry." I slowed my bounce and looked at his face, and for some reason it mattered that the sadness was still there. I could *feel* the ache in his eyes; his melancholy was familiar, a friend we had in common. "I am really, really sorry, Charlie."

His eyes came back to me as he shrugged and slowed as well. "What're you gonna do, right? It had to end sometime. What about you? Are you still with Mr. Skintight Shirt?"

I pictured Zack's hand on Kelsie's lower back as she ordered coffee that morning, and my stomach got tight. I still couldn't believe he shared grins and the sound of milk steaming with *her* now. I was fine with him moving on, but why did our moments have to move with him? I sighed before sliding into a *Who cares* grin and saying, "Nope—we broke up too."

"Must be something going around, huh?" he said, and I could tell by the rigid set of his jaw that he was *over* this mindless small talk that pressed on his wound.

"I guess," I murmured, unsure of what else to say.

"You two aren't jumping!" The DJ sounded like he was eating the microphone as he called out Charlie and me.

I rolled my eyes and Charlie kind of smirked, but we both started jumping again. He put his hands into the pockets of his flight suit and said, "And the parents? How's the divorce thing going on your end?"

"My mother is seeing someone now, so that's fun," I said, unsure why I was actually answering his question. He was obnoxious Mr. Nothing, a stranger I didn't know or particularly care for, yet I kept going. "And my dad seems to be losing his verve for buying expensive plane tickets, so God only knows when I'm going to visit him again."

"Their dating is the worst, isn't it?" He gave me another one of those looks that spoke volumes, like the one he'd given me for a split second on the plane three years ago, and he said, "My mom has a boyfriend who pretty much lives with us right now, and I can't tell you how much I love it when he eats my Pop-Tarts. Like, just the sight of him at the table in the morning puts me in a murderous rage."

I laughed at that, a genuine, feels-good-to-the-core laugh, because I felt seen. Someone, even if it was just Charlie from the plane, knew exactly how I felt. "For me it's soda. He drinks gallons of regular Coke, but then I can't—"

"You can't make your halfsies," he interrupted, his mouth turning up in a small smile.

A startled laugh escaped me. I was shocked that he would immediately remember the soda and get it. "Bingo."

Also—wow—was that a *genuine* smile?

The music stopped and the DJ was back to deep-throating the microphone. "All right, squadron, let's bounce on out of here, grab ourselves a doughnut, and head to the Milky Way for launch."

"I'm assuming that's a training room?" I muttered, disappointed that our parental-horror-story exchange was over before it'd begun. I couldn't explain it, but our fleeting moment of commiseration had felt *good*.

It was nice to have a partner in suffering.

God—how weird was that, that I actually *wanted* to talk to Mr. Nothing?

Maybe I was coming down with something.

"Or they're slingshotting us into orbit," he said, looking at the deep-throating DJ with an expression so disgusted that it made me want to laugh. "Either way, it's probably gonna be painful."

"Probably," I agreed, and Nekesa joined us as we exited the trampoline area and were ushered down the hall.

Once we got to the Milky Way, we were split up into four groups: Red Dwarfs, White Dwarfs, Protostars, and Red Giants.

Charlie asked without raising his hand, "Because we're all stars. Seriously?"

I could hear people snickering, but the perky lady in charge of our training class gave him a wide Miss America smile, totally unfazed by his snark. "You got it, hon. We thought it would be real excitin' to use the stars for our four teams."

He put his hands into the pockets of his pants and looked down at his feet, almost as if he was working hard to keep his sarcastic thoughts to himself.

That's new.

Although, to be fair, Charlie actually seemed like he'd completely changed from the last time I'd seen him.

He was taller, but not in a typical he's-grown-a-little-in-the-past-couple-years way. No, Charlie had to be, like, at least six foot three now—he was *big*.

Not only that, but his face had changed. The dark eyes still twinkled with trouble, but the face they were set in had popped from boyish softness into chiseled edges.

He had that whole contradiction thing going on, I supposed. Boy *and* man. Mischievous *and* intense.

The promise of multitudes.

Yeah, Nekesa was right—he was *very* attractive.

Not to *me*—God, no—but objectively speaking, he was a handsome guy.

I pulled out my phone—*no messages*—and after a brief perusal of the crowd, my eyes went back to Charlie.

Who was *listening* to the speaker like an interested new employee.

Wow—he really *had* changed.

The woman went on to list off the teams and their designated training rooms. There was no explanation on *how* the group was split up or what it meant, but Nekesa and I were Protostars, staying in the Milky Way, while Charlie was called to line up with the Red Giants, who were headed to Mars. He shrugged and followed his group out of the room, and I was torn between being a tiny bit disappointed that he was gone and massively relieved I wasn't going to have to work with him all the time.

Because even though he appeared to have grown up a little, and we'd just shared a decent human moment, there was surely enough Mr. Nothing left in him to drive me mad on a daily basis.

Once the Protostars were alone, we were each given a big red shield with a *P* to affix to our uniforms. We were told that our group was the administrative band that would hold the front line of fun together. We would train to become front desk clerks, concession stand reps, restaurant hostesses, and Funcierges (fun concierges). Pretty much any job that involved a little responsibility and customer fiduciary interaction fell to our team.

I was slightly offended when Mr. Cleveland, our trainer, explained that our group scored high in professionalism but very low on the fun vibe. He said our love language wasn't socialization but rule-following, and though that might sound like a drag—the man literally used that word—we were essential to the success of Planet Funnn.

He mentioned that the other teams had roles such as "audience exciter," "waterslide daredevil," "snowball fight instigator," and my favorite, "karaoke influencer," so I imagined their training curriculum would differ wildly from ours.

About an hour into an incredibly boring PowerPoint presentation on the history of our parent company (Funnnertainment, Inc.), the side door creaked open and Charlie walked in, loose-limbed and looking totally chill with the fact that he was interrupting our very large group.

Mr. Cleveland stopped speaking. "Can I help you?"

If it were me, I would've died of embarrassment as the eyes of the entire Milky Way rested upon me. But Charlie was relaxed. He put his hands into the pockets of his flight suit and said, "Yeah. Um. Apparently there was a mistake. I guess I'm supposed to be in here."

"You're a Protostar?"

I rolled my lips inward, wanting to laugh at Charlie's face; he grimaced like Cleveland had called him something vile. Charlie said, "Well, those are the words that they told me to say. So, um, I guess yes."

Mr. Cleveland gestured to the open seat in the front row. "Then have a seat."

"Awesome," Charlie said, dropping into the chair.

"Your timing is perfect, son, because we're just about to go over the Funnnertainment Employee Handbook." The man chuckled loudly for a half second, very clown-like, before adding, "Buckle up, Protostars, cuz it's about to get real."

I bit down on my lip to hold in a groan.

Nekesa rolled her eyes and mouthed, *Real boring.*

Mr. Cleveland started reading word for word through the handbook. I pulled out a pencil and took notes—because what else was there to do. He went over the dress code (uniforms only), the payroll system, and employee benefits before we finally broke for lunch.

I'd never been happier to stand.

Everyone had a voucher to get a free meal in the food court, so Nekesa and I—and the rest of the monster-sized training group—started down a long and endless hallway that led to the Galaxy of Funstaurants.

I lowered my voice and said to Nekesa, "Maybe we should ditch now, before lunch."

"What?"

I glanced over my shoulder. "It wouldn't feel right to take the free lunch if we're quitting."

Nekesa looked at me like I'd just confessed to a squirrel obsession. "*Quitting?* What are you talking about? This place is totally bonkers."

"Which is why I said what I said."

"What is more hilarious than this place, Bay? I could work at a grocery store where customers yell at me because their coupon won't work, or I could be a Protostar whose quarterly review involves learning a line dance. That, my friend, is gold and should be treated as such."

It was such a Nekesa thing to say.

Sometimes best friends were like twins separated at birth. But Nekesa and I—not so much.

She was outgoing, hilarious, and always down for a good time. She sewed her own amazing clothes, she took ballroom dancing classes for fun, and she'd punched someone in the mouth once. She was like the heroine in a zombie movie who'd be wielding a stake and yelling, *Come and get me, you zombie pussies!*

I was . . . well, *not* that. I was perpetually trying to keep up with her. I'd be the girl too busy yelling *Wait* and flipping through the Zombie Rule Book to notice the zombie hovering behind me, about to eat my brain.

"Well, I've never even heard of the Bopper Shuffle." I scratched my eyebrow and felt uneasy at the thought of working for a company whose core values were *fun* and *belly laughing*. "It is ludicrous that my potential pay increase should hinge upon cheesy choreography."

"You're just scared because you suck at dancing," Nekesa teased, nudging my side with her elbow.

"It's a ridiculous assessment!" I *did* suck at dancing—Nekesa said I was too repressed to enjoy it—but that didn't change how absurd the assessment was.

"Nekesa?"

She and I both turned around, and a short-but-built guy

with curly blond hair ran up beside her. I expected her to make a smart-ass comment because he was wearing a pinkie ring and a fake Rolex, but instead she squealed, "Oh my God—Theo!"

And she rarely squealed.

Her face lit up as she smiled at this stranger like she was genuinely happy to see him.

The dude, wearing a space suit that matched ours except for the purple *R* patch, smiled and said to Nekesa, "Let me guess— you're a Protostar."

"We both are." She gestured to me, but neither of them actually looked at me as they started walking again and I followed. "What made you assume that?"

"Our trainer said Protostars are pretty much buzzkill know-it-alls," he teased, "and that is like the actual description of Nekesa Tevitt."

I opened my mouth to argue, because he'd described the *opposite* of Nekesa, but he added with a laugh, "Just kidding— they obviously have you on the wrong team."

"Right?" She reached up and gathered her hair in her hands, like she was making a ponytail. "It's the wrong team, but I'm glad because I want to be with Bailey."

She gestured to me with her head, and once again, neither of them looked my way. She said, "I still can't believe you're here. When did you guys move back to Omaha?"

"Last summer. I go to Kennedy Prep."

Ah, Kennedy Prep. So the Rolex might actually be real.

"How come I haven't seen you at mass?" Nekesa let go of her hair, looked at me, and explained, "We used to be CCD buddies."

I wasn't Catholic, but a surprising number of my friends in Fairbanks had spent their elementary years going to those weekly classes at the church too. I didn't even know what *C-C-D* stood for, but we'd never really been a church family either.

"We go to St. Patrick's now." He looked a little embarrassed and added, "It's closer to our house."

"Ooh—uptown," she teased.

They shared a smile, and I wondered what their history was. CCD was way before I moved to Omaha, so I didn't know Nekesa back then. But their vibe today felt a little flirty, which was weird because Nekesa was wildly in love with her boyfriend, Aaron.

I was probably reading it wrong.

I tuned out their catching-up chatter as I saw food approaching. I was starving but also mildly nervous about what kind of culinary offerings this place was going to have. Would an establishment whose core values were *fun* and *belly laughing* really care if their snacks were FDA approved?

"I heard there's a hidden pub, just beyond the Galaxy of Funstaurants, that has better food than all the other places put together."

I turned to my right, and there was Charlie. *Where did he come from?* I looked up at his face—damn, so tall—and was still torn between dreading the sight of him and finding a strange comfort in his presence.

It was a little unnerving, wondering when Mr. Nothing was going to show up and cancel out this *Charlie.* So I just said, "Really?"

He leaned in a little closer, his lips turning up into a slow smirk. "It's designated as a kid-free zone, so they put it in a separate corridor. The DJ told the Red Giants about it in confidence, but since I'm now of the House of Proto, betrayal of the Red Giants is my duty."

"Nekesa—did you hear that?" I nudged her with my elbow and turned to my left. "Bar food up ahead."

Charlie muttered, "You left out the part about my dutiful bravery."

"I know," I replied, not looking back at him.

I heard him say "Ouch," and it kind of made me want to laugh.

Nekesa glanced at me and then looked back at Theo. "Bar food up ahead."

Theo shook his head. "Constellation Pizza has calzones in the shape of Saturn. Rumor has it the rings are made out of breadsticks. You *cannot* miss out on that, Nekesa."

She looked back and me and Charlie. "You guys, come on. Planetary pizza? We have to do that shit."

Charlie shoved his hands into the pockets of his flight suit and turned to face us, so he was walking backward. "I'm sticking with bar food—Saturn pizza is too nauseatingly cute for me. Feel free to join me, Bailey, if you'd rather have fries and amazing conversation than fuckshit pizza."

Did he just invite me to join him for lunch?

And if yes, why? Why would he do that?

"I believe the first is possible," I said breezily, even though my mind was turning, clueless of how to make sense of this version of Mr. Nothing. "But not so much the second."

I really wanted bar food, but I wasn't sure I wanted the company that came with it.

"Oh, come on—we can finish whining to each other about our nightmarish home lives." Charlie turned back around and slowed his pace, so he was walking right beside me. He lowered his voice so he was just talking to me and said, "Vent together now so we don't kill later."

He didn't *look* like he was messing with me. His eyes were on mine, but he looked like he was waiting for my answer— nothing more, nothing less. Was it possible he'd grown up?

I knew I'd probably regret it, but as I looked at Nekesa and Theo, deep in their conversation about people I'd never met, I sighed and said, "Fries it is."

CHAPTER EIGHT

Charlie

I hadn't expected her to say yes.

Yes, I'd been trying to convince her, but now that she was leaving her friends and walking with me toward the pub, I wondered if it'd been a mistake. She was all about doing things the right way, ordering her food with shit on the side, and overthinking, whereas I just wanted to take a load off and eat a burger.

I didn't want her to make lunch feel like work.

And I didn't want her to get the wrong idea either.

"So," she said, glancing at me as we walked toward the pub's entrance. "What made you want to get a job here?"

The truth was that I'd applied at this idiot-zone solely to piss off my mother's boyfriend. He'd convinced her that I needed to get a responsible job so I didn't waste time "scrolling apps" and "gaming" (the guy was *such* a douchebag) all day, so I got a job at the city's largest dipshittery just to give him a wicked case of the eye rolls.

And man, did it work.

"It was this or Chuck E. Cheese, and that mouse gives me the fucking creeps." I didn't bother with a legit explanation because I knew she didn't care. Bailey was, for all intents and purposes, a stranger, yet I knew enough about her to know she had no use for me whatsoever. "Same question but your turn."

She gave me a tiny smile, one of those polite little numbers that didn't quite reach her eyes. "Nekesa and I applied out of boredom, but now I'm strongly considering quitting."

"Because you suck at bouncing?" I said, trying to make the smile reach her eyes.

"Because it's so stupid," she said, looking at me wide, like she wanted me to commiserate. "Right? I mean, there is a person whose title is *audience exciter*. I don't think I can work at a place where adult humans approved that job title."

That made *me* smile, even as she blinked fast in her uptight way. "I can see that about you."

We walked up to the order counter, and Bailey asked, "Does that mean you like it here so far?"

"God, no." I looked at the menu board, and my stomach growled. "It's a complete and utter shitshow. My car needs gas, though, so I will unfortunately be sporting a flight suit whether I like it or not."

"That's the one thing I don't mind," she said, sounding mildly amused. "I kind of like the cut of these jumpsuits."

That brought my eyes to her body, which was a mistake

because the last thing I wanted was for her to think I was checking her out. I quickly raised them to her face and was relieved that she was looking at the menu, not me.

Whew—avoided the trap.

But as I looked at her pink cheeks, I was a little taken aback by how pretty she was. I mean, I had eyes—I'd known she was attractive the times we'd met. But there was something about the freckles on her nose and the way she blinked like she was continually processing things that I found . . . interesting.

"What are you going to order?" She tucked her dark hair behind her ears and said, "I think I'm just getting fries."

I shrugged and cleared my throat. "Yeah, I'm just getting a few burgers and a couple fries. Maybe some onion rings and a hot dog. Step aside, Glasses—let me show you how it's done."

"This should be a real treat," she deadpanned, and as I moved around her to place my order, I realized that I could breathe deeply for the first time in weeks. She was twenty things that annoyed me, all rolled into one, but there was something oddly relaxing about being around her.

Maybe it was the slight sparkle that she always had in her eyes, like she was expecting magic to appear at any given moment. That wide-eyed hopefulness kind of made *me* feel hopeful, which was dangerous but mildly intoxicating.

We got our food and grabbed a table, and as she rambled to fill the silence while squeezing every drop out of three ketchup packets like a lunatic, it occurred to me that I didn't want her to feel like that. Like she didn't know how to act around me. Like she was waiting for me to be a dick.

I wasn't *always* a dick, for fuck's sake.

"So how bad was it?" I asked, unwrapping one of my burgers and reaching over to grab one of her fifteen ketchup packets. "Tell me all about the divorce."

She stopped squeezing, and her eyebrows went down. "Why would I tell *you*?"

"Because I know how absolutely hard it sucks and I get it." I squirted the ketchup onto my wrapper, then dipped my burger into the condiment. I could tell she didn't trust me—hell, we were basically strangers so it made sense—but I'd never forget the way she looked on the plane when I'd mentioned divorce.

For a split second, her prickly demeanor had evaporated entirely.

The crinkle between her eyebrows, the hard swallow, the way she'd sucked in a deep breath—it felt like I'd punched her in the stomach.

She'd recovered, but her face had haunted me afterward.

So much so that here I was, trying to assure myself that she was okay.

Fucking weird, that. I said, "We're like soldiers, comparing scars and stories of our shitty battles. People who haven't been there don't understand, but we do."

She made a noise, like she didn't necessarily agree, but her eyebrows returned to normal as she said, "That's actually a terrible analogy."

"Agreed," I said, taking a bite, "but misery loves company and I'm a miserable piece of shit. So tell me everything."

CHAPTER NINE

Bailey

"What's weird is that it seems like everyone but me is cool." I set my elbow on the table and rested my chin on my hand while Charlie finished his third cheeseburger. "I feel like I'm the only one, besides little kids, who can't just adapt to the divorce and adjust."

That was the total truth. I was seventeen, for God's sake, and I'd be out of high school next year. Like a grown-ass person. So why did it still make me unbearably sad when my dad wasn't around for school events? When the art club had a showcase and our work was hung in an actual gallery, I'd watched for him all night like he was going to just hop on a plane from Alaska to surprise me. Spoiler: he did not.

And why, when my mother's boyfriend came over and sprawled out on our couch, watching TV in his socks like he was part of my family, did I close myself in my bedroom with the all-encompassing homesickness that felt like it was physically choking me?

Charlie shook his head and took a sip of his soda. "At least you seem to keep it all inside like the type A, repressed person you are."

"First of all," I said, surprised that not only was I sharing my story with him but I was actually *enjoying* the interaction, "I'm not repressed."

He was the second person to call me repressed in the past half hour; *that* was an ouch.

"Second of all," I continued, "how would *you* know if I was type A?"

He gave me an irritating *I know everything* look as he shoved a few fries under the bun of his burger. "Anyone with eyes can see that you are. And that's okay—it makes for peace, if nothing else. I go off like all the time, so not only does everything just straight-up suck, but my mom, my sister, and the douche boyfriend are always pissed."

"Like how?" I asked, genuinely curious. "How do you go off?"

He grabbed the pickle spear off the corner of his plate and stuck it under the bun as well and said, "I'm just honest. When I see *Clark* in the hall in the middle of the night, I say, *Dude, why don't you stay at your own house like you aren't a mooching loser?* And when my dad cancels on me because his girlfriend's kid has a Little League game, I tell him that he's a shitty father for choosing her kid over me."

"Wow." I sat up straight and stared at him in awe. I couldn't imagine that kind of confrontational interaction—God, it gave me anxiety just thinking about it—but I respected Charlie's ability to *not care* about other people's feelings.

I mean, I might be able to daydream about that kind of honesty, but when it came down to it, I just didn't like making people unhappy. I wanted my mom—and my dad, when he remembered I existed—to be happy and I wanted to be the one to *make* them happy.

Rocking the boat might feel good for about five seconds, but I knew myself well enough to know that the guilt that followed would be unbearable. I said, "I cannot believe you say those things."

"It isn't received well." He took a bite of his overstuffed burger and looked at the two girls behind me. "But it's the truth."

"I can't believe I'm saying this, but you're kind of my hero." I sat back in my chair and crossed my arms, studying him. I could actually picture him saying those words, and something about it made me sad for him, even as I respected his ballsiness.

That made his mouth turn up into a snarky half smile as he wiped his hands on his napkin. "And you don't even like me."

"I know." I couldn't stop *my* smile—his mischievous ones were contagious—and I shook my head. "But this is revolutionary stuff. Can I live vicariously through you?"

"Why be vicarious? Burn some cities down with your own rage." He took another bite of his hamburger.

"Yeah, um . . . no." I took a sip of my chocolate malt, wishing I could be gutsy enough for honesty. I wanted to, I really did, but there was no doubt I would remain nonconfrontational. I stirred my drink with the straw and said, "I don't think it helps with anything."

He dropped the rest of his burger onto his plate, like he was finished. "It makes you feel better."

"But does it?" I thought back to the way Charlie had been each time I met him. "I don't see you rolling in happiness with the freedom that your words have given you."

"Maybe I am on the *inside*," he quipped, wiping his hands before dropping his napkin onto his plate.

"Really?" I dipped a fry into the pile of ketchup.

"Chicks dig my churlishness." He reached over and stole one of my fries, batting my fry out of the way so he could drench his stolen one in ketchup first. Oddly enough, there was something about the way he behaved as if we were actual friends that made me interested in learning more about him. "I wouldn't want to screw that up with happiness."

I gave him a very unladylike snort. "I don't think it's quite as appealing as you think it is."

"Oh, come on," he said, his eyes sparking like he wanted to grin as he chewed. "The first time we met, when you were all owl-eyed and brace-faced, you didn't fall a little under the Charlie spell?"

I shook my head, remembering how much he'd irritated me. "I definitely did not."

"Seriously?" His eyebrows scrunched together, and he looked at me like I'd confessed to being an alien.

Which made me want to laugh, because how could he be so

unaware of what a total jackass he'd been? I said, "Why is that so hard for you to believe?"

"Because I'm rakishly charming," he replied, although the slight tilt of his mouth told me he wasn't wholly serious.

"Oh, is that what you are?" I said, exhaling around a laugh. "I guess I missed that."

He barked out a quick chuckle, and for a minute it was great. For that brief, fleeting moment, it was *nice* with us. And then he said, "Wait. I'm not hitting on you."

"Oh my God—gross." I shook my head as the annoyance returned. Why did he feel the need to say things like that? *Still the same Mr. Nothing.* I said emphatically, "I *know.*"

"Okay, good." He pushed his plate toward the center of the table and added, "And I second the gross."

I couldn't believe his nerve; not just the *gross* comment, but the overall disclaimer that he wasn't hitting on me. "Why would you even say—"

"I don't know." He held up a hand to stop me from talking, then raised the other one as well. "I'm pretty sure no two people have ever been as disinterested in each other as we are, but I just wanted to make sure."

"Oh, I can definitely confirm." I thought back to the Fairbanks airport and said, "Honestly—the first time we met, I was in awe of how irritating you were. Like, I don't think I knew just how obnoxious a person could be before that day."

"Same," he said, nodding in agreement.

"*What?*" I narrowed my eyes at him. I hadn't been remotely obnoxious that day. If anything, I'd been a pathetically quiet little mouse. "I wasn't irritating."

He moved his straw around in his cup and said with a feigned scowl, "You wouldn't let me cut in line because of rules. Irritating as fuck."

I was about to explain to Charlie how there was nothing the least bit irritating about following the rules when Nekesa interrupted, appearing beside our table with Theo. "Hey! Guess what? Mr. Cleveland sat with us at lunch, and when Theo told him he's majoring in accounting next year, good old Cleves transferred him to Protostar. So he's on our team now too."

I looked up at the two of them and was mildly annoyed by this news. Theo seemed fine, but Nekesa and I had taken the job together—as a team—and his presence was really messing with the vibe.

"Wow." Charlie leaned back and stretched. "So you got upgraded? I got demoted to Protostars just because I said glitter was the devil's calling card."

Nekesa snorted. "You said that?"

"Respect." Theo gave Charlie a slow grin of appreciation. "There was an entire section in the Red Giant handbook on the endless joy of glitter bombs. I can't believe you actually said that out loud."

"Listen to what you just said and tell me I'm wrong." Charlie crossed his arms over his chest. "'Endless joy of glitter bombs'— are they kidding with that?"

Charlie and Theo started talking between themselves, and I glanced at Nekesa. "Are you sure we shouldn't quit and find normal jobs?"

"Normal sucks," Nekesa said, and I got distracted for a second by Charlie and Theo. They were doing that whole low-talking, smart-ass grin-wearing thing guys did that usually equated to a conversation about breasts, and I rolled my eyes.

I just *knew* I wouldn't approve of their conversation.

Nekesa reached down and grabbed my cup. "Can I have a sip?"

Charlie looked up from his conversation with Theo and said to Nekesa, "Only if you like a malt made with vanilla ice cream but only *half* a spoonful of malted and two squirts of chocolate syrup instead of three. And half whipped cream, no cherry."

I hadn't realized Charlie had heard my order *at all*, much less heard it and remembered every little detail. A part of me was impressed by his perfect recollection, but a bigger part of me was taken aback by the way he acted so familiar with me.

Because we didn't know each other at all, right?

So why did it feel like we kind of did?

"So on-brand for my girl." She lifted the cup and took a long drink before saying, "Ooh—but so good. Do I have time to get a malt?"

I said, "No," and at the same time both boys said, "Yes."

Nekesa stuck out her tongue at me, and I glanced down at my watch. "Well, be fast. I don't want to be late."

"Such a Protostar," Theo teased, and I couldn't believe he was self-assured enough to mock *me* when we'd only just met.

"Takes one to know one," Nekesa said, "Mr. Private School."

"Did you really just say that?" Theo said, giving Nekesa a flirty smile. "Miss Public Education?"

"I think I did," she said, grinning.

"Looks like someone upped the attitude since we last met." I watched as Theo tilted his head and gave her an appraising look. "I'm not sure if I'm scared or if I like it."

"Oh, you're scared," Nekesa replied, meeting his gaze before turning and walking to the counter to order.

"I think I'm both," Theo said, laughing as he followed behind her. "I'm scared and I like it."

As soon as they were out of earshot, Charlie said, "Those two are *so* gonna hook up."

"You are *so* wrong," I quickly snapped at him. Even if she was being a little flirty, that didn't mean she was going to cheat. "She's got a boyfriend."

He gave me a level stare before saying, "So what?"

"So she's super happy with Aaron, that's what." Typical Charlie, assuming the worst. "Theo's just an old friend."

"An old friend who looks at her like *that*."

I followed his gaze over to the counter, where Nekesa was laughing loudly about something. And, okay, Theo was staring at her.

Pretty intently, actually.

He was staring at her as if she'd just told him the most wonderfully shocking thing he'd ever heard in his life. His eyes were very nearly sparkling, for God's sake. Still, I said, "He's looking at her like he thinks she's funny."

"Trust me, if those two start working together, they'll be banging it out in under a month."

"You're disgusting," I said, not at all shocked by his cynical assumption. It was exactly what Charlie in the plane would've said, as well as Charlie at the movie theater. He might have changed in some ways, but his penchant for assuming the worst remained the same.

"I'm right, though. Even if she's happy with Aaron the Great, those two have entirely too much fun together for it to stay platonic."

"So you still subscribe to the same idiotic theory about friendship?" I wasn't sure why I was even posing it as an inquiry when his opinion was obvious.

"It's not a theory, Glasses—it's a fact," he said, stretching out his long legs under the table. "And coworkers are the worst, too, by the way, because they don't realize they're becoming 'friends' until that 'friendship' turns into attraction, which ultimately becomes a hookup."

"That's a trash theory." I watched just over his shoulder as Theo and Nekesa laughed together as they stood in line. *He's wrong, right?* I said, "I guarantee you, no matter how much those two might work together, nothing will happen between them except friendship."

"Care to make a wager?" he asked, his eyes twinkling with excitement even as his mouth stayed in its patented snarky half smile.

"On what?"

"Gimme your phone," he said, holding out his palm.

"What?" For some reason, I pulled it from my pocket and handed it over. "What are you doing?"

"Putting in my number so we can work out the details of our

bet later." He glanced toward the counter. "Shhh—here they come."

He finished entering his number before dropping my phone onto the table.

I stared at my phone as if it were a loaded gun, because, *What the hell?* Suddenly I had Mr. Nothing's phone number—*definitely wasn't on my new-job bingo card for today*—and also he wanted to make a bet on my friend's fidelity.

I was getting whiplash from all the WTFs.

"You guys ready?" Nekesa gave me a weird look, and I knew she'd seen Charlie messing with my phone.

I snatched it up, feeling like I'd been caught misbehaving.

"Yep—let's go," I said, standing up so fast that I knocked over my chair. It landed with a crash when it hit the tile, and I wanted to disappear when all heads turned toward me.

Shit.

As I bent to pick it up, it occurred to me that this job might not turn out to be the *mindless fun* that Nekesa thought it would be.

CHAPTER TEN

Bailey

"Mom?"

I walked into the apartment and closed the door behind me. My mom hadn't planned on going anywhere that night, so the silence meant that she was probably asleep already.

Which was kind of a bummer, because I'd been looking forward to the brownie batter party, but also a relief because if she was asleep, that meant there was definitely no Scott underfoot and I would have the place all to myself. Mr. Squishy came over and rubbed against my calf before dropping flat onto his back and rolling from side to side.

"Hey, Squish." I stepped out of my shoes, then rubbed his fluffy belly with my foot before he got spooked by a nonexistent something and ran down the hall.

"Freak." I went into the kitchen, opened the fridge, and took out a can of RC and a can of Diet Rite. I was wide awake after my weird day of training and kind-of-fun evening with Nekesa and Aaron at the bookstore, so I was excited to just stretch out on the couch and mindlessly binge-watch *The Bonk*. I grabbed a glass out of the cupboard and a bag of Doritos.

I was just pushing the door to exit the kitchen when I heard, "Bay, is that you?"

I gritted my teeth, stopped, and dropped my snacks onto the counter as if they'd been burning my hands. The cans tumbled into the sink. "Yes."

"Come here, will ya?"

I breathed in through my nose before going into the living room. I wanted to scream as I saw Scott all stretched out on the sofa with only the muted television lighting the room. He was lying on his side, watching football in his stupid white crew socks.

Why can't he keep his damned shoes on?

"Where's my mom?"

"She went to bed."

So why the hell are you still here? He was giving me a sleepy half smile, like he'd been dozing before I showed up, and his obvious level of comfort in our house made me clench my fists so tightly that I knew I'd have crescent-shaped marks on my palms when I escaped to my room.

"Your mom said you'd be home by eleven."

I blinked and my cheeks got warm. "Yeah?"

He glanced at his watch. "It's past eleven, Bay."

Bailey. It's fucking Bailey. I tucked my hair behind my ears and said, "We, um, got a little carried away at the bookstore."

"Don't worry—I'm not going to tell your mom." He gave me a smile that I think was supposed to be warm and adulty. "But you should probably get less distracted next time so she doesn't worry, don't you think?"

My face burned, and all I could manage was, "Yeah. Um. I'm going to bed."

But inside, I was raging. This man was speaking to me about my mother? *Scott* was talking about her like she was his primary concern, like it was *his* job to make sure she was happy?

I clenched my jaw and had taken one step when he asked, "Did you have fun?"

I stopped. "What?"

Again with the fatherly smile. He asked, "Did you guys have a good time shopping?"

I smiled back as I daydreamed about pushing him off the couch. With a cattle prod. "Yeah."

"Good." He snuggled back into the couch pillows. "Night, Bay."

MY NAME IS BAILEY, YOU SHOELESS DOUCHEBAG! I wanted to roar it like a bloodthirsty hellbeast, because only my friends and my mom got to call me that.

But I just said, "Good night."

As soon as my door closed behind me, I gritted my teeth and threw my head back in a silent scream. It was so unfair. Wasn't your house supposed to be the one place where you felt *at home*? Like, relaxed and comfortable? My heart ached with homesickness whenever I thought about the house back in Fairbanks. Not because of the home itself, but because it seemed like a lifetime ago that I'd lived with the wrapped-in-a-blanket comfort of knowing that at any given time, the only inhabitants of the place were the members of my family.

No dates, no boyfriends, no coworkers who liked to yell *Whoo* when they had girls' night at our apartment. I missed my home being *my* home so much that I rarely allowed myself to even remember life before the split.

It hurt too much.

I flipped on my little TV, but Scott's presence had ruined *The Bonk*. I was too worked up to get lost in trashy reality TV. I tossed my phone onto the bed and changed into my pajamas— my dad's faded old *Global Weather Central* T-shirt that still went down to my knees—as I silently raged.

I felt like I was going to explode.

My phone buzzed, and I didn't recognize the number that popped up. But when I opened the message, it was from Charlie.

Hey, Glasses.

Even though he'd said he was going to text me, I couldn't believe he actually kept his word. I stared at the phone in my hand like I'd never seen a phone before, wondering how to proceed. *Do I answer and engage with him? Do I ignore it and pretend it never happened?*

I felt too *ragey* about Scott to think rationally.

But as I flopped down onto my bed, I thought about what Charlie had said about his interactions with his mom's boyfriend. Did he really just go off whenever he felt like it? I could never do that, but imagining it was sublime. Calling Scott a peckerface and telling him to put some shoes on his gnarly feet? That was some euphoric kind of daydreaming.

Instead of responding to his "hey," I went wild with oversharing.

Me: My mom's boyfriend just called me out on being late. She's asleep, as in down for the night in her bedroom, but he is still here watching TV. Is there a way to kill him without getting caught?

There were immediate texting bubbles, and then—

Charlie: Just ask him why he's still there and throw in the word "loser." Tell him he's gotta go.

I couldn't believe I was smiling, but I was. The idea of that conversation was just too funny. I texted: **I can't do that.**

There were more conversation bubbles and then they disappeared.

Just as my phone rang.

It was Charlie.

Almost on instinct, I let my phone slip from my hand.

Why is he calling me?

My heartbeat picked up as I retrieved the phone, unsure yet again on the best way to proceed. Talking to Charlie on the phone, instead of just texting, seemed like a big bump up for us on the friendship scale and seemed somehow unwise.

But for reasons I didn't have time to explore, I answered.

"Hello?" I said, *beyond* hesitant about this unexpected form of communication.

"Quit being a wuss. Go out there and get it done."

I lifted up enough to kick the throw pillows off my bed before flopping back down. "I don't like confrontation."

"Do you like hiding in your bedroom?" he asked, his voice sounding deeper over the phone.

"Well, no."

"And you can't just give up your territory, by the way." I could hear music in the background, and I wondered what he was listening to. "As soon as he conquers the living room, he's only going to advance and take more space. Before you know it, you'll be living in an occupied state where he is the king. Stand your ground."

I turned over onto my back, amazed that anyone's brain worked that way. Love him or hate him, Charlie was definitely his own person. I said, "He's not *advancing*, you psycho. This isn't a war."

"The hell it isn't." It sounded like he was moving around when he said, "I fought hard but not until it was too late. Now the jackass practically lives here."

"Ugh." Three stains formed a flower shape on my ceiling, and I wondered what had caused it. "That's a nightmare."

"Right?" I heard him bite into something crunchy.

"So he's there *all* the time?"

"Every minute."

"Does he act like he belongs in your family?"

"What?"

"Like, is his role that of your mother's roommate, where he stays at your house but that's kind of it, or does he tag along if you guys decide to eat out?"

He sounded like he was smiling when he said, "You sweet little naïve child, hoping for some fictional version of the best.

78

The answer to your question is that Clark is ever-present. He eats with us, watches TV with us, rides in the car with us, texts us, and shares his every dickish opinion with us. Last week, for example, he went to conferences with my mom, asked my trig teacher if it was possible for me to come in early for extra credit, and then he came home and casually mentioned that I wasn't applying myself."

"Shut *up*," I said, horrified *for* him. How utterly intrusive.

"Trust me, I wish I could."

"That's the worst thing I've ever heard," I said, staring up at those ugly ceiling stains.

"Which is why you need to stand your ground."

"You're right."

"But, Bailey," he chastised, his tone downright fatherly, "you're not even going to leave your room, are you?"

I shook my head. "Nope."

"You're just going to hope for the best?" he asked, sounding disappointed in me.

"That's right."

"Well, I've got a news flash, Glasses—the best never comes."

"So." I rolled over onto my side and realized I didn't want to get off the phone with him. Apparently, when facing depressing Scott thoughts and certain insomnia, I was desperate enough to grab on to ol' Charlie. "You're just as positive as ever. Like a freaking ray of sunshine."

"I'm still a realist, yes," he said, sounding incredibly serious.

"Well, I'm just going to trust that my mom will bore of Scott over time and then maybe take a hiatus from dating for a while."

I was counting on that.

He made a noise of dissent, like a snort or an exhale, before saying, "Yeah, that'll happen."

"Well, if it doesn't, I'll just go back to the murder plan."

"Smart. You'd probably be one hell of a killer."

"Why would you say *that*?" I grabbed the remote from my nightstand and started flipping. "I just told you I hate confrontation."

"It's the half-diet, half-regular thing with your soda. You're meticulous, like a total sociopath. You'd probably chop up a body on a tarp and individually wrap each section in ziplock baggies and newspapers. While wearing rubber cleaning gloves. Wouldn't even spill a single drop of blood."

"Oh my God," I said, laughing in spite of myself. "That's pretty dark, even for you."

"You're the murderer."

I sped through the channels until I found a rerun of *Psych*. "Says you."

"Listen, about the bet—" he started, and I cut him off.

"Yeah, I don't think it's a good idea," I said, feeling guilty for even discussing it.

"It's not—it's a *great* idea." He dove right in like he was excited about the wager. "So here's what I'm thinking. Since we're all going to be working the front desk, it'll be cake to see them in action. I say we give it thirty days or a hookup, whichever comes first."

I crawled under the covers and repeated, "Nope. I have no desire to make a bet with you about my best friend."

"What if I said your refusal to wager has nothing to do with that."

I sighed. "And I suppose you're going to tell me what you think it actually has to do with."

"You got it."

Charlie's confidence in his own opinions was truly remarkable.

"The real reason you don't want to make the bet is because Nekesa is your friend and you know you should have faith in her. But deep down, you also know the truth about love. You try to deny it, like a little kid convincing themselves that they *didn't* see their parents putting Santa labels on the presents under the tree, but it's there, deep in your psyche."

"You don't know jack about my psyche," I said as I rolled over and snuggled deeper into the covers. "We're not all jaded like you."

"You saw her and Theo," he continued, ignoring me, "and you know that as much as she might like her boyfriend, she has chemistry with that prep school jackass. Love is fickle, and everyone—even Nekesa—is capable of infidelity when faced with chemistry."

"Wrong," I muttered, then added, "And you're a ghoul, by the way."

"I'll take your flippant insult as your compliance." And before I could say no, absolutely not, Charlie's deep voice asked, "So what're you going to give me when I win?"

This time I didn't try to hide my irritated sigh. "No idea." I took off my glasses and set them on the nightstand. "I've got sixty-eight dollars in my bank account and a visually impaired cat, so I'm afraid it's slim pickings. But you're not going to get it, so I'm not too concerned."

He was back to crunching something again. "Let's just say that when I believe what will happen happens, you have to be at my beck and call for an entire week. If I need a ride somewhere, you have to squeal up to my house as soon as I ring. If I need someone to swing into Baker's and buy me a Snickers bar and a box of triple-XL condoms, you are my smiley little rubber Snickers wench. Work for you?"

"First of all, you're disgusting and you wish." I laughed in spite of myself because when he wasn't being negative, he was funny in his own way. "But fine, because it's NEVER. GOING. TO. HAPPEN. Instead, you'll be scooping Mr. Squishy's litter box every day. You'll be my smiley little litter box wench."

"Three things," Charlie said. "First, I'm not worried about losing. Second, that is *such* an idiotic name for a cat. And third . . ."

He paused, not finishing his statement until I finally asked, "What's the third?"

"The third is that *of course* you have a cat. I have never met anyone in my life who's more of a 'future cat lady' than you."

I turned off my lamp and closed my eyes. "I'm sure you mean that to be insulting, but I accept it as a compliment because cats are awesome; thank you, Charlie. And I'm going to sleep now. G'night."

"Cats are the worst, actually." He scoffed and said, "And g'night to you too, Glasses."

As tired as I was, it took me forever to fall asleep after we hung up. There was some morsel of truth in Charlie's notions about love.

Logically, I knew better.

But his example about chemistry had been true with my parents. No one cheated, but exposure to chemistry outside of their relationship had shown them that they no longer had it.

And it'd been true with Zack, though beer had played as big a part as chemistry.

I knew Charlie was wrong, but his words had given voice to that tiny part of me that questioned everything.

And that voice didn't need any encouragement.

CHAPTER ELEVEN

Bailey

I walked into the kitchen the next morning, starving and half-asleep and totally regretting my decision to ignore the alarm the first three times it went off. I had to be at Planet Funnn in thirty minutes for day two of training, so I was going to have to wolf down my bagel, throw my hair into a ponytail, and put on makeup when I got there.

"Good morning, my sole offspring," my mom said, not looking up from the newspaper that was on the table. The room smelled like the Folgers coffee that she guzzled by the pot, and I wondered if we had enough almond milk for me to make it into a decent cold brew.

"Good morning, matriarch," I muttered, opening the pantry and grabbing the package of everything bagels. I pulled one out and put it into the toaster, and I was reaching for a plate when IT happened.

Scott walked into the kitchen wearing plaid pajama bottoms and a faded white T-shirt that I could see a forest of chest hair through. "Well, good morning!"

"Oh my God." I yanked down my sleep shirt (even though it went to my knees) and crossed my arms over my braless chest. "Um, I didn't know—"

"It's, uh—it's okay." He held up a hand and gave me the world's most awkward smile, looking mortified. "I have a daughter your age so . . ."

He shrugged and looked like he wished the room would swallow him.

"You're fine," he mumbled. "I have to go shower anyway."

And then he turned and walked right back out of the kitchen.

I think I stared at the spot where he'd appeared (and quickly disappeared) with my mouth hanging wide open, but I'm not sure. Time stopped and sounds got furry as the ramifications of everything slapped over me. He'd stayed the night. He had stayed the night . . . with my mom . . . in our apartment. Like he lived there. Like he belonged there.

What did it mean?

Surely this wasn't just going to be a onetime thing, right? My heart raced as I wished so badly that it was, even though I knew better. Was he slowly moving in now—was that it? And shouldn't my mother be worried about what this said to me about sex or something? Shouldn't someone be protecting me from that kind of bullshit?

And side note: What did his having a daughter my age have to do with the fact that I wasn't wearing pants—or a bra—in front of him in our kitchen? Did he really think the fact that he had offspring in my general age vicinity mattered? Since I wasn't related to this jackass of a man in any way, shape, or form, I was going to have to disagree with him and say that it wasn't okay for me—at seventeen—to be nipping out and bare-legged in front of his fortysomething ass.

"Bay, honey."

My mom's voice—soft and gruff with morning—made my head swivel around. I foolishly thought she was going to save me. Apologize, rescue, or at least comfort me in this most disconcerting of breakfast scenarios. Her pretty face was half smiling, but she was looking at the spot where he'd just been standing, not at me.

I said, "Yeah?"

"Why don't you go put on some pants and we can all have breakfast together?" She glanced at my face and gestured toward my room with her chin, whispering, "You should probably get dressed *before* coming out when there are people here, kiddo."

"Oh my God, that is disgusting." Nekesa rummaged through her purse in the passenger seat while I drove. "YIKES! He stayed the night? What did your mom say when he just walked out of her room in the morning? Did she warn you?"

"No." My head was bouncing with all of Nekesa's questions that I had already asked myself a million times that morning. "She acted like it was normal and like I was somehow in the wrong for doing exactly what I do every single morning."

"I cannot believe Emily didn't step up for you."

"Right?" I said, realizing that was exactly what the worst part of the morning had been. My mother taking a step back from me.

"What's his last name?" Nekesa took out her phone. "I'm gonna look up this weaseldick and see what his story is. Scott what?"

"Hall." Nekesa was acting psychotic, but it felt good to have someone in my corner. She might be outrageous, but I also knew she'd stab someone in the face with an ice pick (her words) for me. "Scott Hall."

I slowed and took a right at the corner, driving too fast but determined to be on time for work.

"Found him."

I glanced over, and she was scrolling.

She said, "He's got a Facebook. Profile pic is a normal dad-ish kind of thing."

She scrolled a little more. "No weird political rants, no sexist posts, nothing pervy so far. Looks like he's got a daught—"

"Our age, remember?" I said, still seething inside from the awkward encounter.

"Oh my God."

"What?"

"Wait," Nekesa said, bringing the phone closer to her face. "Hang on for a sec."

"What?" I glanced over, dying to know what she'd found.

"Holy shit!" She yelled it and glanced up from her phone, her mouth dropping wide open.

I was scared and hopeful, all at once. Had she found a

criminal record? A rap sheet that would make my mother insta-dump Scott? I said, "Will you please tell me what you're freaking about?"

She shook her head and looked legit nervous. "I don't think I can even say it."

I welcomed the red light over the upcoming intersection so I could slam on my brakes. "For the love of God, what?"

"Okay, don't freak out." She breathed in through her nose before holding out a hand to calm me and saying, "His daughter. Is. Kristy Hall."

"No, no—it's a common last name," I said, trying to believe it even as a huge knot formed in my stomach. "He lives on the other side of town, way outside of our district. The name is just a coincidence."

"Bailey, it's not."

It was my mouth's turn to drop wide open as I stared at her in disbelief. There was just no way. I said, "If there is a God, you are lying to me."

"Not lying, sweetie—look." She held out her phone, and sure enough, there was an adorable picture of Scott and Kristy Hall.

Together.

Kristy Hall—was the universe kidding me with that?

Kristy went to our school; she was pretty and wildly popular, and she *hated* my guts. Which was weird in that I kept to myself and a large portion of the population didn't even know who I was. I was off the radar to most of my classmates, but if Kristy saw me, she couldn't stop herself from calling me out.

What are you looking at?

She was a nightmare, and the sole cause of my school anxiety. All because of one stupid, stupid night.

Nekesa had dragged me to a football party. She'd just started talking to Aaron, and she was head-over-heels obsessed. Half the people there had been floor-licking drunk, and since I knew no one, I found a nice spot on the sofa in the corner and I literally read *The Handmaid's Tale* on my phone—all by myself—while Nekesa made out with her new boyfriend somewhere upstairs.

I'd been totally invisible until Callie Booth—Kristy's best friend—had plopped down onto the floor beside me. She was hammered and mumbling incoherently, and then she laid her head on my calf.

I'd pretended not to notice—still very intent on remaining invisible—until I felt moisture on my skin.

I'd glanced down, and it was clear the girl had just vomited.

And her mouth was resting on my bare leg.

Without thinking, I moved my leg. I just jerked it out of the way of the vomit, not giving any thought to the fact that once I moved my leg, her forehead might slam into the glass coffee table in front of her.

But worse than Callie's terribly loud head-bang and resultant groan was Kristy walking into the room the instant it happened. One minute I'd been minding my own business, and the next Kristy Hall had been screaming at me in the middle of the party, "Did you just kick her in the head?"

Even just *remembering* that moment made my blood pressure spike and my cheeks get hot, because it had been straight out of a bad dream. I had been terrified. If Nekesa hadn't come downstairs that very minute, I'm fairly certain I would've been clawed to death by screaming banshees in letter jackets.

God. Kristy Hall.

I was going to have to find a way to ensure my mother ended things with Scott before Kristy calling me a bitch over morning bagels became a distinct possibility.

God. Kristy Hall.

CHAPTER TWELVE

Charlie

As soon as I pulled into the parking lot, my phone buzzed.

I almost ignored it for multiple reasons. First, I knew it would be my mom, and I was too tired to deal with her. Clark was in her ear all the time with parental advice, so it'd become commonplace for her to text me about ways I could be a better son, a more thoughtful brother, and a fucking productive tenant.

Thanks but no thanks.

Second, my shift started in two minutes, so just answering the text was guaranteed to make me late, and I didn't feel like being late on day two.

Still, I took out my phone and checked the display.

Becca: Can I call you?

"Fuck," I said under my breath, leaning my head back on the driver's seat and trying to figure out how to answer that question when my pulse was out of control. It was idiocy, but just seeing Bec's name pop up on my phone sent my vitals spiraling every time.

No. What do you need? That would be the intelligent response, the way to avoid getting sucked back into the Becca vortex, but I wasn't intelligent.

No, when it came to Bec, I was the world's biggest dumbass.

I hit the call button and waited for her to answer, wondering what she wanted to talk about. We'd broken up a few months ago, but she still randomly texted me when I was "on her mind" or something reminded her of me. So even though we weren't anything anymore, and last I'd heard she was talking to Kyle Hart, I found myself having hours-long random text exchanges with her every couple weeks.

"Hey, you," she answered, her voice quiet. She wasn't allowed to do anything on Sundays because her parents called it a family day, so I imagined she was still in bed. "I was dying to talk to you. I'm so glad you called."

I looked through the windshield and watched a group of Red Dwarfs walking into the building together. "Yeah?"

"Yes." She cleared her throat and said, "I don't want this to sound weird because it's obviously no big deal at all, but you haven't told anyone that we still talk sometimes, right?"

Fuck. I dragged a hand through my hair and said, "Right."

"Good," she said, relief in her voice. "Kyle said something last night that made me realize that people might get the wrong idea. You know, if they knew we still text."

"Ah," I said, unable to come up with anything else.

92

"No one understands that a guy and a girl can be friends and that's it—just friends," she said, sounding entirely happy as she rambled in that way I'd always found adorable. "Why can't we normalize guys and girls having platonic friendships with each other?"

Because they don't exist.

"Listen, Bec, my shift starts in a minute so I have to go," I said, taking the keys out of my ignition and feeling like a fool. I knew—I fucking knew—that relationships and love were sinking ships of bullshit, but for some reason, that knowledge went out the goddamn window every time I engaged with Becca.

"Oh, okay," she said. "Well, have fun at work."

"Sure," I said, opening my door.

"And please don't tell anyone about—"

"*Bec.*" I said it through gritted teeth, less upset than just . . . done. Just fucking done and exhausted with motherfucking emotions. "Got it."

I shook my head as I disconnected the call, because it sucked being right all the time. Bailey thought I was a cynical asshole, but the truth was that she was just further behind me in line. Eventually she'd get to the front and see it all, and I kind of envied that she wasn't there yet.

I kind of wished she could stay back there forever, blinking fast and clinging to her blissful notions.

I popped a TUM as I headed for the building, counting on the sheer idiocy of my new job to make me forget about life.

CHAPTER THIRTEEN

Bailey

"Well, if you're not going to kill him, you could make the guy's life so miserable that he never wants to return to your apartment."

"How so?" I looked at Charlie, then at Nekesa and Theo. We were on our first break, sitting at a cafeteria table in Planet Funnn's Supermassive Fun Hole, and since Nekesa had no filter, the boys were now totally up to speed on the embarrassing thing I'd done at my first booze party, how much I was hated by the popular girls at our school, and the crushing reality that my nemesis could potentially move in with me in the not-so-distant future.

"The possibilities are endless." Charlie's voice was quiet and kind of gruff, like he was bored. Or surly. He took a long drink of his Rockstar and said, "You can sit between him and your mom on the couch every single time he comes over. You can find out what he hates and do *that* like all the time. Conversely, you can find out what he loves and ruin it."

"Example, please," I said, intrigued by this notion of subterfuge.

Nekesa grinned and said, "Oh my God—he's right! If you know he loves football, and he's coming over on a Monday night, you make sure you're already watching a documentary on, like, Hurricane Katrina when he gets there. Bonus points if you get your mom super into it so when he shows up, there's nothing else for him to do but watch the depressing documentary."

"Ooh," I said, thinking that didn't sound too difficult.

Charlie added, "Or if you find out he's allergic to dogs, borrow mine for an hour and we'll let him run all over your house. The Undertaker sheds like a son of a bitch, so we'll roll him all over the sofa so that the next time the boyfriend lies down to watch TV, he'll have a massive asthma attack."

"I'm not sure what's more unbelievable here. The underlying darkness of you guys' childish *Parent Trap* ideas," I said around a smile, "or the fact that *his* dog is named the Undertaker."

Charlie's mouth turned up. "What? My little sister loves wrestling."

I wondered what Charlie was like with his sister. Was he sweet and protective, or kind of an asshole? Honestly, I could see both.

"My uncle got the Undertaker's autograph last summer," Theo added proudly.

That made Nekesa giggle and flick a straw wrapper at him. "Aw, does widdle Theo wike westling?"

"That's it." Theo tugged on her hair and said, "One too many *widdle*s today."

They were all smiles and breathless laughter, which made me glance at Charlie.

Who gave me a knowing smirk and a slow nod.

I narrowed my eyes into a squint and shook my head as if to say *No way*, even though Nekesa and Theo really *were* flirting all over each other, but the squint was rendered meaningless when Theo tickled Nekesa. He tickled her, she squealed, and Charlie ditched subtlety as he stood and mouthed the words *TOLD YOU* while wearing a cocky, all-knowing grin.

Gahhhh. It was infuriating, the way he always thought he was right.

The four of us spent the entire day learning how to work the front desk. The majority of our responsibilities would be checking the guests in and out, and answering the switchboard. It didn't seem difficult, but it didn't necessarily seem exciting, either.

Toward the end of the day, we had to take turns role-playing. I was killing it, totally slaying as a desk clerk and impressing my trainer with my skills. I knew it didn't matter, but I *liked* doing a good job.

Only, every time Charlie played a guest and I was the desk clerk, he used ridiculous accents and terrible voices to try to make me laugh. I was able to hold it together and be professional, but when he attempted to channel a Frenchwoman with a very high-pitched voice, a tiny laugh escaped.

"Miss Mitchell," the trainer said, not looking amused in the slightest by Charlie's shenanigans, "the reality is that there *will* be guests at our establishment who are unusual. Are you going to crack up every time they ask you for a room?"

I glanced at Charlie; was *I* actually the one getting in trouble? I couldn't believe it; it was day two, and he'd already gotten me on the naughty list. I pressed my lips together and took a deep breath before recovering with, "Of course not. I'll, um, I'll get it together."

The trainer gave me a nod but still looked annoyed.

I turned to Charlie to glare, but he gave me a wink that made glaring impossible. Because uh-oh . . . something about the intimate wink did *things* to my stomach. I cleared my throat and looked away.

What the hell was that?

I cleared my throat again and decided it wasn't anything more than hunger, making my stomach growly.

When we finally got off work and the four of us were walking to our cars, my mom texted.

Scott and I are hungry for Godfather's. Does pizza work for you for dinner?

"Dammit," I whined, putting my phone into my pocket as instant dread filled me at the thought of more forced proximity. "He's already over at my house."

"He probably never left," Charlie said. Nekesa and Theo were too busy talking to even notice we were speaking.

"Shut up," I said to him, hating that thought. "Not helpful."

"Seriously, just make the dude's life hell." Charlie waved a hand in the air as he said, "It's so easy."

I wished it was. I wished it was easy and I wished it would work. "Maybe I *do* need to come up with a plan."

"Hell yes," Charlie said enthusiastically. "A control freak like you should definitely take some notes."

I wanted to deny that I was a control freak, but I knew that with Charlie it was pointless. It would result in ten minutes of back-and-forth that would end in him thinking he was right, even though he wasn't.

No, the bigger point was whether or not I wanted to be proactive in the Scott situation. Whether or not I wanted to *do* something to try to shake him from our lives.

Ugh, just the thought of it all stressed me out.

The idea of plotting something was immature; who was I, Lindsay Lohan (and Lindsay Lohan), employing childish shenanigans in order to get my long-lost parents back together? I wanted to think I was better than that.

And what if somehow it worked and Scott walked away? *I* wanted that, but what about my mom? I couldn't stand the thought of anything making her sad, so was I really considering spearheading her heartbreak?

But just as I thought that, I remembered the brownie batter party that didn't happen last night. Instead of my mom and me, hanging out together the way we always had since she'd split with my dad, Scott's ass had been on our couch and he'd put my mother to bed before I'd even gotten home.

And it wasn't about the brownies—I wasn't *that* selfish.

It was about what had survived the divorce. Our family had imploded, but my mom and I having brownie parties still felt like some descendant of that, some tiny fragment that had survived the crash. Connecting me to the family we used to be.

I was fine with her dating—I didn't want her to be alone forever—but Scott was an imminent threat to all the brownie parties I held on to for dear life.

"Will you help me? Like, for real, not being a smart-ass?"

Charlie looked surprised for a second, and then he shrugged like he didn't care. "Sure. I was going to hit Zio's on my way home, so if you want to tag along, we can map out your annoy-him-until-he-leaves strategy."

"My mom and Scott are ordering pizza, so I should probably—"

"Cancel with them and go with me." He looked down at me with raised eyebrows. "Duh."

"How would this help?" I asked, noticing that he really *did* have a nice face in spite of his Mr. Nothing disposition. *Man, would I love to put mascara on lashes that long.* It just wasn't fair that he was born that way.

"Chaos. Tension," he replied, reaching out a hand and patting down the curl on the right side of my part that had been wildly uncooperative that day. "Throwing a wrench into their we-happy-three plans."

"Okay." I smacked his hand before pulling out my phone to text my mom. I said to him as I opened my contacts, "Just let me drop off Nekesa first."

"Theo," Charlie said, his eyes on me, "do you think you can give Nekesa a ride home so Bay and I can go strategize her destroy-the-boy plan?"

"Of course," Theo said, looking like he didn't mind a bit.

Charlie murmured "Of course" at a volume that only I could hear.

"Thanks," Nekesa said, also looking like she had no regrets about being rerouted to Hot Theo.

Shit, maybe Charlie was right about them.

I followed Charlie downtown and parked at a meter spot, and by the time I got inside the restaurant, he already had menus and a table.

"So." I sat down, pulled off my cross-body bag, and said, "Do you think this can actually work?"

"Doing anything is better than doing nothing, right?" he asked, crumpling his straw wrapper into a perfect tiny ball before flicking it in my direction.

"I suppose," I said, still unsure if that was actually true. Unsure what I was even doing here with him.

A waiter came over and took our orders, and then we got right to it. Charlie was full of ideas on how I could make our apartment an "inhospitable environment" for my mother's boyfriend, and we wolfed down pizza while I rejected each and every ridiculous idea.

"I can't do that," I said, full-on cackling when he suggested I start hiding Scott's stuff. Charlie had a way of being cynically dark and absurdly funny, all at the same time, and apparently that was my sense of humor's sweet spot. Most of the time I wasn't sure if he was serious or kidding, but the sarcasm in his deep voice made it funny, regardless. I shook my head and pulled a piece of pepperoni off my slice. "I just can't."

"Why not?" he asked, picking up the red Coca-Cola cup that was half-full of Mountain Dew. "If he loses his glasses every time he comes over, he might stop coming over, right?"

"Seems oversimplified," I said, wishing it wasn't.

"What is happening on your plate right now?" Charlie asked, setting down his soda and gesturing with both hands. His eyes were narrowed, like he couldn't believe what he was seeing, but his lips were turned up just a little when he said, "That is pizza desecration. You should be ashamed of yourself."

"No, it's not." I looked down at the pile of toppings and said, "I eat it all. I just like to eat the cheese and toppings first, then the crust."

"Why?" He reminded me of Airport Charlie as he gave his head a disgusted shake and added, "Seriously."

I sighed. "Do you really want to know, or do you just want to mock me?"

He reached out a big hand and grabbed one of my black olives. "Both."

"Okay." I smacked his hand and said, "If you eat it all together, you don't really taste the crust because of the topping flavors. This way, you get to enjoy the flavors of beef and pepperoni and olives and onions, and then you get to enjoy the texture and yeasty flavor of the crust."

His mouth slid into a small grin that almost looked appreciative. His dark eyes were kind of twinkly when he said, "It looks disgusting, but what you said kind of makes sense."

I lifted my chin, feeling somehow vindicated. "I know. Right? Try it with your pizza."

"Try—"

"But drink water first." I slid his water closer to him and said, "Palate cleanser."

His eyes were a little squinty—I sensed a laugh in there—but he didn't say anything. Instead, he did exactly what I said. He took a big drink from his water, slammed down the cup, then gave me ridiculous eye contact—like we were in a staring contest—as he first took a bite of his topping, then his crust.

"I'm right, right?" I asked, setting my chin on my wrist. "It's way better."

He sat back in his chair and watched me, without a word, his head tilted like he was trying to figure something out. He wasn't smiling anymore, didn't look teasing, but he didn't look unhappy, either.

He looked . . . analytical.

I cleared my throat and felt warmth on my cheeks. "Whatever. *I* know I'm right, even if you're too—"

"Amazing," he said, his face still unreadable.

"Not the word I was looking for, but—"

"No," he said, his mouth sliding into a smile. "Your pizza methodology. Is amazing."

I blinked. *Is he mocking me?* "Are you saying that you agree with me?"

"I'm saying that I feel like I've never tasted pizza before. Thank you, Bailey Mitchell Glasses, for showing me your ways."

"You're welcome," I said, and it was impossible not to give in to a huge smile of victory. I didn't want him to know how much I enjoyed his compliment, so I said, "Now back to the devious plan."

His eyes stayed on mine for another second before he gave a nod and grabbed his soda. "About that. Let me ask you something."

"God."

"Do you really think you'll have the coconuts to do any of these things we're planning? You're kind of a pathetic people pleaser."

"No, I'm not," I shot back, sounding more defensive than I wanted to, but dammit—I felt a little attacked. Because *what was it with that*? Just because I was *nice* and preferred to avoid conflict didn't mean I was pathetic. Nekesa called me that— *pathetic people pleaser*—all the time, and even Zack had eluded to it when we were together.

"Easy," Charlie said, putting up his hands like he was being held up. "I didn't mean it."

I raised an eyebrow, my irritation instantly diffused by his overdramatic facial expression. "Really?"

"Okay, I probably meant it," he said, his unapologetic smile making him look like a mischievous little boy. "But back to the question at hand. Are you brave enough to rock the boat?"

"I don't know," I said, giving the question honest consideration. I had a very hard time with confrontation, so he was right to question my abilities. "I mean, I *want* to."

He made a noise and shook his head. "Not good enough, bruh."

"I *know*," I whined, stirring my drink with its straw and actually meaning it when I said, "I wish I was more like you."

"I knew it." He leaned back in his chair and crossed his

arms over his chest, which was so wide, I wondered if he was a swimmer, and he said with teasing smugness, "I'm your role model."

"Hardly."

"If you want to call me *Uncle* Charlie, or Mentor Charlie," he said, smiling in a funny way that made me want to smile back, "you totally can."

"I'd rather eat glass," I said, pulling off the sharp retort even as I wanted to laugh. "Can we get back to the business at hand?"

"Sure," he said, his eyes moving all over my face before focusing on my gaze. "Well, in my opinion, the first thing you need to do is dig deep and find your inner asshole."

"Oh, wow."

"Strike the language," he said quickly. "But you know what I mean. Just be a dick."

"No one's as good at that as you." I looked at him, at his naturally sarcastic face, and said, "Oh my God—come with me."

"What?" His dark eyebrows knotted together.

"Yes!" It was brilliant. "I'll be braver with you there—"

"More brave," he interrupted. His brow was still furrowed, but the playful glint was in his eyes.

"And you can bring *your* surly attitude too." I didn't want us to be *mean* to Scott, but I felt desperate to do something— *anything*—to slow things down. I was terrified that my life was about to change yet again, and I couldn't let that happen when I was still adjusting to the first change. I just needed more time before my mom got serious—with *anyone*. "We'll be the dynamic duo of assholery."

"Lame superhero names," he muttered, watching me closely like he was thinking a million things.

"I'll let you be the bigger, badder one," I teased, tucking my hair behind my ears, dying to know what was going on in his head.

"Oh, you'll *let* me." He rolled his eyes. "What's in it for me?"

Now I rolled my eyes. "You really *are* a dick. How about you're just being a nice friend?"

"Coworker," he corrected, and I heard the vibration of his phone as he pulled it out of his pocket and glanced at the notification.

"That's right—coworker," I said, feeling a little *weird* about his correction. I didn't care about being Charlie Sampson's friend, but it felt like a tiny rejection every time he made it clear he'd never be my friend. "God forbid you admit you were wrong about the friendship thing."

"Right?" His jaw clenched as he looked at his phone, and then he turned off the screen and dropped it onto the table. Not angrily, but like he was *done* with it. His gaze came back to mine, and even though he gave me his smart-ass smirk, it didn't reach his eyes when he said, "I'd rather die than be wrong."

"I'd die to prove you wrong," I teased, "so we're kind of similar on this front."

"Only not."

I reached across the table, grabbed his sleeve, and gave his arm a shake, desperate to convince him and also bizarrely compelled to shake that detached expression off his face. "Please do this. Please. Please. Do it. Do it."

That made his mouth curve into a slow, wide smile as he set one very big hand on mine, trapping it against his biceps. "You're begging—I like this."

"So you'll do it?" I asked, a little taken aback by the power of his grin. *Or maybe it's the power of the grin/muscular-arm-under-my-palm combo.*

"I'll follow you to your house and stay just long enough to stir the pot." He exhaled dramatically, shook off my hand, and said, "I'll let you watch the master, and hopefully you'll pick up a few things."

"Are you finished?" I asked, staring pointedly at his empty plate. "I want to get rolling on Operation Ditching Scott."

"So impatient," he said, reaching out a hand and messing up my hair. "My bright-eyed student."

"My dumbass instructor," I said, smacking his hand before fixing my hair. "Let's go."

CHAPTER FOURTEEN

Charlie

What the fuck was I doing?

Going to her house??

I'd been serious about trying to help her, mostly because Bailey seemed so wide-eyed and trusting that she was going to be shattered when reality reared its ugly head. I knew we weren't going to be able to stop it, because *life*, but at least if we fought, she wouldn't feel helpless.

I fucking *hated* feeling helpless.

Because helplessness was a little like waterboarding (I said *a little*). Someone else has all the control while you feel like you can't breathe and like it's never going to stop.

Logically you know it will—*eventually that bucket is going to be empty, right?*—but that doesn't help the panic when the dousing is constant.

God, I'm so fucked-up.

But helping her was one thing.
Going to her *house* to help her?
Terrible idea.

CHAPTER FIFTEEN

Bailey

"Does my hair look okay?" Charlie asked.

I stopped digging for my keys and looked at Charlie, who was giving me a goofy smile and patting his head like he cared. I shook my head and muttered, "You're stunning."

"Why, thank you."

When I got the door unlocked, I took a deep breath before walking inside. No one was in the kitchen, but I could hear my mother's voice in the living room.

"Be a dick," Charlie muttered, his voice deep in my ear, and it made me shiver. Which made him say, "I felt that."

I turned and looked at him, blinking fast at the sexy grin lining his face. He had one of those half smiles that suggested he knew a *lot* about all the things I knew only a little about. He said, "What? I didn't mean anything by it. I was just stating the fact that I felt you get a chill."

I swallowed and hated that my cheeks were insta-hot. "Okay."

"From my mouth's closeness," he teased, and I would've gotten irritated if his words weren't followed by the laid-back chuckle that I'd heard him use all day at work with Theo.

Casual. Harmless.

"Bay?" my mom yelled. "You home?"

"Yeah," I said, grabbing Charlie's sleeve and pulling him into the living room with me. He grunted quietly in response to my bossiness, and I said, "Sorry I'm late."

But when we got fully into the room, I let go of his arm and crossed mine tightly over my chest, hating what I saw. My mom was leaning on Scott on the couch, her feet tucked underneath her like she'd never been more comfortable in her life. He was wearing flannel pajama pants, a baggy T-shirt, and those motherloving white crew socks that made me irrationally angry.

God, what if I'm too late to stop this from becoming our new normal?

"Oh." My mom looked surprised at the sight of Charlie. "Hey there, person I don't know."

"Yeah," I said, tucking my hair behind my ears. "This is Charlie—we work together."

"Hi, Charlie," my mom said, and when I glanced over at him—

Holy crap.

Charlie gave her the world's most charming smile. It wasn't the hitched-up-on-one-side, lazy grin that I'd seen so far, but a full-on smile that belonged on an ad for whitening toothpaste. Squinty eyes, pronounced dimples; he looked *nice*, for God's sake.

I stared at him, fairly certain my mouth was hanging open as he grinned and said, "Hi—it's really nice to meet you."

My mom's smile stretched all the way up to the top of her head—she was positively glowing as she looked at Charlie. Scott stood and held out a hand. "Hey, Charlie. I'm Scott."

Charlie's charming grin melted down into his sarcastic smirk as he shook Scott's hand. "Nice to meet you. You're Bay's dad?"

I bit down on my lip; he was such a shit.

"No," Scott said, looking mildly uncomfortable. "I'm a friend of her mom's."

"Friend, huh?" Charlie said, letting his eyes roam down over Scott's pajama pants and stockinged feet. "Okay."

"Let's get a soda," I said, practically pulling Charlie into the kitchen. As soon as we rounded the corner and were out of their line of sight, I looked at him with wide eyes.

And then he grinned. He grinned like he was victorious, and I dissolved into giggles that sounded ridiculously high-pitched as I tried to make them quiet.

"You are the *worst*," I said, trying to talk and laugh quietly.

"Did you see his face?" Charlie asked, still smiling. "I think he wanted to hit me."

"Shhhshh—listen."

My mom was talking quietly, and we both craned our necks to hear.

"Oh, he didn't mean anything by it," my mom said in a placating tone, which made Charlie throw an elbow into my ribs.

"Oh yes, I did," he whispered, sounding crazy-proud of himself.

"Oh yes, he did," Scott murmured, sounding petulant. "Trust me, I know teenage boys."

I rolled my eyes and so did Charlie.

"Can you just be nice to Bay's friend?" my mom asked. "No big deal, just nice."

My mouth dropped wide open at my mom's snarky tone, and Charlie raised his hands in the air like he'd just won the match. *Oh my God—could his plan actually work?*

"I have to go now," Charlie said, looking down at me with a half smile, "but you're welcome for the awesomeness."

"Noooo," I begged, grabbing his arm and shaking it. "You're doing the Lord's work here."

"Seriously—my mom will freak if I'm late."

"Fine." I let go of his arm. "But can we do this more often? Like, will you come hang over here and just be awful?"

"Sounds like a party," he said, his dark eyes traveling over my face before he stepped around me. "I've got to go home and study," he said, leaning to see into the living room as he called out to my mom, "but it was really nice meeting you."

"You too, Charlie," my mom said, but Scott didn't say a word.

Charlie left, and when I went into the living room, they both looked at me questioningly.

"So Charlie is a coworker, huh?" My mom gave me a funny little smile, like she wanted to pump me for info but knew it was too soon after Zack for her to push romance. She glanced at Scott before saying, "He's really cute."

I pictured his face, and yeah—he *was* really cute.

112

Really cute and really just so irritating.

"We're just friends."

"Thank God," Scott muttered, and when we both looked at him, he said, "What? I just thought he seemed like a little smart-ass. Which is great for a friend, not so great for a boyfriend."

"Wow," my mom said, giving him a confused look with her eyebrows furrowed and her lips pursed.

"What?" Scott asked, his eyes moving from her to me and back again.

"Nothing," she said, giving her head a shake. "I just did not expect *you* to be the one in this apartment with hard-and-fast boyfriend rules."

He set his hand on her knee, made a goofy face, and said, "I am an enigma, don't you know that?"

"I guess I forgot," she said, smiling and dragging a hand through her hair. "You know . . . that you're an *enigma*."

She made an obnoxious face at me, like *Get a load of this guy*, but I couldn't laugh or even smile because I was frozen. I was frozen as I watched them happily laugh together.

God, am I too late?

How was I supposed to jump in front of the Mom-Scott train when it was chugging along so well? I desperately wanted her to be grinning and happy, I really did, but I just didn't want some guy to be the one responsible.

I didn't want *him* to be responsible.

Not because I was like some third grader screaming *You're not my dad* to every man my mother dated; I was good with her having a social life. She's my favorite person in the universe and deserves every good thing.

But on the other hand, like, dammit if I wasn't a twelfth grader who knew exactly how quickly things changed. My father introduced me to Alyssa—a girl he was "seeing"—via FaceTime on a Friday in September, and by the end of that month, he'd completely stopped calling and texting me.

Total radio silence, which, for silence, was overpowering in its utter nonexistence.

How hard was it to send a random text every once in a while, just to let your CHILD know you were thinking about them?

And that was the rub, honestly.

He obviously just *wasn't*. Thinking about me.

I saw on Alyssa's socials yesterday that he and Alyssa had just come back from Hawaii.

So sue me for wanting to slow things down.

"I'm going to bed," I said, needing to get out of there. "G'night."

I made a quick break for my room and tried not to dwell on what was happening, but I was unable to put it out of my head as I changed into shorts and a T-shirt and climbed into bed.

What if he moves in?

I knew it was way too early for that, but I couldn't push the thought out of my head. What the hell would I do if Scott moved in? The thought of someone—anyone—moving into our life made my stomach hurt.

My phone buzzed just as I was flipping for something to watch on Netflix.

Charlie: Did they say anything about me?

I texted: **Scott thinks you're a little smart-ass and is very glad I only like you as a friend.**

Charlie: Coworker

I groaned in the darkness and responded: **Oh yes, that's right. How dare I presume, right?**

Charlie: I'll forgive the presumption.

Me: Oh, thank you.

Charlie: So let me ask you a question, Glasses. Obviously we're both single right now—are you looking? Are you into anyone?

I didn't know what to make of his question. It made sense that he'd wonder—I'd wondered the same thing about him— but I felt lame when I responded with:

I guess I'm open to looking, but I'm not into anyone right now. HBU?

Charlie: Same.

I remembered how happy he'd looked at the movie theater when I'd seen him the year before, and I texted: **Are you still hung up on Movie Promposal Girl?**

Charlie: Yes and no.

I couldn't believe he'd actually answered the question in some kind of serious way. I typed: **What does that mean?**

Charlie: It means I'm not hung up on Bec—she looks happy with her douchebag and I've decided her eyelashes are too long, anyway. I mean, what kind of freak wakes up every morning looking like Clarice the Reindeer?

Me: Who?

Charlie: The reindeer who thinks Rudolph is cute. Her name is Clarice. Remember? Cuuuuuute??

I snorted. **I would've assumed you were born far too jaded to enjoy holiday Claymation specials.**

Charlie: Confession—I'm a sap for the holidays. I don't know what it is, but I really get off on Christmas.

That made me laugh. **Perhaps you should rephrase.**

Charlie: As if anyone would misunderstand and think I spank to the holidays—come on, Glasses. BUT FINE. I thoroughly enjoy the season of giving.

I scrolled to comfort TV—*Schitt's Creek*—and selected the turkey-hunting episode. Then I texted: **So if you're over her, what's with the "yes and no"?**

Charlie: I'm over HER, but I'm not over the shitty feelings about getting dumped. I don't want Becca back, but I also don't really want to get out there and do it all again.

I totally related to that, except I *did* want Zack back.

Our circumstances were completely different, though, because Zack and I should never have broken up. We had a stupid little inconsequential fight, and if he hadn't gone to a party where there was a LOT of beer, we would've gotten back together the next morning and everything would've been fine.

But instead, he'd gotten so hammered that he made out with Allie Clark.

He came over the next day, begging me to forgive him because it was the keg's fault, but I gave him the bird and kicked him out.

But it should've been temporary.

I'd known at the time that I was going to forgive him eventually. I just couldn't right then. I was so angry. And disappointed, now that I look back on it.

But instead of coming back to beg my forgiveness one more time, Zack started seeing Courtney Sullivan. I *knew* it was a rebound thing and that he still loved me, and as soon as they broke up, we would get back together.

Only now he was seeing Kelsie.

I texted: **I didn't know you then—what happened?**

Charlie: She decided that there was someone else that she felt a stronger connection with.

Me: UGH.

I couldn't imagine getting dumped *for* someone else; it was bad enough just seeing Zack with someone else *after* our breakup.

Charlie: Right? Like it wasn't about me, but just how hard she vibrated around someone or something. Bullshit answer.

I agreed, although a tiny part of me wondered if she'd been letting him down easy by saying that and the truth was actually that she'd hit her limit of Mr. Nothing's dark sarcasm. Still, I was supportive and texted: **Total bullshit answer.**

I heard Mr. Squishy scratching at my door, so I had to get off the bed and go let him in.

Charlie: At least I got custody of Scarf.

I climbed back onto my bed and texted:

Please tell me you didn't pull a Gyllenhaal.

Charlie: She tried pulling a Jake on ME, but I went over and reclaimed it. Not gonna have her being reminded of innocence and thinking it smells like me.

I sat straight up. **Holy shit, Chuckles—are you a Swiftie?**

Charlie: Settle your ass down. I just thought the Red rerelease was really good.

Me: I'm speechless. Christmas and Taylor Swift. You're an enigma, Charlie.

CHAPTER SIXTEEN

Bailey

The next few weeks fell into a pattern that pretty much just rotated between school, work, and Charlie. Charlie and I seemed to get scheduled every Tuesday and Thursday night, whereas Nekesa and Theo were the Monday/Wednesday team. The four of us worked together on weekends, which meant that Charlie pretty much texted me throughout the entire weekend shift about the Nekesa/Theo vibe.

Charlie: That is the TWELFTH time she's touched his arm since we started.

Me: You're a psycho.

Charlie: You need to count HIS touches, Glasses.

Me: Why would I do that?

Charlie: Data. It's all about the data.

Me: What does that mean?

Charlie: If you don't know, I'm not going to tell you. Just start counting.

And I did. Charlie always had me doing stupid things that were pointless and silly, things I never would've done and should've said no to, but it was easier to just play along with Charlie's games.

"Salted Nut Roll," Charlie said, staring at the shirtless man in swim trunks who was approaching the vending machine.

"Nope." I looked at the dude's chest hair and *knew* I was going to win this time. "He's all about the Funyuns."

I leaned on the counter of the registration desk, beside Charlie, straining to see.

Charlie had come up with a game—Vending Machine Bet— where we wagered on what the guests were going to purchase when we saw them approaching the machine.

It was just one of *multiple* games Charlie would come up with that helped us pass the time at the front desk. I wondered if Charlie hated being bored, the quiet that came with being bored, or the idea of having it just be him and his thoughts, because he sure put a lot of effort into making up things to do to avoid whatever it was he wanted to avoid.

"Do you think a guy that serious about manscaping," Charlie said quietly, out of the side of his mouth, "would *ever* introduce Funyun dust into his chestal thatch?"

I snorted. "Be nice."

"I am," he said, still watching the guy. "I have mad respect for anyone who chooses to keep it bear-thick on top and nonexistent on the bottom. He marches to his own drum."

"Shhhh," I said, watching intently as the man fed dollar bills into the machine.

Charlie shifted the weight of his body to lean fully on me and make me stumble. "*You* shhh."

"Stop it," I said, but we both froze as the man pressed his selection.

"Yes." Charlie pumped a fist in the air. He leaned his face down closer to mine and said, "Who's the winner, Bay? Is it you or me?"

"Has anyone ever told you you're insufferable when you're winning?" I asked, unable to hold in the smile as he acted like a child.

"Then I must be insufferable all the time," he said, his grin wide and cocky.

"You actually are. That is the perfect way to describe you. Constantly insufferable."

When we weren't working together, I was pretty much just begging him to come over because one of two things happened when he did. Either he came over and it made Scott quiet, which made me feel like Charlie was buying me time by slowing their relationship progression, or he came over before Scott got there, and magically, Scott never showed up.

Almost as if he doesn't want to come over when Charlie is there.

That being said, my mom still seemed happy with Scott and things weren't falling apart. But for someone dealing with their relationship on a day-to-day basis, anytime Scott wasn't there, I considered a win.

Which was how I ended up owing Charlie a favor.

I was studying in my room on a random Wednesday night, with music cranked in my AirPods so I couldn't hear Scott and my mom in the living room, when Charlie texted.

I need a favor, Glasses.

I texted: **What's the favor?**

Charlie: I want you to go with me to a party Friday night.

What? That made me hit pause on the song. He wanted me to go to a party with him? *With* him? We didn't really do things like that; we only hung out at work and at my house. Why would he want me to go to a party with him? I texted: **What????**

Instead of him texting back, my phone started ringing. Which, to be fair, was something Charlie did all the time. If something required explanation, he almost always bailed for the phone call.

I answered with, "What kind of a party? Like a child's birthday party?"

I wanted him to say yes to that, because I didn't want this to be something that made things weird with us.

"Like I'd subject you to that kind of torture," he said, his voice quiet and a little hoarse, like he'd been sleeping. "It's just a small party at one of my friends' houses."

A small party at one of his friends' houses?

Without thinking, I said, "Okay, but we don't do that."

I walked over to the window and closed my blinds, trying to explain without sounding like I thought he was into me. "We've never crossed school and friend lines."

"That's why this is called a favor," he said, and he cleared his throat. "My ex and her douche will be there—and I so do not care about that—but I also don't want to seem pathetic. If you go with me, I can relax and have fun without worrying about looking sad."

Okay, that didn't sound bad. I was relieved he wasn't asking me out, even though for some reason a tiny knot of *something* was in my stomach. "Will I have fun?"

"Of course you will—you'll be with me."

"That isn't the reassurance you think it is," I said, wondering what his friends were like. "I'm fairly certain you're the most obnoxious person I've ever met."

"Wrong," he said, and I thought I heard a dog bark in the background. "It's a known fact that repressed people mistake 'fun' for 'obnoxious' all the time."

"Obnoxious people mistake 'normal' for 'repressed' all the time," I replied. "Get it right."

"Oh, Glasses, you're adorable when you're in a huff."

That made me smile, which I was glad he couldn't see. The boy did *not* need to know that his sarcastic boobishness was amusing at times. I said, "It's like you're *trying* to make me say no."

"Pleeeeeeeeeease say yes," he begged. "Please, please, please, please, please."

"Are your friends, like, keg-stand party people," I asked, my mind switching over to the idea of the party itself, "or are they more of the playing-board-games party people?"

I wasn't a partier. I didn't have strong opinions about it either way, but my friends and I didn't hang out with people who got together to drink beer. Zack and his friends were big drinkers, but he'd never taken me with him to a party.

"This gathering will be everything," Charlie said, sounding

happier since I'd yet to say no. "Keg in the front, trivia in the back, probably a few bros with bongs hiding somewhere upstairs."

"So I'm going to get an MIP, then."

"If you go with me, Bay," he said, his voice soft and quiet and surprisingly genuine, "I guarantee your safe return."

Every time he called me "Bay," it made me feel a little weird. Which, honestly, was weird in and of itself, because Nekesa and my mom called me that *all the time*.

But when Charlie said it, it made me feel closer to him than we actually were. I cleared my throat and said, "You remember the story of my one booze party, right?"

"Puke chunk on leg—yep." His voice held a tinge of amusement when he added, "I promise I will not leave your side."

And for some reason, I could tell he meant it. Which surprised me with its reassurance.

"Well," I said, "how will I know what to wear if I don't know any more details? Like is it a pj party? Costume party? Will there be a seven-course meal involved? Fancy silverware?"

"Stop overthinking it, Glasses." I could practically hear Charlie's eye roll through the phone. "You look cute in that black-and-white sweater that you always wear with jeans and the boots that squeeze your toes."

That made me pause. I had never considered that Charlie ever—EVER—noticed how I looked or what I was wearing. I'd always felt—since way back at the airport in Fairbanks— that he just saw me as something like the annoying, uptight friend of his sister.

I said teasingly, just to make sure things didn't get awkward,

"Are you into me, Sampson? Are you secretly obsessed with me and have my entire wardrobe memorized?"

"Give me a break," he said, still sounding like he was amused. "Just because I notice how you look doesn't mean I'm into you, Glasses."

"Whew."

"Although I *would* like it if you pretend to be marginally potentially into me at the party."

"You are really blowing my mind tonight."

"Why? I just want to show up at the party with a cute girl that appears to be my date. It doesn't mean I want to lick your neck or call you my girlfriend; it just means I'm an insecure little bitch about the party. Okay?"

I laughed—I couldn't help it. He just sounded so unhappy to call me cute and also so disgusted with himself for caring about appearances.

It was ridiculous, but the fact that Charlie thought I was cute *meant* something to me. He was an obnoxious butthead, but since he didn't like a lot of people, it felt good that I registered.

"Yeah—keep laughing, it's hilarious," he said, and I could hear the smile in his voice. "You're a real dick, kid."

"Oh, come on, Charlie—I am not." I laughed, and I realized that I actually *wanted* to help him. "And fine—I'll go with you."

"Seriously?" he asked, sounding surprised even though I thought it'd been obvious the whole time.

"Sure," I said, cracking my back and wishing I didn't have more studying to do. "I don't know any of your friends, so I don't have to act cool."

"Can you please act a *little* cool?"

"What are we talking here?"

"Okay." His voice was deeper now and he sounded comfortable, like he was lying on a couch, watching TV. "I would prefer no bathroom accidents and no public vomitings."

"I think I can accommodate you on that. How do you feel about spontaneous show-tune outbursts?"

"As long as it isn't Gershwin," he said, sounding disgusted. "Can't stomach Gershwin."

"Are you a communist?" I asked.

"Communists hate Gershwin?"

"No one hates Gershwin," I said, wondering how it could be fun to talk to Charlie on the phone when he was such a royal pain in the ass most of the time. "Hence the communist assumption."

"You should be careful with assumptions, Glasses."

"I know. Forgive me."

"I will," he said, "but only because you're pretending to dig me Friday night."

I closed my book, got up from my desk, and proceeded to flop down onto my bed. "That is going to be the hardest challenge of my life. I should be immediately nominated for an Oscar on Saturday morning if I pull it off."

"Oh, you'll pull it off," he said, sounding almost flirty as he teased. "I'll make it so easy that you'll forget you don't actually dig me in real life."

"Impossible," I said, snuggling into my blanket.

"Wait and see, Glasses," he said. "Just you wait and see."

CHAPTER SEVENTEEN

Charlie

I shook my head as I slid my phone into my pocket, knowing I was a complete and total dumbshit for inviting Bailey to the party.

I'd told her that I wanted her to come so I didn't look pathetic to Becca, which was true, but the bigger reason was to show Bec that I was moving on.

I walked into the kitchen, opened the fridge, and grabbed the gallon of milk.

"Did you try TUMS?"

I turned around, and my mom was standing in the kitchen doorway. I nodded. "Yep."

"Did you try any of the exercises Dr. Bitz gave you?" she asked, looking concerned as she walked over to the sink and grabbed a wineglass from the drying rack.

I swallowed and didn't want to answer. I hated that question, hated that the question was even a *thing*. Because as much as everyone liked to spew words about the importance of taking care of one's mental health, it felt like a fail, having this problem.

And it wasn't even a fucking problem.

I overthought things, and the result was fucking annoying acid reflux. That was it—no big deal. But something about it made me feel like I was broken, especially when my mom tried to help by bringing up mental *exercises* that the *therapist* thought could help me.

But again—it was no big deal.

"Yeah," I said, closing the fridge and taking the milk to the table, where my cup was. "It's no big deal. I think it's just because I had leftover pizza for dinner."

"Oh, good," she said, looking relieved as she grabbed the bottle of red wine on the counter and poured a glass. "We went out for chicken before you got home."

"Glad I missed it," I said, giving her a reassuring smile. "I hate chicken."

"I know," she said, giving me one of those big Mom smiles that made me happy and melancholy, all at the same time. "You always have."

"Someone has to be the genius in the family," I replied.

To which she quipped, "Talk to me when your calc grade goes up."

"Touché."

After she went upstairs, I started thinking about Friday night again as I pounded milk (my homemade acid reflux prevention that never worked).

I'd been avoiding hanging out with *anyone* since the Becca

breakup, mostly because I didn't want to see her or hear people ask about what happened. I only agreed to go to Chuck's on Friday because he was moving the following week and it might be the last time to see him.

But now it felt like an opportunity, I thought as I chugged milk like a frat boy with a can of beer during rush.

I was too much of a simp to actually *tell* Bec to stop texting me unless she wanted to get back together, but it was how I felt. I was glad she was happy (sort of), but I had zero interest in becoming her fucking bestie.

So maybe if I *did* something like this, it might send the same message: *Charlie is available for boyfriending if you realize you miss FaceTiming him in the dark at 3 a.m., but he's got other options if you're only interested in platonic messaging.*

I wasn't planning on lying and telling people that Bailey and I were a thing, but if Bec wanted to make her own assumptions and respond accordingly, well, I couldn't do a damn thing to stop her, right?

I poured another glass of milk and set down the gallon.

But I also couldn't ignore the part of me that was the tiniest bit excited to seeing Bailey outside of work and our partnership to destroy her mom's relationship. What was social, let's-go-hit-the-town Bailey like?

Who was Bailey, aside from *Glasses*? And why was I so fucking curious to find out?

Something about her had drawn me in the very first time we'd met, and God help me, there was something I *liked* about interacting with her.

We had nothing in common. NOTHING.

Still, I'd never forget the nerd in glasses at the airport, clearing her throat and repeatedly saying *Excuse me*. There was something ballsy in her rule-following repression that I found entertaining, something sweet in the way she wouldn't let me cut but felt bad about it.

Bailey wasn't like other people.

So even though I knew she'd likely drive me fucking nuts at the party, why was I looking forward to it?

CHAPTER EIGHTEEN

Bailey

When Charlie texted me Friday night to let me know he was at my house, I messaged my mom, **Hanging out with Charlie at his friend's house**, and walked outside. I didn't even have to wonder where Charlie was parked because he started honking.

Loudly.

Incessantly.

I rolled my eyes and ran over to his black Honda something, pulled open the door, and climbed inside. "You are a jackass."

Sitting relaxed behind the wheel, Charlie grinned wildly, like he was having the *best* time messing with me. His eyes were warm and all over me—my face, my outfit, my legs, and back up again—and the appreciative gaze brought out the butterflies in my stomach.

Then he said, "Holy shit, you wore *exactly* what I told you to wear. You are such a good girl."

I reached for the seat belt after I slammed my door, the butterflies calming as he looked away from me and into his rearview mirror. "Do you really want to cause me to go back inside and change?"

"I'll shut up," he said, putting the car in reverse and backing out of the spot. "But it looks good. You look really nice."

"Did you just compliment me?" I asked, buckling up.

"Weird, right?"

"I don't know how to deal with it, honestly." And I also didn't know how to deal with him looking like that. I'd known T-shirt Charlie, hoodie Charlie, and flight suit Charlie, but this Charlie . . .

Whoa. He was wearing a plaid button-down—was that Ralph Lauren?—a nice watch, jeans, and *really* good shoes.

But that wasn't the *whoa*.

The *whoa* was the combination of the smell of his soap and the way his thick hair looked like he'd run his hands through it a hundred times. The close proximity of Charlie *trying* put him on another level I wasn't used to dealing with.

Like, Charlie Sampson was cute, but Party Charlie was *hot*.

He glanced at me, and the corner of his mouth tilted up. "Well, don't get weird on me. The outfit looks good, but the fact that you probably have everything in your purse lined up by shape takes away a lot of the attractiveness."

"There it is." I pulled down the visor and looked in the mirror. "So what's your ex's name again?"

"Huh?" He glanced over again, then returned his gaze to the road. "Oh. Becca."

"Becca." I reached into the pocket of my jeans and pulled out my lipstick. "Are you guys civil to each other?"

He made a scoffing sound and switched lanes. "For God's sake, I'm not some melodramatic puffball. Of course we're civil."

I looked at his face, which was all seriousness as he drove down Maple Street. "Really?"

"Yes."

"Really."

"Yes." He shook his head like I was a moron. "Knock off your bullshit. I treat her exactly the same as I treat you."

"Oh, so you're kind of a sarcastic prick, but funny enough to make it acceptable."

He raised his eyebrows and nodded. "Pretty much."

"Got it." I put on lipstick, flipped the visor back up, and turned toward Charlie. "And what are your friends like? Loud? Quiet? Funny? Snobby?"

"*My* friends are pretty chill. And funny."

I don't know why, but I nervously asked him, "Do you think they'll like me?"

He gave me a quick glance and looked like he wanted to laugh; it was in the squint of his eyes when he said, "You might've changed on the outside, but you're kind of still the brace face from the airport, aren't you?"

"No, I most definitely am not," I said defensively, irritated that he was mocking my moment of insecurity. "But you, Charlie—you are absolutely still the know-it-all jackass that I met in Fairbanks."

"Whoa," he said, and now he did cough out a little laugh as he slowed for a stoplight. "Calm down. I *liked* the brace face."

"And now you're lying," I said, turning in my seat to face him better. "Because we've already established that we hated each other."

His eyes moved from my face to my hair and back to my face again before he said, "How could I forget?"

"I mean," I said, tucking my hair behind my ears and thinking back to that day, "I was just a nice girl, trying to safely maneuver my first solo flight, and there *you* were, being a jerk and macking on a girl in the security line like a mini–Hugh Hefner."

"First of all, 'macking'?" he said, hitting the gas after the light turned green. "Do better, Glasses."

"Yeah," I agreed. "I don't know where that came from."

"Second of all, Hugh Hefner was an asshole. Young Charlie, on the other hand, had enough game for Grace Bassett to make the first move with that airport kiss."

"Really?" I didn't hide the sarcasm in my voice. "I don't believe it."

"Trust me, she begged for that kiss."

"That's what you want me to think."

"Touché."

When Charlie pulled to a stop in front of a nice-looking cookie-cutter split-entry house at the top of a cul-de-sac, I got a few butterflies. There were three cars in the driveway and a few on the street, so though it didn't appear to be a huge party, it was bigger than my usual four-friend get-togethers.

It was like Charlie knew I was nervous, though, because as

he pulled a little roll of TUMS out of his pocket and popped two into his mouth, he said reassuringly, "I'll make it fun—I promise."

We got out of the car and walked toward the porch, and I wondered what he'd be like at the party. Who *was* Charlie Sampson with his friends?

"It'll be quick and painless. Don't worry." We went up the two porch steps, and Charlie pushed open the front door like he'd been there a hundred times. There was loud music playing—"Nobody Knows" by the Driver Era (I loved the *X* album)—with people floating around everywhere.

I followed him inside, taking a deep breath and reminding myself that this didn't matter. I didn't know anyone at that party, so they could all hate me and it wouldn't even count.

We walked by two guys on a couch, listening to a pretty blonde tell them something that appeared to be fascinating. A group of people on my right huddled around the dining room table, which was covered in cards and beer cans, as others watched whatever game they were playing with deep interest. We wove through more people standing around laughing or caught in light conversation. Following Charlie, I quickly eyed the kitchen, my hungry stomach wondering if that's where the snacks or chips or some kind of delicious dips resided, before figuring this wasn't a party where casserole dishes filled with any sort of seven-layer jalapeño popper dip existed.

It was exactly what you'd expect from a party, yet it wasn't out of control.

But it was early.

People glanced at us as we passed, and I couldn't shake the feeling that all eyes were on us. I tucked my hair behind my ears, tugged at the hem of my sweater. Yes, I was starting to feel a bit insecure, which was probably why Charlie leaned closer and murmured into my ear, "Let's go in the kitchen."

It was in the kitchen—I was right; ZERO dips—where a tall blond guy said, "Fucking finally, Sampson. I was starting to think you were blowing us off."

Charlie gestured toward me. "I had to pick up Bailey first."

"Finally we meet Bailey." The blond guy, who was leaning casually against the counter, flashed me a nice grin. "I'm Adam—I'm sure he's told you all about me—and this is Evan and Eli."

I floundered for a second, totally taken aback as I glanced toward the two guys sitting at the table. *Charlie mentioned me to his friends?*

"Hey," I said, smiling and pretending like I'd previously known of their existence. "Nice to meet you guys."

"What do you think of this shirt?" Evan asked, pointing at his pink button-down.

"Christ, man, can you shut up about the shirt?" Adam muttered, grinning and shaking his head.

"I would but you won't," Evan said loudly.

Eli laughed and said, "It's fucking beautiful, dude—just shut up about it already."

"I like it," I said, unsure if *Evan* actually wanted my opinion.

"Beer?" Adam asked.

"No, thanks," Charlie said. "Bay?"

"No, thanks," I agreed, looking at him and wondering if he usually drank and was just saying no because of me. Regardless, I was glad he wasn't drinking that night. I wasn't anti-booze, but I was a little too much of a control freak to handle the idea of losing my inhibitions in front of other people.

"I gotta be honest," Eli said, "I pictured you a little more, uh—"

"Ugly?" Evan looked at Eli and nodded his head in agreement. "Same."

"*What?*" I looked at Charlie. "You told them I'm ugly?"

"No." He laughed.

"No," Eli said. "He just talks about you like you're some guy he works with. He failed to mention that you're—"

"Not *that* ugly?" I said, looking at Charlie, unable to hold in a laugh.

"Exactly," Eli said, looking relieved that I hadn't taken his words the wrong way.

"Charlie," someone yelled from the living room. "We need you."

He looked at me and said, "Care to be the official phone-a-friend with me?"

"Huh?"

"Charlie is a trivia god, so everyone wants him on their team," Eli said, picking up the can of Ultra in front of him. "So much so that he's become a free agent, where players can pay to phone-a-Charlie."

I looked at him in shock. "Is this true? Are you smart?"

"I'm a genius," he said, so typically Charlie.

"He actually is," Eli said.

"Shut *up*." I mean, Charlie was obviously an intelligent person, but he'd never struck me as someone who would care enough to do well in school. People with attitudes like his usually ditched class and slept during lectures.

Was he *seriously* a genius?

"Charlie!" The group at the dining room table all yelled like their favorite person in the world had just walked in, but he gave them a half smile and lifted a hand in the air as if this was normal.

Actually, it seemed like *everyone* was happy to see him, and not just because of his apparent trivia prowess. Just about each person we passed as we went into the living room smiled and shouted a "Charlie!" in his direction. As if Charlie were their old buddy back from some sort of long trip.

I wasn't sure what to make of it. *I* liked Charlie—wow, I actually *did* like Charlie—but it was somehow surprising that so many other people did. I would've imagined him being too much of an acquired taste for the general population. Kind of an IYKYK type of guy.

"Sampson!" A guy in a black-and-white T-shirt and red jeans—and a full beard—screamed. "When Tad said you were coming, I couldn't believe it. I haven't seen you out in forever."

"I work every weekend," Charlie said, then looked at me. "This is Bailey, by the way."

"Hey, Bailey," he said, grinning like I was fantastic just for being *with* Charlie. "I'm Austin."

"I love your pants, Austin," I said, wishing I'd taken Eli's proffered beer just so I had something in my hand to make me look like I fit in. "Bold choice."

"Right?" he agreed, looking down at his red jeans. "The way I see it, these babies send a message that I know exactly who I am."

"You are Red Jeans Man," I said around a laugh, instantly taking to Austin. He looked like the kind of guy who was always smiling. And there was some sort of positive energy surrounding him, which was a definite contrast to Charlie's aura. *These two are friends?* I guess opposites do attract.

"Also known as Questionable Choices Man," Charlie added. "Or perhaps Fashion Don't Dude."

That made Austin cackle and launch into a story about someone they knew.

But as I engaged with his friends, I wondered why Charlie hadn't been *out* in a long time. He worked weekends, yes, but I knew that he was off every single Friday night.

So, what was he doing with his free time? Was he home alone, pining over his ex? Did he have some sort of family obligation that kept him away from his friends? Why had he been MIA?

He was obviously a social person, if the party's reaction to his appearance was any indication, so what was the deal?

And why am I so curious?

"Oh my God, it's Charles!" a tiny redhead squealed, then ran over and grabbed Charlie in a big bear hug. She looked overjoyed to see him. "You've come back to us!"

She looked at me and said, "Hi. I'm Clio."

"Bailey," I said, grinning wildly, because it was impossible not to. Clio had a warm smile, the kind that reached the corners of her eyes and made them crinkle. She just *projected* kindness. I could feel my shoulders relax.

"Bless you, Bailey, for getting this asshole to quit being a hermit."

Seriously, what is the story with Charlie's apparent hermitatude?

Charlie put his hand over Clio's face and teasingly pushed. "Just because I have a life doesn't mean I'm a hermit."

"Whatever." She reached around him and grabbed a can of Old Milwaukee off the coffee table. "Sit down and get ready to feed us the answers."

We sat down on the couch, and Charlie leaned closer to me and said, "Just pinch my leg or something if you're bored, and we'll go."

"Like this?" I asked, pinching his leg hard.

He gave his head a slow shake and said, "You are *so* lucky I'm a nice guy. If Eli did that, I'd drop him."

"Wow—so macho," I said under my breath, pulling my phone out to make sure neither of my parents had texted.

I heard Charlie laugh as Clio started telling me the rules of the game. It was like Trivial Pursuit, but made for our generation. All the questions were about things everyone was familiar with, but they hinged upon the tiniest of details.

What color robe was Jess wearing when she and Nick had their first kiss on New Girl?

Every time a team lost a point, they had to stand on the dining room table and perform a song selected by the other players. I teamed up with Clio, and everyone in the house seemed to gravitate over to the living room to get in the game.

Charlie was, apparently, a mercenary. If a team didn't know the answer, they had the right to pay him a dollar for his help. And shockingly, he was right every single time he was called to serve. So when Clio and I were unsure about the answer to *List the exact wrappings around Michael Scott's foot after he grilled it in his Foreman*, Charlie bumped his leg against mine.

I looked at him, and he gave me an obnoxious eyebrow waggle. "You might want to consider sliding a single into my rhetorical thong on this one, Glasses."

"I'm queasy now—thanks a lot."

"Do you have a buck, Bailey?" Clio asked me. "Because he might be right. I know Michael Scott's got Bubble Wrap, but I can't remember what else."

I couldn't. I couldn't pay Charlie when he was looking so smug, and when he started chanting "Pay the Chuck, pay the Chuck"—and everyone joined in with him, I had to take a stand.

"We don't need to pay the Chuck," I said, looking at Charlie and raising my eyebrows. "Michael Scott's foot was wrapped with clear plastic Bubble Wrap, and that is all."

"Judges?" Charlie asked, and I did a double take at his face. He looked *very* pleased, so I knew I'd made a mistake.

"Bailey is right," the blond girl with the answer card in her hand said. "It *is* wrapped in Bubble Wrap."

"Boom," I said.

"But," she added, dropping the card and grinning. "That Bubble Wrap is held in place by clear packing tape."

"That's not a wrapping," I yelled, arguing as the room

exploded into laughter and noise. "Tape isn't part of the wrapping; it's the adhesive."

Charlie shook his head, laughing, and said, "Why didn't you listen to me?"

"Because I'd rather sing on a table than let you be right," I replied.

"Get up and come on," Clio said to me, smiling a tipsy grin. "We're up."

"I mean, I'm just here with Charlie," I tried as she grabbed my arm and pulled me to my feet. "As a guest. I shouldn't be subjected to the same—"

"Come on," she said, pulling me toward the dining room.

"Charlie," I said, looking back at him. "Shouldn't you save me?"

"I tried," he said, smiling, "but you didn't want to dip into the proverbial G-string."

"What song?" Clio asked, using a remote to turn on the karaoke machine after we climbed on top of the dining room table.

Everyone started yelling out suggestions, and then Charlie said, "'All Too Well.' The ten-minute version."

CHAPTER NINETEEN

Charlie

Everyone cheered, and Bailey looked at me like she wanted to stab me in the face. Her eyes narrowed and her brows went down, and it occurred to me that I was 100 percent comfortable with her glaring at me.

I kind of liked it, to be honest.

Getting under her skin was my new favorite hobby.

What she didn't get *this* time, however, was that I was doing her a favor by choosing that song.

The music started, and again—everyone cheered.

But then—as I'd suspected—the entire house started singing along with Clio and Bailey. It was like a Taylor yell-along that everyone was totally into.

You almost ran the red 'cause you were looking over at me.

Bailey was smiling and laughing, sharing the microphone with Clio, and I was a little impressed by the way she was rolling with it. I would've expected Miss Hall Monitor to be intensely nervous, but she actually looked relaxed.

"I thought you said she was a dork," Eli said, grabbing the spot on the couch beside me. "She's hot."

I glanced at Eli, and he was watching her, smiling, and something about it felt wrong.

"I never said she was a dork." I went back to watching the entertainment, and Bailey was kind of yelling now, her nose scrunched up. *"Fuck the patriarchy" / Key chain on the ground.* "I said she was uptight and a little nerdy."

"Well, it works for her," he said, and I didn't like the way he said it. As if her looks were the most important thing about her.

What the hell was wrong with me?

Chill the fuck out. I needed to chill the fuck out. The only reason Eli's attitude was hitting wrong was because I felt protective of Bay.

That was it.

Eli was fine.

"Yeah," I agreed. She might've been hella irritating, but she did look really fucking cute, dancing around on top of the table.

It was a little disconcerting, to be honest.

Just as I was thinking that, she looked at me. Her eyes got squinty as she grinned and sang, which made me smile back, and then she screwed up the words. She sang the wrong word— never *lovely jewel*—loud as fuck into the microphone, and I don't know what my face did, but it made her start laughing.

And something about it got to me.

Which was why I was laughing and singing along like a

fucking chump when I shot a quick glance over my shoulder and caught the amused smiles being exchanged between Becca and Kyle as they entered the party.

Fuck *me*.

CHAPTER TWENTY

Bailey

I was in the middle of laughing my ass off—while singing—when I saw *it* happen.

One minute Charlie was giving me a funny grin and singing along to "All Too Well," and the next his face completely changed.

His smile disappeared like a door slamming shut, and his Adam's apple bobbed as he swallowed. I looked back at the couple who'd just walked in behind him, and—holy crap—it was her. The gorgeous girl from the movie theater.

Charlie's ex-girlfriend.

Just as fast as his face had changed, it changed back. Charlie turned his attention back to me and smirked, but it didn't touch his eyes. I was glad the song was ending, because I didn't want to sing it anymore.

It felt like the worst possible accompaniment to seeing your ex with her new boyfriend.

"Thank you very much, Omaha," Clio said into the microphone, grinning at me as she added, "And I pray to God we won't be back up here again this evening."

She dropped the microphone, and we jumped down from the table to a smattering of applause.

"That was *awful*," Eli said, slow-clapping and smiling from his spot next to Charlie on the sofa. "But ten out of ten, would recommend."

"Gee, thanks," I replied, but my eyes were on Charlie as he looked uncomfortable. He was all cool with his ankles crossed and his arm resting over the back of the couch and lips turned up into a smile, but his discomfort showed in the tightness of his jaw and the dullness of his stare.

Just as I sat down beside him, Becca and her boyfriend walked up.

Shit.

The guy grinned down at Charlie and said, "Sampson—how's it going?"

The guy—like the rest of the world—seemed genuinely happy to see Charlie.

Charlie's ex-girlfriend did too. She smiled. *Warmly.* Like he was an old friend. It was a happy, kind, entirely unaffected smile, and I imagined that smile, coupled with her fingers linked between her boyfriend's, had to feel very super shitty. I couldn't help but feel bad for Charlie.

"Your mom knows," Charlie said, a smirk on his face that told everyone he was kidding and they were buddies and ha-ha-ha it's a "your mom" joke. "Ask *her*."

The guy started cracking up and Charlie's ex smiled, and I was surprised that I seemed to be the only one who could see his words for what they were. Everyone thought Charlie was hilarious, but he used humor and snark as a total defense mechanism.

All the time.

I guess I'd already noticed it whenever he talked about his relationship with his parents, but suddenly it was clear that it was his go-to move in any situation.

Of course, if I told him that, he'd probably mess up my hair and mock me for trying to be Freud, but, God—it was textbook.

And now that I'd seen it, it was all I could see.

Which is the only way to explain why I smiled up at the new boyfriend and said, "I'm Bailey, by the way. Charlie's . . . *friend* . . . ?"

I looked at Charlie, my head tilted just a little, as if sharing an inside joke about whether or not I could be called his friend. His dark eyes moved over my face for a split second, and then he *got* it, his mouth sliding into a slow, flirty grin that actually made my stomach do a little dip.

Holy shit, Charlie could be *sexy* when he wanted.

It was something about the squint of his eyes, the way he looked at me lazily, mischievously, almost as if he wanted to steal me away for multiple uninterrupted hours.

Ahem—*wow.*

I brushed away that unwelcome awareness because the bigger thing was that his eyes were alive again. I don't know why I hated seeing him unhappy so much, but for some reason, I did.

"I'm Kyle and this is Becca," the guy said, and I smiled and nodded and tried my best not to stare at her.

But it was impossible.

Because I was trying to reconcile her with Charlie. More so, I was trying to reconcile the idea of someone who Charlie liked enough to have a hard time getting over.

Because he might've brought me along under the guise of appearances, but I wasn't an idiot; this was all about her. Charlie was one of those rare people who genuinely didn't give a shit about what people thought of him, so the fact that she made him care mattered.

"You just missed 'All Too Well,'" I said, trying to play the part of a laid-back party girl, when in reality I *hated* chatting with strangers because I was awkward as hell.

"Oh, we caught the end of it," Becca said, talking to me even though her big blue eyes kept bouncing between Charlie and me. "You didn't phone-a-Charlie?"

That made her and Charlie share a smile, and there was something about it that I did not like. Memories were being shared in that gaze, recollections of interwoven moments, and my stomach knotted as I witnessed the fleeting second of *something*.

I don't know why, but I really hated that *something*.

It probably had to do with the fact that, against my better judgment, I didn't like the thought of him being sad.

Surely that was it.

"Bay's too stubborn to ask for help," Charlie said, and then he kind of leaned into me. Like, technically it was just a shoulder-nudge, a bump, but it spoke of an intimacy that Charlie and I did *not* have in real life. "I believe her exact words were that she'd rather sing on a table than let me be right."

That caught me off guard, and I laughed, surprised he remembered what I'd said. I shrugged, and I don't know what came over me, maybe it was this bizarre need to protect him from emotional scars, but I snaked my arms around his left biceps and squeezed.

Yes, I gave him an arm hug as I said, "I stand by my decision."

Charlie looked at me, the tiniest crinkle between his eyebrows the only sign of surprise, and then he said, "Hold up, you have an eyelash."

My breath stilled as his face moved marginally closer and his free hand came up and softly touched my cheek. It was only a split second, but it felt like a freeze-frame as our eyes met and held.

What is happening? I took a deep breath and felt a little unsettled, my heartbeat skittering in my chest as his gaze swept over me from point-blank range. Brown eyes held me like a spell, a hex that rendered me incapable of looking away as his jaw flexed and unflexed.

But then, as if a switch were flipped, the freeze-frame ended. The noise of the party returned, Charlie straightened, and we were back to chatting with his former girlfriend and her new man.

Only, instead of dropping his hand, he let it come down to rest on my thigh.

And not passively, but almost in a grab, with his thumb and forefinger applying the slightest pressure.

I looked down at his long fingers and wondered why my

stomach was going wild with butterflies. Why was the sight of Charlie's hand on me causing utter chaos to my insides?

What. The. Hell?

Realizing that I was looking down at his hand, I quickly brought my gaze back to his face. Charlie was giving me a totally normal smart-ass grin, and I realized that I'd been getting a little caught up in the fake game.

It's Charlie, you idiot.

Only, I could still feel his fingers on my thigh.

Ahem.

Becca looked directly at Charlie's hand, then raised her eyes and said, "Do you know where Brittany is? She was bringing our beer."

"In the kitchen when we got here," he said, and I couldn't help but notice the way his eyes seemed to drink her in when he looked at her. Did he have any idea how much of his heart was in his gaze when he looked at her?

And why did I find it a little annoying?

"Britt," she yelled, grabbing her boyfriend's arm as she headed for the kitchen. "Where you at?"

As they walked away, I let go of Charlie's arm and did anything but look at him. I wasn't sure how to deal with whatever strange things had been afoot between us. I knew that I'd just gotten a little caught up in our game of pretend, but would he know that's all it was?

"Glasses."

"Hmm?" I said, trying to look casual as I raised my eyebrows as if interested in what he was going to say. "What?"

When I dared to meet his eyes, he was giving me a funny look. It was . . . sincere, maybe? He let go of my thigh, cleared his throat, and said, "You went above and beyond. Thanks."

"No problem."

"Come on, Clio," Charlie said, following Clio out the front door. I shut it behind us as he tried to get her to listen to him. "Be a good girl."

"I'm fine," she said—well, *yelled*, smiling as she stepped off the porch and into the front yard.

"Nope." Charlie jumped off the porch and landed in front of her. He bent his knees, so his face was at her level (he was like a foot taller than her), and he said, "I'm not going to be able to sleep tonight if I let one of my favorite humans get behind the wheel when she's clearly buzzed. Please let me drive you, because I need my fucking beauty sleep."

The way she beamed at him made me smile, because what else was there to do?

The jerk from the airport was ridiculously charming.

Actually—that wasn't it.

It wasn't *charm* that was melting Clio and me, it was kindness. The jerk from the airport clearly cared about his friend and was committed to taking care of her.

Dear God, it was almost *too* nice, like sunshine on a spring day. So completely wonderful that you want to stare and soak it up, but that only results in burned corneas and impaired vision.

We got Clio loaded into the back seat, and when we were buckling our seat belts and he started the car, Charlie said, "By the way. My friend Eli asked me if he can ask you out."

What? I knew to be cool and act like I'd been there before, but what I really wanted to do was say *Are you sure?* and *Did he get me confused with someone else?*

Not that I didn't think I was worthy of interest, but I hadn't really engaged with Eli, aside from a few random sentences.

"Why would he ask *you*?" I said, mainly to sound cool as I worked through my shock that he'd noticed me at all. "What are you—my dad?"

Charlie put the car in drive and pulled away from the curb. "I'm his friend, and he just wanted to make sure I wouldn't care. Settle your ass down."

I peeked back at Clio, who looked like she was asleep sitting up, and tried to determine how I felt about this turn of events. Charlie's friend was cute and seemed nice enough, but he also wasn't Zack.

"What's Eli like?" I asked Charlie, deciding not to shut it down entirely before I had all the facts.

"Oh my God, I love Eli," Clio said with her eyes closed. "He's hot and super nice."

That made me grin at Charlie.

"I think you'd like him," Charlie said, looking into the mirror before switching lanes.

"You do?" I looked over, for some reason surprised, and his face was unreadable in the dashboard lights. "Really?"

"Sure," he said, his wrist casually draped over the steering wheel. "I mean, *I* like him, he's a handsome guy, and you're not into anyone else, right?"

"Right," I said, looking out the windshield into the darkness and picturing Zack.

But I must've made a face, because his eyes got big and he said, "Holy shit—who? Who are you into?"

"No one," I lied, but Charlie wasn't buying it.

"Oh, come on, Glasses," he said, his eyes twinkling with mischief. "I don't know any of your dude friends, so you can tell me. Is there some new guy that makes your little heart go pitter-patter?"

"Oh, it's nothing like *that*," I said dismissively, so far away from pitter-patter that it wasn't even funny.

"Wait," he said, shooting me a quick glance before returning his eyes to the road. "Are you still hung up on your ex?"

"No!" I said, *way* too defensively. I glanced into the back seat and then repeated in a much quieter voice, "No."

"Holy shit, you *are*," Charlie said, his eyebrows rising all the way up his forehead. "I can tell."

"How can you tell? That's ridiculous," I said around a little fake laugh, trying to play it off.

"I just know." Charlie glanced at me for a split second, and his face went kind of serious, the curve of his mouth flattening, and he gave a shrug as if to accentuate that he couldn't explain it.

"Because *you're* still hung up on Becca," I said, in almost a whisper.

He didn't agree, but he didn't deny it either as he stopped for a red light. Charlie held my gaze before asking, "So do you guys talk? What's the deal?"

For the most part, I didn't discuss Zack and me.

For multiple reasons.

I didn't want to hear opinions on how I needed to move on or opinions on Zack's character, and I definitely didn't want to be judged as a clinger because I couldn't let him go.

I would probably say those things to someone else in the same situation, to be honest.

But the thing about relationships was that no one else knew the quiet, tiny moments that belonged exclusively to you two. *Those* were the things that made you hold tight because you were the only one he'd shown that side of himself to.

No one else knew.

The time we goofily whisper-sang all the words to "A Groovy Kind of Love" together when he snuck me up to his bedroom and then I was stuck because his mom wouldn't go downstairs; the way he got *actual* tears in his eyes when I told him about the way my parents used to fight all the time; his propensity for kissing me when I was midsentence because he said he couldn't bear to wait another second; and U2's *Rattle and Hum* album—which he bought when we went to Homer's together, and said that Bono surely wrote "All I Want Is You" for us.

A thousand inside jokes stood between my heart and closure.

But I knew those thoughts made me sound like a lovesick child, so it was easier to just keep it all in my own head.

Which was why it was really strange that at that moment, it felt safe to share with Charlie. I gave a half shrug and said, "No. He's seeing someone else now."

I would've expected Charlie to snicker about how pathetic I was, but he didn't. He gave a little nod as the light turned green, and instead said, "So why aren't you over him?"

"I don't know," I said defensively, irritated that he sounded just like Nekesa.

"No—I'm not being a dick." He held up a hand as if trying to reframe his words. "What I mean, um, is that most of the time, if a couple has a normal breakup, even if there are still feelings, they each move on. So if a smart girl like you can't move on, there's usually a reason. An extenuating circumstance."

I narrowed my eyes, wishing I could see into his brain. "What do you mean?"

"Take me," he said, looking embarrassed and lowering his voice. "Bec still texts me all the time—only as a friend—but sometimes it feels a *lot* like when we were together, and it's a bit of a mindfuck."

"Oh, shit," I said, picturing Becca's face, wondering if she was playing games with him. I'd met her for only a minute so I had no idea, but I hoped she wasn't intentionally keeping him on the line, keeping his heart tied up with her so he couldn't move on.

"Right?" He half smiled, but it wasn't happy or amused. It was self-deprecating, as if to say *I am a stupid man*. "So I was just wondering if there is a *reason* for you to still be hanging on."

I looked at his pain-in-the-ass Charlie face and thought how strange it was that this was more of an emotional conversation about the breakup than I'd had with Nekesa or anyone else, for that matter. I took a deep breath and said, "With us, the breakup was a mistake."

He raised an eyebrow.

"I know—that sounds like a typical ex-girlfriend thing to say. But it's true." I went on to tell him about how I'd broken up with Zack when I was mad, fully expecting we'd get back together, but Zack had taken it as the final death knell for our relationship and started dating. As Charlie pulled the car to a stop in front of a house—Clio's, presumably—I said, "So I kind of feel like we aren't done."

"Ah." He looked like he wanted to say something but was holding back. His eyes moved over my face as he asked, "And you'll take him back if he asks you to?"

That . . . was a good question. I felt like it was a yes, but Charlie's question made me realize that I still had some issues with the way Zack had been able to just move on from *me*. If he cared about me even *half* as much as I cared about him, shouldn't it have taken a little time? Shouldn't he have tried harder before giving up?

"Probably," I admitted, knowing it was the wrong answer while also knowing I meant it. "What about you? Would you take Becca back if she asked?"

"Here!" Clio popped forward, leaning up between our seats, and said, "We're here! This is my house."

"That is correct," Charlie said to his tipsy friend, but his eyes stayed on me. He gave me a little closed-mouth smile, like an acknowledgment of our shared heartaches, before pulling the keys from the ignition and opening his door. "Let's get you inside, Miss Clio."

CHAPTER TWENTY-ONE

Bailey

I opened the door to the apartment and was surprised to see that the living room lights were still on. My mother was rarely awake at midnight, so I shot Charlie a look of dread. I'd gone inside with Clio to make sure she made it quietly up to her room—which she did—but that had made me nice and late.

We cut through the kitchen, and when we stepped into the living room, my mom and Scott were sitting side by side on the couch. The TV was on, but they were looking at me like they'd been waiting for me to appear in the doorway.

"Hey, night owls," I said, pasting on what I hoped was a laid-back smile. "I thought you'd be asleep by now."

"Bay," my mom said, looking pissed. My heart hiccupped a bit—she rarely got mad at me—and she said, "Midnight means midnight."

"I know, and I'm sorry." I glanced at Scott, who was glaring at something behind me.

Some*one*.

He looked like he was trying to kill Charlie with orbital laser beams.

"We ended up having to give one of Charlie's friends a ride home at the last minute—that's the only reason we were late."

"But it's your job to factor that stuff in when accounting for your curfew, sweetie." My mom crossed her arms and said, "Part of that whole if-you're-old-enough-to-stay-out-till-midnight thing."

"I know." *Why is she busting my ass?* My mother was usually incredibly understanding, especially since I rarely went out aside from coffee shop/bookstore visits. "It was last minute. Charlie could see she wasn't okay to drive, so he took her keys and insisted—"

"The girl was *drunk*?" Scott asked, as if I'd just proclaimed that the girl had murdered someone.

I felt my forehead wrinkle as I wondered why the hell Crew Socks was inserting himself into my life. I cleared my throat and said, "Well, I wouldn't call her *drunk* exactly—"

"But she'd been drinking." Scott looked at Charlie again, then at my mom, before he asked me, "Were you at a *booze* party?"

Charlie made a noise, like he found Scott's ridiculous verbiage funny, as I said, "No. The girl had been drinking, but we weren't at a *booze* party."

Scott looked at my mom expectantly, as in *Let her have it.*

Which really pissed me off. Who did he think he was, her *husband*? What right did he have to guide her toward his parental expectations?

And as if the entire scenario wasn't bonkers in and of itself, the reality was that Scott's snarky daughter partied *all the time*.

My mom looked uncomfortable as she said to me, "This can't happen again, Bay."

It felt like she was acting, like she was saying that because she knew he expected her to, which pissed me off even more. My mom was a strong woman—why would she let him treat her that way?

"That's *it*?" Scott said, looking at my mother like she'd just high-fived me for being late.

"*Yes.*" She gave him a look of annoyance that made me want to applaud. "Bailey's always been responsible. I trust her judgment."

"She hasn't always been hanging out with Mr. Funny here, though."

"*Scott.*" My mom looked at him like she was embarrassed by his immature name-calling.

"How would you know who I hang out with?" I said it quietly, but I surprised myself by saying it at all. I hated confrontation, but I hated this *stranger* butting into our business even more. He knew nothing about me, and the fact that he dared to butt in felt so intrusive, it was almost suffocating.

Somehow it felt like an insult to my *dad*, too, which didn't make sense but added to the painful burning sensation in the center of my chest. I said, "You're new here—I don't think this is your concern."

"I'm gonna take off," Charlie said, and when I turned around, the expression on his face surprised me. His cheeks were a little pink, and he looked uncomfortable.

Not at all like his usual cocky self.

Almost as if Scott's attitude toward him had bothered him.

I felt oddly protective of Charlie at that moment, and I offhandedly wondered why that kept happening. He was cocky and obnoxious and surely didn't need my protection, yet when I saw his face at the party—and now in my living room—he seemed vulnerable. And it tugged away at me.

"Thank you for the ride, Charlie," I said, wanting to add *AND FOR BEING THE KIND OF GUY TO INSIST ON GIVING CLIO A RIDE HOME* but knowing that wouldn't help the situation.

After he left, I went to bed, livid that Scott (a) thought he had any business worrying about my life, (b) was a jerk to Charlie, and (c) was obviously sleeping over every night indefinitely. I was so mad, and also so sad, because it felt like I had zero control. I felt like everything was changing—yet again—and there was nothing I could do.

But then I heard it.

I was lying in my bed, buried in the worn old quilt I'd had since Alaska, when I heard them. Scott and my mother were arguing about *me*, and Scotty didn't sound happy.

Holy shit, is it actually working?

"If you don't put your foot down, she's going to start walking all over you."

Oh, no, I'm not. I snuggled deeper into my pillow and thought, *But it isn't your business if I do.*

"No, she's not," my mom said, sounding irritated and tired. I felt bad for the last part, for having a hand in making her tired.

She was my favorite human in the universe, and I didn't want her to be anything but wide awake and happy.

"I know it seems like she won't, but look at Kristy. She's an out-of-control snot, but she wasn't always."

Holy shit, he talked about his daughter that way?

"Bailey is *not* like Kristy," my mother snapped, sounding insulted. "They couldn't be more different."

So my mom knew Kristy . . . ?

"I know, Em," Scott said, sounding apologetic, "but trust me—she was a sweetheart until she hit middle school, when Neal and Laura totally lost control and let her run wild."

"But your brother's a slacker, come on," my mom said. "Not the same thing."

Wait. What?

"True. But I'm telling you, guys like that Charlie—"

"Will not turn Bailey into your bratty niece," she interrupted.

His niece? Kristy was his *niece*? Relief washed over me as I lay there, smiling in the dark and wanting to screech like a happy . . . well, animal who screeched when they were happy.

Kristy wasn't his daughter—holy shit!

Yes, I was screaming into my pillow and kicking my feet.

"He's a good kid," I heard my mom say, and I felt lucky that she was the nonjudgmental person that she was. "You just got a bad first impression. You'll see."

Strangely enough, she'd hit it right on the head. Charlie *was* actually a decent person.

You just had to get through a hell of a lot of bullshit to see it.

Yes, I'd been wholly convinced that Mr. Nothing was an

irredeemable ass. I would've bet money on the fact that he was trouble with a capital *T*, yet the more time I spent with him, the more I realized that he wasn't.

At all.

I still wasn't sure what exactly he *was*, but I was definitely starting to see what he *wasn't*.

CHAPTER TWENTY-TWO

Charlie

"Who's going to go get us a pitcher of Coke?" Nekesa asked.

Planet Funnn's front desk crews were allowed a complimentary pitcher of soda every shift, which led to a complimentary argument during every shift.

Nekesa looked at Bailey, knowing she'd cave because Bailey always caved.

"Not me," Theo said from his spot on the floor, where he was crouched and trying to unjam the printer for the third time that day. Theo was an idiot with the tech skills of a senior citizen, but I wasn't about to help him.

"Fixing" the printer kept him marginally less talkative than usual.

"Not me," I muttered, "because I got it last time."

"That doesn't count because you were working alone." Bailey rolled her eyes at me, looking at my propped-up feet and the book in my hand as if they disgusted her.

I said, "You know you're going to do it."

"Yeah," Theo said. "Just go, Bailey."

"Ugh—I'll go, you bag of dicks," Nekesa said, splitting a glare between Theo and me. "*I'm* allowed to walk all over Bay because of our history, but *you* cannot."

I actually felt like *I* was allowed to walk all over Bay because she'd push back—hard—if she didn't like it.

Theo stopped fucking with the printer. "I'll go with you, because there's no way you can carry it without spilling."

He was terrible at flirting, yet Nekesa seemed to be all about it.

"I can too." Nekesa laughed, grinning at Theo.

Bailey was watching them intently, a tiny crinkle in her forehead, and I swear to God I could hear the chaos pinging around in her brain. She knew her friend was flirting, could see the chemistry between Theo and Nekesa, and she was desperately trying to find a way to intervene.

Trust me, Bay, I thought as she tucked her long hair behind her ears, *coworkers cannot be platonic friends.*

"I don't think so," Theo said in a nauseating singsong voice, and then the two of them were off, wandering down the hall that led toward the Funstaurants.

Yeah—it was only a matter of time for those two.

Bailey pulled her phone out of the pocket of her flight suit, and I said, "Don't do it."

"Do what?" she said, looking startled by the fact that I was onto her.

"Don't get involved." I set down my book and dropped my feet to the floor. "Nekesa is a big girl."

"I don't care about your bet," she said, biting the inside of her cheek as she put away the phone and logged into reservations to check for cancellations.

"Really."

"As much as you do," she corrected. A long-suffering sigh was followed by a throat-clearing and then, "Anyway, Nekesa *is* a big girl, a big boyfriend-loving girl."

"Uh-huh."

"Stop that," she said through gritted teeth, swinging her gaze to mine. "She *is*."

"Sure she is," I said, stretching out the words just to irritate her. "You just keep thinking that, Bay."

"I will . . . ," she murmured, trailing off in that pouty way that made it hard *not* to smile. "Why don't you go back to your Murakami and leave me alone?"

I was super into the latest Murakami—as in, I couldn't put it down in spite of the things I hated about it—and when I mentioned it to her yesterday, she told me she'd never heard of the author until Joe Goldberg mentioned him.

Which led to me admitting I'd never heard of Joe Goldberg, which led to her spending thirty minutes telling me about the You books by Caroline Kepnes.

She offered to loan them to me, which I politely declined.

I offered to loan her my other Murakamis, which *she* politely declined.

"You can keep your highbrow lit," she'd said, raising her

chin in that defending-my-stance way she had. "I prefer lighter reading."

And by "prefer lighter reading," she meant that she read five or six romance novels.

A *week.*

How did I know that?

Because I'd crept on her social media, of course.

Bailey the Introvert had *thousands* of followers on her bookish account, a place where she posted pictures and reviews of books she'd read. Her posts were smart and funny and engaging as hell, and even though *I* knew that side of her, it was wild to see her being bold when she was so . . . controlled and concerned in real life.

She was a fascinating contradiction.

"Excuse me."

Bailey and I looked at the desk, and a tiny blond woman in a floral swimsuit cover was waiting with a scowl on her face. She seemed ready to Karen the shit out of us, and I stifled a sigh.

"Oh. Hi." Bailey went to the counter and said, "Can I help you?"

I could tell just by looking at the woman that she was about to walk all over Bay.

"Yes," she said, clearing her throat. "There is a tall boy in the World of Water who cut in the waterslide line. Not only that, but he looks entirely too old for the slide."

"Okay . . . ?" Bailey said, obviously waiting for the rest of the story.

The woman glanced at me, then brought her snooty gaze

back to Bailey. "I would like him removed."

"Um, removed . . . ?" Bailey said, sounding confused. I could see only the side of her face, but I knew Bailey's brow was creased, even without the visual confirmation. "Did anyone give him a warning, or—"

"No, maybe *you* could," the woman said, raising her voice and scowling even harder. "Don't ask *me* to do your job."

I stood, feeling strangely protective of Bailey as the lady snapped at her.

The woman couldn't have been over five feet tall, but she had that perfectly coiffed way about her that screamed of money and power. Shiny red manicure, big diamond ring, lipstick with a swimsuit, Louis Vuitton beach bag—it looked like the whole package.

"I—I wasn't," Bailey stammered, her cheeks turning pink. "I was simply—"

"I'll talk to the kid," I said, moving to stand beside Bailey. "You said he's in World of Water?"

The woman nodded, looking appeased. "Yes."

I said facetiously, "I'll go take care of that little whippersnapper in just a moment."

But then she replied, "Thank you," gushing and laying some serious *See, that's how you treat a customer* eye contact on Bailey before going back down the hallway.

I felt like shouting, *"The whippersnapper" was sarcasm, you hag!*

"Whippersnapper?" Bailey gave me a look that showed exactly how nauseating she found me. "I think I just puked a little in my mouth."

I stepped closer. "Quit lying. I was charming as fuck."

"If 'charming' means 'annoying,'" she said, biting her lip and trying not to smile as I towered over her, pretending to be threatening, "then yes, you were totally that."

"Bailey Glasses Mitchell, are you telling me," I asked, smirking and using my index finger to poke the tip of her nose, "that you don't even know the meaning of the word 'charming'?"

She said around a breathy laugh, "I just know that you are not it."

We were both grinning, and for some reason, I felt an invisible string pulling me closer to her as she smiled up at me.

"For someone who I recall having unflinchingly rigid rules about line cutting," I said, not moving as the crinkle of her nose did something to my stomach, "your reaction was surprisingly lax."

"Yeah, um," she said, her voice suddenly a breath away from a whisper, "I think the airport situation had more to do with the cutter than the cutting."

"Did it, now?" I said, fighting the urge to lean closer. But, fuck. I *wanted* to lean closer.

Only . . . this was Bailey.

We were at work.

There was definitely an undercurrent of electricity in the very small space that existed between the two of us—*shit, shit, shit*—which is what made me take a step back and say, "Time for me to go kick some whippersnapper ass."

"Yes," she said, blinking fast and clearing her throat as she turned back to the computer. "Go kill some whippersnapper ass."

CHAPTER TWENTY-THREE

Bailey

Kill whippersnapper ass???

Dear God, I was a bumbling idiot.

I went to the back room to get another ream of printer paper while Charlie headed toward World of Water, and every cell in my body was misfiring as I tried remaining calm. My cheeks were hot and my stomach was wild with butterflies as I crouched to reach the bottom shelf.

Charlie had been flirting with me.

Charlie Sampson had been flirting with me, and I'd been flirting back.

Holy shit.

I had *liked* flirting with Charlie.

Holy shit, holy *shit*!

What did it mean?

The tiny exchange kept replaying in my head as I loaded the

printer. The smirk, the gravelly sound of his voice when he'd said *Did it, now?*, the way I'd been leaning closer to him as he touched my nose.

What in the actual fuck??

I wanted to text Nekesa, but she was suddenly the last person whose opinion I wanted about workplace flirtations. I was in a lather as I threw myself into busywork, wondering what Charlie wanted and what I wanted and what about Zack and what about Becca and dear God it was Charlie! I took a deep breath, happy to be distracted as Nekesa and Theo returned. But a second later Charlie reappeared, looking absolutely casual and normal as he popped a pink TUM into his mouth and said, "Problem solved."

I cracked open the stapler and started filling it, forcing my eyes to stay on that task. "What'd you do?"

He came around the desk and said, "Kicked a little tail."

I snorted and focused on the staples. "Meaning you said 'Stop it'?"

He clicked into reservations on his computer, not even looking in my direction. "Meaning I pretended to talk to the kid while the rich lady watched me from the other side of the pool. I didn't actually say a word."

"Wow—such a powerful man," I said, closing the stapler.

"Right?" he replied.

I did glance up then, and Charlie was looking at me. I couldn't read his expression, but I somehow felt marginally better when he teased in the usual Charlie way, "You owe me for taking care of it, Glasses."

"I don't think I do," I quipped, trying to gauge the situation.

"She was going to destroy you, so I took one for the team and walked all the way down to World of Water, just to save your ass." He shook his head and added, "I'll accept a crisp twenty-dollar bill or a Snickers bar from the machine; either-or works for me."

"Yeah, I actually think you earned a big bag of squat or a box of air," I said, going around him to fill the other stapler. "Either-or works for me."

I heard him laugh, and then everything reset in normal mode.

I convinced myself that the entire episode was a product of low blood sugar because I'd forgotten to eat before work.

All in the imagination.

Right?

That night, after I got home from work, my mom and Scott were sitting at the kitchen table, waiting for me. They were all happy smiley, super excited, which immediately made my stomach fill with dread.

"Hey, guys—what's up?" I dropped my bag in the entryway, slid out of my shoes, and went over to the fridge. "Just finish a rousing game of Chutes and Ladders or something?"

They both laughed, way too excitedly, and then my mom said, "Scott has a surprise for us."

I opened the refrigerator door and looked inside, seeing nothing as I waited for the surprise that I just knew I was going to hate. "Yeah?"

"Fall break is next week," she said, "and since you're already going to be out of school, Scott thought—"

"Whaddya say we go to Breckenridge?" Scott interrupted,

beaming as if he'd just announced they'd won the lottery.

"What?" I closed the door to the fridge, and my chest got tight as they looked at me expectantly.

I'd never skied, and my mother had never skied, so I wasn't sure what exactly their plan was. Scott's daughter (who wasn't Kristy—yayyyyy) would also be out of school; were they trying to get us all to go on a trip *together*?

Because no—that wasn't happening.

I felt dizzy as nervousness and dread came at me fast, fear of their intentions hitting me like a punch. Were they trying to start the Brady Bunch transition with this? Was this "trip" the beginning of something?

Everyone I knew had been to Breck, and it sounded amazing. Charming mountain village, picturesque cabins—I'd always wanted to go there, to be honest. But I wasn't about to let Scott think he could take us all on some family vacation like we were a family.

God, I was getting that suffocated feeling again just looking at the two of them, smiling at me. Because my mom looked so fucking happy. What was I supposed to do with that? I *wanted* her happy; I wanted her to be happier than she'd ever been in her life.

But at what cost?

Scott posed a threat to the comfort in my life. Not comfort as in something that pampers, like nice sheets or soft slippers, but comfort as in the part of your life that provides healing. The part of your life that you can relax and take some kind of comfort from when the rest of the world is on fire.

The part of your life that you can burrow into.

Our life—the one we'd carved out post-dad and pre-Scott—was the comfort.

Which made Scott the anti-comfort.

The potential agent of change in a place that desperately wanted to remain unchanged.

Shit.

"Scott rented a condo that is right on the main street, with a balcony that comes out on the roof of a restaurant," my mom said, her voice rising as if nothing had ever sounded this fun before. She ran a hand through her long blond hair, and it occurred to me as I looked at her that I hadn't even noticed that she was wearing it down.

What the hell was with that?

She was all ponytail, all the time.

Now she was wearing her hair down? Was this for *him*?

She continued trying to sell me with, "We thought it'd be nice to see in October, when the leaves are starting to turn. Just a little three-day getaway. What do you think?"

I think I might bawl like a toddler, right here and right now.

I'd known this was all possible, Scott's dropping anchor in our lives, but suddenly everything was happening too fast.

Out of nowhere, another awful thought came at me. If Scott put down roots, would that serve to further oust my father from my life? Would he see it as a reason to become even more absentee than he already was?

"Um." I tried for a smile and nodded. Like, a lot. Nodded as if my head might fall off my neck because it was so untethered.

"I mean, it sounds amazing, but I think I have to work. You guys should totally go, though."

I saw my mom's face fall. It'd always just been an expression—"her face fell"—until that moment. Her wide smile dropped into a weak horizontal line, and the squint of her eyes went away, leaving her wide-eyed with disappointed surprise. Her voice was thick when she said, "Surely you can get someone to work for you."

"They're actually kind of short-staffed," I lied, hating myself but hating Scott more. "But I can check."

"I'd love to teach you to ski," Scott said, smiling. "If you want to learn, that is."

I looked at my mom. She *knew* I'd wanted to learn when I was little, and it felt like a betrayal that she'd obviously told him. I curled my fingers into balls and said, "Yeah, um, I'd love to, but I don't think it's probably going to work this time."

"Come on, Bay," he said, tilting his head and talking to me like we were buddies. "It'll be epic, I promise. Just blow off work—you'll never hear me say that again—and come with us."

Us. I was getting so damn sick of him referring to himself and my mother as the *us*, when my mother and I were the *us* and he was just the dude who wouldn't go away. I breathed in through my nose and said, "Maybe next time."

My mom said, "Bailey, I don't think—"

"*I don't want to go, okay?*" I hadn't meant to, but I snapped at her. I didn't know where it came from, but I also didn't want to take it back, either. I pressed my lips together before saying, "I have to go study."

I went into my room and closed my door, feeling like garbage. For yelling at my mom, for disappointing them about the trip, and mostly for the inescapable fact that things were definitely progressing with Scott and pretty soon his presence in our life would be constant.

I could *feel* it now.

I blinked back tears—stupid, immature tears—and wondered when life would stop changing up on me.

I flopped down onto my bed and turned on the TV with the remote.

"Bailey." My mom knocked on my door like I knew she would, because we weren't the kind of people who could just let it lie. "Can I come in?"

"Sure." She came in, and I knew she was going to make me. I just *knew* she was going to make me vacation with Scott, and I didn't know what to do. It surely wasn't that big a deal—a weekend away—but I remembered what Charlie said the first time we talked on the phone.

He's only going to advance and take more space.

"Are you okay?" She closed the door behind her, came over, and sat down on the edge of my bed. "It's not like you to snap like that."

"I'm sorry," I said, meaning that part of it. I looked at her face—the blue eyes, the pale eyebrows, the mouth that had said everything I'd ever needed to hear for the whole of my life—and I felt desperate. It was so babyish, but I felt a desperation to hold tight to our *us*.

"I don't get it, Bay," she said, reaching out to run a hand

176

over my hair. "He was so excited when he got the idea because he wants to get to know you better. He thought it could be a relaxed way to just have some fun together."

"I know," I said, trying to come up with words that didn't make things worse between her and me. "But I just don't feel ready to go on a *vacation* with him yet."

"It's not like that," my mom said, crossing her arms. She was wearing her *I'm the problem* T-shirt, the one she'd bought the day after *Midnights* came out. "It's just a casual, fun weekend where we get out of town. No bigs."

"Just the three of us?" I asked, bracing myself for the mention of a daughter.

"Well," she said, pursing her lips. "I suppose if you wanted to take Nekesa, that would be okay."

"Really?" She'd obviously misunderstood what I was asking, but God, if I could take Nekesa, that might make it okay. She and I could ditch them and have fun in Colorado, and even when we were all together, it wouldn't feel as much like a forced family event. "I could?"

She shrugged, and I felt a little guilty that she was having to make concessions. "I don't see why not. The condo has two bedrooms and a pullout sofa in the living room, so as long as she doesn't mind the couch, I think it'd be fine."

"Wow." I pushed my hair out of my face, relief flooding through me. "That will make it so much, um, I mean, a little bit less . . ."

I had no idea how to put it into words without making her feel bad about Scott.

"I get it, Bay," she said, and I could tell that she did. Which made me hug her, because as much as I didn't dig Scott, I also loved my mom and didn't want to make *her* unhappy.

It was a fucking terrible tightrope of guilt to walk.

I grabbed my phone and texted Nekesa as soon as my mom left the room.

How would you like to go to Colorado?

I was getting whiplash from my own emotions, but as I waited for her response, I realized that if she was able to go, I was actually a little excited for a Colorado getaway.

Only if she can go.

Yes, Scott would be there, but Nekesa always made everything better, and I knew this would be no exception.

Nekesa: I am packing my plaid shirt and Docs as we speak.

That made me smile as I walked over to my dresser. **You think I'm kidding but I'm not. Scott is taking me and my mom to Breck for a weekend and they said you can come.**

Nekesa: I thought we hated Scott.

That response made me feel like garbage, and I texted: **We don't hate HIM, we just hate the way he's weaseling into our lives.**

Nekesa: That doesn't sound very different from what I said.

I texted: So are you coming or not???

Nekesa: Let me ask my mom. BRB.

I held my breath as I dug for mountain-wear, and then I

squealed when Nekesa came back with: **When do we leave??** ☺

The next morning, even though the sight of Crew Socks in the kitchen made me as irritated as ever, I thanked him for the trip.

"It's nice of you to invite us and to let me bring a friend," I said, genuinely meaning that. My mom was the one who threw out the Nekesa option, not Scott, and he easily could've said no or been a dick about it.

Instead, he smiled and said between bites of his everything bagel, "The more the merrier. Only . . . no more. That's plenty. The four the merriest and no others . . ."

"Rolls off the tongue," I said, which made him laugh.

As he walked out the door, he texted me a link to the condo on Vrbo so Nekesa and I could look at the pictures, which led to an hour-long FaceTime where we discussed outfits, activities, and logistics.

We had to work on Saturday morning—just a half shift, so Scott and my mom were going to leave early in the morning, and we'd drive out when we got off. In my opinion, this was a total best-case scenario, because we wouldn't even have to spend any time in the car with him.

As long as something insane didn't happen, like Scott proposing to my mother on the slopes, this could actually be a great trip.

CHAPTER TWENTY-FOUR

Bailey

The night before we were supposed to leave, Nekesa called me, crying.

"Oh my God—what's wrong?" I asked, sitting on my bed, watching a rerun of *Monk*.

She was sniffling and trying to keep it together, but the moral of the story was that she'd come in an hour late the night before (because she'd fallen asleep at Aaron's house) and gotten into a fight with her parents, and now they wouldn't let her go on the trip. She was grounded indefinitely, only allowed to leave the house for work and school.

I knew the proper response would be something nurturing, words to make my best friend feel better.

But *oh my God, I couldn't go without her*! I just couldn't.

"What if my mom calls your mom?" I asked, desperate. "Do you think that might help?"

"No," she said, still crying. "This is big-time. I'm seriously grounded for *months*."

"Noooooooo," I groaned. It was too late for me to get out of the trip now, and I'd been so nice to Scott for letting Nekesa come along that he was totally going to push the whole I-want-to-be-your-pal agenda in her absence.

"Listen, I know you won't want to," she said, sniffling before loudly blowing her nose, "but what if you take Charlie?"

"Whaaat? What? WHAT!? *No.*" That was ridiculous. *Right?* It was ridiculous. I couldn't take *Charlie*, dear God. That was batshit bonkers. My voice was a little high-pitched when I asked, "Why would I do that?"

"Listen." She cleared her throat and said, "I mentioned the idea to Theo, and he agrees that it could—"

"When did you talk to Theo?" I interrupted. *She told Theo she was grounded before even telling me?*

"I just got off the phone with him."

Whoa. I tried to sound casual when I asked, "You guys talk on the phone now?"

"Sometimes, but it's no big deal," she said, brushing it off. "Aaron knows and he's fine with it."

Should he be? I wondered how to proceed, because even though it wasn't my business and she didn't sound concerned, it felt like my friendly duty was to intervene.

"Are you sure that's a good idea?" I said, trying to keep my voice light and breezy. Though I was anything but.

I knew Charlie would tell me to butt out, but Nekesa's happiness was more important to me. I needed her to slow down and think before she had regrets. I said, "Don't you think Theo is rather flirty with you?"

"Nah, he's just a playful guy," she said, and I could tell she truly believed it. "So anyway. Back to the trip. Call Charlie."

Huh. That was a quick change of topic, but . . . okay. I decided to dismiss it and focus on the current tragedy at hand.

I let myself flop back onto my mattress, starting to freak out at the mere idea of Charlie and me in Breckenridge. "I cannot take him on this trip—come *on*."

"You don't want to go alone, and he's your other bestie. Why *not*?"

There were a million reasons, starting with the fact that he was *Charlie Sampson*.

Also—my other bestie?? Where. When. Why? How???

"Not only should you take Charlie," she said, "but what do you think about pretending to date him?"

"*What?* Have you lost your *mind*?" I said, a little too loudly, when my mom and Scott were asleep in the room next door. I lowered my voice and said, "No *way*."

I couldn't even *imagine* it. It was weird enough when Charlie asked me to go to his friend's party with him for support in dealing with his ex. But this was different. Pretending to be into Charlie romantically? Exploring what *that* entailed? No. No way.

Just the thought of it filled my stomach with nervous stressful butterflies, but it didn't matter because it wasn't happening.

No *way*.

"You two always say you're only friends, right? Like, no chem whatsoever . . . ?"

"Right. Absolutely no chemistry," I said, which was true. *For the most part.* There might've been a small workplace flirtation that elevated my blood pressure, but it'd already been established in my mind that it was nothing. NOTHING. Two humans that happened to stand close together, and body temps naturally increase in moments like that. It was science. And NOT the chemistry kind of science.

Still, that didn't mean I wanted to embark upon a weekend full of awkward false affections. No, no thank you. I added, "I'm actually feeling queasy at the mere thought of me and Charlie."

"So who cares, then? Fake date the hell out of him. Do you realize the amount of tension that can be added to the Breckenridge weekend if you show up holding hands with Charlie?"

Holding hands? That felt . . . dangerous somehow.

"Nekesa, dear, this is real life," I said. "Not a Hallmark movie." Fake dating happened in movies, not in the normal world. It was wild that this behavior was even being suggested, and especially by my practical friend Nekesa.

"Just do it," she said, sniffling. "What do you have to lose?"

God, Scott *would* absolutely lose his shit. It could even ruin the whole trip for him, which the good part of me didn't want but the desperate part of me did. "But couldn't I add the tension *without* fake dating him? Not that I'm even considering this, but his presence alone would make things testy. I don't think I'd need to pretend to be into him."

"Bay, you know so little about men," she said, finally sounding like herself again. "My little sweet baby."

"Screw you," I said around a laugh, mostly because she was right. I knew very little about men.

Except for Zack. I knew everything about him.

Nekesa laughed—and then sniffled again—before saying, "I just mean that your dad hasn't been around since you've been old enough to date, so you've been spared male stupidity."

Nekesa was being helpful and sweet, but her succinct summation of just how long my dad had been absent caused a pinching feeling in my sternum.

I swallowed and pictured my dad's face. "I suppose that's true."

"There's this primitive, cavemanish thing that happens to fathers when they see guys they don't like around their daughters. They become like hissing cats, peeing on your sweaters."

"I don't. Even. *What?*"

"And even though Scott's not your dad, since he already hates Charlie, Theo and I predict he will go full-on defecating-on-every-cardigan if he sees Chuckles holding your hand."

So why did those words continue to make my stomach dip? Why did just imagining it feel like I was treading into deeper waters? Even if it wasn't real.

But maybe more importantly—Nekesa and Theo had discussed me and Charlie? Had she brought it up, or had he? And why would Theo be weighing in at all?

"And don't you think—even if his presence does nothing to forward the Scott agenda—that Charlie would be fun to vacation with? I mean, this is the guy who created Garbage Tether, a game that makes us fight for trash duty because it's so fun. He makes you enjoy taking out the trash, Bay! He'd be a riot on a mountain retreat."

"What are you doing?" I asked, my voice rising an octave at the situation's absurdity. "Why does it feel like you're trying to set something up with me and Charlie?" My Spidey senses were tingling.

"That's not it, Bay—trust me," she said, and I could hear her little brother in the background. "I'm just trying to think of a way for the mountain weekend to still be good for you."

"Hmm," I mumbled, not sure I was buying it.

"And he really *would* be a blast on the road trip."

She wasn't wrong. As *Charlie* as he could be with his cynicism, he really *was* hilarious.

Hell, an entire house party had essentially broken out into applause at the sight of him.

I could hear Nekesa's impatience growing. "Sooooo . . . ?"

I took a big breath, the weight in my stomach getting heavier at the thought of this, at the realization that I was seriously considering this. Traveling with Charlie felt wildly intimate—regardless of what Nekesa said—and I wasn't sure how to be casual about it.

"Soooo . . . for starters, I'm not sure I know how to ask him. I don't want him to get the wrong idea."

Honestly, if he said, *Do you want to go to Colorado for the weekend with me and my family?* I'd definitely be concerned that he was into me. And—God—I would hate it if he thought that.

I would *die* if he thought that.

Charlie wasn't even comfortable calling me his friend. We were *coworkers only* in his mind, even though we both knew it was more than that, because that was the only way he could cope with the reality that his hypothesis was wrong.

"I've got you," she said, sniffling again.

"And what does *that* mean?"

"Theo and I have . . . uh . . . actually been texting him in a group chat since we came up with the idea a half hour ago, so I think I can safely say he'll respond well."

"*What?* A half hour ago?" I sputtered. "How come you went to them with all of this before coming to me?"

"Because I know you, Miss Overreaction," she said, and I could hear a smile in her voice. "I wanted to come up with a plan before I told you so you didn't freak out about having to go with just Scott and your mom."

"Nekesa!" My heart was hammering in my chest, panic rising. "Not cool!"

"It's all done from love, my wonderful, sweet, oh-so-irresistible Bay."

"Don't try to compliment your way out of this," I quickly snapped, but somewhere in the pit of my stomach I was thankful Nekesa broke the ice for me. Okay, so maybe she did know me. Too well.

"I have to get off the phone, but I'm adding you to the chat."

"But do you—"

She had already hung up as my phone pinged from her text.

I looked down at the display as she sent me screenshots of their conversation.

The chain started with Nekesa texting—**I can't go to Breck—Bay is going to kill me.**

After she explained what happened, and Theo tried making her feel better (**catch up on your reading, troublemaker**), Charlie texted—**Bay's gonna be devastated. You sure your parents won't reconsider?**

Something about his concern made me feel warm inside.

Nekesa: Positive

Charlie: So she'll have to spend the trip with just her mom and Sock Boy. Fucking nightmare.

Nekesa: You should go in my place.

It felt surreal, reading their conversation; I felt like I was eavesdropping, even though I had permission.

Charlie: Dude hates me—try again.

I don't know why, but it felt good that his initial response wasn't something like **No way.**

Theo: Wait—that would totally amp the mom/ boyfriend tension, tho, right?

Nekesa: YESSSS OMG GO, AND FAKE DATE

Charlie: FAKE DATE. Are we in a fucking Hallmark movie?? How would that help?

Thank you, Charlie! At least it wasn't just me who thought the idea was totally bonkers.

Theo: If the bf hates you, he'll hate you more if you're holding her hand bc it means you're not going away anytime soon. VERY threatening to his territory.

I rolled my eyes, feeling that claustrophobia again at the thought of me and/or my mom being Scott's "territory."

Charlie: Okay—that would definitely make the guy lose his shit. BUT. Odds are good he'll just say no to me going.

Scott would say that.

Nekesa: Bailey and I were going to drive out after work tomorrow and meet them. So basically he won't know you're coming until you get there, and he can't say no if you're already in Colorado.

Was I—Bailey, who doesn't let others cut in line—ballsy enough to just show up with him? Could I be? Did I want to be?

Charlie: That will definitely add to the tension, holy shit.

And that's when I chimed in with: **DEFINITELY. HOLY SHIT.**

Theo: Bailey's here!

Charlie: Even though it's HOLY SHIT, I'll do it if you want me to, Bay.

I squeaked in disbelief—or anxiousness or nervousness—because this idea felt like something that might actually happen.

And I wasn't sure if I wanted it to or not.

Nekesa: DO ITTTTT I'm dying to hear what happens.

I texted: **You'd seriously give up a few days of break? And pretend to be my boyfriend???**

Seemed like a really big ask.

Theo: He'd pretend to loooooove you.

"Shut up, Theo," I muttered to no one in the darkness.

Nekesa: You're such an idiot. ;)

Charlie: I'd be in Colorado—that's a big old HELL YES from me.

My phone started ringing—Charlie—and I answered with, "But he'll probably be a dick to you the whole time."

"I can handle it," Charlie said, his voice gravelly like he'd been sleeping before the call.

"Hmmm." I seriously didn't know what to do. On paper, what Nekesa/Charlie/Theo were proposing could potentially help my Scott dilemma and make the weekend fun(ish). But there were so many other things to worry about.

My mom's and Scott's reaction when Charlie got there— that was an explosion of unhappiness guaranteed to happen. Traveling with Charlie for eight hours; been there, done that, and it wasn't remotely enjoyable.

And—the biggie—pretending to *date* Charlie.

Our friendship was safe because it was labeled as only that. Friends. Hell, he labeled it *not even* that; he labeled us as just coworkers.

So what would happen when we played relationship for a weekend? It might be fine and just return to normal when we got home, but what if it didn't? What if we crossed a line that we couldn't come back from?

"Bay, if you don't want me to, that's totally fine."

I didn't know *what* I wanted. Taking Charlie sounded like fun and I didn't want to go alone, but the thought of it set off screechingly loud alarm bells.

"Um," I said, opening my nightstand drawer and digging for the coral nail polish while I tried to decide. "Well, for starters,

I'm just afraid you're saying yes to be nice."

"Do I ever do that?" he asked dryly.

I smiled in spite of my nerves because that was a loaded question. He *didn't* do things just to be nice, but he was also surprisingly thoughtful sometimes.

A walking contradiction, Charlie Sampson. "Well, no."

"I think it sounds like a blast," he said, "but if you'd rather not, it's totally cool."

I thought about the weekend, staying in a condo with just my mom and Scott, and I said, "I *really* want you to go, but I wonder if I should ask—"

"Nope," Charlie said, cutting me off. "You do whatever you want about the weekend, but if you ask them, they will *for sure* say no. If we pull up in Breck, though, with you in my car, they can't really send me back."

There it was again—the ginormously ballsy move that I wasn't sure I could pull off. I closed the drawer and flopped back onto my pillows. "That is positively diabolical."

"Thank you."

"And terrifying," I added. "I know you're *Charlie*, but doesn't the thought of just showing up make you nervous?"

I expected him to say no, but he didn't.

"Of course," he said matter-of-factly. "But I also know that they're not going to want to throw away their mountain retreat, so they'll decide to deal with it for the sake of preserving the weekend that Scott has already paid for."

He's right. His confidence bolstered mine, so much so that I heard myself say, "Okay, so maybe we should do this."

Did I just squeal?

Holy shit, I couldn't believe we were going to do this.

"Atta girl."

"Shut it." I felt mildly relieved that I'd made the decision, but immediately my brain switched into planning mode.

"Wait—what about your mom? Do we need to ask her if it's cool for you to run off for a few days?"

"Nah." He cleared his throat and said, "She trusts me."

"For *multiple days*? *Out of town*?" I asked, shocked. "That's a whole lot of trust for a kid in high school."

"One of those divorce things," he said, sounding tired on the other end of the phone. "She's so busy with the boyfriend and my younger sister that anytime I'm not in her hair, I think she breathes a sigh of relief."

"Bullshit," I said, feeling a bit of a gut punch for him in that moment. Whether it was true or not, it made me sad that he felt like his mom didn't want him around. "I'm sure that's not true."

His voice was quieter than usual, a tinge more serious, when he said, "You'd be surprised."

I didn't know Charlie's mom, so I tried to assume this was just what she was like and not a sweeping generalization of single parents.

But I'd be lying if I said that a tiny part of me heard his words and didn't think, *What if that eventually happens with my mom and me?*

"It doesn't matter, though," he said, his voice louder and more stereotypically Charlie. "Know why?"

I rolled onto my side and asked, "Why?"

"Cuz I'm going to the mountains tomorrow."

"Have you been before?" I liked the excitement in his voice. He sounded like he was genuinely looking forward to the road trip, and it sparked something in me.

I felt a little excited.

"Not in Colorado, but in Alaska," he said.

"Duh," I replied, picturing the White Mountains. "I forgot your cousins live there."

"Duh, indeed," he agreed. "I miss the mountains. Don't you?"

"Yeah, I do," I said, but I didn't let myself think about home anymore. I'd spent so many hours closing my eyes and picturing my old house, and the only thing it ever did was make me sad.

It was better to forget. I asked him, "Do you ski?"

"No."

"Do you want to try?" I asked.

"No."

"I'm so happy to hear that!" Nekesa had been all about the skiing, but I just wanted to walk around the mountains and drink coffee at charming little shops. There might've been a time when I wanted to learn, but not while Scott was offering to teach me. "I don't want to either."

"Because of your clumsiness?"

"I'm not clumsy." I laughed, grabbing the remote and turning on the TV. "Why would you say that?"

"You just have that *I could fall over anything* look about you."

"Lovely," I said, shaking my head. "Thank you."

"I don't mean it in a bad way," he said, his deep voice teasing over the phone line.

"How could that ever be said in a good way?" I quipped.

"I just meant that with your skinny legs and big feet, you sometimes remind me of a puppy."

"Oh my God." I laughed. "This just keeps getting better and better."

"What?" he said with a smile in his voice. "Puppies are cute. Puppies are adorable. People loooooove puppies."

"Uh-huh," I said, clicking into Netflix.

"Did I annoy you enough to make the nerves about Colorado go away?" he asked.

I leaned back against my pillow. "I can't believe you're going with me. It's a little surreal, to be honest."

Wildly, absurdly, overwhelmingly surreal.

"I know. I'm excited for Colorado, but I'm not sure about road-tripping with you."

"What?" I found *You've Got Mail* under Romantic Comedies and clicked it on. "Why? I'm a dreamboat road-tripper."

"I've traveled with you before, remember?"

Of course I did. He knew it. I knew it. Even if it felt like a lifetime ago.

I said, "Which is why *I'm* dreading this. Me, though—I'm a fantastic traveler."

"Come on, Glasses," he chided, and I could almost *see* his teasing smirk. "I bet you have every stop timed out, snacks packed in little baggies, and playlists created specifically for where you are on the map."

It was a little jarring, how well he knew me.

And ugh. I liked it.

He knew all of my neuroses and hang-ups, and not once did I feel that he was disappointed or turned off.

I *liked* when he teased me about them because it made me amused by them too. Comfortable with them. It felt *good* to laugh at myself instead of being embarrassed for once.

"The stops are merely suggestions," I said, "you're wrong about the snacks"—he wasn't—"and I think it's amazing to have a musical accompaniment for every leg of your journey."

"You sound like an insane person. Also, since I'm driving, I control the music."

I couldn't even imagine what Charlie listened to. *Bo Burnham, but rap.* "That's not fair."

"Neither is the fact that I'm driving," he said, trying to land his point.

"I can take a turn," I replied, even though I didn't want to.

"And let you threaten the sanctity of the bond between me and my vehicle?" he asked. "I don't think so."

I chuckled quietly, watching on the TV as Tom Hanks navigated New York in the fall, and asked, "What are you doing right now?"

"Watching Lawrence Welk and touching myself."

"First of all, ewwwwww," I said, laughing in spite of myself. "Second of all, Lawrence Welk?"

"Stroking my beard, you pervert—get your mind out of the gutter." He sounded like he was smiling when he said, "And I lost the remote, if you must know, and my TV always goes back to public television when I turn it on."

"So you're seriously lying there, watching an ancient show where a bunch of people stand around singing, because you're too lazy to look for the controller?"

"Pretty much."

"So when you say 'stroking your beard,' you actually mean that you're touching your pathetic little chin hairs, right?"

"Now, come on, Bay, no need to get nasty," he said, and I liked the way his voice sounded when I could tell he was smiling. "Those hairs are concrete evidence of an impending beard."

"Doubtful," I teased.

"Evidence of my manliness," he replied.

"Facial hair is *not* evidence of manliness," I corrected, "not that what you have on your chin even qualifies as such."

"I cannot believe you're so hateful about my beard," he said, feigning outrage but failing because I heard the laugh that slipped out.

"I cannot believe you're doubling down on calling that a beard."

He asked, "Do you want me to shave it before tomorrow?"

That surprised me. "It's your face, and you can do whatever you want."

"But your vote is . . . ?" he asked, and I wondered if he actually cared what my opinion was.

"Shave it," I said, picturing his face. "It's not that the hair is offensive, per se, but you have a nice face and the beard hides that."

Silence and then . . . "Oh my God, you're so in love with my face."

LYNN PAINTER

"Shut up and stop making me queasy." I leaned back against my headboard and said, "Objectively, you have a very nice face that other people probably enjoy."

I heard him laugh again. "But not you."

"God, no." I actually thought it was funny that I was friends with someone so objectively attractive but so *whatever* to me. "Sometimes I squeeze my eyes shut when we're together, just so I don't have to see your eyes and cheeks and that atrocious nose."

He laughed again. "Okay—confession."

"Ugh—I hate those."

"I know," he said. "The worst."

"Go ahead, though," I pressed.

"Okay. So. When I saw you at the movies last year, before you opened your mouth and reminded me of what a pain in the ass you are, I thought you were hot."

I coughed out a laugh. "Did you seriously just say that you thought I was hot until you remembered my personality? Is that supposed to be a compliment?"

"Come on, Bay, you know what I mean." His voice was a little crackly when he said, "I looked up, thought, *Damn, she's pretty*, and then I was like, *Oh, holy shit, it's the whackjob from the plane but with normal hair*."

I *did* know what he meant. I'd felt the same way when I'd seen him. "Awwww—thank you, Charlie."

"So . . . ?"

Oh my God, he wanted me to return it. I admitted, "Okay. When we saw the promposal, I thought you looked kind of cute and kind of jacked. But only until you looked at me. Then I was

196

like, *Oh shit, oh shit, I need to run because I hate that guy.*"

He chuckled, a deep, scratchy thing that made me want to make him laugh more often. "Oh, Glasses, you never hated me."

I rolled onto my side and snuggled into my blanket. "Trust me, on that flight, I hated you with the white-hot intensity of a thousand suns."

"For which you would've requested special sunscreen that was half-organic, half-regular."

"Whatever." I looked over at my suitcase and said, "So what are you doing when we get off the phone?"

"Laundry and packing," he said. "Are you leaving your car at work while we're gone?"

"No—Theo's going to give Nekesa and me a ride in the morning."

"Really," he said, sounding smug.

"Shut it, they're friends," I defended, even as I knew they were getting too close.

"Sure they are," he said. "I'm sure you saw the adorable winky faces she used when addressing Theo in the group chat."

"I send winky faces to my mother," I replied, even though the winky faces had totally been red flags to me. "Doesn't mean anything."

"Sure it doesn't."

"Are you going to be this annoying on the drive to the mountains?" I asked.

"Probably?"

I let out a long sigh. "I'm hanging up. G'night, Charlie."

He sighed, louder and longer than mine. "G'night, Bailey."

CHAPTER TWENTY-FIVE

Charlie

I can't believe I'm doing this, was all I could think—on repeat—the day Bailey and I were leaving for Breck.

The morning shift flew by with its usual boredom, but I couldn't ignore the fucking annoying twirl of nerves rippling through me as I waited for her to change. Why had I agreed to this ridiculous plan?

Did it sound fun? Yes.

Did it sound like the kind of scenario that could go wrong in a thousand different ways?

Hell fucking yes.

And so the last thing I needed before jumping into a car with Bay for hours on end was Theo and his bullshit smile swaggering toward me.

"Holy shit, bro," Theo said, grinning and shaking his head as I leaned against my car, which was parked under the canopy in front of the hotel. "This should be a slam dunk."

"Huh?" I *liked* Theo, liked him as in I didn't want a meteor to fall from the sky and crush him, but I didn't particularly enjoy talking to the weasel. He was the stereotypical prep school kid who enjoyed stirring up trouble because he'd never had to face any consequences in his entire life.

He was wearing the required uniform that we all wore, but the dude accessorized with a pinkie ring, a huge watch, and shoes that had *Saint Laurent* scrawled across the side. If this were a movie, I'd say they'd been a little heavy-handed in costuming the prep school kid—no subtlety whatsoever.

Especially when he spoke like he'd never been unsure of himself a day in his life.

Wouldn't that be fucking nice.

He came a little closer and lowered his voice. "The bet . . . ?"

I was confused for a second and thought he knew about the bet Bailey and I had. But then . . .

SHIIIT.

"That was a joke," I quickly snapped at him and his perfectly pomaded hair, as I suddenly remembered lunch on our first day at work, when Theo said something to me about Bailey being wound too tight for any guy to stand a chance with her. And then before I'd known what an actual sleaze he kind of was, I joked that I could do it.

"I bet you a hundred bucks that you can't get her," he'd said, and because I didn't like his cocky smile, I'd replied with, "You're on."

But the last thing I had any interest in doing was pursuing Bailey.

For money, for fuck's sake.

I said it just to shut him up.

But I knew Bailey would never understand that. Why would she?

So finding out I'd bet that I could "get" her—yeah, she'd lose her shit if she ever found out.

"What the hell is wrong with you, man?" Theo said, his face twisted in amused disbelief. "You're going away with her for the weekend. Now's your shot."

"I'm not looking for a *shot*." I glanced over his shoulder, wishing he'd shut his fucking mouth. Not only did I not want Bay to hear him, but I didn't want someone else to overhear and think I was a prick like him. "Like I said, it was a joke."

"Getting nervous that you can't make it happen?" he asked, smirking like a creep.

I had a million smart-ass comments I wanted say at that moment, but guys like Theo were unpredictable. If you said the wrong thing and managed to wound their fragile ego, there could be hell to pay.

"No," I said, lowering my voice so he'd take a hint. "But I *know* it won't happen if she overhears you."

And boom—it worked. Theo's face slid into a sleazy grin and he nodded. The dude lowered his voice and said, "Slam dunk."

I was relieved when he walked away (after a fucking absurd bro-handshake that included a shoulder bump), but that didn't mean there wasn't still stress pinging around inside me.

Something about the road trip had me on edge. I couldn't put my finger on whether it was the blowup that was sure to happen with the adults when we arrived in Breckenridge, or some . . . something that had everything to do with spending an entire weekend alone with Bailey.

I was . . . *unsettled* as I got into the car and started it up.

And that feeling didn't go away when Bailey came out in a hooded sweatshirt that looked like it was going to swallow her whole, her hair in a slick ponytail, and a huge pair of sunglasses on and ready.

Damn. The on-edge feeling ratcheted up to an inching-toward-the-end-of-the-cliff level of on-edge as I watched her approach the car. Swear to God I heard Taylor Swift's voice say, "Are you ready for it?"

Let the games begin.

I reached into my pocket for the TUMS and popped a few into my mouth. I saw Bailey's eyebrow lift, which made my mother's anxious voice—*Find your calm, Charlie*—swim in my head.

"You do realize that if Mr. Cleveland sees you parked here, he'll lose his shit," she said, opening up the passenger-side door and climbing into my car.

"I'm not worried about Cleveland. I *dare* him to censure us."

"Wow." She reached for the seat belt, her ponytail brushing her shoulders. "Are you a badass?"

"Obviously. You haven't realized that by now?"

"Somehow I missed it," she mused. And I relaxed a little.

"I don't see how." Good. This felt very normal for us.

"Are we getting snacks before we get on the interstate?"

"Duh." I put the car in drive and floored it out of the parking lot. "Are we getting snacks—as if that's even a question. What kind of a moron do you think I am?"

CHAPTER TWENTY-SIX

Bailey

"Okay—I'm exiting here," Charlie said.

"Whatever." I shrugged. "Get gas wherever you want; see if I care."

"I will," Charlie said, his mouth twitching into an almost smile. "Just wanted to warn you, in case you need to stretch or something."

"No, I'm good, but thanks." I sat straight up, moved my purse, then slid my feet back into my shoes. "Maybe *you* should stretch."

"As if, Glasses. Come on."

We'd been driving for six-ish hours, and we'd created a ridiculous game that was going to get me killed. Every time we stopped, we raced to the bathrooms. *Literally.* Whoever could sprint to the bathroom, use the facilities, wash their hands, and be the first to get back and touch the car was the big winner.

That person didn't have to pay for gas or snacks, and they also got to drive and control the radio.

Unfortunately for me, he'd won at each stop.

And last time my foot had gotten stuck in the dangling seat belt I'd yanked off the minute we'd stopped, leaving me with a hole in my leggings and a bloody knee as I'd chased Charlie into the gas station.

It was a little unfair because he had no qualms about yelling "Look out, look out" and basically running over people, whereas I couldn't bring myself to keep up the sprint when faced with oncoming foot traffic.

This time was going to be it, though. *This time* I would win.

"Okay—three gas stations up ahead. Which one do you want?"

"Don't," I said, rolling my eyes. "Don't give me the pity choice. Just because I have yet to win doesn't mean you need to feel sorry for me."

"Oh, honey," he cooed, coughing out a laugh as his eyes stayed on the road. "But I *do* feel sorry for you. That's a nasty strawberry on your knee."

"That you poured hand sanitizer on!"

"To keep away infection," he said, smiling, and I let it go. He'd been kind of sweet after the fall. I could tell he felt really bad. It was a little bit adorable.

"Eddy's Hot Stop," I said. "Go, asshole."

"Atta girl," he said around a laugh as he hit the blinker.

I don't know why, but there was something about the way he said "Atta girl" that made me feel warm *everywhere*.

I stared out the window as he turned into the lot and headed for a gas pump. The rule was that no one could start until the car was put in park.

"You look tense," he said, slowly cruising toward the covered fuel pumps. "You all right there, buddy?"

"Don't distract me," I said, glancing over at him.

Which was a mistake, because he was grinning as if he'd never seen anything more amusing than me, poised and ready to jump from the car. "Wanna know why you'll never win this game?" he asked.

"Oh, but I will," I replied, biting the inside of my cheek so I didn't smile back at him.

"It's because you lack the killer instinct."

"I do not," I said, leaning forward as he started slowing.

"Yes, you do," he said, and even without looking I could *hear* the smart-ass grin in his voice. "If you run into the bathroom and there's one open stall and two of you ladies, are you going to push the other chick out of the way?"

Of course I wouldn't. But I said, "If it means beating you, then yes."

"Liar," he drawled, and the way he said it brought my eyes back to his face again.

There was a challenge in his dark eyes as they met mine, in the wicked smile that turned up his mouth. If it were anyone else, looking at me like that, I would call it wildly flirtatious.

But this was Charlie.

This was just the thrill of competition.

Right?

He jammed the shifter into park, and our doors flew open. We each leaped from the car and full-out sprinted toward the gas station doors, and for once I was a hair ahead of him.

"I'm right at your heels, Glasses," he said, trying to distract me.

"Shut up." I pushed the door with both hands, not yielding at all as I ran into the convenience store. The people in line at the counter looked at us as we flew past, but I kept my focus on the bathrooms.

"Coming hot on your left," Charlie breathed, and the sound of him chasing me was downright predatorial.

"Staying hot on your right," I panted.

The bathrooms waited for us at the back of the gas station, and we didn't even slow as we each plowed through our respective door. I flew into a stall, hurried, splashed through the world's fastest hand washing, and ran back out, ignoring the stares as I sprinted past the Pepsi coolers and blasted out the door.

I had a clear path to his car, and there wasn't a sprinting Charlie in sight.

I was finally going to control the radio.

I ran all the way up to his car and slapped the hood with both hands—as per the rules—before jumping up and down, even though I was standing by myself next to his car.

Only, after ten more seconds, I wondered what was up.

Where the hell was Charlie?

The couple in the car on the other side of the gas pump was giving me *Is she high* side-eye, so I gave them a closed-mouth smile and got into the car.

While wondering where the hell he was. Was he okay? Had something happened? Was he in trouble? Just when I was reaching for my bag to find my phone, it started ringing.

"Gah." I fumbled and fished it out, saw Charlie was calling, and raised it to my ear. "You lost. Come out and accept your shame."

"I can't," he said, and his voice sounded . . . *weird*.

"What's wrong?" I asked. "Are you sick?"

"No," he said quietly, then said, "Well, yes, I kind of think I will be soon."

"What?" My heart sped up at the sound of Charlie sounding . . . *off*. "Are you okay? What can I do?"

He sighed and muttered, "I dropped my keys."

"Um." *What?* "So pick them up . . . ?"

He sighed again. "That's the thing. I can't."

"Did they fall down a hole or something?"

Oh God. How were we going to get to the condo before midnight if he'd dropped his keys down a hole?

"Or something. They're in the urinal."

"What?" I looked over my shoulder at the gas station. "So . . . shouldn't they be easy to grab?"

"I, um." He cleared his throat, sounding very uncomfortable, and said, "I *can't*."

I sat there for a half second before saying, "Charlie, are you telling me your keys are right there in the urinal, but you can't grab them?"

It was quiet for a moment before he said, "Yes."

I didn't know what this meant, but I knew him well enough

to know this was *something*. I asked, "Is anyone else in the bathroom?"

"No."

"I'll be right there."

I grabbed my purse, got out of the car, and went back inside the convenience store. I felt like an idiot as everyone I'd sprinted past a minute earlier stared at me, but I kept my eyes trained on the bathrooms in the rear of the store.

"Charlie?" I approached the men's room and opened the door a crack. "Am I good to come in?"

"Yeah," I heard him say.

I opened the door, and when I got inside, I found Charlie looking miserable. He watched me with one dark eyebrow raised, his hair tousled like he'd been dragging his hand through it. Oh, how I wanted to give him so much shit.

But I didn't. I couldn't.

I couldn't help the lump in my stomach. Seeing Charlie being . . . *un*-Charlie was surprisingly unsettling.

I said, "First things first. Did you pee *on* your keys?"

The corner of his mouth kicked up the tiniest bit. "Of course not."

"And they're . . ." I gestured with my chin to the urinal beside him.

"Yes." He moved so I could see his keys sitting in the urinal. It looked clean-ish, and I was surprised he hadn't just grabbed them. Yes, gas station urinals were beyond disgusting, but I'd pictured it much worse. He said, "I moved too fast when I ran in here and missed my pocket entirely."

"Oof." I stared at the urinal before shrugging and committing to the task at hand. "I'm going in."

"Oh God," he groaned, his strong nose crinkling like a little kid's when presented with an unwanted vegetable. "So gross."

And just then I wanted to hug Charlie. I knew nothing about *why* he was physically incapable of sticking his hand into the dirty urinal, but I knew him well enough to know that he'd rather do just about anything than have someone witness what he surely perceived as a moment of "weakness."

"Why don't you go buy our snacks—because I'm the winner," I said, hoping to make him smile. "And fill up the car. I'll be out in just a sec."

His eyes went serious again. "You sure? That's pretty disgusting."

I nodded. "It's no big deal. Get me Twizzlers and a white Rockstar, please."

"You got it."

When I came out to the car a few minutes later, after bathing his keys in hot soapy water and then a follow-up hand sanitizer shower, he still looked conflicted. "Listen, Bay, about what happened—"

"I don't care, Charlie," I groaned. "Did you get my licorice?"

He got a crinkle between his eyebrows. "It's in the front seat, in the console."

"Sweet. And my energy drink?"

"Same place," he said.

"Excellent." I crossed my arms and said, "So, I don't really want to drive; I just want radio control. Cool?"

He gave a nod. "Cool."

We got into the car and hit the road, and we were quiet for a solid two minutes before Charlie said, "I feel like I need to—"

"You don't." I reached out my arm and stuck a Twizzler into his mouth, and watched his jaw as he immediately started chewing without question. "Never happened, unless you *want* to talk about it, in which case I'm happy to listen. Now, on to more important things: Do you prefer country or pop?"

"Can I say neither?" he asked, taking one hand off the wheel to hold the end of the licorice. He looked away from the road for a second, his eyes sweeping over my face with a thoroughness that made me feel like he was looking for something.

"You can say it, but it won't change the fact that those are your choices," I explained, feeling my cheeks get hot.

He groaned before saying, "Pop, I guess."

"Pop it is." I took over the radio, searching for the most annoying music I could find, and time flew by as Colorado gave us a lot to look at. The aspens were bright yellow, dotted across the mountains that our highway wove through, and all of a sudden I remembered why people moved away from Nebraska and never came back.

The place was breathtaking.

"Look at that," I said, pointing to a stream running parallel to the highway. "It's so gorgeous."

"That's twenty-one times," he said, reaching for the can of Red Bull in the cup holder. "That you've said that."

"I know, but it's impossible to stop."

"Obviously," he said, and I knew he agreed with me.

Something about the scenery and the mountain air made us both more relaxed, made us both feel like we were on a full-on vacation.

"I almost don't want to get there—is that weird?" I asked, biting down on my piece of licorice.

"No," he replied, taking a drink. I watched his Adam's apple move while he swallowed, and something about the motion seemed . . . *sexy?*

Yeah, that was weird. Not sexy, you idiot.

"You don't know what's going to happen when you get there, and you *hate* that." He set down the can and said to me, "Here in the car, there is no mystery. It's just a road trip with your amazing coworker."

"That's probably it," I agreed. "Not the amazing coworker piece, but the rest."

"The part I'm looking forward to," he said, reaching out a hand for more licorice without looking away from the road, "is not thinking about anything from home for the entire time. I want to wake up every day and only worry about how I'm going to irritate Glasses."

I pulled a Twizzler from the bag and held it out in front of his face.

He bit down on it, then turned his head and grinned at me in a way that did things to my stomach.

I cleared my throat and turned my eyes out the window. "What things don't you want to think about?"

"Bay." He made a noise of protest, something that sounded like a growl-groan combo. "If I say it, then I'm thinking about it."

"But we aren't there yet, so it's allowed," I verified.

I thought for sure he would change the subject, but instead he said, "The number one thing I don't want to think about is Bec and Kyle. The number two thing I don't want to think about is the fact that my mom is pregnant."

"What?" I stopped chewing. "When did you find out? Why didn't you tell me?"

Charlie's forehead crinkled as he tilted his head to the side. His sunglasses were so dark that I couldn't see his eyes, but I knew my question had surprised him.

"My mom mentioned it last night," he said, "but it's no big deal."

"I mean, you're going to have a new sibling," I said, trying to make him excited. "That's a *really* big deal."

"Yeah," he said tightly, and I couldn't read what he meant by that.

"Are you bummed?" I asked quietly, as if the lower volume would make everything better. "I mean, if I found out my dad was having another kid, I think it would freak me out."

"Really?" he replied, his emotions still unreadable.

"Yeah. I mean, things with him are already weird and distant, so how would a new kid in his life ever help that?"

"Can we not talk about this?" he asked on a sigh, but it wasn't unkind. He just sounded exhausted about it all. "I'm happy for them and I'm sure it will be great—my sister is fucking over the moon—but I just haven't wrapped my head around it yet."

"Sure." I crossed my arms and propped my feet on his dashboard. "So let's talk about Bec."

"You little shit." Charlie glanced over at me, shaking his head

211

and grinning as he reached out a hand and knocked down my feet. "How about we talk about Zack instead?"

"Ooh, no thank you," I said, glad he was smiling again. "Hard pass."

"Any movement with him?" he asked, pulling off his sunglasses and dropping them onto the dash. "Conversations that felt promising, looks exchanged, anything like that . . . ?"

"Actually," I said, "I don't really ever see or talk to him."

"What?" His face got all screwed up. "How are you hung up on him if you never see or talk to him?"

"I'm hung up on the *memory* of him," I said, wondering why it felt more comfortable trying to explain it to Charlie than it did to Nekesa. "And the fact that we aren't done."

"Yeah, I'm familiar with that last part," he said, reaching out to flip the radio even though it wasn't his turn. "But how are you ever going to reconnect if you don't have any contact?"

"I don't know," I said. "I'm sure we'll run into each other sometime soon."

"Do you have the same friends?" he asked. "I see Bec all the time because we have the same friends."

"No, um," I said, not wanting to sound like a dork. "We kind of hang in different crowds."

"He's not a super reader with a billion online buddies?"

That made me look over at him in surprise, because I'd never told him about my bookstagram account. "Are you on Instagram?"

He grinned but didn't answer, instead saying, "Why? Do you want to be my friend?"

"I'm already your friend, moron," I teased, a little shocked that he'd obviously found me on social media.

"Coworker," he corrected. That made me roll my eyes, which made him chuckle.

Just then my phone buzzed. Nekesa.

My parents are treating me like I killed a man.

"I feel so bad for her," I said to Charlie, "that she's not on the trip."

"But if she were here, you wouldn't have me," Charlie said, driving with one hand draped over the wheel.

"True," I said, texting her back. "At least she's got Aaron and Theo to text and keep her company."

Charlie made a noise, and I looked over at him. "What?"

He shrugged and said, "Do you like Theo?"

"I mean, yeah," I said, even though I found him to be a little annoying. "He's fine."

"I don't really trust that guy," Charlie said, which surprised me. He and Theo always seemed to get along when we all worked together on the weekends.

"Is this about the bet?" I asked.

"What?" he asked, his voice rising a few octaves. His eyes narrowed as he glanced away from the road and at me. He looked . . . I don't know, different when he said, "What are you talking about?"

"THE bet . . . ?" What the hell was *that*? "Hello?"

"Right, right," he replied, in a much calmer tone, "but what would my not trusting him have to do with *that*?"

I shrugged and grabbed my drink. "No idea."

"So . . . you should text Zack."

"*What?*" That brought my eyes right to his face, but he continued to drive as if he hadn't just bombshelled the suggestion that I text my in-a-new-relationship ex-boyfriend.

"You should text him right now, while I'm with you, so you don't lose your nerve. Why wait?"

"*Why wait?*" I turned my body so I was fully facing him in the front seat of the car, so he'd have no question about the *What the hell* expression on my face. "Well, for starters, he has a girlfriend."

"So?" he said with a shrug, looking wholly confident that the girlfriend wasn't a concern. "You're not asking him out. You're just going to reach out to him as a buddy."

"We aren't buddies. I've never been his buddy."

"Quit being literal and quit being scared. Text him something chill like *Do you know my Netflix password?*"

"Why would he know my Netflix password?"

He gave his head a shake, like *I* was an idiot, and said, "He doesn't. But he doesn't know that you don't think he might."

"I'm sorry—how is this going to help things?"

"It's the reconnection," he said, sighing. "You text him what I said, and he responds that he doesn't. Then you say *Dangit—I didn't think so but I thought it was worth a shot.*"

I still didn't see how that would help anything.

"He will—of course—give you a *Sorry bro*, and then you have the chance to say something funny and make him think about you."

"Think about me how?" It was a pointless plan, an idea without merit, but still.

"That is up to you. Send him the first text," Charlie said, "and I'll Cyrano the rest as we go."

"No," I squealed, not at all interested in involving Charlie with Zack but for some reason giddily excited about something. "It'll never work."

"It will *absolutely* work for its purpose," he said, staring out at the road in front of him.

"Which is . . . ?"

"Which is reminding him that you're funny and interesting."

"Charlie—"

"Just text *Hey, it's Bay—quick question*."

"I was never Bay to him, for the record."

"Such a shame," he said, his brow furrowing like he didn't understand.

It was a strange response, but even stranger was the fact that I liked it. It felt like he was defending me somehow. I said, "Is it?"

He looked away from the road to give me a pointed glance before saying, "Fine. Text *It's Bailey—quick question*."

I don't know what got into me, but I pulled up Zack in my contacts. I was squirrely and giggling as I said to myself, "I cannot believe I'm doing this. 'Hey, it's Bailey. Quick question.'"

"Send," he said, loudly and with a half smile. "Hit send, you chickenshit."

I took a deep breath, squealed again, then hit send. "Holy shit, I hit send."

"Atta girl." He laughed, which made me squeal again.

"I can't believe I just sent that," I said, and then conversation bubbles popped up. "Oh my God, he's responding!"

"Breathe," Charlie said, his eyes on the road.

"Easy for you to say," I mumbled, staring at the phone.

Zack: What's up?

I muttered "Holy shit" under my breath as I texted: **Weird question, but do you know my Netflix password?**

"I did it," I said, looking over at Charlie. "I asked him about the password."

"Quit acting like you just initiated nuclear war or something," he replied with amusement in his voice. "This is no big deal."

Zack: No idea. Am I supposed to?

"What'd he say?" Charlie asked, in response to the noise I made in my throat.

I told him, and he said, "So just say no but add something cute."

I squinted. "I thought you were going to Cyrano this for me. 'Add something cute' is not freaking Cyrano!"

"Calm down, Glasses." Charlie tilted his head, his eyes still on the road. "Just say, uh, *No but we were hoping* and add an emoji."

"That's not cute," I said, a little disappointed.

"Your usage of the word 'we' will make him assume you and a mysterious someone are hanging out, and the smiley face will make it seem chill and absolutely *not* like you're hitting on your ex. Trust me on this."

I rolled my eyes but typed exactly what he said while he broke the rules and changed the radio station.

Me: No, but we were hoping. I'm somehow getting it wrong. ;)

I wondered what Zack was thinking, getting a text from me, and his face was all I could see as I waited for his response.

Which was almost immediate.

Zack: Do you want mine?

"Whaaat?" I yelled, reading it again and feeling like it had to mean something. "He asked if I want to use his!"

"Duh," Charlie said, sounding unsurprised. "Now just go with something quick and funny that gives you the last word. Like . . . *Haha no. I think I'll just act out the entire third season of* Breaking Bad *instead. Thanks, though.*"

"Okay, first of all, I've never watched that show. Second—"

"I know you haven't," he interrupted. "Anyone who knows you knows you haven't."

"I don't get it," I said, wondering why I was even taking advice from him. "So why—"

"Silly child," he said, glancing over at me as he interrupted yet again. "That tiny joking reference tells him you're likely with someone who *does* watch that show."

"A dude," I said, my mouth falling open at his genius. "I'm making him think I'm with a dude."

"Bingo," he said, looking pleased with himself as he gave me a smug smile. "Saying without saying."

I started typing his exact words, in awe of Coach Charlie. As soon as I hit send, I said, "You are quite the manipulator, Mr. Sampson."

"We all have our gifts, Miss Mitchell."

A second later another message came in.

Zack: I'd pay money to see that.

"Ohmygod," I squealed, freaking out that it worked. That we'd actually reconnected. I read the response to Charlie, begging, "Tell me what to say now, you diabolical genius."

"Nothing," he said, slowing as our exit approached. "Send him a smiling emoji but nothing more."

"Won't that be a waste of this entire conversation?"

"Hell no." Charlie sounded deep in thought when he said, "If there's one thing that I know, it's the power of stringing someone along."

CHAPTER TWENTY-SEVEN

Bailey

When we finally pulled into Breckenridge, the town all lit up with twinkling lights in the darkness, we devised a plan. I was going to go into the condo and tell my mom that Charlie was with me, not Nekesa, and he was going to wait in the car for five minutes. Hopefully my mother could lessen the initial blow to Scott, and we could get on with the weekend.

Shit, shit, shit. How on earth was I going to tell her? It occurred to me at that moment that we'd all been idiotic teenagers to think this was a good idea. They were going to *freak* that I'd brought a boy, and they were going to *double-freak* that the boy was Charlie.

What in God's name had I been thinking?

And I was a dick. I was a total dick for tricking my mom. Because messing with Scott's happiness was whatever, but messing with my mom's was something else entirely. We were a team, just she and I, and we'd never snuck around and lied to each other.

Shit, shit, shit, what the hell have I done?

"Relax," Charlie said as he looked for a parking spot. "I can almost *hear* your internal freak-out."

"Because this was a terrible idea," I said loudly. "What the hell was I thinking?"

"Breathe," he said, and when I glanced over at him, something about the reassuring look on his face made me calm down just a little. "It's going to be fine."

"I doubt it," I said, nodding, "but I'm going to go with that."

As he drove in the direction of the condo, I realized that *Charlie*—Charlie Sampson, Mr. Nothing—had made me feel calm. Yes, we were becoming better friends, but certain moments felt bigger somehow.

He found a parking spot across the street from the condo, and after ten minutes of panicked breathing, I unbuckled and got out of the car.

"Wish me luck," I said, my hands shaking.

"Good luck," he sang in a silly voice. "Don't fuck it up, Glasses."

"Shut up," I sang right back.

After I walked around to the back of the building, I found their door—unlocked—so I pushed it open and stepped inside. "Hello? Mom?"

I walked through what appeared to be the laundry room and into the kitchen, which was all unfinished rustic wood, and I couldn't believe my eyes.

The condo was incredible.

The living room had high ceilings with big wood beams, and one entire wall was a stone fireplace that happened to have a fire burning inside of it that very minute. The furniture was brown leather, and the place felt like a ski chalet.

I loved it.

"Bay?" I heard my mother yell from upstairs. "Is that you?"

"Yep," I yelled back, my momentary distraction giving way to the nervous fear that'd been there first. "We just got here."

"That was fast," she said, and I heard her feet coming down the stairs. "I can't believe you're here already."

She hopped off the last step and grabbed me in a hug, and I could almost *feel* how relaxed she was. Guilt washed over me like a wave as I realized I was about to ruin that, and I rambled, "We actually left earlier than planned because we didn't want to do the mountain roads in the dark."

"Good idea." She glanced behind me and asked, "Where's Nekesa?"

"Yeah, um," I said, grabbing her elbow and pulling her closer so we could talk quietly. "About that. There was a slight change of plan."

"What happened?" she asked, looking worried.

God, I was such a piece of shit, because my mother looked super concerned about the welfare of everyone when I was about to spring an unwelcome surprise on her. I looked at her raised eyebrows and big blue eyes and hated what I was about to tell her.

"Well, um, Nekesa got grounded last night and couldn't

come. I didn't want to drive here all alone," I said, so nervous that every word was hard to say, "so I brought a *different* friend."

"Oh?" She still looked happy and chill. "Who?"

Clearly she was waiting for me to say someone who was a girl and also not her boyfriend's least favorite teenager.

I swallowed and forced myself to say it.

"Charlie," I said, keeping my voice low as I looked behind her for any sign of Scott. "I brought Char—"

"Charlie?" Her eyes got huge and she said, "Are you freaking kidding me?"

"I didn't know what to do when Nekesa canceled," I replied, talking fast. "I didn't—"

"Oh, no, you don't," she said, pointing her finger at me as her voice got higher and louder and her mouth tightened. "You have a phone—that I pay for. You should've called me. Don't pretend this was somehow your only option!"

I tried talking in a calm voice. "But Charlie's my friend and has a reliable car. Is it really that different from Nekesa?"

"Yes!" She crossed her arms and started pacing. "It's bad enough that you brought a boy—any boy—with you. You're too smart not to know that would matter. But not only did you bring a boy, you brought the boy that Scott hates on Scott's vacation—are you kidding me with that?"

"I know," I said.

"That is seriously rude," she said, almost yelling. "In addition to everything else that's wrong with this plan, it is rude and entitled. *Oh, I guess they'll just have to go along with what we want.* How can you be so okay with behaving like that?"

My cheeks were hot and I felt like total garbage, because she was right. "I'm so sorry."

She shook her head fast, pissed off. "Save it for Scott."

"Where is he, by the way?" I asked, realizing that if Scott were there, her yelling would've brought him to the room.

My mom stopped pacing and chewed on the corner of her lip. "He ran to the market."

I watched her face as she tried working through it, and I hated the twisting guilt I felt at the sight of her jaw clenched.

"I mean, he's here now—can't we find a way to make it work?"

She gave her head another angry shake, like she couldn't believe this was happening. "File that under *things Bailey and Charlie were counting on*."

Not wrong, I thought.

"Okay." She dropped her arms to her sides and said, "Here's the plan. *You're* going to get out of here, and I will tell Scott when he gets back."

"So . . . do you want us to just wait in the car, then?" I asked.

"Bailey, I don't care *where* you wait," she said, mom-glaring me so hard that I felt her stare in my guilty soul. Her teeth were clenched as she said, "Do you know how mad I am at you right now?"

"I know, and I'm sorry," I said lamely, wishing there was a way for her not to get hurt by this.

"That means nothing today." Her eyes roamed all over the condo, like she was looking for an answer, and then she said, "Just go drive around or something."

"We can do that," I said, nodding, anxious to please her.

"And then I'll text you when you're good to come back," she said. "Not that I'm looking forward to that enjoyable reunion."

"I'm so sorry," I repeated.

"Spare me," she said, still looking mad but intent on her plan. "Now get out of here."

I wanted to cry—seriously—because I hated her being mad at me.

Especially when I knew I deserved it. I left, feeling like a trash human, and Charlie was standing behind his car with the trunk open when I crossed the street.

"Hey," I said.

He looked up and smiled. "Hey."

"My mom is *so* pissed," I told him, my stomach heavy with dread and guilt as I kept seeing her angry face.

Ugh—her *disappointed* face.

I walked over to where he stood, and after he closed the trunk, his big, warm hand found mine.

My eyes shot up, jolted by the feel of his fingers linking around mine, and he stepped a little closer. "I was thinking. It's probably time we start this whole charade, right?"

Everything else faded away as I felt the skin of his palm press against me. My breath was shaky as I gulped down cold mountain air and thought, *Ohmygod.*

A car pulled into the lot, but I barely noticed because I was flustered by the intimacy of Charlie's hand. The slide of his big fingers around mine, the heat of his skin; it felt far more risqué than just holding hands.

This was Charlie, and this was pretend, but the racing of my heart and the butterflies in my stomach meant a tiny part of my body had apparently missed the message.

"This is a little jarring, don't you think?" I asked, looking up into his brown eyes under the golden glow of the streetlight. "It feels like I should be smacking your hand and telling you to knock it off."

"Totally." He laughed, and I liked the way the corners of his eyes crinkled when he grinned down at me, like we were the only two people in the world sharing this absurd joke. "I kind of thought you might junk-punch me out of habit."

"I've never junk-punched you," I said around a smile.

"I've never tried holding your hand before, though, so . . ."

"Fair," I agreed, and it occurred to me at that moment that I wasn't emotionally prepared for this . . . electricity. My head knew we were going to be pretending all weekend, but I hadn't anticipated the sparks that would go off when he smiled at me like that.

This would take some getting used to.

"So what exactly did your mom say?" he asked.

Move on, Bay—this is Charlie.

"She was pretty heated." I told him what she said, but instead of driving around, we decided to walk to the cute coffee shop we'd seen when we pulled into town. We grabbed our jackets out of the back seat and strolled, and even though it was a little chilly, it was one of those perfect autumn nights where as long as you were moving, it was comfortable.

"I'm starving," Charlie said as we sat down at a table. "Maybe we should get food before we head back."

"No. My mom said after they booked the trip that the kitchen would be fully stocked and we can make whatever we want." I took off the lid to let my mocha cool and said, "I don't need to do something else to piss her off, so let's just eat their food when we're allowed to return."

He wrapped his big hands around his cup and muttered, "Okay."

"You're not stressed about Scott, are you?" I asked. "I'm sure it'll be fine once the shock wears off."

"I'm not worried," he said, unzipping his coat. "I just hope he's not the level of asshole who ruins your mom's vacation by being a pouty dick."

"See, that's what really stresses me out about our plan." I slid the cup sleeve down as I tried coming to terms with the fact that there was really no way for us to disturb Scott without it affecting my mother's trip too. "I don't want my mom to be unhappy, and if my plans work, she'll be unhappy in the short-term."

"But," he said, lifting his cup off the table and giving me a serious look, "if *she's* happy, you're not. Look out for number one, Glasses."

I rolled my eyes. "You sound like a mobster."

"Thank you."

"Not a compliment."

"Says you." He took a gulp of his coffee, set down his cup, and said, "Let's talk about our fake dating."

"Yeah, I suppose we should," I said, nerves fluttering in my stomach at the prospect. I sipped at my drink and asked, "Do you have a plan?"

"Not a plan, per *se*," he said, "but an idea."

He leaned closer, and it occurred to me that Enthusiastic Charlie was one of my favorite versions of him. His eyes were practically dancing as he said, "Here's what I'm thinking. When Scott accepts that I'm here, we return to the condo. Shortly thereafter, when he's dealing with the unfortunate existence of my presence, we hold hands. That will send up all the what-the-fuck flags, and that's probably good for tonight."

I was horrified, and terrified, but he somehow managed to make me cough out a laugh as I pictured Scott's reaction. "I kind of feel bad for poor Scott."

"Poor Scott indeed," he agreed, his mouth in a big grin. "Unless—do you think we should do *more*?"

"More?" I asked, my laugh settling into a smile as I let my eyes drink in Happy Charlie.

"More," he said, his eyes locking into mine, his mischievous smile morphing into something more intense, "than hand-holding."

I don't know what got into me, but I lifted my chin and asked, "What kind of more are you thinking?"

"Bailey Rose," he said, his voice lowering to a hot rumble as his mouth stayed in a sexy smirk. "Are you asking me to list the types of PDA we can throw at Scotty?"

My phone buzzed, making my heart leap in my chest. *Dear God, what in flirtation was that?* I pulled it out of my pocket and yes—it was my mom.

I talked to Scott, and he's okay with Charlie being here IN CONCEPT, but we're going to have to lay down some ground rules.

Relief rolled through me, relief that they weren't going to make Charlie drive back alone or stay at a motel by himself for the weekend.

"Look," I said, holding out the phone, trying to read his mind as he read the text. He didn't look like anything other than normal Charlie, so perhaps the moment I'd imagined was just him clinically considering our next steps, PDA-wise.

"I almost feel sorry for them," he said, the smile returning to his face. "They think we're only friends, but they still need to guarantee—because they're responsible adults—that we're painfully aware that we can't sneak into each other's bed and bang one out in the Rockies."

"Oh my God." I laughed, horrified as always by the shocking pictures Charlie liked to paint.

He was a damned artist that way.

He continued, grinning like a fool. "They'll lay down those rules, we'll agree, and they'll feel great about themselves. And then . . . *dun dun dunnnnn*—they'll witness us holding hands and snuggling on the couch. They're going to lose their shit."

I laughed, but *snuggling on the couch*? The thought of that made my palms sweaty and my stomach light. Charlie's hands *on* me? My body curled against his body?

Gah—snuggling with Charlie Sampson seemed dangerous, like an activity I should avoid at all costs.

But that was just me—I wasn't cut out for fake dating. I

was the kind of person who didn't even like hugging family members, so how on earth was I going to snuggle with Charlie?

"Right?" he asked, looking at me expectantly.

"What?" I realized I'd drifted away into my own thoughts, so I gave a tiny nod and said, "Yes. Right."

He smirked like he knew what I'd been thinking, which was impossible. He couldn't have known, yet the glimmer in his eye made me wonder if he'd been thinking about couch snuggling as well.

"Grab your coat, then," he said, and I realized he must've asked me if I was ready to go.

We walked back to the condo, neither of us in a hurry for "ground rules" discussions, and I took a deep breath before opening the door.

"Quit worrying," Charlie said. "It's vacation time, Mitchell."

I looked over at him, seemingly unconcerned about anything, and I let out my breath.

He was right.

I was on vacation, and I was going to have a great time.

Even if it killed me.

CHAPTER TWENTY-EIGHT

Bailey

"Scott?" I yelled.

"Yeah?"

"Do you want spaghetti or fettuccini?"

I heard him mutter something to my mom—they were in the living room—before he said with a smile in his voice, "Spaghetti, please."

"Told you," Charlie said, grabbing a box of pasta from the cupboard.

"I really would've pegged him as a fettuccini man."

"When he's alone," he said in a quiet voice, "I bet he's all about the elbows."

"That sicko," I said, sticking a spoon into Charlie's sauce to slurp off another sample before dropping it into the sink beside my other four sampling spoons.

When we'd gotten back to the condo, Scott and my mom

greeted us at the door with a list of ground rules. He didn't look mad, though, which really took me by surprise. Of course, when he said *Once it's lights-out, you're not allowed to leave your room* and Charlie snorted, that made him glare, but he still seemed pretty stuck in the "happy vacationer" role.

Which I didn't want for the sake of our plan, but for my mom's sake, it was probably good for the first night.

After the listing of the rules, they gave us a tour of the place, and everyone got in a surprisingly good mood.

Charlie shocked the hell out of me by volunteering us to make dinner.

"If you two want to relax, Bailey and I can make dinner. It takes no time for me to whip up a batch of my mom's quick spaghetti sauce—you've got the ingredients in the pantry—and I'm sure Bay can handle boiling a pot of water."

Scott and my mom looked at us like we'd offered them millions, and I looked at Charlie like he'd lost his mind.

So we were off to a good start.

"This is really good," I said, a little shocked that Charlie could make a spaghetti sauce from scratch.

"I'm pretty sure my Italian grandmother taught me to sauce when I was a toddler," he said, pulling a roll of TUMS out of his pocket and popping one into his mouth.

"Prodigy." I grabbed the pasta from Charlie, opened the box, and dropped it into the boiling water. "Do you still see her a lot?"

He gave me a look as he chewed. "Now is not the time."

"To talk about grandmothers?"

"To remind me of shitty things." He opened the utensil

231

drawer, pulled out a big fork, and handed it to me. "Also, this is for stirring, not stabbing."

"Thank you." I took it from him and said, "Why are you always popping TUMS, by the way?"

Something crossed his face as he said, "What?"

He looked guilty or surprised or . . . I don't know . . . something.

"You're always eating antacids, Sampson."

"Oh, that." He shrugged and said, "I get heartburn sometimes."

"It's just heartburn sometimes?" I asked, not wanting to pry but also *really* wanting to know more about him. "Then why did you look all weird when I mentioned TUMS?"

"Can you shut up about my afflictions, weirdo?" He gave me a patented Charlie smirk and said, "Now please hand me the garlic salt, Nosy."

"Are you sick?" I asked, hating the thought of that.

"Of your line of questioning?" He stirred the pot and said, "Absolutely. But physically? No."

I gave him the garlic salt. "You're a very complex fellow."

"Don't I know it," he said, and then started barking orders like he was the head chef.

He was surprisingly capable in a kitchen.

Make a sauce, whisk out the tomato paste, do the conversion of how much jarred minced garlic equals a clove; he was a professional.

I pretty much only made microwave things and frozen pizza at my house.

When we drained the pasta and had everything ready to serve, Charlie moved in close. He tugged on a strand of my hair with his right hand, smiling down at me like we shared a secret, and warmth spread through me.

The coziness of the condo, the smell of the marinara, the grin in his eyes as we conspired together—it all linked up to make the moment feel like hot chocolate after a day in the snow.

"Shall we serve?" he asked, letting go of my curl to reach for the sauce.

Lksjflskjfksljfklsdjfklsd, I thought, my breath stopping in my chest.

"We shall," I replied, feeling buzzy from his touch as I grabbed the big bowl of noodles and followed him toward the table on wobbly legs.

I don't know what I'd expected, but dinner was okay. Yes, I got a stomach knot every time Scott teased my mom or called me Bay, but between Charlie's ridiculous stories and my mother's hilarious responses, that nonsense was kept to a minimum and the meal was actually kind of nice.

Weird, right?

Somewhere around eleven, my mom made up the pullout sofa for Charlie and we all went to our respective beds. I'd just turned off the light to go to sleep when my phone buzzed.

Charlie: When are we going to start dating?

I stared at the phone in the darkness and wondered what it would feel like to have Charlie Sampson say that *for real.* Obviously, I didn't want that, but still . . . I couldn't stop myself from imagining it.

Because Charlie's emotional contradictions . . . *intrigued* me.

He teased relentlessly and was the funniest person I'd ever met, yet I knew for a fact that he listened to Conan Gray and Gracie

Abrams on repeat all the time (I had his Spotify password).

He was brazen and outgoing with his friends, yet sweetly vulnerable when discussing himself.

And even though he was cynical Mr. Nothing, I was starting to suspect that his cynicism existed not because he was *un*feeling but because he felt things so deeply. His family issues, his ex-girlfriend—he hated love because he hated the way his love for them had felt.

When Charlie got that horrible, awful look on his face when he talked about Becca, I couldn't help but imagine what it must've felt like—for Becca—to have all that emotion pointed in her direction.

To have Charlie Sampson look at you the way he'd looked at her at the party?

Dear God, the swoon.

I looked down at the phone in my hand, at his question, and my brain returned from its brief excursion to Charlietown. Ahem. **When are we going to start dating?**

The thought of doing it—fake dating—still made me nervous, but I texted: **I suppose tomorrow—we're only here for a few days, right?**

Charlie: Agreed. And we should get it rolling first thing—no reason to wait, right?

Me: What do you have planned? Feeding each other breakfast?

Charlie: That's EXACTLY what I have planned, only I'll be sitting on your lap.

That made me snort. **YOU will be on MY lap?**

Charlie: It's more interesting that way.

Me: True.

Charlie: After that I thought I could just carry you around all day like you're a baby who doesn't know how to walk.

That made me start laughing, all by myself in the dark. I texted: **Can we be serious for two minutes?**

Charlie: Doubt it but I'm listening.

Me: Is there anything I should know about you—or we should know about each other—as fake boyfriend/ girlfriend?

Charlie: My favorite thing about you is the way you always bite the inside of your cheek when I tease you.

I made a noise in my throat and texted: **what???**

Charlie: For real. It's like you don't want me to know I got to you. But Glasses—the minute I see your move, it's like the gauntlet has been thrown and I can't stop until you're smiling at me.

Another noise—something like a squeal—emanated from me, unbidden.

Because that was an incredible answer.

I tried to think of a snappy retort, some sarcastically charming something, but I couldn't come up with anything.

What were words again?

I gasped when my phone buzzed.

Charlie: . . . . . . ? No response?

I held the phone, but literally had no words.

Charming Charlie had rendered me speechless.

CHAPTER TWENTY-NINE

Charlie

Goddammit.

I stared at the phone, waiting for Bailey to respond and wondering when in the hell I'd lost all common sense. Had I seriously just admitted to the one person in the world that didn't mindfuck me on a regular basis that I liked making her smile?

I was a moron.

Yes, Charlie, you should absolutely admit that you like making her smile. That is a brilliant way to ensure your coworker exits your life.

The phone lit up in my hands.

Bailey: Well my favorite thing about you is the way your voice gets deep and crackly when you're tired.

Well, shit. I rolled over, the bar of the pullout sofa totally digging into my back, and I texted: **The only thing you like about me is my voice??**

Bailey: Not what I said. I said it's my FAVORITE thing, because you're relaxed and mellow when your voice gets like that. Your edges soften a little.

My edges.

I wasn't sure how she knew me so well, how she'd somehow always seen me.

I spent most of my time feeling like everyone in my life didn't get me, yet there was Glasses, seeing right through me.

Bailey: Should I have a pet name for you?

I smiled in the darkness, wondering how best to irritate her. **How about King?**

Bailey: Gross

I pictured her eyebrows scrunching up as I texted: **Lover?**

Bailey: You're making me queasy. I'll just stick with Charlie.

I replied: **Or Sex God?**

Bailey: No one in the history of the world has ever used Sex God as a pet name. Can you even imagine?? Example: Can you pick up milk on the way home, Sex God? DOESN'T WORK.

I chuckled and texted: **I would fucking speed to the milk store if you sent me that.**

Bailey: The milk store?

I wanted to laugh as I replied: **You're biting your cheek right now, aren't you?**

Bailey: LMAO that is scary.

Me: But true.

Bailey: Sleep tight.

I smiled in the darkness. **Good night, Lover.**

Bailey: Good night . . . Sex God.

Oh. Fuck.

What was I doing?

CHAPTER THIRTY

Bailey

It was hard to determine what sound—*exactly*—woke me up at one thirty.

It might've been the shattering of the glass, it might've been the squawking, or it might've been the wild wing flapping, but the goose flying through my window was definitely the culprit.

I jolted awake, sitting straight up, and I could see by the outside light's illumination that *something* was in my room, freaking out in the darkness.

Oh my God, oh my God, oh my God!

I was afraid to move because I didn't want whatever it was to see me, but that was a moot point when Scott threw open my door and said, "What the hell was that?"

He flipped on the light, and—*holy shit*—there was a goose in my room.

There was a huge goose standing in front of the now shattered window, squealing maniacally (if that was possible) and kind of hissing.

"Oh my *God*," my mom yelled from behind him as I leaped from the bed and ran toward the doorway. She grabbed me and pushed me behind her, as if to protect me from the bird, as she said, "Are you okay?"

"Yeah," I said, staring over her shoulder.

The bird must've flown right through the window, and even though it was dark, he didn't look injured.

Just pissed.

Again—if that was even possible.

I didn't think I'd ever had an interaction with a goose before, so my goose knowledge was minuscule.

Scott, wearing boxers and his dumb socks, leaned down and picked up one of my tall boots. I watched in disbelief as he crept closer to the goose, like he was trying to sneak up on it, and for a second I wondered if he was going to bludgeon the goose to death with the lefty member of my favorite pair of boots.

But then he started waving it around, waving it in the direction of the bird.

"Scott," my mom scolded, whispering for some reason, "what are you doing?"

"Is that a goose?" I heard from behind me.

"Yes," I said, also whispering for no apparent reason as I watched.

"Oh," Charlie said calmly, as if this was no big deal. "Wow."

The goose did *not* appreciate Scott and started honking frantically while puffing up, hissing as he stared the man down.

Scott kept waving my boot, almost like he was trying to fan the goose, for God's sake, and the man looked like an absolute moron.

But then it *worked.*

The goose took a couple of awkward steps before flapping those wings and flying right out the window.

Where glass had once been.

In an instant, the room seemed incredibly quiet.

And cold.

Scott dropped my boot and slowly walked toward the window.

"No," my mom said, still talking quietly. "Scott. He could come back."

That made him stop and look at her over his shoulder. "He's not trying to *kill* us, Em."

Charlie snorted behind me, which made me cough out a laugh.

My mom shuffled farther into the room, creeping toward Scott, who was looking out the window. His hands were on his hips as he surveyed the landscape below, and after a moment Scott said in a loud announcer voice, "The goose has left the building."

"Listen, you two," my mom said, her hair sticking up as she stood there in her nightgown. "I need your promise that you're going to follow the rules."

I didn't look at Charlie—I couldn't—as I stood there in my flannel duckie pajamas, holding my pillow to my chest.

"Of course we will," I said, suddenly exhausted. "Even if we had bad intentions—which we don't—there is no door to close. No privacy. I wouldn't mack on some guy in the middle of the living room when anyone could walk in."

"I'm sorry, did you just say 'mack on' again?" Charlie asked, a smirk in his voice. "I thought we killed that."

"Hush," I growled, just wanting to go back to sleep.

My mom said, "One of you can have the pullout sofa, and the other will have to sleep on the floor. There's a pile of sheets and blankets over there, on the chair."

After the goose's exit, Scott—who was obviously the hero of the night whether I liked it or not—covered the window with cardboard and duct tape. The owner of the condo promised to have someone out to fix the window in the morning, but cold air poured through that hole so I was promptly relocated downstairs.

To the same living room where Charlie was sleeping on the pullout sofa.

Hence the rule paranoia.

"Well, then, good night," my mom said, turning and heading for the stairs.

"Good night," Charlie said in his super-nice kiss-ass voice. "Sweet dreams."

"I want to vomit," I said, shaking my head. "You are such a suck-up."

"I like your mom," he said, still sitting on the pullout bed, where he'd been since the goose incident. "And I want her to like me. Is that so wrong?"

"Nauseating, but not wrong," I said, finding it a little sweet as I looked over at the blankets. "So which one of us gets the bed?"

His eyebrows went down. "You do. Duh."

Now *my* eyebrows went down. "What does *that* mean?"

"It means I'm not going to let you sleep on the floor while I get the bed."

"Oh my God, that's so sexist," I said, putting my hands on my hips. "If I were a dude, I bet you'd let me have the floor."

"It's not sexist. It's friendist," he replied matter-of-factly.

"Come again?"

"You're such a pervert, Glasses."

"Charlie."

"I just mean that you're my friend," he said in an irritated voice, "and I don't want you to be uncomfortable. So you should get the bed."

"But if I were your *dude* friend—"

"Fine—sleep on the floor, dude," he said, annoyed. "Good night."

"Wait."

"I thought so," he said, wearing a smug smile.

"First of all, thank you for recognizing that we are, in fact, friends," I said, unsure why his usage of the f-word in regards to me felt like something big, "and second—maybe we should rock-paper-scissor for it."

"Dear God, 'friend' is easier to say than 'coworker'—settle your ass down."

"Whatever you say," I said in a singsong voice, unwilling to let it go.

"And think about this for a second," Charlie said. "What will your mom—and King Dipshit—think of me if they come down here for a glass of water, and they see that I didn't give you the bed?"

Ooh—he definitely had a point. "They'll think you're a jerk."

"And the trip was bought for you, not me," he added.

"Also true," I agreed.

"So this is your bed, Mitchell, and I'll make myself a floor pallet."

He stood, and my eyes froze on his pajama pants.

"What?" he asked dryly, like he had no idea why I was staring.

"Nothing," I said, pressing my lips together and shaking my head. "I just, um, really like your pants."

Charlie was wearing pink flannel pajama pants that had red hearts all over them. The pattern might've been a *little* unorthodox for men's pj's, but it was the fact that he was six and a half feet tall and they were at least four inches too short for him that made it *quite* the look.

"They were a gift from my little sister," he said, pointing a finger at me. "So if you mock them, you're a monster."

"Not mocking," I said, trying my hardest not to laugh while also finding it really freaking sweet that he wore pants his sister gave him. "They're actually incredibly sexy. Shows *just* enough ankle to tease yet stay classy."

"Oh, I know." He put his hands on his hips as if to strike a pose. "My heart pants bring *all* the girls to the yard."

"Sure they do." My eyes moved up to his shirt, and his chest in that Henley actually *was* sexy. It was just a faded old shirt, but the soft fabric clung to his obviously defined and surprisingly wide chest, and I couldn't stop stealing glances at it.

It was just so . . . broad.

And solid.

I mean, he even had that pectoral-cleavage ridge thing.

Was Charlie shredded?

Gahhhh—what is wrong with me?

I nodded dumbly, struggling to remember what he'd just said as I attempted to return to normal after the brain detour through Charlie's physique.

He interrupted my thoughts with, "Give me a sec to put new sheets on the pullout, and then you can move in."

"Did you," I said, grinning at his ultra-helpful persona, "*do* something to the sheets?"

"No." He scowled, looking offended.

"Then I think I can handle sleeping on the sheets you laid upon for under an hour."

He raised his eyes from the pullout to me. "You sure?"

"Yep."

He walked over to the stack of sheets and blankets, then glanced at the floor. A look crossed his face, just a flash of what I'd seen in the gas station bathroom, and I said, "Charlie, just take the bed. I'm good sleeping anywhere."

He scowled—again—at that. "Fuck, Bay, please don't be nice to me like I'm—"

"What if we make a bed out of couch cushions?" I spoke over him on purpose, because his having some issue with germs didn't matter to me. It didn't matter, and I didn't want him to think I'd even noticed. "That way you're not on the floor, even though you're sleeping on the floor. Get it?"

"Bailey." He swallowed and said, "Stop."

"Charlie." I crossed my arms and said, "If you want me to pretend I don't know, I totally will, because I don't want to make you feel weird. But you're my friend. If it were Nekesa instead of you, I'd just help her find a way to be comfortable."

"Coworker," he corrected, making a noise like he begrudgingly agreed while his smirk reappeared. "And you mentioned couch pillows . . . ?"

I went over and started grabbing the discarded sofa cushions off the floor. "Let's just make a little mattress with these."

I dropped them onto an open area of floor at the other end of the living room, and Charlie grabbed the cushions from the two big chairs by the fireplace and added them to my pile. He picked up and unfolded what looked to be a king-sized fitted sheet.

"Y'know, you're a pretty decent coworker," Charlie said, giving me a look that felt important. Meaningful. It felt like he was acknowledging that our friendship was more than work, even though he was saying the literal opposite.

"I know," I said, and after I helped him make the floor bed, I climbed onto the pullout. "Do you care if I turn on the TV? I'm kind of wide awake now."

"Nah," he said, and then he hit a light switch that plunged the room into darkness, aside from the glow of the television. I could hear him settling onto his cushions.

"Is that comfortable at all?" I asked, stopping on an old episode of *New Girl*.

"Not too bad," he said, his voice quiet in the darkness.

"Nick Miller is the GOAT," I said.

"Winston," he corrected, "is the total underrated GOAT."

We watched for a while, quietly commenting and laughing at the show, and I was almost asleep when Charlie said, "For the record, I'm not a full-scale germophobe."

I stared into the darkness. "For the record, I wouldn't give a shit if you were."

"I just, like, I just get skeeved about public restrooms and the thought of sleeping on a stranger's floor. I'd happily eat a meatball off the counter or lick your finger; that wouldn't bother me at all."

"You did not just say that." I laughed, snuggling a little deeper under the covers and wondering why it didn't feel awkward, having this impromptu sleepover with Charlie. I was sleepy and comfortable, absolutely relaxed; the opposite of awkward.

"Seriously, though. I don't even own hand sanitizer or wipes," he said, sounding like he desperately wanted to convince me.

But he didn't have to. I knew nothing about Charlie's situation, but I'd had my own terrible experiences with panic attacks so I *got* it. Just because his brain made his body have physical reactions to certain things didn't mean he was . . . I don't know . . . anything other than what he was supposed to be.

I said, "I dare you to eat a counter meatball."

"Probably cleaner than your fingers," he teased. "Rumor has

it you jammed them into a urinal today."

"I did. I was like, *These fingers are so clean. I wonder if there's a filthy urinal in which I could soil them.*"

He laughed, and I rolled over and closed my eyes again. "Thanks again for coming with me, Charlie."

"Thanks for inviting me," he said, and I really hoped he meant it.

Because I wanted him to be having as much fun as I (surprisingly) was.

"G'night, Charlie," I said.

"G'night, Bailey," he replied, his voice deep and crackly in the dark of the living room.

CHAPTER THIRTY-ONE

Bailey

I woke to the smell—and sounds—of breakfast.

Opening my eyes, I blinked, reached for my glasses, and got my bearings.

Living room pullout sofa—*got it*.

I looked to my left, but Charlie wasn't over there, on the floor, where he'd spent the night. The cushions and bedding were all stacked up in the corner like he'd never been there.

I grabbed my phone—seven thirty.

No text from Zack, not that I was checking.

"Good morning, sunshine," I heard. I turned to my right, and there was Scott, sitting at the table, drinking coffee.

"Good morning," I said, giving ol' Scott a smile. It was hard to be irritated by his presence at breakfast when he'd procured the vacation for us and also rescued us from a killing-by-goose.

"Your mom and Charlie are making breakfast, so I hope you're hungry."

"I could eat," I lied, pushing my hair out of my face. I wasn't a breakfast person at all, so I'd just be happy if I could find some liquified caffeine for now. I got up and went into the kitchen, and as soon as I hit the doorway, I wanted to laugh.

My mom was sitting on a stool, talking about the Kansas City Chiefs' defense, and Charlie was making scrambled eggs.

"Good morning," my mom said, smiling.

"Wow," Charlie said, his eyes almost twinkling as he looked at me. "Good morning, Bedhead."

I flipped him off.

He laughed.

My mom smiled and said, "There's Frapp in the fridge."

"Oh, God bless you," I replied.

"So, Emily—do you think they even have a shot if he's out all season?" Charlie stirred the eggs and talked football with my mother, who was a die-hard Chiefs fan. "I mean . . ."

I opened the fridge and grabbed a bottle of mocha Frappuccino, unable to believe I'd just heard Charlie call my mom *Emily*. When exactly had they become best friends? It was a little adorable, but it made me uneasy.

I didn't want my clueless mother to form a bond with my fake boyfriend.

That couldn't end well, right?

"I mean, he's just one guy, so of course they have a shot, but it'll be a lot harder without him," my mom said.

I couldn't watch them for another minute because it made me feel too guilty.

The Frappuccino lid came off with a click as I said, "I'm going to go shower."

"But breakfast is almost ready," my mom said.

She knew I never ate breakfast, so she was saying that just to make sure I didn't hurt Charlie's feelings by not eating his food. I cleared my throat and said, "I'm not hungry yet."

"But Charlie made this entire spread," she said, looking at Charlie like he was Santa Claus.

"I'll for sure have some when I'm done," I reassured her.

"Go fix that hair," Charlie teased, and I liked the relaxed expression on his face. But I also wondered how he was so comfortable hanging out with my mom and making breakfast.

I worried about it as I showered, but I pretty much worried about everything while I showered. I worried about the "plan"— now that we were here, would it actually work? And if it did, would it result in my mom being devasted?

And what was happening with Charlie? There had been multiple *moments* with him yesterday, and I wasn't sure if it was just me, overthinking, or if it was something more?

"No." I said it out loud in the shower as I poured shampoo into my palm because *no way*. There was nothing going on between me and Charlie aside from complex emotions that had everything to do with each of our individual battles and nothing whatsoever to do with "us" as a whole.

He wouldn't even use the word "friend" in regards to me, for God's sake; he definitely wasn't feeling something romantic.

By the time I convinced myself to chill and go back downstairs, things weren't so relaxed anymore. The three of them were sitting at the table, my mom and Scott eating breakfast while Charlie talked about his mom's boyfriend (and Scott's face got red).

"He's not a bad guy," Charlie said, lifting his coffee mug to his mouth. "But shouldn't he be at his own place with his own kids, instead of crashing at my mom's every night?"

Holy *shit*. I couldn't believe he said that.

"Any eggs left?" I asked as I walked into the room. "I'm starving."

My mom looked incredibly happy to see me, Charlie gave me an amused grin, and Scott looked ready to fight.

"I'm on it," Charlie said, taking a gulp of his coffee and standing. "They've eaten already, but I was waiting for you."

We went into the kitchen, and the minute we crossed through the doorway, I heard Scott loud-whisper to my mom, "I do not like that kid."

"Oh, he wasn't talking about you," my mom defended, her voice in that motherly singsong tone that was good at soothing tempers. "I asked him about his mom, and he was answering. That's it."

I glanced at Charlie, who winked at me. Then his eyes narrowed the tiniest bit before he quietly said, "Wait. C'mere."

"What?" I asked, stepping closer to him even though I wasn't sure why. I lowered my voice and said, "What are you doing?"

He gave me a look, his head motioning with a tiny nod toward the dining room table, and I realized what he was doing the minute he put his hands on my waist. We were technically *in* the kitchen, but the open floor plan had a wide entryway that left the majority of the area visible.

We were totally in their line of sight but conceivably unaware that we were being seen, so if they stopped arguing and glanced toward the kitchen, they would see our fake datery.

Of course, all *I* could focus on was the heat of Charlie's fingers as he lightly squeezed my waist. My breath felt trapped in my throat as I looked at his mouth and he whispered, "We should kiss."

"What?" I hissed in a whisper, my cheeks growing hot. "Are you serious?"

"I mean, if you're scared you'll fall for me, I get it," he whispered back, his mouth curling into a cocky grin. "But he's gonna lose his shit and it will be puh-fucking-erfect."

He was right about Scott, given what'd just happened in the dining room. The timing was perfect. I knew that, but every single nerve ending inside me was shorting out at the thought of kissing Charlie, of Charlie Sampson kissing *me*.

I raised my arms to his shoulders, wanting to be brave enough to go big even as a thousand butterflies went wild in my stomach. Nervousness shot through me, but I calmly said, "Let's do it, Sampson."

His mouth came down on mine, and my brain did a quick inventory of the sensory details; the faint pressure of his fingertips as they slid to my lower back, the sound of a fork scraping over a plate at the table, and the smell of bacon on the stove. I sucked in a breath, ready for a big, huge, real-life-looking kiss.

But first Charlie fed me an appetizer.

His eyes stayed open, crinkled at the corners as we shared laughing eye contact over this secret, and his teeth clamped onto my bottom lip. I swear I felt the reverberation of that nibble in every nerve ending of my body before he opened my mouth with his, angled his head, and gave me a full-scale kiss; closed eyes, shared breath, warm lips.

I forgot everything—breathing, pretending, thinking—as he kissed me like it was the break of dawn and he'd dreamed about me all night long. *This is Charlie* was the only conscious thought that crossed my mind, but the words failed to remind me we were only fake kissing when I could hear the unsteady rhythm of his breathing.

It sounded just like *my* unsteady breathing, and something about that similarity curled my toes and made me clutch at his shoulders.

When he pulled back and looked down at my face, I blinked fast, trying to catch up. *Where am I again?* Everything swirled around me, nerves and pleasure and *What the fuck* and doubt, until his mouth slid into a naughty grin.

Such a naughty grin.

"Holy shit, Glasses," he said, his hands squeezing my waist as his dark eyes were wholly squinting with his smile. "I am an incredibly good kisser—not to be cocky but it's just a fact—and take it from me, you are *very* talented."

My knees felt weak, and I wasn't sure I could keep my eyes open as I looked up at his flirty gaze. Finally finding my voice, I managed, "I'm not sure if I should thank you or slug you for that glowing critique."

"I thought you were getting eggs," Scott barked from the other room, but I couldn't pull my eyes away from Charlie.

"We are," Charlie said to Scott while still giving me that impressed grin.

I glanced over at the table and—holy *shit*—my mom and Scott were both staring at us in shock. My mom's mouth was literally hanging open, and Scott looked like he'd just figured out that the butler did it.

I grabbed a clean plate from the drying rack with unsteady hands and said quickly, "I just need to warm them up in the microwave."

Charlie ignored them and said to me, "Holy shit, Mitchell— do you realize what this means?"

I gave him a *They're looking at us* face and moved away from him, needing distance as I walked over to the skillet, which was out of their line of sight. "I'm afraid you're going to tell me."

He came over, leaned against the refrigerator with that long, tall body of his, crossed his arms, and said, "We can totally use this weekend to hone our craft because we're emotionally unaffected by each other."

I felt my eyebrows go down but quickly erased that tell, not wanting him to know what I was thinking. But . . . *emotionally unaffected by each other?* Had he been in the same kiss as me? Because I was a lot of things at that moment, but unaffected was not one of them.

I scooped a few eggs out of the skillet and onto my plate. "I'm sorry—what?"

"Think about it," he said, and when I glanced up at him, he

was still grinning that stupid grin. "The only time people ever kiss is when it matters, right? There's never any practice, any training to get better; it's a failed system. But you and I—we can become fucking Olympic-level kissers, Bay, because we have the opportunity to train."

I set down the big spoon and picked up the plate, unsure if I was understanding his meaning. Did he want to practice kissing? *Together??* I forced my voice to sound super casual and said, "You have *got* to be kidding."

"Listen." He straightened and grabbed my plate in his two big hands, his dark eyes bright on mine. "Wouldn't it be cool to try new things and get honest feedback? You can bite down on my bottom lip and lick the corner of my mouth—potential new sexpot move—and I can tell you, *Nah that feels weird* or *Holy shit you just changed the game.*"

I looked at him and blinked. Was there a carbon monoxide leak in the condo? Because he was saying ridiculous things, and those ridiculous things were making me flushed and light-headed. *Lick the corner of my mouth.* I cleared my throat and attempted to sound matter-of-fact when I said, "Absolutely not."

"You're not listening. I can attempt to tie your tongue into a knot with my tongue, and you can tell me if it feels like I'm trying to eat your mouth or if it makes you tingly." Charlie was getting amped up about the idea, his eyes alive like when he was coming up with new games at work. "Please tell me you'll consider this attempt at bettering ourselves, Baybay."

Tie your tongue into a knot with my tongue. I looked at his mouth.

Cleared my throat.

"Never call me *that* again," I said, doing my best to seem calm and cool when I felt like I was slipping underwater, getting pulled down by this wickedly strong chemistry I was suddenly having with him.

I let my eyes run all over his face—dark eyes, long lashes, strong nose, stubborn chin—but I couldn't seem to find Mr. Nothing. All I saw, when he gave me that playful half smile, was the Charlie who knew how to make marinara and talk football with my mom.

And kiss like he knew very, VERY dark secrets.

Fuck.

Get a grip, Bailey.

I pressed my lips together and forced myself to ignore the chemistry and focus on his words. *Bettering ourselves.* I could tell he thought it was a great idea, but he was out of his mind. I was okay with fake dating, but I was *not* going to let him use me to make him a better kisser for other girls.

What the hell was wrong with him?

Actually, what was wrong with *me* for caring?

"My apologies," he said, looking anything but apologetic.

"And I will *not* be using you for 'kissing practice.'"

His mouth dropped open like he hadn't even considered the idea that I'd refuse. "Why not?"

"Why *not*?" I asked incredulously. "Because the whole point of kissing is sharing it with the person you care about. If I'm concerned about improving my game, I'll practice with someone I'm into when the time is right, thank you."

Zack, perhaps.

Yes, Zack.

Of course Zack.

"Oh, Glasses," he said, looking disappointed in my answer. "You're wasting an incredible opportunity with that wide-eyed idealism of yours."

"Says you," I replied, unsure why I felt disappointed.

"You're going to regret it, but whatever." Charlie straightened, seeming entirely *unaffected* by everything, and asked, "Do you want some bacon?"

Wow—he was just so quick to move on, wasn't he? I rubbed my lips together—*coffee and toothpaste*—and said, "Yes, please."

CHAPTER THIRTY-TWO

Charlie

Bailey and I spent the day hiking while her mom and Scott went skiing. Scott seemed irritated that we were going out on our own instead of hanging with them, but I held Bailey's hand and supported her I-have-no-interest-in-learning-to-ski agenda.

"Look at this," she said, leaning down over a stream. She cupped her hands together, dipped them into the creek, then lifted the cold water to her mouth. "Drinking in the wild like a true mountain man."

"You do realize that a mountain lion could've totally crapped in the snow, which melted and sent that fecal water downstream and into your hands?" I asked, in awe of her ability to *not* think about how disgusting that was.

She shrugged, grinning up at me. "It's cold and delicious. I'm thirsty, so I'm good with poop water."

I shook my head, equal parts horrified and impressed.

Because as uptight as Bailey was about some things, she was so fucking chill about others.

I was constantly surprised by her willingness to roll with the punches.

Which was probably where the kissing idea came from. It was immature as hell, because nothing said middle school quite like "Let's practice kissing," but that kitchen kiss was fucking addictive and I'd been desperate for my next fix.

Kissing Bailey was supposed to be like everything else was with her. Entertaining, a contest of wills, a back-and-forth that was oddly satisfying; those are things I would say when describing our friendship.

But the kiss was something else entirely.

It was hot and sweet and a little bit wild, with her fingers on my shoulders and the smell of her shampoo in my nose. She'd been the opposite of uptight, and to be honest, it was really fucking with my mind.

"Here." I held out my water bottle and said, "My germs are better than poop water."

"Are they?" She blinked up at me in that way she had, like she could see every single thing I was thinking and she disapproved of most of it. But she took my Smartwater and said, "I mean, your mouth was on my mouth, and now my mouth was on poop water. So if I drink this, and you kiss me later, your mouth will be pooped in with the very next—"

"Stop," I said, shaking my head as she reasoned like a toddler.

"Fine," she replied, looking pleased with herself.

My eyes got a little stuck on her for a second because she

looked so damned cute. She was wearing jeans, a thick brown sweater, and a plaid scarf in her hair, which should've been boring, but on her, it worked, especially when she wore those old-school movie star sunglasses.

There was a vibe to the way she dressed, the whole I-don't-think-that-cardigan-even-fits-her-but-damn-she-looks-perfect kind of thing.

Fucking cute, but it was Bailey.

This happened to me sometimes when I looked at her. One second she was Bailey, crinkling her nose in irritation with me while doing something like reorganizing the apps layout on her phone, and the next she was a girl with curly dark hair, long eyelashes, and freckles that begged to be counted.

She was like a one-person *Freaky Friday* or something.

It'd be a little concerning if her too-smart mouth wasn't always there to remind me that she was, down to her core, still the cute blinking brace face from the airport in Fairbanks.

CHAPTER THIRTY-THREE

Bailey

After hiking all day, I was ready for a shower when we got back to the condo. We were going to a fancy steakhouse for dinner, so I got ready in the bathroom upstairs, since the window in my room still hadn't been fixed. I took my time, really leaning into wavy curls and dramatic eye makeup. I don't know why, but it felt important that I look good.

I was in the middle of drawing eyeliner tails (sharp enough to kill a man, of course), leaning up to the mirror and full-on concentrating, when my mom appeared in the doorway and whispered, "When did you and Charlie start dating?"

I looked at her in the mirror, and she looked rightfully surprised by what we'd thrown at her over breakfast. I was a terrible liar and immediately couldn't remember if we'd come up with a backstory. I just said, "On the way here, kind of."

"Oh." She nodded and watched me, like she was reconciling

it in her head. "So it's new, then."

"Brand-new," I agreed.

"Ah." I don't know why, but that seemed to be the right answer. She looked relieved that we hadn't been in some secret relationship she'd been unaware of. "Well, I like Charlie a lot, but make sure you take it slow, okay?"

I nodded and gave her a convincing "Okay."

But after she walked away, *take it slow* kept pinging through my brain. Because even though, in the overall scheme of things, we were taking it very slow (because it wasn't real), the chemistry between us felt crazy-fast.

Maybe because we'd gone from almost-friends to sleeping in the same room and kissing over breakfast. It was whiplash-fast, which was probably why I felt so unsteady around him.

That was why.

Just that.

The hike—when no one else was around—had been comfortable, so as I put away my makeup and sprayed my hair, I reminded myself to stop getting worked up.

It was all pretend. Charlie seemed to have no problem turning it on and off, and I was going to channel that energy and not worry about every spark that flew, because it was just a side effect of our superb acting.

Or something like that.

Once I pulled on my black dress, I ran down the stairs to look for my shoes in my suitcase.

"Wow." Charlie was at the bottom of the stairs, and I nearly ran him down. He grabbed my upper arms to stop me, and then he smiled, his eyes strolling all over me.

"You look incredible, even though I don't like you that way," he said in a deep voice, his fingers applying the softest pressure to my skin. "Seriously, Glasses."

I didn't know if this was part of the faking or not, but the tone of his voice made my toes curl. Because regardless of how he meant it, I *wanted* him to mean it.

A compliment from Charlie was like the equivalent of three from another human.

"Shut up, loser," I said, reaching out a hand to tug on his tie. He looked hot—he did—in black pants, a plaid button down, and a black tie. "You look like someone I'd call cute if I didn't know you drink poop water."

"Aww." He let go of my arms and tugged on one of my curls instead. Then he looked at my mouth, raised his eyebrows, and asked, "May I, Girlfriend?"

Whoa. There was that superb acting again, because something about him calling me his girlfriend made warmth squeeze me like a hug. I looked up at his lips and *Ohhh—he wants to kiss me again.*

Just a game—enjoy it and quit overanalyzing.

I gave a nod that made his eyes crinkle around his smile as I said, "Of course, Boyfriend."

His hands moved to my cheeks and his mouth lowered, and stopped just above mine. "What do you want here? Romantic and sweet, or hot and heavy?"

"I get to order like I'm at a drive-up window?" I asked, joking because my heart was suddenly pounding in my chest.

"Yep," he said, giving me more of his charming grin. "May I take your order?"

I thought through my choices, and then came up with, "Okay. So pretend you're obsessed with me, and I just told you that I'm moving to Moldova in the morning. This will be our one and only kiss, so you have to make it epic."

"Why Moldova?" he asked, his eyebrows scrunching together in confusion.

"Why *not* Moldova? I mean, it's coastal, right?"

"I don't think so." There was a smile in his voice as he said, "And doesn't it cozy up to Ukraine?"

"Does it?" I breathed, my stomach getting a bat-sized butterfly as his eyes were so close, I felt like our lashes could brush. My voice was barely there as I said, "I can't remember."

"I honestly have no idea," he agreed, moving even closer, his response low and deep.

"About that kiss," I whispered, his eyes making me feel more daring than I actually was.

His hands tightened on my cheeks, and his mouth came down a little hard on mine. *In a good way.* He gave me a wide-open mouth kiss, angling his head perfectly to make the kiss feel deeper, hotter.

Holy *shit*.

When Charlie kissed, there was no hesitation. It was like he somehow knew exactly what I wanted and magically delivered it with just a little more than I'd even known to want. A shiver slithered through me as that talented boy somehow used suction to crank it even hotter, and my hands came up to rest on his chest.

He made a noise—*a growl?*—and he said against my lips, "I like feeling your hands on me while I kiss you."

"Yeah?" I whispered, moving my fingertips the tiniest amount over his shirt.

"Oh yeah," he said, and the look in his eyes made me a little breathless.

His mouth came back to mine, his teeth scraping over my bottom lip, and—

"Christ," Scott said, walking into the room from the kitchen. "Can you two please cool it on the PDA?"

I jumped back from Charlie, but his hand casually moved to my hand, his fingers sliding between mine.

"Sorry," I said, rubbing my lips together as my cheeks burned.

"Same," Charlie added.

I looked at him out of the corner of my eye as a warm, bubbling buzz thrummed all around me. I wanted to laugh, to giggle like a moron, as his big hand squeezed mine.

My mom came down the stairs at that moment, breaking up the tension as Scott told her how gorgeous she looked. It was disgusting and I wanted to slap his grinning face, but I also couldn't help but recognize that my mom looked blissfully happy.

Damn, damn, damn.

The bubbles I had from the kiss popped and went flat as I watched the two of them. She deserved to look that happy. I *wanted* her to be that happy.

But it wasn't as simple as happiness, because what if that happiness changed everything?

Because my dad had seemed happy when he'd started seeing

Alyssa, but just a few months later, he stopped attending our weekly Zoom chats and kept forgetting to respond to my texts.

He remembered to pen funny replies when Alyssa tagged him on Instagram, but he couldn't seem to remember to reach out to his one and only daughter. I hated it so much, but it would be a thousand times worse if that happened with my mom.

Because my mom was more than just a mom to me; she was my everything.

So what happened to our *us* if she and Scott became the big *US*?

We loaded into his car, and he drove to the restaurant. I was quiet in the back as they talked about the chef who'd be cooking that night, and Charlie leaned closer and said, "Can I give you some kissing feedback?"

"*No.*" I felt my eyebrows screw together in irritation, both at the way my worries were ruining my fun and at the idea of Charlie criticizing the way I kissed.

But then—dammit—I needed to know. "Okay—what?"

"Be careful with that breathy little noise you make when a guy kisses you," he said quietly, his voice making a tiny shiver slither down my spine. "It's a little too sexy, and might give someone the wrong idea."

"I'm sorry, but (a) I don't make a breathy little noise, and (b) if I did, are you seriously slut-shaming the sound?"

He grinned so big, it was like a laugh. "Um, (c) yes, you do, and (d) not at all. It's a fantastic sound that almost made me forget who I was kissing. But with great sexy sounds comes great responsibility."

Almost made me forget who I was kissing. I didn't like that phrase, even though it was how this was supposed to work. The whole thing was pretend, but for the love of God, no one wanted to hear that the person they were kissing liked forgetting who they were kissing.

I just said, "Got it."

"By the way," he went on, his voice rising to a normal volume, "I read about this gold-mining ghost town that's only like an hour away. We should check it out tomorrow."

"Ooh, for sure," I said, torn between being disappointed by how easily he was able to move on and being a little excited about another day of exploring on our own.

"I was hoping you'd reconsider skiing," Scott said, looking expectantly at me in the rearview mirror. "And go with us tomorrow."

"Oh." I looked at his face in the mirror and felt like garbage. He was a decent guy, and I was trying to sabotage him, his relationship with my mom, and his vacation. Guilt gnawed at me as he looked at me like someone who was really trying.

Charlie gave me a look, eyebrows cocked to remind me I was supposed to be avoiding Scott's attempt at father-daughter bonding. I inhaled through my nose and said, "Well, um, maybe Charlie and I can go there with you guys and hang out for part of the day, and *then* take off for ghost towns?"

I saw Charlie slowly shaking his head in my peripheral vision, disappointed, as Scott beamed and said, "We'll take it."

"You're so soft," Charlie whispered, but I just ignored him and looked out the window.

How was I supposed to be mean to the guy all the time when he kept doing nice things?

Dinner was incredible.

The food at the old-school steakhouse was over-the-top (in a good way).

Bread and salad and spaghetti and steak and potatoes—it was like three entire meals in one, and I devoured it. My dad was the meat eater in our family, so aside from a random burger here and there, we didn't eat a lot of beef anymore.

Hence my attempt to wolf down every last bite.

My mom and Scott had enough wine to make them happy and not exceptionally aware of Charlie's and my presence.

Which was what made it so fun.

First, Charlie and I made wagers on what the people at the table beside us would order. I won the most points, which meant that when we got back to the condo, Charlie was going to have to do all the dishes I'd left in the sink. It seemed like a cruel thing to do on vacation, but bets were only bets if everyone was held accountable.

Charlie's words, not mine.

After that, we fell into a game of making each other's food unpalatable. We hadn't intended for that to become an activity—it just happened organically. First, I told Charlie to try my twice-baked potatoes, but as I held my fork in front of his face, the potatoes fell into his prime rib's au jus. As penance, I had to try a bite of lumpy au jus, which made me gag and made us both giggle.

Then I poured horseradish into his risotto and made him sample it, which led to more giggles as he shivered in disgust. By the time Scott paid the bill, my stomach hurt from quietly laughing so hard.

The four of us took a walk around Breckenridge after dinner, and I was happy Charlie was pouring the fake boyfriending on thick by putting his arm over my shoulders, mostly because his body was warm and mine was not.

"Do you always have to hang all over each other?" Scott asked, looking at Charlie but wearing a teasing grin for once. "I mean, last week you were just friends."

I laughed because he was right, and so did Charlie as he said, "True, but once your eyes have been opened, you can't unsee what you've seen."

"Did you really just say that?" I teased. "That was, um . . . heavy . . . ?"

"With bullshit," Scott said.

And my mom added around a laugh, "With *total* bullshit."

"Maybe," Charlie said, looking at them, "but the bottom line is, now that I've seen what Bay could be to me, seeing her as just a friend is impossible."

I *felt* his words, felt the power of their potential as we walked. My stomach flipped over as I breathed in his cologne and felt his warm arm, anchoring me against him.

I allowed myself for a half second to pretend he meant what he'd said.

My mom's voice crooning "Awwww" pulled my eyes wide open.

"Wow," I whispered sarcastically to Charlie, hoping he hadn't noticed the way I'd melted into him. "So good."

But. Was it strange that at that moment, I wanted his words to be true? This whole thing was just a game, and the real Charlie Sampson was a huge pain in the ass, but in that mountain moment, under the gorgeous moonlight, I wanted fake Charlie to be real and to mean what he'd just said.

Oh my God, oh my God, oh my God.

I needed to get myself together.

None of this was real, and I needed to stop forgetting that.

"Right?" he said to me, but his mouth was straight, his eyes serious before he pulled them away and turned his head.

When we got to the town square ice rink, my mom and Scott decided they wanted to skate, even though they totally weren't dressed for it. Charlie and I stood off to the side and watched them for a few minutes, skating in dress clothes and looking fairly adorable in spite of their age.

"I don't think our fake dating is having an effect at all," I said, watching Scott gesturing wildly while my mom laughed.

"We just need to go harder," Charlie replied. "Cause more friction."

"Do you really think it matters?" I asked, feeling discouraged as I stared at the old people having more fun than me.

"Would you rather do nothing?" he asked.

I glanced at him out of the corner of my eye.

"Seriously. Risk versus reward," he said, sounding very sure of himself. "The risk isn't high—unless kissing is risky business— so why not keep trying?"

I tilted my head and turned to him. "So you're saying—"

"We could stand here and watch them skate, or we could stick with the plan and make them uncomfortable."

Did he want to kiss me again?

"Let's do that," I said, a little too quickly, but the truth was that *I* was dying to kiss *him* again.

Actually, I assured myself as I let my eyes wander over the dimple in his chin, kissing Charlie was a great idea. Because there were always sparks when you kissed someone new the first few times; that was natural.

So it stood to reason that the more I kissed Charlie and made the newness wear off, the less sparky it would be and the more clinical it would become.

This, I thought as he looked down at me, *this* was a plan.

"Atta girl." Charlie grabbed my hand and led me over to a huge pine tree. We were still in public, but the tree gave us a little privacy. I felt the trunk against my back as he lowered his mouth toward mine, so close that our breath mingled, and then he stopped.

Hovered, his dark eyes hot on mine.

Sending electricity to every nerve ending in my body as he waited for me to make a move.

I set my hands on his chest, feeling bold as I caught his lower lip between my teeth and dragged them along the edge. His breathing was a little ragged when I licked at the corner of his mouth, and then I angled my head the tiniest amount and closed my eyes, feeling a wild confidence that was new and downright intoxicating.

Charlie had been still the entire time I'd been toying, but just like that, he moved in closer, pressing my back against the tree as his mouth took over. It was like when summer sprinkles give themselves over to the crack of thunder, abruptly switching from a light tease of rain to a lightning-fueled downpour.

His hands clenched on my face—not painful, but more of a flex—and his body moved even closer as his lips and teeth and tongue went wild over mine. The game was forgotten and technique left behind as he kissed me like I was moving to Moldova and this was the last time we'd ever be together.

He kissed me like he'd been holding back for years and was finally giving in.

No kiss, in the history of civilization, had ever been that good, and I grabbed his shirt in both of my hands and did my best to give back as perfectly—and thoroughly—as I was getting.

A noise broke through the storm, and I could hear people walking in our general direction.

Charlie pulled back and watched me, his eyes traveling all over my face. He didn't grin or make a joke, and his voice was gravelly when he said, "They're watching us."

"What?" I asked, touching my lips with my index finger. "They are?"

His Adam's apple moved as he swallowed and nodded. "They stopped skating and they're talking. *Dramatically*."

"Seriously?"

"Oh yeah," he said, looking toward the rink. "Trouble in paradise, I think."

"Um, that's really great," I mumbled, still stuck in a post-kiss stupor. I tucked my hair behind my ears and rambled, "Yes. Great."

That brought his eyes back to my face, and his mouth slid into a slow half grin. "You are fucking gorgeous when you're kiss drunk, Mitchell, did you know that?"

I grinned back at him, feeling hot in spite of the chilly fall evening. Drunk was exactly how I felt; blissfully, tipsily, giddily under the influence of Charlie—both his kiss and the unexpected compliment. His smirky *fucking gorgeous* felt, to me, like he'd called me the most beautiful thing he'd ever seen.

"I did *not* know that," I said, biting the inside of my cheek to hold in the giggle. "Thank you."

He reached out and ran his finger over my cheek, muttering "My favorite thing" before turning away from me and yelling, "It's cold, Emily—can we go home and have cocoa, or are you skating all night?"

CHAPTER THIRTY-FOUR

Bailey

"Glasses?"

I lay there on the pullout sofa, staring up at the ceiling. "Yeah?"

"You know there's nothing wrong with liking him, right?"

"Who?"

"Scott." Charlie's voice was thick with sleepiness as he said, "It doesn't change anything with your dad if you like him."

"*What?* Charlie." I sat up and looked in his direction, even though I couldn't see more than his form in the dark. I didn't want him to say that, because I was already struggling to keep my resolve in the whole get-rid-of-Scott plan. "Aren't you the one who's supposed to be helping me sabotage his relationship?"

"Settle your ass down," he said, amusement in his voice. "I am here to ruin his weekend—no worries. But, honestly, he's a nice guy, and if you change your mind, there's nothing wrong with that."

"Well, I'm not." I shook my head and tried to forget how much of a "nice guy" Scott was, because it didn't matter—it wasn't about that. My concern was about preserving the normalcy of my life, the comforting sameness of my family unit of two. "Changing my mind. I don't care how nice he is. I don't want him moving in and changing everything."

"And that's fine," he said. "Now lie back down like a good girl."

"Screw you," I said as I did exactly what he said. I rolled onto my side. "So what's the story with your parents, Charlie?"

I suddenly wanted to know more about my partner in crime. "I know the basics, that your mom's boyfriend sucks and now they're pregnant, but you never talk about it more than a generalization, whereas I complain all the time."

"It's boring shit," he said, but his tone made me think he was trying hard to sound bored. "After the divorce, my parents absolutely focused on their futures, never looking back. My dad is remarried and expecting a baby with his wife, and my mom has been desperately trying to make that happen with Clark. And now they're having a baby."

I didn't want to push, because the last thing I wanted to do was remind him of unhappiness, but suddenly I found myself thirsty for Charlie backstory. "Do you like your dad's wife?"

"She seems nice enough, although I really only visit twice a year, so how the hell would I even know?"

"Yeah, what's with that?" I toed off my socks under the covers and said, "I don't want to sound like a whiny little kid, but I don't get our dads. Everyone in the world acts like it's normal and fine, but to me, it seems absolutely bizarre that a parent would be cool living in an entirely different state than their kid."

"But they have responsibilities, Bailey," he said, his voice full of sarcasm. "Careers and real estate and health club memberships that they can't just cancel."

"Such bullshit." I snorted and pictured my dad's golfing buddies. "I'm not asking to be the center of his world or anything, but shouldn't it bother them, never seeing us? Shouldn't it give them an uncomfortable little pain just under their breastbone, every time they picture our faces?"

"Glasses," Charlie said, a sweet, sympathetic lilt in his deep voice. "Do you get a little pain under your breastbone every time you picture your dad's face?"

We were rarely serious, so maybe it was tiredness that changed things for me. But instead of joking, I answered honestly.

"Every single time," I said, feeling that melancholy creep in as I remembered the way my dad's laugh sounded. He laughed like Santa, slow and deep and loud, and part of me wondered if he even knew what my laugh sounded like.

My throat was tight as I explained, "It's almost like panic, like I'm afraid if I don't see him soon, I'm going to forget what he looks like. Or he's going to forget all about me."

"Honey," he said, and it made me blink back tears in the dark. Charlie calling me *honey* was sweet and reassuring and hit me so hard in that emotional soft spot that I had to pretend I hadn't heard it.

"Stop, I'm fine," I said, my voice tight.

That kind of sweetness could annihilate me.

LYNN PAINTER

"It's okay to not be fine. When was the last time you talked to him?"

My heart felt like it was beating a little heavier, all of a sudden, as I focused on the big thing I'd been avoiding focusing on. "That's the thing. Nekesa pointed out that I'm always the one who instigates, the one who calls and texts him first, so I decided to prove her wrong. I decided to wait until *he* reaches out to *me*."

"Aw, shit," he said. "How long has it been?"

I swallowed. "Four months and three days."

He didn't say anything, and I felt stupid. I knew Charlie didn't judge me, but *I* judged me. I was a fucking senior, goddammit, and it was pathetic that I was homesick for my dad like a thumb-sucking kindergartner.

I closed my eyes, wanting to push back the emotions, but then Charlie was there. The pullout bed dipped, and then his arms were around me in such a Charlie way that I laughed out my shock. He threw a long leg over me and physically hauled my body closer so he could big spoon me while he murmured, "Like I can sleep with this bullshit going on over here."

"Charlie." I laughed. "Go sleep—I'm good."

"Nope," he said, tightening his grip. "You're not good until Charlie spoons you for a solid ten, trust me."

I started giggling. "You're an idiot."

"Your hair smells like balsam needles," he said, inhaling deeply. "And despair."

"You know what despair smells like?"

"Hell yes, I do."

We got quiet then, but it was comfortable.

I lay there, sad and relaxed in his arms, and I didn't want to speak or move or do anything to change the moment. My heart was racing because he was holding me, and that response seemed to be my new normal, but better than electricity was the way I felt insulated in Charlie's concern, blanketed in his warm support.

I almost thought he was asleep until Charlie said, "I'm sorry your dad's a selfish asshole."

"He's not, though," I said, letting my eyes close, suddenly exhausted. "He's just really busy."

"You deserve better," he said, sounding offended on my behalf.

"So do you," I said, meaning it. I turned over, so I could see his face, and I almost wished I hadn't, because his smart-ass mask was nowhere to be found. He looked sweet—vulnerable—and a rush of fondness went through me. "You're not nearly the jerk you purport yourself to be."

I saw his throat move around a swallow before he said in a gravelly voice, "Trust me, I am."

"Charlie," I said, smiling as I looked at his face. Those dark eyes, slashing brows, that prominent nose—I loved his face. I mean, I *liked* his face. My heart was in my throat as my gaze moved all over him, traveling everywhere. I didn't dare bring my eyes back to his, yet I couldn't keep them away.

He was looking at me, his gaze intense as if he'd been waiting for me to see him. I felt like I couldn't breathe as those dark-as-night eyes dipped to my lips, and then his face was moving closer to mine.

I felt light-headed as I watched him because I knew—I just *knew*—that this was no longer a game of pretend.

And it didn't make sense, but I didn't want it to.

This was *Charlie's* mouth coming down on mine. This was *my* lips, opening for him in the yawning darkness of the living room. My shaking hands moved up to his shoulders as I felt his big, warm hands on my hips, and my breathing went choppy as his went deep.

My mind went wild as he kissed me, playing a montage of Colorado Charlie memories that made me *feel* things for him. The way he'd grinned when we sprinted through multiple gas stations. The vulnerability he'd shown about whatever anxiety issues he was dealing with.

His calm *Is that a goose* question while Scott wielded footwear.

And the way he'd pulled me into his arms when I was sad— oh God.

He lifted his mouth for a second—only a breath away—and said, "Bay."

But he didn't just say it. His voice was deep and hot, and he spoke my name as if it were a curse or an exaltation, something that moved him, for better or worse.

He angled his head, his fingers clenching against me in a way that made me feel the heat of his hands through my flannel pants, and then he sent full-sex kisses into my mouth. I felt like my heart was going to explode as he fed me long, hot, deep tastes that made my toes curl under my blanket.

I gripped his shoulders harder, needing, which made him lift his head again. He didn't say anything this time as he looked down at me, and it didn't feel like he needed to. The eye contact was somehow sweet, questioning, and hot, all at once.

His mouth lowered, but before our lips touched, Charlie's head jerked up. "Did you hear that?"

"What?" I hadn't heard anything, but I was also wildly disoriented, as if just regaining consciousness after a year in a coma, so I probably wouldn't have heard a freight train.

His eyes met mine, and I wished I could see what he was feeling, what he was thinking.

"Shit!" Charlie leaped off the pullout and fell to the floor, then scrambled over to the floor bed and covered himself with the blanket.

Then I heard it.

Footsteps on the stairs.

I lay there, my eyes squeezed shut as I pretended to be asleep, and Scott came down the stairs. I listened as he lumbered into the kitchen, and I heard him open a cupboard and turn on the sink. It felt like an eternity as he shuffled around in there.

Hurry the hell up!

Meanwhile, my brain was starting to chant on an endless loop, *What the hell just happened what the hell just happened WHAT IN THE LITERAL HELL JUST HAPPENED ON THE PULLOUT?*

Scott came out of the kitchen, and my heart actually started pounding *harder* when I heard him go up the stairs and close the door.

I held my breath and waited.

Was Charlie going to come back?

"Holy shit, that was close," Charlie said from the floor on the other side of the room. "He would've flipped if he'd come down a minute earlier."

"Yeah," I said, unsure of what I should say. He sounded . . . *normal*, which was good, because I could easily picture him freaking out about this, and that was the last thing I wanted.

However, did I want him to be *unaffected* after what'd just happened?

I didn't think so, because I was unbelievably *affected*.

"I'm turning on the TV," he said, and I could hear the covers rustling. "If that's okay."

"Um. Yeah," I said, pulling the covers up to my chin. *Is he not going to say anything at all?* That was strange, right? It was bizarre to behave as if that didn't just happen, right?

Of course, there was no way *I* was going to bring it up.

No, it was much better to just lie there, wondering. *Was* he unaffected, or was he affected and unhappy about it? Was he regretting it? Was he chocking it up to additional practice time?

I rolled onto my side, so I was facing away from Charlie's floor bed, and clenched my teeth to stop myself from sighing.

Because I knew without a doubt that I was going to be awake all night, neurotically wondering what the hell had just happened.

CHAPTER THIRTY-FIVE

Charlie

Generally speaking, I considered myself to be a smart dipshit.

I could ace a calculus test (when I wanted to) and get every answer right on *Jeopardy!*, but I wasn't always good at making mature decisions.

See: Bailey Mitchell.

I stared at the TV, but I wasn't even listening to the episode of *Seinfeld* that was playing because my brain wouldn't stop screaming, *WHAT THE FUCK IS WRONG WITH YOU?*

The volume was so loud that I could hear nothing else.

What the fuck is wrong with me?

Kissing Bailey under the guise of fake dating—that was fine. Fucking funny, actually, that she and I were able to derive a little salacious pleasure from our plan to sabotage Scott. That, my friend, was what you called bonus material.

But kissing her because I looked into her eyes and just wanted to?

Such total dipshittery.

Because nothing good could come of it. I was certain Bailey was lying on the pullout, losing her shit this very second. She would freak out, things would get awkward, and everything would change.

It was asinine that I'd been careful enough to label her "coworker" instead of friend, just to ensure there was a mutual understanding between us, yet stupid enough to try to absorb her sadness into my body through osmosis because I didn't like hearing her sound unhappy.

But her face; God, her face had been too much.

She'd looked at me through teary eyes, and all at once I'd seen someone whose scrape I wanted to kiss better, the funny friend I needed to convince of her worth, and a stunner whose lips beckoned to me with promises of deep, satisfied sighs.

Combine that with the emotional punch of connecting with every fucking word she'd used to describe her feelings about her family life, and what else could I do but kiss her?

Thank God for Scott, trudging downstairs like an unwieldy bear at a sleeping campsite, because I didn't know what would've happened if we hadn't been interrupted. I couldn't speak for Bailey, but I knew *I* had lost total contact with my smart side. Dipshittery was in control, and I'd been a thousand percent focused on diving into the deep end and drowning myself in Bailey Mitchell.

What the fuck was wrong with me?

I had no choice. I had to fix this.

CHAPTER THIRTY-SIX

Bailey

"You sure you don't want to try?" Scott asked.

Scott and my mom were all smiles in their ski gear, and I told myself that her glowing face was all about this much-needed vacation, as opposed to a response to spending quality time with Scott.

"No, thanks," I said, pointing toward the chalet café next to the lift. Charlie and I rode with them instead of going out on our own, aborting ghost town plans to make my mother happy, and we'd all had breakfast together at the Blue Moose before she and Scott changed into their gear. "I plan on reading by the fire with cocoa in my hands all day, only stopping to wave whenever you bunnies reload."

"Charlie?" Scott raised his eyebrows. "You're more than welcome to join us."

Ugh—he really *was* a nice guy, asking even when Charlie was a total pain in his butt.

"Thanks," Charlie said, his fingers clenching between mine as he held my hand. "But if someone doesn't keep an eye on this one, God only knows what she'll do."

They headed out for the slopes, and we went inside. I had a huge knot in my stomach, worried things were going to be awkward with us after what'd happened on the pullout sofa. I still had no idea what to think about what I'd felt for him, but I would prefer figuring that out on my own while our friendship remained unchanged.

God, *please* let things be normal.

Charlie's phone rang when we got to the front of the line, and when he looked at the display, he said, "It's my mom. Would you mind ordering for me so I can take it?"

I made sure my face remained cool as I said, "Sure."

"What can I get for you?" asked the barista in the ski cap.

I placed our order and went to the other end of the counter, but I kept stealing glances at Charlie, who'd moved to stand beside the windows at the front of the store.

Was it his mom, or was it the ex that wouldn't leave him alone?

And why did the thought of it being his ex make the knot of nerves in my stomach feel even heavier? She had nothing to do with me.

That thought made me pull out my phone and check my messages—still nothing from Zack—before putting it back into my bag.

A few minutes later I watched Charlie put his phone into his pocket before he came over and stood beside me. "Sorry about that. Apparently she just realized that she isn't sure who my friend Bailey is, so she's melting down about my safety."

"Is it okay now?" I asked, remembering the way he'd sounded when discussing his family.

"Oh, yeah," he said, grabbing our drinks as the barista set them down. "I told her you're an uptight rule-follower, so now she's thrilled."

I gave him an eye roll and turned, heading straight for the big fireside sofa.

"You seriously want to read all day?" he asked, setting his mug on the end table before taking off his jacket.

"It sounds amazing to me, but if you'd rather do something else . . ." I shrugged and trailed off as I set down my mug and plopped onto the couch.

His eyes narrowed. "What is up with you today? Since when do you want to do whatever I want to do?"

I shrugged again. "I'm just trying to compromise since it's our last day."

"You're freaked out about the bed kiss," he said, smirking like it was amusing to him.

"No, I'm not," I said, not really knowing how to act. It was good that he didn't seem freaked, but then again, shouldn't he seem *something* about it?

"Oh, yes, you are—don't lie to *me*, Glasses, come on." He propped his feet on the coffee table and said, "Admit it."

"Okay." I pushed my glasses up my nose and turned my body so I was facing him. "I *do* feel a little . . . *confused* by the kiss."

"Well," he said, still looking unaffected. "Sometimes shit happens."

He looked so casual, so not concerned about it, that I wondered if the emotions had been all in my head. "Seriously? *Shit happens* is your analysis?"

His smirk disappeared and he swallowed, looking . . . something. Uncomfortable, maybe? Nervous? He picked up his coffee and said, without looking at me, "Christ, why do we have to analyze it at all?"

"We don't," I said, desperately wishing to know the *truth* about how he felt. "'Shit happens' says it all. Everything that needs to be said has been covered with the brilliant 'shit happens.'"

That made him look at me, but his expression was unreadable, aside from the tiny motion of his jaw flexing.

"What?" I asked, regretting my sharp tone because that *definitely* wasn't going to restore normality with us. I forced myself to mimic one of his sarcastic little smiles, desperate to diffuse the tension, and said, "Quit staring at me, weirdo."

"Sorry." His dark eyes moved over my face, and a smirk appeared for the briefest of seconds before he raised his coffee to his mouth. "Now start reading that book to me."

"What?"

He took a drink, his eyes a little crinkly with mischief, before he leaned forward to set his cup on the coffee table. "I didn't bring a book, so you're going to have to read aloud."

"Why would I do that?"

"Why wouldn't you?" He glanced down at my book. "Are you ashamed of what you're reading?"

"No." I was rereading *Dodging the Duke* for like the twentieth time in my life. "But I doubt it's your jam."

"Historical fiction?"

"Historical *romance*," I clarified.

"Porny?"

"Not really."

"Then read it aloud."

I rolled my eyes and said, "Only if you read the duke's lines."

"Is he cool?"

"Oh yeah."

"Hot?"

"On fire."

"Fine," he said, shrugging. "I'll do it."

"Shut up." I couldn't believe it. "Seriously?"

"I'm only doing it because you were so confident that I wouldn't. Can't have you being right, can I?"

He scooched closer to me on the couch so we could both see the pages. I opened the book, caught him up to what was happening and where I'd left off, and then I started reading.

"'She smiled,'" I read out loud. "'Her cheeks were pink as their eyes held, but surely it was only due to the warmth of the room.'"

I looked up, and his dark eyes were doing that mischievous twinkling thing. He cleared his throat and said in a ridiculous British accent that made him sound like a chimney sweep from *Mary Poppins*, "'Miss Brenner, would you care to see the gardens?'"

It started with giggles, and after another page of this, we were both cackling. Leave it to Charlie to make reading into a noisy, hilarious, absolutely *not* relaxing activity. It seemed like something Charlie would tire of quickly—one of his little games—but he actually got into the book.

We sat on that couch for a couple hours—literally—laughing and obnoxiously reading. And when Charlie got up to refill our coffees, I realized that he might've just given me the perfect date.

I mean, we weren't on a date and it was morning, but if I read about this coffee shop excursion *in* a book, I would be creating a whole Pinterest mood board on it because it was one of those kicking-and-screaming-into-my-pillow scenes in a book.

They're reading together in a coffee shop!

I watched him pour a splash of cream into his Americano, and I wondered if Mr. Nothing was gone forever. Because when I looked at him now, I saw only my friend Charlie. He still confused the hell out of me, but he was nothing like the jerk I'd once thought him to be.

Weird how things could change so much in such a short time.

Maybe I needed to stop overthinking things with him, making rules and judgments about who he was, who I was, and who we were together. Because if I hadn't rolled with Charlie's *shit happens* explanation of last night, we wouldn't have had this perfect morning.

Shit happens.

He looked at me then, screwing his eyebrows together in a *What is that weird expression you're wearing all about* face as he walked over with our coffees in his hands, and I didn't even try to hold back the smile that took over my entire face.

Because I had a new motto. A new way of thinking.

Until we crossed the border and left Colorado behind, I

wasn't going to overthink anything. About Charlie, about my parents, about Zack . . . about anything. Every action that was going to happen, every word that was going to be said—all of it would now be attributed to shit happening.

And that would just be that.

Shit happened in Colorado.

End of story.

Eventually we left the café and wandered through town, but when it got a little crowded with tourists, we decided to go for a hike. I was glad Charlie suggested just hitting the trail behind the condo without going inside first, because it seemed like a terrible idea to be home alone with him.

Not that I thought something would happen—we'd been cool all day—but I wasn't sure my relaxed shit-happens attitude could survive that kind of inner turmoil.

The trail was stunningly beautiful—pine trees and gurgling streams and friendly chipmunks—and hiking through the steep terrain was just as fun as it'd been the day before. On the way back, though, my legs were screaming.

"Can we sit?" I asked, pointing to a clearing with a fallen log that begged to be sat upon. "I need a break."

"Do you want a bear to eat you?" he asked, his teasing eyes hidden behind his sunglasses.

"I want to sit, Charlie," I whined. "My legs are tired. I will risk a bear attack."

"No." He stopped walking, stepped closer, and tilted his head. "We're almost to the condo, wherein you can plop down onto the sofa and never get up."

"Don't say 'wherein,'" I said around an eye roll. "And how are you not tired?"

That made his lips turn up. "I'm incredibly fit, Glasses."

"Spare me."

"Do you want a piggyback ride?" he asked, full-on enjoying himself now. "I can carry you down the mountain like you're a sleepy toddler who needs a nap, if your little legs can't make it."

"I should take you up on that just to punish you," I replied, pointing a finger toward my log. "But right now, that log needs me."

"It wouldn't be a punishment. I'll just consider it my workout for the day." He turned and bent his legs. "Get on."

Normally my brain would've melted down into a puddle of neurotic worries at that—*What if I'm too heavy? What if he thinks I'm out of shape? Will I spontaneously combust from being attached to Charlie's body?*—but instead I thought, *Shit happens.*

You get tired, your friend is in great shape, he carries you down a mountain—shit happens.

I jumped onto his back and wrapped myself around him.

"Atta girl." He laughed and immediately started walking. His pace was much quicker, meaning I'd been slowing him down, but I wasn't going to concern myself with that thought because *shit happens.*

Also, was it weird that I liked how strong his grip was on my legs?

Yeah, probably, but shit happens.

"Thank you," I said, noticing the way his neck smelled like a bar of soap, "for sparing my legs. I was surely about to die."

"Surely you were," he agreed sarcastically, then tilted his head. "Shhh."

I didn't speak but had no idea *why* I wasn't speaking.

"Shit—do you hear that?" he whispered.

I said, "What?"

"Shh . . . listen."

He stopped walking, and that was when we heard a cat meowing.

I looked at the trees in front of us, saying nothing, as Charlie looked above him and said, "Oh no, little guy."

I followed his gaze upward, and holy crap—the tiniest little gray kitten was *way* up on a tall branch.

A very tall branch.

"Oh no," I said as the furball kept mewling. I slid off Charlie's back. "How's he going to get down?"

I don't know what I expected from Charlie, but without a word, he started climbing the tree. Thankfully, it had a knotted old trunk, but that cat was *high,* and Charlie was out of his mind.

"Charlie," I said nervously. "You can't climb all the way up there."

"Sure I can," he cooed, using a soothing baby talk voice so as not to scare the cat. "It's just a little farther."

I squinted into the sun as he kept climbing higher.

"I'm coming, little buddy, so you wait for me, okay?" he said, climbing higher still. "I'm going to get you down, get you a warm blanket and some food, okay?"

The kitten just kept meowing, and I just kept listening

in disbelief as Charlie spoke to that cat in the sweetest voice. Something about his low croon settled into my belly, making *me* feel soothed, even as he idiotically climbed way too high in that super-tall tree.

"I know, buddy," he said, and my heart turned to warm liquid as I watched Charlie's entire focus settle on the well-being of that little cat. "It's creepy as hell up here, right? But I got you, don't worry."

My heart was in my throat as I watched him climb higher and higher. "Be careful, Charlie."

"I am," he said, in the same soothing voice he was using on the cat. "Almost there."

How did I ever think he was a jerk? Charlie Sampson had the softest, sweetest center, in spite of the fact that it was surrounded by crunchy cynicism, and I felt an odd sense of pride as I watched him move closer to the kitten.

Because how many people would just start climbing in this situation?

He got to the branch below the kitten and started talking even more. "I'm going to grab you in a sec, and I'm going to need you to not freak out too badly, okay? A scratch is fine, but please don't leap down and hurt yourself."

I took a couple steps over to stand directly underneath him, incredibly stressed about how high he'd climbed. Maybe if he fell on *me*, instead of the ground, he wouldn't die.

He reached out, and—thank God—got the cat on the first try.

And instead of trying to get away, the little pile of fluff buried his head in Charlie's collar as he petted him.

"Good job, buddy. Such a good boy, sitting still and waiting for me." Charlie's mouth was right by the kitty's ear as he said, "You are such a good kitty."

I watched him, dangling from the side of a tree while cuddling and nurturing that tiny little animal, and it was undeniable.

I had huge feelings for Charlie Sampson.

Shit.

CHAPTER THIRTY-SEVEN

Bailey

The road trip home was the same as the way there—fun, relaxed—only it had the added bonus of Charlie's adorable cat, Puffball. A name I earned the right to give by winning the what-will-they-order-for-breakfast challenge before we'd hit the road. Charlie wanted to talk to his mom before bringing the cat home, so my mom had suggested we bring it to our apartment and he could come get it once he had permission. It was disgusting, how protective Charlie was of the cat, and I was utterly obsessed with this soft side of him.

After we brought the cat back to the condo, Scott ran to the market and came home with a disposable litter pan, food, and a cat toy, and the three of them—Scott, my mom, and Charlie—gushed over the fluffy feline all evening.

The damn cat had ruined everything.

Because now, in addition to being emotionally distracted by

the beautiful way Charlie was a total sap for that cat, I could no longer avoid the obvious as I watched them love all over the kitten.

Scott was a decent guy.

He was sweet and thoughtful, even giving Charlie a chance in spite of all the things Charlie had done to antagonize him.

So how could I keep trying to mess things up? Especially when my mom seemed to really like him?

It was giving me stress, but when I thought about him being in our lives forever, that stress accelerated to the nth degree.

So much for the whole laid-back shit-happens vibe.

But as we flew over the interstate, I felt better than I had the night before because I now had a solid plan.

After lying wide awake for *hours* on that pullout sofa, thinking about my feelings for Charlie and obsessing about why they were terrible, the answer came to me.

It didn't matter.

It didn't. Who cared if I had a few new-and-confusing feelings for Charlie?

I'd gotten all tied up in the feelings themselves—*What do they mean? Are they real? How can we be friends when I am suddenly crushing on him so hard?*—before realizing that it wasn't *about* the feelings themselves.

It was about what I did with them.

And I wasn't going to do *anything* with them.

Because I knew Charlie didn't feel the same way about me that I felt about him. I knew he *liked* me, I was pretty sure he had fun hanging out with me, and I was absolutely certain he enjoyed kissing me.

Gawwwwwwwd, the way he kissed.

But I'd never seen his face change when he looked at me the way it'd changed when he saw Becca at that party. And after the rejection I'd felt when Zack moved on after our breakup, I wasn't willing to settle for "pretty sure" and "liked."

I wasn't willing to settle at all.

So I was going to take what I'd learned from my parents—the fact that feelings eventually faded, especially when new feelings were introduced—and ensure a change of heart.

"So I have an idea," I said when we entered Lancaster County and I knew we'd be home in an hour.

"Uh-oh," Charlie said, popping a few orange TUMS into his mouth.

"No uh-oh," I argued. "No uh-oh at all. I was just thinking that now that the trip is over, it might be a good time for each of us to actually date in real life."

When I said the words, I realized that—holy shit—I *meant* it. Not just as a Charlie-Bailey diffuser, but maybe it was time for me to try to move on from Zack.

"What?" he said, his voice tight as he glanced over at me, a wrinkle between his eyebrows.

"Not each other," I quickly added, noting the look of horror on his face. "But . . . people."

He rolled his eyes and looked back at the road. "Really, Glasses?"

"You said Eli wanted to ask me out, and I have a friend—Dana—who is gorgeous and smart and funny." I tried sounding nonchalant as I said, "We should double-date it up."

"First of all, please never say things like 'double-date it up,'" he said, chewing his antacid.

"Agreed. I regretted it the second it exited my mouth."

"Second of all, what the fuck?"

Charlie looked irritated, which felt kind of good. *Is he hurt by the thought of me going out with someone else?* Was he mad that I was suggesting it after the weekend we'd just shared? I aimed for super chill when I casually asked, "What the fuck what?"

"What the fuck *what*? You have a gorgeous, smart, funny friend, and this is the first time you're mentioning her?" His eyes stayed on the road, but he looked amused as he said, "You've been holding out on me."

Heat flooded my face—hell, my entire body—and I was embarrassed by how quickly I'd fallen into wishful thinking. I ignored the unwelcome feeling in the pit of my stomach and said, "I guess I didn't know you were looking."

He did look at me then, but his expression was unreadable. "I guess I didn't either."

God, how was it possible that I missed my fake boyfriend already?

"So let's set it up, then," I said, remembering that forcing this was the best way to put our friendship back on solid ground, without any weird emotional tie-ups.

"Let's," he said. "We should do something stupid, like bowling."

"Bowling's not stupid," I muttered. "I was in a Saturday-morning bowling league in elementary school, and it was the funnest."

"A nerd says what?"

"Whatever," I said, looking out the window. "I was on the Saturday Strikers, and we ruled."

"I can't hear through all the static of your lameness. Are we bowling or what?"

I shook my head and said, "We're bowling."

He glanced over and raised an eyebrow. "Now, you know you can't kiss me when we're on dates, right?"

I coughed out a laugh. "I am aware, yes."

"I'm sure it'll be tempting, now that you've tasted the Charlie Special, but—"

"Ewwwww—the Charlie Special sounds like a tongue sandwich on toasted bread," I interrupted.

"Tasty," he muttered.

"And *you* are the one who needs the kissing reminder, since you couldn't keep your mouth off me over the weekend," I teased, reaching into my bag for the SweeTarts.

"I really couldn't," he agreed, which made me look up from my bag in shock. His eyes were on the road, crinkled at the corners, when he grinned and admitted, "I fucking loved the kissing portion of our game."

"Same," I said, surprised by the honest admission from both of us.

He gave a nod. "Too bad you passed on the intensive training."

"I think we had ample practice."

He was quiet for a minute, then said, "Yeah, anything more intense probably would've killed me."

I liked his face when he said that. It was soft and funny, like he was being candid about his own weakness. I didn't know what to say to that, so I turned around and looked over the seat at the cat carrier. "Awww . . . Puffball's asleep."

"He had a rough weekend," Charlie said with a little smile. "He needs his rest."

When he finally pulled in front of our building, my mom and Scott were there, unloading their car. It was good, because I didn't know how to *not* be awkward with the goodbye after everything.

But when Scott grabbed my stuff, my mom grabbed the cat, and we waved goodbye to Charlie as he drove away, I was instantly homesick for him as I watched his car disappear.

I wasn't ready for our trip to be over.

When we got into the apartment, I ditched them as quickly as possible. Puffball and I took our things, went into my room, and closed the door, happy to be alone with our thoughts. Mr. Squishy kept meowing at my door—he knew something was up—but I ignored the old cat because I knew my mom would shower him with attention. I flopped onto my bed and pulled out my phone while the kitten walked around on top of my pillows.

I had a *lot* to tell Nekesa.

But before I'd even finished my first message, Charlie was calling.

I rolled onto my back as I answered, "Are you even home yet?"

"Yeah," he said, and I could hear voices in the background.

"I'm home, but I didn't know the boyfriend was bringing his kids over. So I need to talk to you and my cat before I lose my shit."

"Freaking boyfriend," I said through gritted teeth, hating that *that* was what Charlie returned home to. After all of our talks in Colorado, I felt like I knew him better than I had before. Now I knew this *bothered* him—a lot—instead of assuming he didn't care because he was a sarcastic dick about it. "Want to come over?"

"I think I owe Scott a few hours without me," Charlie said. "He could've been a huge asshole to me during the trip, and he actually wasn't."

"God, I hate when you say things like that," I said, mostly because I was feeling the same way about Scott.

"I know, I'm sorry." I heard a door close, and now it was quieter. He said, "Let me talk to my cat."

I reached a hand across the bed, grabbed the fluffball, and set him on my chest. "Say hello, Puffer."

The cat raised his little face to the phone as I held it out, then rubbed his chin against it.

"Sorry—I don't think he wants to talk right now," I said, scratching the little guy's head as he walked in circles on my chest.

"Put the phone to his ear," Charlie said.

"Okay," I said, and held up the phone. Charlie started talking, and even though I couldn't hear what he was saying, I could tell he was using *that* voice. And—seriously—the kitten started meowing, looking agitated and excited and like all he wanted was for Charlie to appear.

I took the phone back, laughing as the kitten started

ramming his face into the space between my ear and the phone. "Oh my God, this guy loves you so much, it's disgusting."

"Will you FaceTime me? I miss him."

That made my mouth fall open and I gasped. Loudly. "Charlie Sampson, you are absolutely a gooey, soft cinnamon bun for this puffball."

"Yeah, I know."

"I just never imagined you being so . . . sweet."

"I'm sweet, like, all the time."

"Never, actually, but okay."

"Show me my cat."

"Fine."

I hit the button, and a second later he was popping up on my phone.

"Hang on," he said, and I felt like gasping all over again when I saw him standing in his bedroom in just a pair of shorts and no shirt. I'd always thought he looked like he might be shredded under his clothes, but *hoooooly crap*, the boy obviously took working out very seriously.

He ducked out of the frame for a second, and then he was back, pulling a shirt over his head. "Where's my boy?"

I scooped up the cat and held him directly in front of the phone.

"Hey, little buddy," Charlie said, and my heart pinched as I watched him grin at the kitten. Seeing Charlie's face look like *that* felt like a reward or something. He kept talking to Puffball—cooing, really—and then he said, "Okay—put Glasses on the phone."

I laughed and set down the cat, so Charlie and I were looking at each other.

"If you ever tell anyone what a pathetic fuck I am for that cat, I will kill you."

"I won't tell anyone," I said. "Just Dana."

"Oh, yeah." I watched as he sat down on his bed and said, "Did you set that up yet?"

"Okay—we *just* got home. But you have to talk to Eli *first*. If you don't make that happen, you don't get Dana."

He gave me a smart-ass smirk and said, "I'll text him in a sec."

"Do you think I'll like him?" I asked.

"Didn't you talk to him at the party?"

"Yeah, but you really *know* him. Do you think he's my type? Do you think we'll have things in common?"

He narrowed his eyes, like he was thinking about it, and then he said, "Yeah, I actually do."

"Sweet."

"What about your friend?" Charlie raised his eyebrows and said, "I mean yes, we're both pretty and funny and smart, but do we have *other* common interests?"

I rolled back over and said, "She's totally sarcastic, like you, and she's a volleyball player."

"How would volleyball apply to *me* exactly?"

"Obviously you both like doing sporty things."

He raised an eyebrow and looked amused. "Obviously?"

I rolled my eyes as my cheeks burned. "You have the chest of someone who enjoys sweating, and you know it."

"Baybay," he teased, leaning his face closer to the camera,

"were you checking me out?"

God, had he always been that sexy? It was FaceTime, for God's sake, and my breath hitched like he was going to lean in and kiss me. I cleared my throat and said, "I'm telling Dana you're a conceited asshole. Goodbye."

He laughed and said, "I'll text you after I talk to Eli."

CHAPTER THIRTY-EIGHT

Charlie

"Sorry about my parents," Dana said as she buckled her seat belt.

"No worries," I replied, starting the car and putting it in reverse. Her perfume smelled good, and I wondered what it was. "They seem great."

They *did* seem great, even though they'd interviewed me for ten minutes, but I didn't give a rat's ass about Dana's parents. Honestly, I was dreading this entire double-date evening, even though Dana seemed pretty cool.

Why? Oh, yeah—because I was a fucking idiot.

I'd *known* that men and women couldn't be friends. It was something I considered to be a universal truth. But somehow, with Bailey, lines got crossed. One minute we were just coworkers who irritated each other, and the next she was putting her hand in a fucking urinal for me.

We fell into the trap and became "friends" for a hot minute, but somewhere along the way—*of course, you dumbass*—I became obsessed with the way she blinked fast when she was surprised, the breathy sound of her laugh when she was sleepy, and the way she somehow knew when something was going to upset me, even before I did.

Somewhere between Omaha and Colorado I'd fallen truly, madly, fucking ridiculously hard for Bailey Mitchell. She was all I could think about, all the time, and sometimes it felt like I'd do anything—*anything*—just to make sure she was happy.

So yeah—it was kind of like a fucking slap when she mentioned setting me up with Dana, but that slap had been necessary. It was like the splash of cold water that reminded me I had no interest in anything more with her because *more* never lasted.

Everyone I'd ever known—every-fucking-one—had told me I was wrong. Every single person tried to convince me that true love and happily ever afters were a possibility.

But it was simply not true.

Yes, there was the obvious baggage in my life to which a therapist could attribute my beliefs: my parents fell out of love, every person I'd ever dated had fallen out of love, my grandparents had all split up—even my aunts and uncles had RIP'd their marriages.

Anyone related to me wasn't a part of the HEA crowd.

You could argue with me all day about the merits of true love, but in my opinion, it wasn't worth the risk.

It always came to an end.

And then there was nothing.

When Bec and I *used* to sit next to each other in bio, we laughed and screwed around and texted secret jokes about what the acronym of Mr. Post's first name (Uwe) stood for. I looked forward to that class because she made it fun.

It felt good to have someone to have fun with.

But after we dated—and subsequently broke up—we didn't *speak* in that class anymore. She looked at her phone or talked to Hannah (who sat on the other side of her) every day, and I . . . felt alone.

Every fucking day.

Fuck.

But that was why Bay and I needed to go back to being "annoying coworkers." It felt good, being with her, and I didn't want to lose that.

Man, I sound fucking insane.

"They're wildly overprotective," Dana said, and I could see in my peripheral vision that she was looking at her phone.

"So did I see a picture of you in a *rat* costume on the wall?" I asked, forcing myself to make a damn effort. "That's kind of a bold costume choice for a little kid."

"No." She laughed, setting her phone on her lap. "I mean, yes, you did, but that was from when I was in *The Nutcracker*. Ballet, not Halloween."

"Ah," I said, nodding. "Makes a little more sense."

"Yeah," she said, and then she picked her phone back up.

It was pretty much that way the entire drive to the bowling alley, a Q&A session with no chemistry whatsoever. There was nothing wrong with her, but it just didn't feel like we were connecting.

As we walked into Mockingbird Lanes, though, I wondered if I was just tired. I'd barely slept last night, and the dog had woken me up at the ass crack of dawn, so maybe it wasn't a lack of chemistry but a lack of my ability to *feel*.

"Bailey!" Dana yelled, lifting up an arm to yell across the crowded bowling alley.

I followed her gaze and saw Eli and Bailey, standing in front of the shoe counter.

Fucking fuck, my ability to *feel* was apparently just fine.

Bailey was wearing jeans, a thick wool sweater, and the new tortoiseshell glasses that she kind of hated but I thought were cute as hell. The off-white color of the top made her dark hair seem shinier than usual and made her eyes look a brighter green. Eli leaned down a little bit to hear her, and I knew he could smell the freesia lotion she always used.

I reached into my pocket and pulled out the roll of TUMS. *Can you just fucking inject them straight into my veins, Universe?*

"Come on," Dana said, and I hadn't realized I'd just been standing there, staring.

I followed her through the crowd, and when we reached the shoe counter, Eli gave me a wide grin and said, "Have you ever had a broken bone?"

"What?" I stole a glance at Bailey, who was watching me with a tiny crinkle between her eyebrows.

"I was just saying to Bay that the way you chomp down antacids must give you superstrong bones, right? With all the calcium?" he said, and Dana gave a little chuckle of support. "As long as I've known you, chomping those TUMS."

"I'm sad to report that I've broken two fingers, a wrist, and an elbow," I said, my face getting hot. "So your theory is shit."

We all laughed as the four of us got our shoes and went to our lane, and I tried to ignore the way Eli's comment made me feel, because I didn't need a fucking acid reflux spiral. I'd had an appointment with Dr. Bitz that morning, and even though I felt like a child when she kept repeating, *There is nothing wrong with you, Charlie; it's just the way your body reacts to stress*, I found myself replaying it in my head.

I kept trying with Dana, but I felt zero interest from her whatsoever. It seemed like she was way more into hanging out with Bailey and Eli than getting to know me, which I was absolutely fine with.

Meanwhile, Bailey looked like she was trying really hard with Eli, and I *hated* that.

I hated that she was trying hard, because what did that mean?

But most of all, I hated that it was making me so fucking jealous.

CHAPTER THIRTY-NINE

Bailey

Why did Charlie have to wear that T-shirt?

I sat there at the scorer's table beside Eli, clueless as to what to say to the guy because we literally had nothing in common and struggled to get past one-word answers. But every time Charlie bowled and stretched out upon release, a tiny strip of skin between the top of his jeans and the bottom of his shirt was exposed. It was nothing risqué—at all—but it reminded me of how shredded he was, of how hot he'd looked, shirtless, when we'd FaceTimed so he could talk to his cat.

It reminds me of how it felt being close to him.

Charlie got a strike, then turned and walked toward our little seating area.

"Looks like he's forging a comeback," I said to Eli, watching Charlie walk off the lane.

"Yeah," he replied, also staring out at the lane.

"You're up," Charlie said to Dana, giving her a teasing smile. "But maybe try to knock the pins *down* this time."

"Haha," she said, smiling back as him as she stood and walked toward the ball return. "Cocky words coming from the man who currently has a sixty-seven."

Why was her flirting so irritating? I *wanted* her to like Charlie, but did she have to be so . . . so . . . giggly?

It was giving me a stomachache.

"I'm holding back to make you look good," he announced. "You're *welcome*, Dana."

She giggled at that, and I needed one of Charlie's TUMS.

"And you're welcome to polish my ball when I'm done," she retorted, lifting her chin and giving him a smile that made my fingers clench.

God, could the date get any more annoying?

Twenty minutes later, I realized the answer to that question was HELL YES.

"I cannot believe you were at that show," Eli said, smiling and showing his very perfect teeth. "What a small world."

"Right?" Dana said, laughing as she picked up her soda. She was almost as tall as Eli as she stood beside him and said, "There were only like fifty people in the place, tops. What are the odds we were both there?"

"You're up, E," Charlie said, sitting at the scorer's spot beside me. He muttered under his breath, "More bowl, less talk."

I watched my date, my tall and handsome date, pick up a ball and get ready to approach the lane.

"Don't trip again," Dana teased, which made him turn

around and give her an adorable fake glare.

He bowled a strike, and when he came back, Charlie said, "Take my spot."

Eli sat down beside me to take over scoring, and Charlie said, "Hey, Eli—did I tell you that Bailey used to live in Alaska, too?"

Eli looked at me. "You did? Where are you from?"

"Fairbanks," I said.

"Ah—I lived on Eielson Air Force Base," he said, pointing to himself. "Practically neighbors."

"Cool," I replied, nodding.

And then we both smiled and looked at the lanes in front of us.

Think, you idiot—think of something interesting to say. Eli seemed cool, and I needed to get my shit together so I could forget about the way Charlie made me feel.

Charlie knocked down eight pins, and I asked Eli, "Do you ever go back?"

"No," he said, and then he looked over his shoulder and said, "You're next, Dana—better start getting pumped."

"To kick your ass?" She smiled and said, "Yeah, I'm already on it."

Dammit. Since the minute Dana and Eli had teamed up to mock Charlie when he dropped his ball, there had been a super-flirty vibe between those two. It seemed like no matter what I said, or whatever hilarious thing Charlie did, those two only had attention for each other.

I wanted to scream, *Look at ME, Eli!*

Charlie went again and hit two pins, but when he turned

around, I was the only one watching. Eli was gesturing for Dana to go, and she did some sort of adorably dramatic bow that made him laugh loudly.

"Your friend is totally falling for me," Charlie murmured dryly as he walked by and went over to his drink.

I got up and followed him, since Eli was so into trash-talking with Dana.

I made sure neither of them was looking before I said, "Eli has zero interest in me, by the way."

"Yeah, I noticed," he said. "I wouldn't take it personally, though; your little buddy didn't even laugh when I told her about the butter."

"What?" He'd dropped butter on the floor that morning, and then stepped on it, slipped and fell, and somehow ended up with butter in his eye. I'd cried actual tears when he'd told me the hilarious story. "I think these two are wanks for not being into us."

"Same."

"Still try, though," I said, watching Dana throw her head back and laugh at Eli. "She's really great, and I think you'd hit it off. Y'know . . . if Eli weren't here."

He looked at me like I was deranged, but said, "I'll try. And E loves the Chicago Cubs. Maybe talk about that and lure him in."

"You think I need baseball to get a guy?"

He just gave me a look.

"That's insulting," I whined, elbowing him in the ribs ever so lightly. "Maybe I should give him a taste of the Bailey Special."

That made his eyes smile, even though his mouth didn't move. "Cow tongue on toasted bread?"

I lowered my voice, leaned a little closer, and said, "No. It's Moldova but with my hands on his chest."

I expected him to laugh.

Instead, he leaned even closer—or maybe I imagined it—and his eyes were on my mouth when he said, "Don't you fucking dare."

My heart fluttered in my chest at the intensity of his gaze as he towered over me.

"You don't want me to kiss him?" I asked in a near whisper, my breath stuck in my lungs.

"Your call on that." His jaw clenched—flex, unflex—and then he said, "But Moldova is mine."

"You're up, Charlie," Eli yelled.

I blinked fast as we stepped apart and the sounds of the bowling alley returned to my ears.

What the hell was that?

Charlie's face changed then, the intensity sliding into a measured smirk, and he said, "Time to go bowl some strikes and strike out at love."

He walked over to the ball return, leaving me and my entire body thrumming with energy.

After the game, the four of us went into the snack bar for dinner. Charlie and Eli were laughing about some guy they knew as we waited for our baskets of bowling alley food when Dana pulled me aside.

"So . . . do you like Eli?" She looked toward the guys, then back at me. "He is so funny and cute—you're lucky Charlie set you up with him."

"Yeah," I said. "I honestly haven't really talked to him much so far."

She nodded and glanced—yet again—at Eli and Charlie.

"So what do you think of Charlie?" I asked. "Cute, right?"

"Yeah," she said, shrugging. "I mean, he's cool, but I don't really feel like there's a spark."

I looked over at Charlie and remembered his face when he'd been gazing at Becca at that party, the sad smile, and I didn't want him to get rejected his first time back out there. Especially when his friends acted like he'd been a hermit since getting dumped.

"He's so hilarious when you get to know him—give him a chance."

"I don't want to let him think there's a chance when there isn't."

"No, I know." I sighed, realizing that would be worse. "Sorry. He's just my friend, and I wanted to find someone for him."

"I think it's cool how close you are," Dana said. "I'd love to have a guy friend."

I gave Charlie another glance, and as he smiled his smart-ass grin, looking cute in his jeans and long-sleeve tee, I wondered if he'd been right all along. Was it possible to just be friends? Because as I watched him, it was definitely more than friendship I was feeling.

Dammit.

We went back to the table, and the rest of the night pretty much went like bowling. Charlie and I tried showcasing each other, but our dates seemed to be equally disinterested in each of us.

I mentioned the Chicago Cubs, but when Eli said *Are you a Cubs fan?* and I said no, it dissolved into just another awkward attempt at lame small talk.

At the end of the night, as we put on our jackets and gave back the bowling shoes, Dana said to me, "I have to go pick up my car tonight from the shop on Blondo where it got new tires, and I totally don't feel like it."

"I live on Blondo," Eli volunteered, his eyes lighting up like her freshly tired car was the greatest news he'd ever heard. "I can drop you on my way home, if you want."

Dana's face brightened. "Seriously?"

"But you said you'd go with me to Target after bowling," I whined.

"I'm sure Charlie will," Eli said, giving me the metaphorical boot. "Right, Charlie?"

Talk about feeling like an unattractive loser.

"Sure," he said, his eyes on me like he was trying to figure out how I felt about the brush-off. "I want to go see my cat anyway; now I can bring him a toy."

Dana and Eli looked beside themselves with joy as they said goodbye and headed for his car. Charlie and I, on the other hand, walked to his car in silence, each of us lost in our own thoughts. When we got to the vehicle, he said, "Did we seriously *both* get ditched by our dates?"

I stopped as he hit unlock. "Looks that way."

Charlie said, "Did Dana tell you what she said when I asked her about college?"

"No."

"I asked if she was going away or staying local. You know, just to show an interest in her life, right?"

I nodded. "Right . . . ?"

He gave me a funny eye roll. "She said, and I quote, *I'm not looking for a relationship right now.*"

"Shut *up!*" I opened the passenger door and climbed inside the car. "That seems so arrogant, to assume that *you* are, with her."

"And it didn't even answer the question. I still have no idea if she's going to MCC, Harvard, or Clown U, for fuck's sake."

I tried not to laugh.

"And," he said, smiling just a little, "since it's considered rude to shout WHO ASKED YOU TO in someone's face, I had to keep it all inside my tiny heart."

I did start laughing then. "*Who asked you to*—great line."

"It was either that or *Get the hell out of my bowling alley.*"

I was cracking up as he started the car and pulled out of the parking lot. "I mean, at least she addressed you. I was pretty much invisible to Eli all night long."

"I think she spelled him," Charlie said.

"What?"

"Remember those *Descendants* movies? Where Mal spelled King Ben and made him fall in love with her?" He pulled his phone out of his pocket and said, "I bet Dana did that to Eli."

"Because that's the only logical explanation, right?"

"Exactly." Charlie clicked into the Bluetooth to play his music and said, "By the way, since no one loves us and we have no prospects, do you want to go to our fall formals together?"

That made me snap my head toward him. "Are you serious right now?"

Was he serious? He wanted to go to both dances *together*? I'd been working so hard at knocking down my Charlie feelings; could I do the whole formal wear thing with him and not totally lose myself?

He nodded and said, "Sure. It's senior year, so my mom will have a heart attack if I don't go. I'm not into anyone, so at least if I go with you and vice versa, we know we'll have fun, right?"

It sounded reasonable.

Reasonable, and like a recipe for a broken heart. So of course I said, "Sure. Yeah."

You're an idiot, Bailey.

"Cool," he said, the same way he'd respond if I told him I wanted to stop at the gas station to use the restroom.

He turned onto L Street, and I wondered if it'd even entered his mind, the concept that I might be into him. He acted like nothing had changed between us since Colorado; did he truly believe that?

"By the way, I totally loved those movies when I was little," I said, trying to be normal while visions of tuxedoed Charlie danced in my head.

"*Descendants*?" He grinned and said, "It's probably uncool for me to admit, but so did I. The song with Mal and her dad was a banger."

I was laughing when I said, "Did you really just say 'banger'? And mean it in regard to 'Do What You Gotta Do'?"

He gave a deep laugh and leaned back a little to dig into his pocket. "Baybay knows the name of the song. What a wank."

"*You're* a wank."

"A wank who knows every word to that banger," he said, grabbing an antacid tablet as I laughed at him.

That cracked me up, even as I agreed that I did too.

We stopped at Target on the way home, and Charlie made it an altogether different experience than it would've been with Dana.

For starters, he bought hot popcorn at the stand in the front of the store, because according to him, shopping was more fun with snacks. I was barely paying attention while he ordered, just people watching, but then I heard him ask for two small popcorns—one buttered, one plain—and then he asked for the bucket that the large came in so he could mix them together.

"I cannot believe you remember that," I said in a low voice, mostly because the snack attendant looked super pissed about the request.

The smile he gave me, along with those crinkling dark eyes, pinched my heart just a little. "Who could forget about all of Glasses's little quirks?"

The moment held for a half second, him smiling down at me while I grinned back, and then it changed. It felt like we were having some intimate exchange as we stared into each other's eyes, and memories of his kisses immediately flooded into my mind.

320

"I'm out of buckets—is a big bag okay?" asked the attendant.

My head whipped around, and I realized my heart was pounding.

"That's great, thanks," Charlie said, and when he turned to me, his face was calm. Like he *hadn't* felt what I'd felt.

What the hell? He *had* to have felt it, right?

God, was I losing all ability to read chemistry?

"What are we here for, anyway?" he asked.

The whole reason I wanted to stop at Target was because there was a dress on clearance I had non-buyer's remorse about. I told him about it, and as we grabbed a cart so he had something to lean on while we walked, he convinced me to try it on and get his opinion.

I took it into a fitting room, and one second after I closed the door, a piece of popcorn landed on my head. I brushed it off, reached for the button on my jeans, and said, "Knock it off, Sampson."

"I don't like being bored," he said from his spot somewhere outside my door, "and shooting for your little room gives me a challenge."

Another piece of popcorn fell onto the bench beside me.

I picked it up and tossed it over the wall. "Was I close?"

"That was weak, Mitchell," he said. "If I were you, I'd stand on that bench and get a visual. That way you've got a better shot of hitting me."

"You're just trying to get me to look like an idiot, standing on the bench and peeking over like a child," I said, wondering how Charlie could be so much more fun than everyone else.

As I wondered that, a piece of popcorn landed on my head. Again.

I changed into the dress while popcorn rained down on me, and then I stepped up onto the bench.

And when I looked over the door, he was standing right beside it. Like, actually leaning on it.

"That's not a challenge." I laughed, surprised to be looking down at his upturned face. "You're basically just dropping them into my room because you're a giant. Lazy."

"Come out and show me your bargain dress," he said, grinning up at me.

"Okay," I said, feeling that familiar *something* as I hopped down and came out of the fitting room.

"I like the dress," he said, his eyes all over me, and then he did a motion with his finger, telling me to spin around.

I did, and he nodded in appreciation. "Reminds me of something a little kid would wear to recess. Buy it."

"I'm not sure that's the aesthetic I was going for," I said, looking at it in the mirror.

"Okay, then—it reminds me of something that would assure a principal that a new student was a nice girl."

"Oh my God," I said, turning to see the back. "I don't think I want this dress anymore."

"Wait, wait, wait," he said, tilting his head a little and crossing his arms. "I've got it. It looks like something the weird best friend would wear in a rom-com."

"If you're trying to convince me to buy it, you suck at this," I said, going back into the fitting room to change.

"I am *begging* you to buy it," he said, and my heart nearly stopped at the growly sound of his voice. I stood there, frozen in front of the mirror, overanalyzing his comments as was my new normal.

"Is that what that was?" I asked slowly, trying to sound careless and light.

"You know what it was," he said, sounding almost . . . defeated by the words.

What did that mean? Did he like me in the dress and not want to? Because he didn't want to lead me on, or because he didn't want to feel things?

"I'm going to go get the cat toy."

"Um." I blinked at the jarring subject change before pulling the dress over my head. "Okay."

"I'll go to the pet aisle and you can meet me there."

"Sounds good," I said, feeling like he was literally putting distance between us on purpose.

Just as I was opening the fitting room door, my phone buzzed. I fished it out of my bag, fully expecting a message from Charlie about cat toys.

But it was from Zack.

Zack: I have to know. Did you act out Breaking Bad or did you reset your password?

CHAPTER FORTY

Charlie

"Oh my God, Charlie!"

I looked up from the catnip-packed bird in my hand as Bailey was running toward me—literally—and wearing a huge grin. She somehow managed to smile in a way that was both childish (like a six-year-old getting a glimpse of Santa Claus on the roof) and sexy (like a woman who knew exactly what she wanted to do to you), all at the same time.

It made me crazy, swear to God.

"What?" I asked, and then she grabbed both of my arms and gave me a little shake.

"You will not *believe* what just happened, you freaking genius!"

"I like the sound of this," I said, a little disappointed when she let go of my arms.

"He texted," she squealed in a singsong voice. "Zack texted me!"

Huh? That was not what I'd expected her to say, and it felt like I'd just been punched in the stomach. She looked so fucking happy, and the happiness was because her ex had texted her.

Fucking awesome.

"Told you," I said, clearing my throat and trying to ignore the tension flowing through me. "What'd he say?"

She pulled out her phone and read his response, beaming as if she'd never been so happy. "So how should I respond?"

Tell him to go to hell. The guy was clearly a moron and didn't deserve her, but it was better for me if they got back together, wasn't it?

"I'd go with something vague, like *Let's just say you missed one hell of a performance.*"

That made her smile hitch even higher. "That is perfect."

I watched her send the text, making happy puppy sounds that were so adorable, I wanted to hit something, but then she looked up and her smile dropped away. "Wait a second."

"What's wrong?" I asked, torn between being glad she was no longer Zack-beaming and already missing her happy glow.

Her eyes moved over my face, like she was thinking hard. "He has a girlfriend."

I didn't say anything.

"So he shouldn't be texting me if he has a girlfriend, right? And I don't want to be the bitch who's texting someone else's boyfriend."

Bailey's concern-crinkle formed between her eyebrows, and she blinked a little faster.

"Maybe they broke up," I said, trying to make her feel better while hoping—like a total asshole—that it wasn't the case.

"Maybe," she muttered. "I should probably find out."

"Not a bad idea," I replied, knowing I'd lost her. Her mind wasn't with me—with us—anymore. It was with *Zack*.

Why did I suddenly fucking hate that so much?

And as we walked toward the registers, it occurred to me that *holy shit*, they could actually get back together.

Holy. Shit.

In all of the hypotheticals that streamed through my mind on a daily basis, I'd never considered the possibility of it. Not until right now.

And no. No. NO.

What the fuck would that mean for us?

CHAPTER FORTY-ONE

Bailey

"But you've got it under control," Nekesa said with a heavy dose of skepticism, setting her lunch tray on the table and sliding into a seat. "Right?"

"I do." I sat down beside her with my chicken sandwich and said, "It was just another little blip."

"So, let's add shopping at Target to the list of things that give you the Charlie tingles." She looked down at the dress that'd started the whole conversation. "All your little blips."

"It's over now," I assured her, trying to convince both of us. "I was tired that night, bummed about Eli, and touched that he remembered the popcorn. Total fluke trifecta."

It'd been almost a week since we'd gone to Target together, and I'd been totally normal every other time we'd texted and worked together.

"Sure." She opened her milk and said, "Theo knew this would happen, by the way."

"What?" *Freaking Theo.*

"I mean, I haven't told him anything about your actual feelings and what happened in Breckenridge, but he wondered if fake dating would mess up the whole we're-only-friends vibe."

I raised my chin, feeling defensive in the face of Theo's nosy opinion. "Well, he was wrong."

She looked at me with her eyebrows screwed together. "Bay, you *just* said—"

"He. Was. Wrong," I interrupted, holding up a hand.

He *so* wasn't wrong, by the way. The fake dating *had* changed everything. Now Charlie wasn't simply my funny coworker; he was the person I thought about all the time, the person I *wished* would think about *me* all the time.

When I found out Zack *was* still dating his girlfriend, instead of being devastated, I felt only a *little* sad, because I was so Charlie-focused.

Yes, he was the person I had to pretend *not* to have feelings for, because if he found out, it would destroy our just-coworkers status.

"Fine," she said, giving her head a slow shake and reaching for her pizza. "Whatever you say."

"Hey, guys." Dana sat down beside Nekesa, a huge smile on her face. "How's it going?"

For the past week, Dana had been insufferable. She and Eli were gaga for each other, and it was all she could talk about. You could say the sky was blue, and she'd bring up his eye color. You could say garbage smelled, and she would wax poetic about the way Eli's hair smelled.

It was adorable and nauseating, all at once.

"Good," I said, opening my string cheese. "How's life on lovesick island?"

She launched into a gushing story about how she and Eli studied for five hours at Starbucks the night before, and I had to admit that I kind of loved them together. Dana had always been one of my nicest friends—angelically nice to everyone—so it was probably her turn to wear the happy glow.

"Eli said Charlie's mom is going out of town and he might have people over tonight," she said, looking excited. "Are you going?"

Charlie had told me his plan, but he hadn't technically invited me.

Not that I'd go if he had. I'd been working really hard to ignore my superfluous feelings for him, and it just felt like it would be testing that progress if I were to engage with him in yet another new social setting.

Also—if Becca showed and he looked at her like *that*, well, I might just die.

"I doubt it—I don't really know his friends."

"Neither do I," she said, shaking her carton of milk. "But you know me and Eli."

"True. Yeah, maybe," I replied, even though there was no chance of me going.

Zero.

As if he could hear our conversation from his school across town, Charlie texted me an hour later.

Charlie: What're you doing?

Me: Study hall. Reading.

Charlie: Book, please.

I smiled and texted: **The Kingdom of Diamonds and Ash.**

Charlie: I TOLD YOU NOT TO BOTHER!!! It's just royals with magical powers, having sex.

Me: 10/10 would read based off that description.

Charlie: Little pervert.

Me: That's "Lil" pervert, thank you very much.

I still couldn't believe he'd read it. Charlie's mom was a big reader, and when she'd gushed about how great it was, he'd given it a try.

And *hated* it. Ranted to me for twenty minutes last week about how god-awful it was.

I replied: **Reading is subjective. Just because you didn't like it doesn't mean it isn't good.**

Charlie: Sometimes you say the most ridiculous things.

Me: As do you.

Charlie: Btw—if I have people over tonight, you're coming, right?

I looked at the words and felt a tiny thrill that he wanted me to come. Even though he only meant it as a friend, it felt good to know he wanted me there. I texted:

I doubt it. I have to work on my lit paper all weekend.

Charlie: Sometimes you say the most ridiculous things. I'll text you my address.

I wasn't going to go, but his insistence put me in a good mood for the rest of the day.

When I got home from school, my mom was already there, and there was no sign of Scott. She was sitting on the sofa, watching *Poldark* (she'd only just started the series), and when I came in, she grinned.

"Are you off tonight?" she asked, Puffball sound asleep on her chest.

"Yeah—I never work Fridays," I said, slipping off my shoes and leaning down to scratch Mr. Squishy between his ears.

"Yay," she said excitedly. "Scott has something going on tonight, so I thought it might be fun to go out for pizza. Just you and me, like old times."

Nothing had ever sounded better. I dropped my bag and said, "I'm in—let's go."

She looked at the clock. "It's four thirty."

"Fine." I plopped down beside her on the couch and said, "We'll watch two more episodes, and then we're gone."

"Deal."

It was nice, just the two of us. I didn't actually know how long it'd been since we'd had an evening alone, but it felt like comfort and home and everything that was soothing. It was a moment of life unchanged, as if everything new and threatening had been removed from its spot on the horizon, and I wanted to wrap myself in its presence and take a long nap.

We got so sucked into the show that we were surprised by the darkness when we finally turned it off.

"No wonder I'm starving," my mom said as she grabbed her

keys and I put on my shoes. "I haven't eaten since lunch."

"Stupid Ross Poldark," I muttered, which made her head snap up.

"I'm sorry, did you say he's *stupid*?" she asked.

"Oh no." I shook my head, knowing what was coming, as I said, "Yes, I said Ross Poldark is stupid."

She looked at me and grinned, and it was on. The silly, immature game we used to play had returned.

"Ross Poldark is so stupid, he went away to war and left his fiancée with his cousin," she said, locking the door behind us as we left.

"Ross Poldark is *so* stupid," I said as we walked to the car, "that he scythes an entire wheat field in the heat without pulling his hair up into a man bun."

"Ross Poldark is so stupid," she said as she merged onto the interstate, "that he tells his wife where he's going when he sleeps with his ex."

When we got to Zio's, we grabbed a table in the back room, by the big fireplace, and ordered our pizza. It felt so good, so relaxed, to be 100 percent myself because no one else was with us.

It was weird how you could spend a lot of time with someone, but if it wasn't one-on-one, it wasn't the same. It felt like it'd been *ages* since I'd hung out with my mom, even though I spent time with her every single night.

Because Scott was always there.

He didn't *do* anything wrong when he came over, but his presence changed the vibe so much that it was unrecognizable.

I'd missed this so much.

I knew it was melodramatic, but I felt like I could breathe around my mom for the first time in so long.

"Did your dad tell you he's moving?" she asked.

"What?" I hadn't meant to say it so loudly, but I couldn't believe what I was hearing. He was moving?

I looked at my mom, and her expression said it all. He was moving and just hadn't gotten around to telling me yet. I wasn't sure what was more depressing—the fact that I might never go into my childhood home again, or the fact that my father hadn't even thought to tell me.

"He sold the house and is moving to an apartment in the city—you seriously didn't know?"

I shook my head and felt numb as I pictured the living room where Santa had left my Barbie house when I was six and where my parents had laughed hysterically—together—as I screamed with joy. "No."

"I thought he would've told you right away," she said, looking concerned. "When was the last time you talked to him?"

"Um, like, a few months ago . . . ?"

"What?" She looked instantly worried and leaned a little closer. "Did you two have a disagreement or something? How come it's been so long?"

"No argument," I said, trying to act like I wasn't freaking out inside. "I just, um, I was always the one calling him first, so I decided to let him take the lead. You know, I figured I'd wait until he called."

"And he hasn't called in months? Oh, honey." My mom came

around the table, sat down in the chair beside me, and gave me a side hug. "What the hell is the matter with him?"

I shrugged and didn't know what to say, but telling her somehow made his absence better. Less painful. She was part of our trio, so she knew him, knew *us*, which made it feel like she knew exactly how bad it felt.

"Surprise!"

Gahhh! I put my hand on my chest, startled, and looked away from my mom's understanding gaze to see Scott, grinning at us like it'd been years since he'd seen us. He was wearing a suit and tie, all dressed up, and it felt clownish because he'd interrupted something important.

What in the ever-loving hell?

I gritted my teeth, overcome with bitterness that he was there. The most we'd been able to enjoy was a few random hours before Scott was back in our lives.

My mom let go of me and squealed, also like she hadn't seen *him* in an age, and she excitedly asked, "What are you doing here?"

"I wanted some pizza," he said, still with the huge smile.

"Oh my gosh—sit down," she said, so happy to see him. "There's plenty of room."

I watched in disappointment as Scott grabbed the chair across from my mom.

"Okay," he said, sitting down. "If you insist."

He called over the waiter and ordered a bottle of wine, yammering about how it was his new favorite vintage because it reminded him of the night we'd gone to the steakhouse in

Breckenridge. "It was such a special night to me because I had an epiphany while we were eating."

I pictured Charlie and me, ruining each other's food at that restaurant.

"What was it?" my mom asked, setting her chin on her hand.

"I looked at our table," he said, lowering his voice so it was soft and sweet, "where every person was laughing, and I realized that was all I needed to be happy forever."

Spare me, I thought.

"Of course, an hour later I knocked you on your ass on the ice," my mom said, laughing. "So perhaps it was a premature epiphany."

They shared a cute laugh, and I got out my phone, preferring to scroll mindlessly instead of listening to them enjoy each other's company.

I knew I was being a baby but it just sucked.

We'd been having a great time without him.

Now *they* were having a great time without me.

"Bailey."

"Huh?" I raised my eyes.

Scott smiled and said, "Can I borrow your attention for a quick sec?"

"Um, yeah. Sure." *Isn't it enough that you've stolen hers?* I raised my eyebrows and said, "What's up?"

"Well, here's the thing." Scott grabbed my mom's hand, so he was holding it on the table, and he looked at her. "Emily."

Why the hell did he bother me when he's talking to my mom?

He leaned a little closer to her, smiling as he said, "My life hasn't been the same since I met you. Everything is brighter, louder, happier. My daughter taught me what joy is, but you, Emily—you've amplified that joy. A thousand times over."

Wait.

My ears started buzzing and I felt a little dizzy. *No, no, no, no, no, no, no.*

There was absolutely no way this was what it sounded like, especially when they hadn't even been dating very long.

NO.

My heart started pounding when he got out of his chair, dropped to one knee, pulled a box out of his pocket, and extended it toward my mother.

This can't be happening.

God, please, no. *Please don't do it.*

"Will you marry me?"

It felt like the breath was sucked out of my lungs when he said it. My hand raised to my mouth as my mom's eyes filled with tears and she smiled like this was everything she'd ever wanted. I blinked fast, and everything in the restaurant got blurry.

Please say no, I thought, my heart breaking in my chest as he smiled at her with tears in his eyes.

"Yes," she said, laughing and crying, and my chest ached as he took a ring out of the box and slid it onto her finger. "Oh my God!"

He got up and they hugged as people around us clapped, and I had the weird sensation of being all alone in the world. Logically I knew that wasn't the case, but the pinch in my heart and the homesickness in my stomach said otherwise.

I sat there, numb, as the wheels on yet another new life started turning. For the rest of my life, it would be my mom and Scott.

"Can you believe it?" my mom asked, pulling out of the hug to grin at me and hold out her hand.

"I can't," I said, shaking my head and working really hard to come up with a smile. I grabbed my bag from the back of my chair and slung it over my shoulder. "I forgot that I have to go—I have a thing with Charlie. I'll catch up to you at home, okay?"

"What?" my mom asked, her smile dimming just a little. "You're leaving?"

"I just have to do something," I said, blinking back tears while giving her a big smile. "But you stay and celebrate. Congratulations, you guys!"

I headed for the exit, walking as fast as I could because I didn't want to break down and ruin her night.

Somehow, I managed to wait until I turned the corner into a Walgreens before sobbing hysterically.

CHAPTER FORTY-TWO

Charlie

"Check it out," Eli said, opening the cabinet where Clark kept his booze.

"Duuuuude." Austin got a shitty grin on his face as he pointed to the bottle of Jack. "What the fuck is this?"

"Don't even think about it." I reached over his head and slammed the cupboard door. "That belongs to the douche, and I'd rather have my nails plucked out than listen to one of his lectures."

My phone buzzed, and I pulled it out of my pocket.

Bailey: Is there any way you can come get me?

I hated how happy that made me, knowing she was coming to the party. I hopped onto the counter and texted: **I suppose. Where's your car, Glasses?**

Austin pulled a twelve-pack out of his baseball bag and put it in the fridge, and I wondered just how many people those two had told about the party.

Bailey: I'm at the Walgreens on 132nd and Center. I walked here because while my mom and I were having dinner at Zio's, Scott showed up and PROPOSED.

Holy shit, holy shit. I texted: **Did she give him an answer?**

Please don't say yes, I thought.

Bailey: She said yes.

I sent: **Fuuuck. You okay, Mitchell?**

She wasn't; I knew she wasn't. Even though I couldn't see her, I knew exactly what Bailey's face looked like at that moment, and it broke my heart.

Bailey: I ran out of the restaurant and now I'm bawling in the pharmacy, begging you for a ride home. That's okay, right?

Ah. She wasn't texting because she wanted a ride to my party; she was texting because she needed to be rescued.

Made sense.

I pulled my keys from my pocket and got off the counter. Typed: **Absolutely it is. Hang tight—I'm on my way.**

"Party's off," I said as I slid the phone into my jeans, not making eye contact with either of my friends. "I have to go now."

"What?" Austin asked, his voice rising in disbelief. "You're kidding, right?"

"No way, bro," Eli said, shaking his head and pointing at my chest. "What the hell happened? You are *not* backing out, you fucking hermit. We've already called everyone."

"I have to, it's an emergency," I said, having zero intention of telling them about Bailey. "And I have to go *now*. Let's just move it to tomorrow night."

"Fuck *me*," Austin muttered in disgust. "I can't believe you're doing this. Is this about Becca?"

"What?" I asked, watching the play of emotion on Austin's face. He knew he was out of line with that comment, but I could tell he meant it. "What would it have to do with *her*?"

He shrugged and said in a quieter voice, "You tell me."

"She texts, and you jump," Eli said, holding up his hands in the universal *I'm innocent* pose. "I'm not trying to be the asshole here, but it's what you do."

I kind of wanted to hit him, because he *was* being the asshole, but he was also not wrong.

"I really have to go," I said, walking past them as I headed for the front door. "Come on. I'll give you money for alternate plans and we'll do it tomorrow."

"This is such bullshit," Eli growled, sounding almost pouty as he opened the fridge, presumably to grab his beer. "Where the hell am I supposed to take Dana now?"

CHAPTER FORTY-THREE

Bailey

Charlie pulled up in front of Walgreens, and when I got into his car, he immediately gave me a pitying smile. "Awww, Glasses, your face breaks my heart."

I knew my makeup was a little smudged, but his reaction told me how much worse it was than I'd imagined. I'd been so numb as I'd killed time in the pharmacy, waiting for him, that it hadn't occurred to me to pull out my phone and check my face.

"Thank you for coming to get me," I said, closing the door and staring out the window as it started raining.

"Thank you for getting me out of the house," he replied, putting the car in drive. "I was bored as hell, but now I have someone to play with."

"Wait—weren't you having people over tonight?"

"Tomorrow," he said, turning up the radio.

We went to his apartment, and I was glad he let me be silent on the drive there. I knew I was being irrational and emotionally childish, and I'd maybe spoiled what should've been an amazing moment for my mom by leaving, but I didn't want to have a logical discussion about it.

I felt crushed. It was silly, because the world wasn't ending and no one was dying; people's parents got remarried all the time.

But I was devastated.

It probably meant that I was an immature child, but every time I thought about the fact that my mother was getting married, a heavy weight settled on my chest. It was suffocating, this panic that I had about the life changes I could no longer avoid.

I looked out at the night through the wiper blades moving across the windshield and wondered how long I had before everything started, before the tiny fragment that was left of my family was going to be erased and changed into something new.

I took in a shaky breath as I remembered that my dad was moving. On top of this, my dad and his new person were moving out of the old and into the new. It felt like the world was crumbling and changing under my feet, and there was nothing I could do to slow it down.

I wasn't a child; I knew I'd adjust to leaving the old behind.

But dammit, I wasn't ready to let go of it.

Of *us*.

Of life as I knew it.

Very soon—it might've happened tonight, actually—the roles would shift. It would no longer be her and me, with the rest of the world as something we navigated. It would be her and *him*, and I would be part of what *they* navigated together, as partners.

When we pulled up in front of the building, Charlie came around to my side of the car and crouched down to the ground.

"What're you doing?" I asked, not really in the mood for silliness.

"Giving you a piggyback ride." He looked at me over his shoulder, his face earnest and sweet, and said, "Hop on, Bay."

I hesitated, but then I thought, *What the hell.*

I climbed onto his back, and it felt good. Wrapping myself around Charlie's big body felt comforting because it was like he literally—and emotionally—*had* me. He hauled me up the stairs, and I closed my eyes, resting my cheek on his strong back.

Thank you, Charlie.

Once we were inside his apartment, he carried me over to the sofa and dropped me on top of it. Before I could say a word, he looked down at me and said, "This is how tonight's gonna go. You ready?"

That made me feel like smiling. "Ready."

"I'm going to make a blanket fort in front of the TV, wherein I will entertain you with a marathon of my favorite terrible movies. We will eat garbage, have ice cream brought to us from DoorDash like we're fucking kings, and we will not speak of things that shan't be spoken of. Got it?"

I did smile then, even though his kindness sort of made me want to cry. "Got it."

At that moment, the tiniest little white dog I'd ever seen

hopped up onto the couch. I hadn't even heard him before that moment, yet—there he was.

"Hey, puppy," I said, reaching out a hand and petting his small head.

"Bailey, meet the Undertaker."

I looked up at Charlie. "You're kidding me. That tiny thing is the Undertaker?"

He just shrugged and walked away.

He went into the hallway to get blankets, and when he was there, he yelled, "Hey, what's your mom's number?"

I sighed, letting the dog climb onto my lap as I pictured my mom's surprised face as I ditched her. "Seems like a creepy question."

"I just want to text that you're crashing here so she doesn't worry," he said. "And so you don't have to do it yourself."

I hadn't thought far ahead enough to consider crashing at Charlie's apartment, but I was too depressed to overthink it. I gave him the number and sighed. What was I going to do? I mean, obviously I had no choice regarding my mother's marital status, but would I actually have to *live* with him and his kid? Would we move into Scott's house?

Would I have to share a room with his daughter?

I felt the tears coming back as I thought about moving into a strange house with people I barely knew.

"Glasses." Charlie came back into the living room with an armful of blankets, and he said, "Ditch the shoes and the dog, go get snacks in the kitchen, and when you come back, I'll be ready for you."

"Okay." I took off my coat and shoes and went into the kitchen, impressed by Charlie's apartment. It was *way* nicer than ours, and the pantry was full of good snacks. I grabbed Twizzlers, Vic's popcorn, a twelve-pack of Diet Pepsi, and a box of Twinkies.

When I came out, Charlie did an elaborate "Ta-da" reveal of his construction work. He'd used kitchen chairs and storage cubes to make a large portion of the living room into a fort. I watched him as he put two fluffy pillows inside, along with two down comforters.

"You made a floor bed?" I asked, blown away by this sweetness.

He crawled out and looked at my very full hands. "Nice selections, Glasses."

"Thank you," I said, pushing up my glasses with my wrist.

"You may enter my blanket fort." Charlie pointed with both hands, gesturing like he was Vanna White with a prize package.

"You're too kind."

We climbed into the fort and piled the snacks between us as we stretched out on the blankets. In spite of my tumultuous emotions, I was very aware that I was lying down next to Charlie.

Been there, done that.

"So the first selection is one of my awful favorites. *Napoleon Dynamite.*"

"Oh my God."

"I know." He turned on the movie and immediately launched into hilarious commentary that had me cracking up, even more so than I usually did when I watched that movie (it was one of my awful favorites too). We shared snacks as we watched, and he almost made me forget about everything.

When the doorbell rang, Charlie crawled out of the fort and collected our ice cream. A quart of vanilla for Charlie, a quart of chocolate for me, and we lay under the blankets and dug into that stash.

"So, Glasses. You okay?" he asked, his eyes on my face as he held a spoonful of ice cream in front of his mouth.

"Yes," I said.

"Really?"

"Yes."

"Really?"

"Here's the thing," I said, licking off my spoon and feeling my throat get tight again. "Unless he wants to move into our apartment and not live with his daughter, I'm *not* going to be okay."

He swallowed. "I get that."

"Like, how do you do that?" I said, my voice frog-like as I imagined it. "How do you get okay with moving into someone else's house with people you don't really know?"

He didn't answer, but just nodded and let me vent while we ate ice cream.

"And speaking of moving—my dad is moving and failed to tell me. So, like, how do you *forget* to tell your child that you're moving? Even if it was a-okay to never call her, wouldn't she pop into your head when you're telling your ex-wife or packing up her old bedroom?"

Charlie held up his spoon. "Listen. You know I'm all about

being stubborn, but maybe you should call your dad," Charlie said, dipping his spoon back into his ice cream and digging out another scoopful. "He might be a good person to talk to about all of this."

"It's lame," I said, "but I think if I hear his voice, I'll get, like, toddler-level emotional."

"Is that so bad?" he asked, giving me just the kindest, sweetest eye contact.

My vision was blurry again, so I blinked fast and changed the subject. "We should mix. Gimme a scoop of vanilla."

He looked offended. "You want me to share?"

I scooped some chocolate out of my container, then dropped it into Charlie's. "Here. We'll *both* share."

"Not so fast." He grabbed my forearm in his big hand and said with faux outrage, "What if I don't want your scoop?"

"Oh, you want it," I teased, lifting my chin. "It's all you can think about now. You are *obsessed* with how badly you want it."

His eyes dipped down to my mouth as his lips kicked up at the corners. "You little ice cream tease."

I opened my mouth to say *How can I be a tease when I'm giving it to you*—and then I froze.

God, leave it to Charlie to make me forget everything and flirt with him.

He looked at my lips again, like he was thinking hard, and then he said, "Quit distracting me—I'm missing the movie."

At around three, after too much ice cream and two more movies, I looked over and he was sound asleep. He looked sweet—which was quite a stretch from his normal state. His eyes were closed, those long lashes resting on his skin, and his forehead was clear of worry lines.

His mouth was soft, his jaw relaxed, and I wished I could stay in that silly fort of blankets and never come out.

I rolled over and pulled up my blanket. If Charlie was asleep, I might as well sleep, too.

Only it wasn't that easy.

I closed my eyes, but every time I did, the worries about my life and how it was about to change wouldn't stop.

Now that they are engaged, will they want to move in together immediately?

How long until they get married?

Will they go on a honeymoon and leave me to stay home alone with a new stepsibling who's a stranger?

Will I have to meet Scott's parents? Will they want to be my grandparents?

I opened my eyes, but then I just stared at the TV-illuminated wall—and *kept* thinking. Because no matter how much I wanted to just think things like *Everything will be fine* and hope for the best, the reality was that everything I'd worried about was now happening.

I reached for my phone—beside my pillow, where I'd ignored it the entire time I'd been at Charlie's—and flipped it over. I had six unread messages, and I sighed as I clicked into them.

The first five were from my mom:

I love you, Bay—we'll figure this out.

Call me. I love you.

I talked to Charlie and I'm glad you're safe.

I miss you—text or call if you want to talk.

I couldn't read the last one because my eyes were full of tears. I knew I was a baby, an immature pathetic loser, because all I wanted was to cry into my mom's shoulder at that moment.

I wiped my eyes and saw that the other message was from my dad.

Your mom thought you might need to talk. Call or text anytime, Bay—I love you.

I dropped the phone onto the carpet as the tears took over. Even as I knew it was silly, I couldn't stop crying. I lay there in the quiet darkness of the blanket fort, overwhelmed with homesickness—for him, for her, for the family we'd once been. They'd been divorced for years, yet I still felt this gaping hole of grief as life kept changing itself up on me, kept finding new ways to make me melancholy and wistful.

When was I going to be fine with everything?

"Bay."

I felt Charlie's hand on my back, but I didn't want to turn over. It was one thing for him to see me a teensy bit emotional in Colorado, but it was another entirely for him to see me bawling my eyes out. I cleared my throat and tried to sound normal. "Yeah?"

"Roll over."

I sniffled. "I don't want to."

I heard a smile in his voice when he said, "Come on."

I wiped at my eyes with the edge of the blanket and turned over. Charlie was propped up on one arm, so he was higher than me, and I said, "Can you not look at me?"

That made half of his mouth slide upward. "But you look hot with blotchy cheeks and red eyes. I can't take my eyes off you."

I rolled my eyes and coughed out a laugh. "You're such a jerk."

His smile went away and he said, "You shouldn't be crying alone in the dark. You should've woken me up."

"Yeah, sure—I can see it now. *Hey, Charlie—wake up. I'm about to bawl like a baby—you don't want to miss this.*"

Now *he* rolled *his* eyes. "You know what I mean."

I didn't say anything.

"I'm here for you," he said, his face serious in our darkened fort of blankets. "That's what friends are for."

That made me smile. "Holy shit, Charlie—did you just admit that you have friend feelings for me? That I'm not just a coworker?"

His jaw clenched and his eyes traveled all over my face. "Maybe."

"I want you to say it," I teased. "Say 'I have friend feelings for you, Bailey.'"

His eyes were on mine as he said, "I might possibly have feelings for you that are more than coworkerly."

I swallowed, unable to tear my gaze from his. Had he worded it that way on purpose? Was it possible that Charlie actually *did* have feelings for me? Every time we'd shared a "moment," he'd followed it up with something that let me know he wasn't into me.

But . . . was there a chance he *was*? I managed to breathe out the word "Yeah?"

He reached out a hand and toyed with my hoodie string, and I swear to God I felt it in the center of my chest. His eyes stayed on that string when he said, "Yeah."

My heart was in serious jeopardy of pounding out of my chest.

I said, "I thought it was just me."

"It's not," he said, and his dark eyes moved to my lips.

I held my breath as he lowered his head, as the air in the blanket fort got thick and heavy with anticipation. I watched his long lashes as his eyes closed and his mouth landed on mine. I sighed as his Charlie-ness enveloped me and I raised my hands to his face, my fingers memorizing the warmth and softness of his skin.

He made a noise as my fingertips moved on his cheeks, reminding me of his kissing feedback in Colorado. *I like feeling your hands on me when I kiss you.* Talk about a heady awareness.

The pillow was soft under my head as his body hovered along the length of mine, leaning over me, and it felt like his mouth remembered everything and picked up right where we'd left off on the pullout bed in Breckenridge.

His lips were warm, his mouth still sweet from the ice cream as he kissed me. It was slow and deep, catch and release, his tongue and teeth delivering kisses bit by bit, taste by taste.

I could hear the shake in his breath—it matched my own— as his hand released my hoodie string and braced itself on the floor.

The movement brought our bodies closer, put him more directly above me, and I liked it. There was something about the feeling of Charlie stretched out over me that hinted of things to come, things that thrilled me at the very same time they made me nervous.

I moved my hands, wrapping them around his shoulders, which brought his hand closer to me, so he was braced directly above me on his arms. He lifted his mouth off mine, and I opened my eyes, and Charlie looked *hot*, a lock of his hair hanging over his brow as his dark eyes blazed down at me.

The moment hovered, as if someone had said *On your mark, get set*, and then his mouth came back to mine, busier and more insistent. I ran my hands over his back as he kissed me, memorizing the muscular ridges of his shoulder blades with sliding fingertips.

Our mouths got hotter, our breathing more labored, as my hands trailed down to his lower back. I didn't know how a lower back could feel sexy—intimate—when he was still wearing a shirt, but it felt full-on sexual as I ran my hands over the spot where he probably had those lower-back dimples.

I was basically panting as he bent his arms, dropping to what was essentially a plank—a plank that brought our bodies flush together. I could hear my erratic breathing—it sounded loud to me in the blanket fort—as I felt all of him against all of me.

I might've made a noise, and then he moved his mouth down to my neck, burying his head in the side of my collar. I felt his teeth and tongue on my throat, which made me rear up against him in shock, shock that brought our bodies back together with an electric current.

And then—

"We should stop," he whispered, his breath hot in my ear, his teeth on my earlobe.

My eyes were heavy as I forced them open, and he looked

like pure temptation as he stared down at me with brown eyes gleaming underneath disheveled hair, hair messed by my grasping fingers. I sighed out the word "What?"

His warm breath was on my collarbone as he said, "Last night was kind of emotional, and I don't want it to feel like I'm taking advantage of that."

"But you're not," I said, memorizing the feel of his body pressing mine into the floor, of our bodies together leaving an invisible imprint in the soft down of Charlie's floor bed. "This is separate."

"I cannot believe I'm saying this," he said, his voice deep and scratchy, "but I think it's best if we both get some sleep and revisit this another time with more level heads."

He kissed me sweetly, dropping a peck on my lips that felt like an intimate promise, and I nodded. "You're right."

"God, I love when you say that," he teased, grinning down at me.

"You just love me in general," I teased back, lifting a finger to trace the curve of his hard jaw.

"Sure I do," he said, but his grin slid away and he swallowed hard. "We should sleep now, Glasses. Reality comes in a few hours."

"Yeah," I said, a little uneasy with what I saw in his face, but then he dropped another kiss onto my mouth and moved so his arms were wrapped around me, my back to his front, and I told myself it was just sleepiness I'd seen. "G'night, Charlie."

I felt his breath on the back of my neck when he said, "G'night, Bailey."

CHAPTER FORTY-FOUR

Charlie

I heard her breathing slow and I knew she'd fallen asleep.

My breathing, on the other hand, was unsteady on account of the fact that my heart was beating out of my chest like I'd just sprinted a mile. Sleep was a million miles away from where my brain was right now.

My brain was beating the shit out of me.

What have you done? What have you done? What in the hell have you done, you fucking moronic dumbass?

I was fucked.

I was so fucked.

I was so fucking fucked.

Because Bailey was in my arms, smelling like heaven as she snuggled against me like it was where she belonged, and I *ached* for it to be.

God help me, I wanted to be where she belonged.

I wished I could bury my nose in her cocoa-butter hair and stay that way forever, wrapped around the one real thing I'd ever known, but I couldn't.

My throat was tight as I lay there in the dark with her, giving myself ten more minutes before I had to get up.

Get out.

But when ten minutes were up, I gave myself ten more.

I was so fucked.

CHAPTER FORTY-FIVE

Bailey

I wasn't sure where I was when I woke up.

The fort threw me off, with the blankets hanging from above, but as soon as I turned my head and saw Charlie's pillow, I remembered everything.

"Charlie?" I sat up, grabbed my phone—it was nine thirty—patted my hair, and crawled out of the fort. I didn't see him, and it was quiet in the apartment. "Where are you?"

I peeked my head down the hallway. I didn't want to bust in on him changing or anything, so I decided to get a glass of water. As soon as I stepped into the kitchen, I saw his note.

Had to run—just let yourself out.

What? I read it again, flipped the paper over, then wondered what that meant. Why would he leave without waking me up? And *let yourself out* didn't exactly scream that he was buzzing over what'd happened with us the night before, or that he'd run to surprise me with chocolate doughnuts.

I sent him a text of my own.

I can't believe you left me alone at your house, loser. ;)

I felt unsettled by his absence, but I was probably being paranoid.

I waited a few minutes, but when he didn't respond, I put on my shoes and coat and I left. I had no interest in hanging out alone at Charlie's mom's apartment. It felt intrusive and uncomfortable, like I was just waiting to get caught where I didn't belong.

But I realized when I exited the building—the building whose security door locked behind me—that I didn't have a car. Holy crap—Charlie picked me up; how had I forgotten? I didn't want to bug him, since I didn't know where he'd gone, so I texted Nekesa instead.

Is there any way you can come pick me up? I know you're grounded but if you tell your parents my car broke down . . . ?

Nekesa: Your car broke down?

Me: No but it's complicated.

Nekesa: Where are you?

Me: Charlie's apartment.

Nekesa: Where is Charlie?

Me: No idea.

Nekesa: Oh God—I'm on my way. Drop me the address.

While I waited for Nekesa, my mind replayed the night over and over again. And I grew more and more conflicted. Because hadn't we admitted our feelings? Hadn't we moved toward something new?

So what did it mean that my texting buddy had yet to respond?

Quit being paranoid, I told myself.

After Nekesa picked me up, she drove to Starbucks so she could "breathe for an ungrounded five minutes" while I told her what was going on.

And tell her I did; I told her everything.

I told her about the proposal, about Charlie picking me up, about sweet blanket forts, and about making out.

After she choked on her coffee, she scratched her eyebrow and said, "But the only actual words you said were that you had more-than-coworkerly feelings, right?"

Oh God. Those really *were* the only words we'd said.

More than coworkerly. That was hardly a love confession.

Had I been so emotional that I'd interpreted something that was nothing to be something? My heart sank—shit, shit, shit— as I considered what she was saying.

But he'd been so sweet, and I'd felt so close to him; surely it meant more than just "non-coworkerly." The kiss—hell, the kis*ses*—definitely didn't feel coworkerly.

Right?

I swallowed and said, "Right."

She dragged her bottom lip between her teeth and said, "Is it possible he was literally talking about his funny 'we're only coworkers, not friends' shtick?"

"No," I said, doubting myself as I said it. "I mean . . . *yes*, it's possible, but you weren't there. The chemistry—"

"You were alone in the apartment, in the dark, lying together on a bed." Nekesa raised her eyebrows and said, "He's a *guy*, Bay. Sometimes they say things—"

"No." *No.* I shook my head and said, "It wasn't like that. He was the one who stopped things."

"I'm just saying that you two might've seen the night differently, that's all."

I kept hearing her words on the way home—could she be right? *Had* we? Had it been something less meaningful to him than it'd been to me?

And why in the hell isn't he texting me back?

As soon as she pulled up in front of my building, all thoughts of Charlie disappeared because it was time to go face reality.

God, I *so* didn't want to do this.

I knew my mom well enough to know she was going to hug me and tell me that everything was going to be fine.

Because for her, it would be.

She was going to have a wonderful new husband.

Shit—what if Scott was inside? What if they wanted to sit down *together* and discuss it with me?

My stomach hurt.

And what if they'd already decided how our lives would look now?

"Thanks for getting me," I said, unbuckling and opening my door. "God, you don't know how badly I don't want to go inside."

"I get that," she said, giving me an empathetic smile. "Good luck."

"Thanks." I went into the building, climbed the stairs as slowly as humanly possible, and took a deep breath before going into the apartment. I closed the door quietly behind me and said, "Mom?"

I dropped my bag in the entryway and slid off my shoes.

"Bay?" My mom's voice sounded like she was in her room.

"Yeah."

She came out of her bedroom—alone, thank God—and gave me a questioning look. I could read in her eyes that she didn't know if I was mad or sad or normal. She said, "Hey."

"I'm so sorry I left," I said, overwhelmed with guilt as I looked at her face. That was the only proposal she was going to get from Scott, and I felt bad that I'd taken something from that. "I hope it didn't ruin your night."

"It's okay," she said, grabbing my hand and pulling me toward the couch. "How's Charlie?"

I tried swallowing, but it felt like there was a rock in my throat. "You know—typical Charlie."

"Can we talk about the engagement?" she asked, so sweet that it made me sad. Sad for adding stress to her happily ever after, and sad for me, for what I was about to lose.

I nodded, but couldn't manage more than that.

She looked disappointed by my silence, and then she asked, "So do you not like Scott?"

I pictured Scott, teasing Charlie about PDA in Colorado, and I realized that I actually *did* like him, just not his place in my world. I didn't know if she'd get it. I said, "It's not that I don't like him; it's that I don't want what he brings to our lives."

She tilted her head. "What do you mean?"

I took a deep breath and went for honesty.

"I mean that I don't want to move. Like, I'm sure you'll want to move into his house if you marry him, but I don't want to move into a strange house. I don't want to live with him, and I definitely don't want to live with his kid, who is a total stranger. How will that ever feel normal, moving my things and myself into someone else's life?"

I hated that I was getting emotional again.

"It's a nice house," she said, reaching out and running a hand over my hair. "With an extra room that's supercute. And it's downstairs, next to a finished living room and wet bar that no one uses, so it'll be like your own apartment."

My stomach hurt—literally—at the confirmation that we would be moving in with him. My vision got blurry, and I wished I could just turn off my emotions.

"Bailey," she said patiently. "I know change is hard, but I wouldn't agree to this if I didn't think it would be good for you."

I sighed and said, "I know."

Even though I didn't mean it. I knew she had my best interests at heart, but I also knew she was an optimist who lived by the motto of *It will all work out*.

"I know in my heart this will be wonderful, Bay," she said, still petting my hair like she used to when I was little. "Just give it a chance, okay?"

"Okay," I said, nodding.

Looked like it was going to happen, whether I liked it or not.

I tried calling Charlie after my mom and I had a long talk, telling myself that it's what I would've done if we hadn't made out.

But he didn't answer. I got his voicemail for the first time since I'd met him.

I texted him: **My mom just confirmed that we WILL be moving in with Scott.**

And two hours later, he still hadn't responded.

So I hadn't been paranoid.

If it were someone else, it would be possible that he was just too busy to text me back.

But I *knew* Charlie.

I knew his work schedule—he was off today; I knew his texting habits—he always had his phone on him; and I knew his family's schedule—they were out of town and he was home alone.

There was no reason—other than a freak accident—that he wouldn't have responded to me by now. So there was only one explanation.

He was post-makeout ghosting me.

I flopped down on my bed, mortified and confused and sad by what appeared to be Charlie's rejection. Because as unorthodox as we'd always been—first as strangers who didn't like each other, then as coworkers and sort-of-friends—he'd never done anything to make me feel bad about myself.

He'd *always* teased, but he'd never been unkind.

What an asshole, I thought as Mr. Squishy jumped onto my bed with a little *mreow* grunt. What a complete and total asshole.

Because he knew me—really *knew* me. He knew my anxieties and neuroses, and he *knew* something like this would make my brain turn endless cartwheels.

And apparently he didn't care.

Maybe he was the jerk that I first thought he was.

Part of me thought I was ridiculous for being pissed, because Charlie hadn't technically made any promises.

But the angry part of me disagreed, because dammit, he *had* made promises. We might not have labeled what we were, but when he'd kissed away my tears, that was a promise. When he'd held me while I cried, that was a promise.

Maybe not a promise to be my boyfriend, but a promise to be *something* to me.

He *knew* that he'd become my *something*, and it felt so fucking personal that he was fine with just leaving me alone when he knew I needed him. If he were to text me about something happening with his mom and her boyfriend, I'd respond—even this very second—because aside from everything else, I cared about his feelings.

He obviously didn't feel the same.

I felt tears start to sting my eyes as I realized that everything that had passed between us was all just a big lie.

And I had fallen for it. All of it.

How could I be such a fool?

CHAPTER FORTY-SIX

Bailey

I took a deep breath, rubbed my freshly glossed lips together, and opened the door to the employee entrance. Charlie had literally ghosted me the entire weekend, and now we were going to have to work together. I was sad, hurt, and also white-hot pissed. I had no idea how I was going to behave around him.

Or how he was going to behave around me.

My stomach was full of butterflies as I opened the back door that led to the area behind the front desk. I hung my coat and purse on a hook, took a deep breath, and walked through the doorway that led to check-in.

"Hey, Bailey."

I blinked and stared into Theo's face. I took a step back—he was bad about personal space—and asked, "What are you doing here?"

"Oh, that's really nice," he teased, smiling and adjusting his name tag. "Way to make me feel unwanted."

"Sorry," I said, wanting to cut through the bullshit and figure out where Charlie was. "I just didn't expect—I mean, you never work on Tuesdays. Wasn't Charlie scheduled tonight?"

"Yeah," he said, opening the drawer that was full of office supplies. "He's got some kind of conflict this week, so we swapped shifts."

"Oh." I swallowed and watched him grab a box of staples. "What was the conflict?"

"He didn't say," Theo muttered as he opened the stapler and started loading it. "All he said was that Tuesday/Thursday wouldn't work for him."

I stood there, frozen in place, as it hit me.

Holy shit, Charlie was full-on avoiding me. As in, avoiding so hard that he was *rearranging* his work schedule so he wouldn't have to see me. My stomach clenched and I felt queasy as the reality of his absence—of the *planning* behind his absence— slammed into me.

He was willing to do anything not to see me.

What was I, so pathetic that he couldn't stand to be in the same building as me?

Shit—was I?

Had I been so pathetic and desperate as I'd bawled in his arms that (after making out with me first) he didn't even want to see me? Could Charlie really be this cruel?

I worked with Theo, numb, super grateful that it was a busy night. The check-ins were constant because of a national DECA event in town, so I was able to *not* lose my mind thinking about

Charlie as I juggled room keys and activities bracelets.

The minute things finally slowed down, though, I decided to do it.

Screw it, I needed to know.

I pulled out my phone and texted Charlie.

I cannot believe you switched shifts to avoid me. Can we talk? Plz don't ignore this.

I gasped when I saw conversation bubbles. Holy shit, was he finally going to acknowledge my existence? I watched in nail-biting anticipation as those bubbles bounced around.

Then—finally—a text appeared.

Charlie: Can we NOT talk about it, Glasses? Let's just move on.

I reread it three times, the near-vomitous feeling getting worse with every read. *Let's just move on.*

I'd known, but it still felt like a knife to the chest to realize that I was actually right about him. Charlie had been avoiding me after that night and wanted to keep avoiding me.

Oh my God.

He didn't ask about my mom, or how I was doing, or try to brush off that night by saying something cruel in its kindness.

No, he just wanted to move on.

I honestly didn't even know what that meant. Did he want to return to our normal friendship, or did he want to move on from even that?

I went into the storage room to inventory the rollaways, blankets, and cribs, but once I got there, I just leaned my head back against the wall and closed my eyes.

It felt like too much to bear.

He'd always warned me that girls and guys couldn't be friends.

Turned out he was right.

And I hated him for it.

CHAPTER FORTY-SEVEN

Charlie

Shit, shit, shit.

I looked at her message and felt like such an asshole, but what the hell was I supposed to say? The truth? The truth was that yes, I'd absolutely switched shifts to avoid Bailey, because I couldn't handle my feelings.

Or hers.

I turned up the volume on my Spotify playlist, but the music didn't help. Conan Gray just made it worse—he always made it worse, but I was a masochist that way—and Volbeat wasn't doing a damn thing to drown out the thoughts pinging around in my head.

Ridiculously pathetic thoughts that didn't matter even a tiny little bit.

Because I was doing the right thing, pretending that night hadn't existed.

Did I want to ignore reality and just *be* with Bailey? Fuck yes. That night with her in the blanket fort had been . . . shit, was there a word? It'd been everything, and I'd damn near wanted to cry when I climbed out and left her alone.

I'd never meant to kiss her that night. My only goal had been to make her less sad, but when she looked at me with those big eyes that I'd fucking dreamed about, I was selfish. I ignored common sense and lost myself in her, taking everything she gave me while clamoring for more.

Fucking moron.

Because now my selfishness might've ruined everything. If I hadn't kissed her, I'd have her in my life every day—at the very least on every day that we worked together.

But now everything was broken.

She either wanted a relationship, which wasn't happening because it would eventually destroy what we had, or she was so pissed at me for bailing that what we had was already destroyed.

And the terrifying thing was that I didn't have a plan. For once in my fucking life, I had no idea how to proceed. I'd switched shifts out of sheer procrastination, needing to stay away from her until I could figure my shit out.

Because all I knew was that if I saw her right now, or talked to her on the phone, I might very well do something stupid like kiss her again or ask her out.

Beg her to love me forever.

And all of those things spelled certain death for Charlie-and-Bailey.

No, I was going to figure out a way to fix this so things didn't change.

If she didn't hate me so much already that she walked away forever.

CHAPTER FORTY-EIGHT

Bailey

"So you can essentially have the entire basement to yourself." Scott stuck out an arm as if to say *All of this is yours*, and I followed his gaze across the finished lower level of his house. "It'll be like your own place."

I gave him a smile and nodded. "Cool."

My mom gave me a huge supportive grin, and I could tell she was happy I was trying. I'd finally realized I had no choice, so I supposed I might as well start trying to make the best of it.

Scott finished the tour of his house—*our* house in a month— and then he took my mom and me to lunch downtown. They excitedly discussed moving—*one more month and it was done*— and their wedding—*six months*—and the honeymoon they were going to be taking (Bora-Bora), and I jammed French fries into my mouth as quickly as I could.

Because old habits die hard.

Every fiber of my being wanted to fight Scott, to fight all of this change to my life.

Instead, I breathed in through my nose and tried to believe that everything would be fine.

My phone rang while I was eating my last fry, and I picked it up because I could see it was Nekesa.

"Hello?"

"Hey, um, could you come over?" She was crying. "Like, now?"

"Are you okay?"

"Yes," she said, and she sniffled. "No. I mean, physically I'm fine, but—Aaron and I broke up . . ."

She trailed off into crying, and I glanced at my mom as I said, "I'm on my way."

When I got there, Nekesa was home alone. She had ick mascara in the corner of her eye and a bright red nose, and I wrapped her in a hug and ached for her as she cried into my neck.

When she finally calmed down a little, we went into the kitchen and I made her tea while she sat on a stool and told me what happened.

"So the other night, when Theo gave me a ride home from work, he kissed me."

"*What?*" I said, nearly yelling the word. "Theo *kissed* you?"

She nodded miserably. "He did, and I didn't stop him."

I just looked at her, letting her finish, while a sudden rush of guilt made me feel queasy.

"I've felt something for him for a while now, and I was

ninety-nine percent sure it was friendship. But when he went in for the kiss, I, um, I guess I kind of let him. To see."

"Oh my God," I said, blown away.

"I know," she said, shaking her head. "It only lasted for about two seconds, and then I pulled away, definitely knowing I was right about it only being friendship, but when I told Aaron, he *freaked* out."

"You told him?" I knew my eyes were huge as I waited for the rest, but I couldn't shake the feeling that I'd played a hand in this. If I'd said something more to her, or told her that I thought Theo was kind of an asshole, would that have changed the outcome?

"I had to," she said, sniffling. "I had to be honest because I love him, right? So I told him, along with the words 'I'm not interested in him; it was just a stupid moment,' and he lost his shit. He said he's going to kill Theo, and when I told him not to, he started to cry, Bay."

"Oh no," I said, feeling awful for both of them. "He cried?"

"He said he loved me," she croaked, her voice tight, "but that I obviously need something he can't give me."

Why hadn't I pushed harder when I'd seen them flirting? Why had I gone along with that stupid bet with Charlie? The guilt just gnawed at me because I *knew* this was partially my fault.

"Sweetie," I said, putting my arms around her as she cried. "I'm so sorry. I'm sure he just needs time to cool off, and then he'll be back. He loves you so much."

When I let go of her, she wiped at her eyes and took a deep breath. "The thing is, Bay, this is all my fault. I had a boyfriend, and even though nothing was technically going on, I was way too close with Theo."

I swallowed and didn't think I could feel worse.

She shook her head. "All the lines got blurred. God, I wish I could go back and create a little distance, y'know?"

Okay—I was wrong. I could absolutely feel worse.

I couldn't even look her in the eye because I was haunted by all those times my gut had told me to warn her. Though it wasn't my place to tell her how close she could be with her guy friends, maybe I should have at least sucked up the awkwardness and had a conversation with her about it? So I just said, "Yeah."

"Why didn't you slap me?" She rolled her eyes and said, "Next time I'm being an idiot with a boy, will you please slap me? I will consider it the kindest best friend move, I promise."

Yeah—I was obviously the devil and the absolute Worst. Friend. Ever.

"Still no word from Charlie?" she asked.

"No," I said, pasting on a *whatever* expression when just the mention of his name made my heart hurt. "But you don't need to worry about that right now."

"Please? Please let me think about something other than my own mess."

I shrugged, even though apathy was the opposite of what I was feeling. I rotated between wanting to sob because I missed my friend, and wanting to track him down and junk-punch him because I was so angry. I kept my voice casual when I said, "Okay. Yeah, still no word. I think he's officially someone I used to know."

"What the hell, man?" Nekesa said, looking irritated. "I can understand you two being on different pages about romantic feelings, but he was your *best* friend. How can he just bail?"

I scrunched my nose. "*You* are my best friend."

"I know," she said, "but so is he. You two have that insta-friend chemistry."

"Had," I corrected, clearing my throat in an attempt to clear away the tightness.

"Had," she agreed with a sigh. "God, we're pathetic."

"Truth."

"Want to order a pizza?"

We ordered a large pepperoni pizza and ate it straight from the box as we binge-watched *Ted Lasso*. It was total comfort TV and actually made us feel better. So much better, in fact, that when Dana texted both of us, asking if we would join her and Eli that night for their birthday dinner at Applebee's (those two actually shared a birthday—so adorable, right?), we were all in.

After confirming that Charlie wouldn't be there, of course.

We took our time getting ready, curling each other's hair and paying far too much attention to details like winged eyeliner and perfect fingernail polish. I borrowed her red-and-black plaid skirt and fluffy sweater, and she wore a bright orange dress.

By the time we walked into the restaurant, we felt pretty damn good.

Until we saw them.

Dana and Eli were laughing, sitting across from each other, along with a few other people I didn't know. They all looked like they were having a blast, with a few presents piled on the table's center.

But also at the table, in work clothes, like they'd just left Planet Funnn, were Charlie and Theo.

I instantly felt like I couldn't breathe, and I hated him for making me feel that way. I wanted to not care, but the buzzing in my ears and the heat in my cheeks told another story.

"Son of a bitch," Nekesa said to me out of the side of her mouth. "Is the universe fucking kidding with this?"

I barely heard her, because my traitorous eyes were drinking in the sight of Charlie. *God, I just missed him so much*—and it had barely been a week. As much as I'd said that it was fine, the truth was that he'd left a gaping hole in my life.

Not the kissing Charlie—I didn't know *that guy* all that well.

But my coworker/friend Charlie, the one I'd texted thirty times a day and talked to on the phone more days than not, had left me with an aching void.

Had it really only been a week?

"Let's do this," Nekesa said, giving me her *I'm a badass* look. "Let's just sit our asses down and try to have fun."

"That's a tall order," I muttered.

"Just try," she said, and then she walked around the table and took the empty chair between Dana and Theo. The only other vacant chair was the one next to Charlie, and I wasn't sure I was mentally strong enough to force my legs to move in that direction.

Dammit.

It was like he heard my mental curse, and his eyes landed on me. But instead of doing the right thing and looking away—or at least looking awkward—he gave me a smirky smile.

Seriously?

I channeled my inner Nekesa and went over to the vacant seat, even though I would've rather sat in the white-hot flames of hell. I immediately turned my attention to Dana and Eli.

"Happy birthday, you guys," I said, pushing my lips up into a perky smile. "Did I miss the karaoke?"

I could hear Theo saying something to Nekesa about his car being in the shop and Charlie giving him a ride, which explained why he was there when he didn't even know the birthday couple.

"You wish," Dana said, looking so incredibly happy that I was glad Eli hadn't been interested in me. "Starts in five."

"Lovely," I muttered.

I looked across the table, and Nekesa was talking intensely to Theo. I was trying to lean a little closer, not being obvious, when I heard:

"You're going to fall out of your chair if you lean any harder, Glasses."

I glanced at Charlie, and he was giving me the amused grin he'd given me a thousand times before. Which pissed me off. How dare he act like everything was normal? I gave him a very fake smile—the baring of teeth—and turned away from him in my chair.

I was about to say something to Dana when Charlie said, "Are you going to sing?"

I looked at him over my shoulder. "What?"

He gave a nod toward the bar. "When karaoke starts. You singing, Mitchell?"

"Doubt it," I said, wishing he'd just leave me alone.

I heard Eli say something to him, and then Nekesa, Charlie,

and Eli exploded into a conversation. So I just sat there, wedged in between two conversations like a loner loser. I desperately wanted to go home, but I was also so happy to see Nekesa not crying that I was going to shut up and deal for a while in the name of her happiness.

Y'know, since I had a hand in making her sad.

Karaoke began, and I was finally able to relax. Mainly because Charlie had stopped talking, and everyone else had started. Dana and Eli sang "Señorita" by Camila Cabello and Shawn Mendes, and they were actually good.

And even more adorable than before.

They were couple perfection. And it made me sick.

Nekesa went up and did "Party in the USA," which was awful, but everyone sang along so it was fun. I was in the middle of discussing Miley Cyrus with Eli when I heard the notes of the next song start.

No.

I closed my eyes and refused to look toward the karaoke stage.

"Bailey," Charlie said into the microphone, "Bailey Mitchell. Come sing with me."

"Do What You Gotta Do" began playing, and Charlie started singing to the Disney song. Badly.

Hearing him singing that song made me grit my teeth and curl my fingers into fists. It reminded me of what we'd been, of how great we'd been together, and how easily he'd just scrapped it.

And now, because of the convenience of location, he thought we could just pick it back up like nothing had happened?

I got up and headed for the door—I needed to get the hell out of there. I needed air, I needed space, I needed no Charlie. I could feel his eyes on me as I walked, and just as I pushed the doors to exit the building, I heard him stop singing and say into the microphone, "Bailey!"

Nope.

Not stopping, not going back.

I walked around to the side of the building, out of sight, and rubbed the back of my neck with both hands.

"Bailey?" Charlie came running around the corner, and I felt something spark in my chest as he looked confused, like he was somehow shocked that I hadn't wanted to play with him.

"For God's sake, Charlie, can you just leave me alone?" I dropped my arms to my sides and sighed. "You're good at that, so it should be easy."

He made a noise in his throat and his face looked pained. Guilty, like he knew he'd been an asshole. "I didn't leave you alone; I just—"

"You *literally* left me alone at your mother's apartment, and you've ghosted me ever since," I said in a high-pitched voice that I didn't like. "Don't get me wrong—I don't give a shit—but you can't act like you're confused as to why I'm not your friend anymore."

"I knew this would happen," he muttered quietly, almost under his breath.

"Knew *what* would happen?" I barked.

"This," he said, looking agitated and sounding frustrated. "I knew *this* would happen. I *told* you this would happen."

"Are you talking about your idiotic theory?" I asked, my voice growing louder. "*This* didn't happen because we were friends. *This* happened because as soon as we shared a real moment, you freaked out and disappeared."

"I didn't freak out," he said, his voice a little louder as well, "but I could tell that you were going to make something huge out of a kiss, and I didn't want it to fuck up our friendship."

I felt like he'd slapped me with his *I could tell that you were going to make something huge* comment, as if he were the adult in the scenario who knew silly little Bailey was going to fall in love. As if I were a lovesick idiot.

"Uh, for starters, it wasn't just *a* kiss, Charlie, and you know it," I said, blinking fast as I tried keeping my thoughts straight. "But if anything fucked up our friendship, it was you ignoring me. Friends don't do that."

"Friends, friends," he said, his words almost a groan. "It's such bullshit."

"No, your ideas are bullshit."

"Really?" he asked, stepping a little closer. "Because it occurs to me that we've yet to discuss the fact that I actually won our bet. Because it wasn't bullshit at all. I told you a long time ago that Theo and Nekesa were going to hook up, and I was right. You bet on friendship, and you lost because it's impossible."

"Oh my god, Theo *told* you he kissed her?"

So that guy was a dick, too.

"What the hell?"

Nekesa appeared from behind Charlie, where she'd apparently been hidden by his bigger, taller body.

Shit, shit, shit.

"What does that mean?" Nekesa asked, taking a step toward me. "You didn't make a *literal* bet that we'd hook up, did you?"

"No!" I nearly shouted, panicking as she glared at me. I cleared my throat as my heart started pounding in my chest, and I said, "It's not like that." Right? How could I explain. "I mean, there was this . . . *discussion* that Charlie and I had." *Discussion? Jesus, Bailey!*

Her mouth dropped open, and her eyes moved between Charlie and me. "What kind of garbage person makes a bet about their best friend?"

"It wasn't like that," I said, desperate to convince her. "Charlie just thought—"

"Charlie sure likes betting," Theo said.

I hadn't even noticed him standing beside Nekesa, but I could hardly keep up with the conversation, much less the attendance. He looked pissed as he glared at Charlie, which irritated me because this was none of his business. I mean yes, he'd been part of the bet, but I didn't care how he felt about that.

Theo crossed his arms and said, "That wasn't his only wager."

I rolled my eyes—couldn't help it. "No offense, Theo, but I—"

"Fuck off, Theo," Charlie said, looking ready to fight.

"Oh, really?" Theo looked like a smug asshole because he was *smirking* in the midst of all the turmoil. "I should fuck off?"

"Spare us the machismo," I muttered, out of patience.

"Machismo?" Theo barked, his smirk turning into a dickish grin. "He made a bet about *you*, Bailey."

"What?" I didn't get it.

"Theo," Charlie said through gritted teeth. "Shut up."

He looked angry, his face flushed and his eyes burning as he glared at Theo, which made *me* even angrier. I said, "No, *you* shut up, Charlie."

And then I said—

"What are you talking about, Theo?"

Theo was still looking pleased with himself, like he was the puppeteer and was having the time of his life pulling all the strings.

"Charlie made a bet about *you*." Theo said the words loudly, clearly, and while giving me direct eye contact. "With me."

"What?" I pushed my hair out of my face and looked from Theo to Charlie. "What does that mean?"

"Yeah," Nekesa said, looking at Theo with a question in her eyes as Eli and Dana showed up behind her. "What are you talking about?"

Charlie flexed his jaw, watching me.

"Charlie and I made a bet a few months ago," Theo said, speaking to Nekesa now. "It was before any of us were friends. Charlie made a wager that he could get Bailey."

I squinted and said, *"Get?"*

My face got hot with embarrassment as Charlie's guilty gaze went to a spot just beyond my shoulder. His voice was quiet when he said, "It was just talk, Bay. It didn't mean—"

"Oh my God," I said, feeling dizzy—no, *numb*—as I realized the truth. Colorado, the pullout sofa, the blanket fort—that was all him *getting* me to win a bet. No wonder he was gone before I woke up; he'd already won.

Unless—my stomach churned as it occurred to me that everything we'd been through, said to each other, what we shared, was all to "get" me. And what the fuck did that mean?

I felt like such a fool. Had we *ever* been friends, or had our entire "relationship" been him trying to "get" me to win a bet?

"Bay," he replied, his expression unreadable aside from the red splotches on each of his cheeks. "You have to know—"

"Shut *up*." I wasn't a violent person, but rage bubbled inside me and I wanted to hit something.

Some*one*.

Because he was *only* Mr. Nothing. All those times I'd looked at him and thought about how Charlie wasn't at all what I'd initially judged him to be? That was just my own gullibility, my own pathetic wishful thinking.

He was Charlie from the airport, and I was a fool.

"Dana," Nekesa said, jerking my attention from Charlie to her. She lifted her chin and said, "Can I get a ride home? I think it's best if Bailey and I don't share a car right now."

I hated the expression on her face at that moment, because she looked as disappointed in me as I was in Charlie.

"Wait," I said, holding out a hand in desperation as I stepped in front of her. "Please let me explain—"

"You don't get to talk—are you kidding me with that?" Her nostrils flared and she shook her head in disgust. "I'm sorry, Bay, but I can't . . . I just. Why," was all she whispered before walking away. I watched Dana follow her, and I felt like a monster.

"Bailey."

I looked back at Charlie, and his face was serious in a way

I'd never seen. He almost looked *scared*, which was impossible because he'd have to be able to feel something to be scared.

"What, Charlie?" I bit out, trying to keep my emotions contained when all I wanted to do was cry. *"What?"*

"The bet was nothing," he said, stepping closer to me. "I know it was wrong, but I made it before we became friends—"

"Coworkers," I corrected.

"Friends," he insisted.

"Really?" I hated him at that moment for having that face. He was staring at me, his dark eyes intense, and it wasn't fair that his face still felt like a comfortable thing to me. So familiar that I knew his left eyebrow was marginally thicker than the right and he had the tiniest mole just to the left of his mouth. His face looked like the face of my best friend, a friend I could trust with anything. "Well, if that's the case, you were a really shitty friend."

"Don't say 'were.'" He swallowed and clenched his jaw before he said, "We're not past tense, Bay."

"You made us past tense," I said, my voice cracking, "not me."

"Bailey—"

"I have to go."

I turned away from him, my heart pounding and my face burning as I went to my car. I was nearly running, desperate to keep him from saying another word. I couldn't handle hearing anything more. I didn't want to forgive him—couldn't forgive him—because he wasn't friend material.

Not for me, at least.

He'd told me that on the flight from Fairbanks, but I just hadn't listened.

CHAPTER FORTY-NINE

Bailey

The next couple weeks went by in a blur of awfulness.

The apartment became a shell of its former self, with moving boxes strewn all over the place as my mom made frequent trips to Scott's with things like lamps, candles, and photographs. It no longer looked homey, no longer felt like any sort of refuge; it was just a place to sleep until we moved.

But worse than that was the fact that I was suddenly alone.

Nekesa, the friend who'd always been there for me, was gone. No texts, no calls, no hanging out; I was my only company. I went to school alone, shuffled through my classes, then drove myself home.

I don't know that I'd ever felt that lonely in my entire life.

I was sure my online friends would be supportive if I messaged them, but everything felt like too much drama to spill to friends lucky enough to be thousands of miles away.

And it exhausted me just thinking about it, so texting about it would be even worse.

I was considering quitting my job, because even that wasn't the same anymore. I'd transferred to Equipment Check-Out the morning after Applebee's, because I was too much of a coward to face Nekesa and I didn't want to ever see Theo or Charlie again, so now I just spent mind-numbingly boring hours on end handing out things like roller skates and snowboards to kids who didn't look like they washed their hands.

The only good thing was that my dad had started reaching out more. My mother must've really given him an earful, because he was back to texting me all the time.

Dad: Guess where I ate last night?

Me: McKennas?

Dad: Lucky guess. I had the Bailey special, btw.

His words made me think *cow tongue on toast*, but I forced myself to concentrate on my father's reminiscing instead of Charlie's nonsense. **Spaghetti with a side of bologna?**

It was what I always ordered at McKennas when I was five years old, and to this day, my dad ordered it every time he visited the restaurant.

It was weird. I was starting to feel less homesick when he talked about my former city, which I supposed was some sort of progress. It was more like seeing a curling old photograph, a soft reminder of another time in my life. I could smile and picture it, but I didn't feel that desperate desire to fly back immediately and resume my previous life anymore.

That probably meant I was finally accepting that that part of my life was over.

Closure and all that.

Charlie texted me every day, and every day I ignored him.

He'd started with apologies. He peppered me with a slew of apologetic texts and explanations. When I didn't respond, he switched to sharing funny memes, things we would've laughed about together before everything went wrong.

Now he'd moved on to random **I miss you** texts, which always made me want to cry. He wasn't a romantic guy, so when he texted things like **Look what I found on my phone today—I miss you** and included a screenshot of me and his cat—and him—when we'd FaceTimed, it felt like more than a picture.

It felt like he'd felt it too, the magic, and that hurt so much that I started deleting his messages without even reading them first.

Speaking of the cat, my mother delivered Puffball to Charlie's house like we were people divorcing and exchanging custody of our ward. Puffball was a fucking custody kid, for the love of God, and that full-circle unhappy ending was too depressing for words.

That Thursday night, when I was dying of boredom with an hour left in my shift, I heard someone approaching the Interstellar Equipment Station—aka my little hut.

Please don't ask for anything.

All I wanted was to mindlessly scroll on my phone and ignore the world.

"Hey."

I sighed and looked up, only to find Nekesa waiting.

My stomach dropped and my heart started racing; God, I was *nervous* to see her.

I got off my stool and went to the window, not knowing what to say or how to look at her. Smiling felt wrong, but so did *not* smiling. So I just said, "Hey."

Her eyes went up to my hair. "A bun? Really?"

I nodded in agreement with what I knew she was thinking. She had strong opinions on the bun. "Yes, I've given up."

"Listen, I need to check out a boogie board for a guest who's coming in late. Can I get it charged to room 769?" she asked, ignoring my bun rebuttal entirely. "Please."

"Sure." I tabbed through the necessary fields on the computer until I got to the right screen. My face was on fire and my hands were shaking, and I wasn't sure if it was from guilt or fear that we'd never be friends again.

I could tell by the expression on her face that she was going to take the board and go, and I knew I needed to say something.

It was now or never.

But *what*?

What could I possibly say to make her forgive me?

"I'm so sorry." I glanced up from the computer screen and said the first thing I could think of. "I'm a jerk and the worst and totally deserving of your scorn, but I am *begging* you to forgive me."

Her eyebrows went down.

"I know, I know, I know," I said quickly, talking as fast as I could, trying to think of more ways to get through to her while she was standing in front of me. "Even my apology is annoying, right? But I just want you to know that I never hoped or thought you'd cheat on Aaron—"

"Bailey—"

"And I was betting *on* you, not that that made it any better—"

"Can you shut up?" she asked, her eyebrows going even lower. "This groveling is pathetic."

My words froze in my mouth, because I couldn't believe she'd told me to shut up.

But then her mouth turned into a little half smile that made me want to cry happy tears. Actually my eyes *did* fill with tears, because I missed her so much. She said, "What you did was super assy. Like, *super* assy."

I nodded and sniffled. "I know."

"But Charlie told me—after he and Theo fought, by the way—that you took the bet to show him how wrong he was. And he told me you felt shitty about it the whole time."

"I totally did," I agreed, adding, "Not that that excuses it."

God, what had I been thinking? It was surreal to me, that I'd ever gone along with it.

Freaking Charlie.

"Are you okay?" I asked, realizing that she'd been coping with her own loneliness. "About Aaron, I mean."

She puckered her lips and lifted her shoulder. "I guess, yeah, but I miss him."

I swallowed and nodded.

"A lot," she added, looking so sad that I wanted to hug her,

LYNN PAINTER

even though I knew she wouldn't let me.

"Have you guys talked at all?" I asked, wishing I could fix it for her.

She shook her head. "I'm too scared to call him."

Yeah, I definitely understand that. "You should, though."

She just sighed, like she had no idea what to do, then said, "So can I catch a ride home with you after work? My battery's dead, and I don't want to wait for my dad to pick me up."

"Are you kidding?" I said, trying—and failing—not to smile. "Of course you can!"

"Settle your ass down." She laughed.

"Sorry." Relief swept over me like a wave.

The rest of my shift was better, now that I knew things might be okay with us. And when I gave her a ride home at the end of the night and she just launched into a story right away, as if nothing had happened with us, I was ecstatic. It wasn't until we got closer to her house that she turned toward me in the passenger seat and said, "So have you talked to Charlie at all?"

Just hearing his name made my chest ache, and I shook my head and said, "He texts me, but I haven't responded. I'm just going to ignore him until he disappears."

"Are you sure that's what you want?" she asked, and I was kind of surprised. After everything that'd happened, I would've thought she'd want him out of our lives forever.

"For sure," I said, turning into her neighborhood. The sooner Charlie went away, the sooner I could stop wasting hours thinking about him.

Of course, that wasn't really working for me so far.

"So do you want to hear about the fight?" she asked, turning in her seat and tucking her legs underneath her.

"Did they actually fight?" I glanced over at her, unable to imagine such an event since neither of them seemed like brawlers. "For real? Like a physical fight?"

I glanced over, and she was nodding emphatically. "The first time we all worked together after Applebee's, those boys got heated. Charlie was quiet the entire shift—didn't say a single word to either of us—and when Theo said something stupid like *Smile, sunshine*, Charlie went off."

"Went off?" I looked over at her and asked, "What'd he say?"

As much as I detested him, I didn't like the idea of him angry. Ugh. What was wrong with me?

"Eyes on the road," she said, and I obeyed. She continued with "I think he said, like, *Can you not talk to me, you stupid fucking asshole*, which made Theo get all puffed up and go *What the fuck is your problem, man*," she said, doing voices as she spoke.

"No way," I said, in utter disbelief. Charlie was a smart-ass, a chill-vibes kind of dick. He wasn't a yelling-in-your-face type of dude.

Or was he? Did I even know what really went on inside of Charlie Sampson?

I sighed because in spite of everything, I still felt like I *did* know him.

"Yep," she said, and I could see her nodding out of the corner of my eye. "Then Charlie was like *Why did you have to open your huge fucking dipshit mouth to Bailey, you gossipy little bitch*, which made Theo push him. Then Charlie pushed him harder and shoved him against the wall."

That made me slam on the brake as we came to a red light, staring at Nekesa as shock and worry and stress hit me, all at once. My thoughts were riotous as I tried to make sense of everything.

"This can't be true," I said, putting my foot back on the gas and attempting to drive responsibly while dying of shock.

And also stressing about Charlie's anxiety, wondering how many TUMS he was consuming on a daily basis, which pissed me off because he didn't deserve my worry.

But dammit, I just *missed* him.

I missed my friend Charlie, even if he'd been a total lie. I missed the teasing and the way he knew what I was thinking all the time and how comfortable it felt to just *be* around him.

I'd never forgive him for taking away that comfort.

"I broke it up," she said, "because I'm a peacemaker, but not before Theo said something like *You did this to yourself, wagering on everyone like a fucking high-roller idiot.*"

I shook my head. "Theo wasn't wrong about *that.*"

"Yeah, but then Charlie almost twisted his nipple off."

That . . . was not what I expected, and I glanced at her out of the corner of my eye.

"Theo screamed—like full-on screamed high-pitched bloody murder in pain—as Charlie just twisted as hard as he could, and Charlie goes, *You're lucky I'm not violent or that would've been a punch.*"

When I pulled up in front of her house, I put my car in park and just sat there.

Nothing in the world made sense anymore.

She said, "Unbelievable, right?"

I nodded and asked, "So did they make up? Theo and Charlie?"

"Come in and stay over," Nekesa said as she opened the door. "And no, they did not. Charlie quit."

He quit? Charlie *quit* his job?

"Text your mom, and then I'll tell you all about it."

After I got my mom's okay to sleep over, we went inside, and Nekesa told me about how Charlie gave his notice and they hadn't heard from him since. It was ridiculous that I was concerned about him after what he'd done, but I was.

He didn't need any more stress.

We went up to her room and watched old episodes of *Project Runway*, and I felt content for the first time in what seemed like too long. Nekesa was my second home, in a way—not her house but *her*—and things felt a lot closer to *right* with her beside me.

The third episode was starting when my phone buzzed.

It was Charlie.

I still want to take you to fall formal. Please go with me so I can fix this. I miss you.

"Oh my God—he is seriously killing me," I moaned, hating that I could still hear every one of his texts perfectly narrated in his voice. Missing him was bad enough, but when he sent me messages that were exactly what I would've wished for before we fell apart, my heart ached.

Nekesa read the text and made a noise, always the defender. She picked up her phone and sent Charlie a message:

It's Nekesa. Will you please leave Bay alone? You can't fix this. You were right all along—you and Bailey CAN'T be friends. Also—she's going to fall formal with ME. Bye.

I knew I should be laughing or cheering, because he deserved that and he needed to disappear from my life.

But there was still a part of me that didn't want him to go.

Something inside of me wanted to stop her from sending that message, because what if it worked?

"Am I?" I asked about her fall formal comment, trying not to be sad over her words about Charlie and me never being friends.

"You already have a dress, right?" she said, setting down her phone and grabbing the bag of pretzels.

"Yeah." I'd bought one on post-prom clearance last year.

"So why not?" Nekesa popped a pretzel into her mouth and said, "Who needs boys anyway?"

CHAPTER FIFTY

Charlie

I sat back on the bed and stared at the phone in my hand, feeling gutted.

Hollow.

It felt like my stomach was made of lead and was slowly crushing everything else inside me, and no amount of TUMS was going to help.

Because it was finally over.

I'd always known it would happen, but it felt a thousand times worse than I'd imagined.

I was never going to get another text from Bay. I was never going to make her forehead crinkle with my words, or hear her laugh in that surprised way she had when she tried and failed to suppress it, never going to hear her quiet intake of breath when she realized we were about to kiss, and never going to hear her sleepily say *G'night, Charlie* on the other end of the phone.

A thousand tiny nothing moments that were collectively

every fucking thing I'd ever wanted.

And I'd thrown it all away.

That old adage about it being better to have loved and lost was bullshit, in my opinion, because in no fucking way was it better to have and lose. Having and losing felt like slow, painful torture, and it was killing me.

God, how had I fucked it up so badly?

It had absolutely been my intention to blow her off and stop any romantic emotions, but I hadn't meant to *hurt* her, even though I knew that made zero fucking sense. I'd wanted distance to figure everything out, but I hadn't meant to make her feel like she wasn't important to me.

Fuck, I definitely hadn't meant for her to think that she and I were just the result of a fucking frat-boy moronic bet.

Yet here we were.

My phone buzzed in my hand, and my pulse skyrocketed, but disappointment pressed even harder on my solar plexus when I realized that it wasn't Bailey or Nekesa.

It was Becca. **What's up?**

I pictured Becca's face, but that familiar rush of unchecked emotions didn't come. I watched conversation bubbles appear, but I felt nothing.

Nothing but disappointment that it wasn't *her*.

Bec: Just got back from the movies. We saw the new Jurassic flick and it sucked.

She probably went with Kyle, yet I still felt nothing as I pictured them at the theater.

Was that how it worked? You had to get your heart destroyed

again in order to get over the first person who destroyed your heart?

Fucking relationships.

I reached for the TUMS next to my bed and texted: **Just sitting in my room, being depressed because I ruined everything with Bailey.**

Becca: Oh my God I KNEW you were super into her; I told Kyle that after the party! Tell me everything. Maybe I can help.

I lay back on my bed and stared at the ceiling, because what the fuck was this?

Becca had crushed my heart and moved on, yet she was . . . still here.

What the fuck was going on?

I texted: **Why would you do that?**

Becca: Um, because you're my friend . . . ? DUH.

Was I her friend? Were Becca and I *friends*?

That was probably nice, and it should've felt like a full-circle moment, right? *This is when Charlie Sampson learns he's been wrong all along.*

But it didn't matter.

Because who the fuck would I share that little gem with? Bailey was the only one who'd appreciate it, the only one I would want to tell, and I'd ruined everything with her because I was an idiot.

Bailey had been worth the risk, and I'd missed that.

And now I missed her so much, it felt a little bit like I was having a heart attack.

CHAPTER FIFTY-ONE

Bailey

Fall formal was the day *after* we officially moved into Scott's house. Lucy, his daughter (whom I'd met the week before and who didn't seem awful), was at her mom's that weekend, so I was able to put off the stepsister bonding a little longer.

I was grabbing a soda out of the fridge when Scott came in through the back door. The cool autumn breeze snaked in around him. "Hey," I said.

He smiled and closed the door behind him before taking off his coat and putting it on the back of a kitchen chair. "Hey, yourself."

I shut the refrigerator door. It felt surreal that this was the new normal.

"I'm starving," he said, opening the pantry and pulling out a bag of corn chips. "If there's a God, there will be bean dip in the fridge."

"Well, then, praise Jesus, because it's on the top shelf," I replied, reopening the fridge to grab it and toss it toward him.

He gave me a grin as he caught the container. "Smart-ass."

"No, I'm serious," I murmured distractedly. "I feel God in this Chili's tonight."

"Okay." He laughed. "Quoting *The Office* is only going to make me like you more, Bailey, so knock it off."

I blinked in shock, not sure of what he meant by that.

"Oh, come on," he said, tilting his head a little. "I know this isn't what you wanted."

"What?" I asked, fully aware of what he was getting at.

He gave me a knowing smile and dropped into a kitchen chair. "I mean, it's not what my daughter wanted either."

"Scott, I don't—"

"I just love your mom—that's it." He shrugged, and his smile slipped just a little as he opened the bag of chips. "I love her and want a life with her. I don't want to hurt you—or anyone—and I don't want to change your life."

He made it sound so simple, so easy. I didn't know what to say, so I took a sip of soda and made a noise of understanding in my throat, like a hummed version of *I know.*

"I don't expect you to be into this whole combined-family thing from the get-go, but I hope you'll talk about it." He took the lid off the dip and laid it on the table. "If there are things you hate, I want to know. And if there are things you love, I want to know that, too."

"Okay," I said, nodding like we were on the same page, when I just wanted to get out of the kitchen. He was being nice, but I wasn't ready to talk about the reality of the situation, especially not with him. I clutched my soda and nodded again. "Sounds good."

Disappointment crossed his features, making his smile disappear, and I headed for the exit.

I was in the doorway when he said, "My parents got divorced when I was fourteen, Bailey."

That made me stop and look back.

"My mom started seeing a guy a year after they split up, and we moved into his house a few months later," he said, staring into space as if watching a memory being played back. His face was relaxed, like the story didn't hurt him anymore. "I can still remember the way I felt in his house. Like everything was wrong and smelled weird and like I was forced to live with strangers in a house that didn't feel like home."

"Really?" I said, turning around, surprised by his words and the fact that he was sharing that memory with me.

"Oh yeah," he said, nodding as he dipped a chip. "I hated it so damn much. Which, honestly, is why I waited so long to propose to your mom. I don't want that for you."

"Waited so long?" I said, trying to sound teasing when I added, "What's it been—like three months?"

"Uh," he said, tilting his head like he wasn't sure what to say. "Well, here's the thing."

I pulled out the other chair and sat down at the table, curious. "Yes . . . ?"

He made a little noise, his head still tilted like he was considering whether or not he should spit it out. "The thing is,

I started seeing your mom last year."

He looked at me expectantly, as if waiting for my reaction. "But we agreed I wasn't going to come over to your place until things were serious."

Wait a second. *Last year?* I stared at him in disbelief as I tried keeping up. "So you're saying that the first time I met you, you'd been already seeing my mom for months?"

He nodded. "We weren't trying to keep it a secret, but we also didn't want to make it a thing for you if it didn't work out."

I didn't know how to respond to that.

"That's kind of, um, thoughtful," was what I came up with, and I genuinely meant it. He'd stayed away from the woman he was seeing for *months*, just to help her daughter adjust.

"Now, I don't know how things are going to go on a day-to-day basis, but I promise I'll do everything in my power to make it feel like home here, okay?"

"Wow." I nodded and said in a thick voice, "Um, thank you. Thank you for telling me that."

He watched me for a second, and then somehow, he was hugging me the next. It was a big, all-encompassing hug that made me feel a little better about everything.

A little hopeful that things might just be okay.

Nekesa came over and we got ready in the basement, and it felt so good having her back in my life. I felt buzzed on happiness as we laughed and did our hair, and yeah—having the whole lower level at my disposal was *not* the worst. We sucked down mocktails at the wet bar while getting ready all over the rec room.

And after my mom took too many pictures, we met Dana and Eli at Brother Sebastian's for our fancy dinner.

Only, as we were being seated by the hostess, we walked by a big table of kids from our school, and Aaron was one of those kids.

No date, thank God, but still.

"Seriously—what are the odds?" Nekesa said, kind of loud enough for the entire restaurant to hear.

And it was one of those dark, quiet restaurants, big on candlelight, white linen, and quiet ambiance.

We sat down at our table, and even though she was laughing and talking and appeared to be having fun, I could tell by the wrinkle between Nekesa's eyebrows that she was very aware of his presence.

"We can go somewhere else if you want," I said quietly. "I'm great with Chipotle in formal wear."

She gave her head a tiny shake. "First of all, I love you for saying that. Second of all, it's okay."

"Well, let me know if you change your mind."

The waiter came and took our orders, and Nekesa and I got swept into the delightful entertainment that was Dana and Eli. They were telling a hilarious story about her falling down her stairs, finishing each other's sentences, when Aaron walked over.

I was instantly nervous, worried he was going to cause a scene, still not over her kissing Theo. And so I cleared my throat and said, "Hey, Aaron."

"Hey, Bailey," he said, looking uncomfortable, which relaxed me a little. He appeared to be nervous, not confrontational, and I leaned back in my chair and exhaled.

Then he looked directly at Nekesa and said, "Hey."

"Aaron. How's it going?" Nekesa smiled, but it didn't reach her eyes.

"You look stunning," he said, his blue eyes unblinking as they moved all over her face. "Seriously."

Her smile fell just a notch, and she replied with a breathy "Thank you."

"You made that dress, didn't you?" he asked, his eyes wide and filled with pride. "I can tell."

"Aaron?" she said, her tone asking what it was that he wanted.

"I know I said what I said, but I take it all back," he said in a rush, moving closer to her and lowering his voice just a little. I scooched my chair over so he could fit between us as he lowered himself to a squat and said to her with a trembling voice, "Everything sucks without you, and nothing matters but being able to talk to you every day."

Nekesa just nodded noncommittally, but I saw the relaxed set of her lips and knew she was going to give in to him.

Eventually.

"I was a jerk and don't deserve another chance, but this is me, officially begging." He put his hands on the edge of the table and said, "I don't want to interrupt your night, but I just wanted you to know."

I glanced around, and it appeared that half the restaurant was watching as he stood, turned, and started back toward his table. I was hoping she'd forgive him, but I didn't expect her to get out of her chair so fast that she knocked it over.

"Aaron."

Not only did she knock it over, but she literally ran and jumped onto his back.

Without missing a beat, Aaron's hands came up and grabbed her legs, supporting her piggyback landing as if he'd been expecting her. He stopped, slid her to her feet, and turned, and they were both laughing as they looked into each other's eyes.

Then he had her in his arms and they were kissing.

I was so happy for her, for them, but my heart burned with longing. The entire restaurant broke out into applause, and I blinked back happy tears as he hugged her hard and lifted her off her feet.

Aaron got an extra chair and joined us for dinner, which was fun because I loved Aaron but not ideal because it made me feel like a total third wheel, especially when I sat in the back seat of Nekesa's car after he ditched his friends so he could ride with us to the dance.

Once we arrived at the venue, it got even worse.

Nekesa and Aaron danced to every song, and even though she kept coming over to check on me, I told Nekesa that I wanted her to dance. I *did*, but I also felt like a total loser sitting at a table by myself because Dana and Eli were also dancing to every single song.

"Hey, gorgeous," I heard, and when I looked up, it was Zack. "You look amazing."

Of course. I was sitting alone like a total derf, so why *not* have Zack say hello, Universe?

I hadn't responded to him after our tiny text exchange at Target, but that seemed like an eternity ago because things with Charlie had eclipsed everything else in my life.

Zack was wearing all black—black suit, black shirt, black tie—and it occurred to me that his shirt *was* a little tight. Charlie's Baby Gap comment slithered through my head, even as butterflies went wild in my stomach.

"Thanks," I said, my cheeks getting warm. "So do you."

He grinned and ran a hand over the front of his shirt. "Me and the guys wanted to go all Prom Mafia with the black; totally Ford's idea."

I nodded and smiled, unable to remember which of his friends was Ford. "Well, it was a good one."

"Who's your date?" he asked, looking around. "Mr. Breaking Bad?"

I felt a stab of satisfaction at that, but of course, it immediately reminded me of Charlie. I said, "Nah—it's Nekesa."

I glanced over and saw her dancing with Aaron. "Well, it *was*."

He laughed at that, and I realized that everything had changed.

And hadn't changed at all.

Because I still found him to be beautiful. And charming. And kind.

But I didn't *feel* anything.

"Well," he said, his eyes moving down to my dress for a second before returning to my face. "I better get back to the group, but I just wanted to say hey. I miss talking to you."

"Same," I said breathlessly, and as he walked away, there wasn't even a tiny part of me that wanted to stop him.

"Are you guys getting back together or what?"

I looked to my left, and Dana and Eli were coming back to the table. Dana was smiling at me as she said it, and I quickly shook my head. "No, he was just saying hi."

"I heard he and Kelsie broke up," she said, plopping into the chair beside me. "So I wondered."

"Wait, what?" I squinted and asked her, "They did? When did they break up?"

"I think sometime last week." She leaned a little closer and said, "Why—are you interested?"

This was the news I'd been waiting for, yet my we-need-to-get-back-together desperation had left the building.

I literally didn't care.

Before I could answer, Eli asked, "Are you still pissed at Sampson?"

"What?" I looked at his bow tie and wondered how much he knew. "What do you mean?"

"When he had people over, I asked if you were coming, and he said no because you were pissed at him."

God, that's right—he was having people over the day after blanket fort night. I guess I'd forgotten. I gave him a noncommittal "Yeah."

"That's okay, you're not alone," he said, smiling. "Austin was so fucking livid when Charlie called off the party the night before that I still don't think they're talking."

The night before? "There were going to be two parties?"

For some reason that irritated me, thinking of Charlie being a party-bro on the same weekend he broke my heart.

He shook his head. "It was supposed to be Friday night. We brought the beer over, we told everyone, and it was just about to pop when Charlie got a text and was suddenly like *I gotta go—no party.*"

I blinked. "Wait, what? What happened?"

He shrugged. "No idea. He goes, *Something important came up and I have to go*, and he kicked us out."

"But we went to Dave and Buster's instead and it was super fun," Dana said, "so it turned out okay."

I heard a roaring in my ears. Had Charlie called off a party to go get me at Walgreens? I felt a little light-headed as I remembered how quickly he'd said he was on his way when I asked for a ride.

No questions, no *I have to rearrange some things*, just a solid *On my way.*

God. That couldn't be what happened, could it?

But as quickly as that thought formed, the thought *So he could "get" you* negated the action.

Shit.

I made it about an hour after that, but as soon as they played "The Last Time," I had to leave. The entire *Red* rerelease reminded me of Charlie, and just hearing it made me think of pine trees and tree-climbing boys.

I told Nekesa that I didn't feel well and was getting an Uber, and even though she was sweet and offered to take me, I could tell she was having the best night of her life and didn't want to ever leave.

Good for her.

I let out a sigh as I walked through the enormous lower level of the downtown convention center. I felt like I'd somehow failed at fun, and now I had to take the Uber of shame back to Scott's house. I was almost out the door when I saw two security guys standing in the way of someone who appeared to be trying to get in.

"You have to be a West High student, sir. We can't let you in," the bigger of the two guys said.

"I don't want to go to the dance. I just want to fucking talk to someone."

Oh my God! My pulse took off at the sound of that voice. Was that *Charlie*?

I stopped walking and craned my neck to try to see around the guards. Was Charlie here, trying to crash our formal?

"We can't let you in, kid," the smaller guy said. "You need to leave—"

"I just need two minutes," he said, sounding agitated.

"Oh my God, Charlie?" I took a step to the right, and *holy shit*, it was definitely him. My body betrayed me by setting free a hundred butterflies in my belly as I drank him in, letting my eyes soak up the formal wear, as well as the dark eyes and thick hair that I'd missed so fucking much, it was suddenly hard to breathe.

Dammit—my reaction annoyed me, and I said, "What are you doing? Knock it off before you get arrested."

His head whipped around, and he looked at me like he couldn't believe his eyes. His hair was messed up, his cheeks a little red as he blinked, stepped back from the security duo, and said, "Bailey?"

You have no right, I thought. He had no right to say my name like that, like he'd been hoping to see me. He had no right to look at me with his eyebrows up. He had no right to make me ache for him.

"G'night, Charlie," I yelled, pushing the door and going outside.

The cool air pricked at my warm face as I looked for my Uber driver in the darkness. The downtown area smelled like spicy food and fire pits, and I tried to calm my racing nerves. So Charlie was there in a gorgeous suit—no big deal, right?

Surely his presence had nothing to do with me.

"Bailey." The sound of his voice hit me right in the middle of my chest, pinching my heart and filling me with longing for . . . something.

I turned around and there he was, looking like everything I'd been missing as he stood there in his black jacket, his gaze intense. I didn't know why he was there, but I wanted it to be for me at the same time I wanted him to disappear. I breathed in through my noise and said, "What?"

He came closer, so close that I could smell the Irish Spring soap I knew he used because he'd left it in the shower at the condo in Breckenridge. His face was unreadable—closed off and serious—as he said, "I need to make things okay with us."

I shook my head and shrugged, looking over his shoulder because it was too hard to see his face. I had perfect memories of that strong nose, of those chocolate eyes, and remembering it all still destroyed me. "It's too late, Charlie."

"Please don't say that," he said, looking down at my dress distractedly, like he was gathering his thoughts, and then his eyes came back to mine. He put a hand on the front of his coat and said, "I miss my best friend. I miss *you*. The whole reason I ignored my feelings for you and what went down in the blanket fort that night was because I was scared of *this* happening. How's that for irony?"

"It's not irony at all. You made a bet and got caught; that's called a consequence." I sighed, wondering when everything with Charlie was going to start hurting less, and I said, "It doesn't matter."

"Yes, it does." He looked intense, like he was trying to convince me, and then he made a groaning sound and put both of his hands over a different spot on his jacket. "I've never had a good relationship—ever. They all go to shit in a big way. So when I started falling for you, I forced myself to ignore it, to deny it, because I couldn't stand the thought of losing you from my life if we got together and then split up."

"You thought *hurting* me—and ignoring me—would ensure you'd never lose me?" I was pretty sure he was just bullshit spitballing an excuse to get me to forgive him. "You're smarter than that, Charlie—come on."

"I know." He sighed and said, "I thought if I could just avoid you until I had a plan, then I could fix things. But then . . ."

He trailed off, and I knew we were both thinking the same thing.

"The bet."

"The bet had nothing to do with anything—ever; swear to God. It was just Theo being Theo." He flexed and unflexed his jaw while he looked down at me. "You and I, though—we were *us*."

"Us?" I asked breathily, wanting so badly to believe him.

"Magical, comfortable, Colorado us," he said, his voice a little scratchy. "We were everything together."

I shoved my hands into the pockets of my dress, confused as I felt a tiny frisson of hope streak through me.

"Do you know how long ago I fell for you?" He looked like he found himself ridiculous as he said, "I think I fell for you that day at Zio's, when you showed me the proper way to eat pizza."

"You called it pizza desecration," I said, not really even registering what my mouth was saying as I looked at his serious gaze and long eyelashes.

He shook his head, like the memory still baffled him. "I remember watching your face as you patiently explained it to me, and I thought, *How can someone be so interesting and irritating, all at the same time?*"

Was that supposed to be a compliment?

"And then I tried it," he said, his eyebrows scrunching together like he was looking at an equation that didn't make sense. "I tried it with the sole intention of mocking you, but then the flavors hit and you were spot-on and I realized just how *unique* you are."

"Unique," I repeated numbly, still unsure of his point.

"Bailey, you are, hands down, the most engaging person I've ever known."

My heartbeat skittered in my chest as he spoke the words like he really *had* fallen for me. "Engaging?"

"Wholly." His eyes burned into mine and he said, "When you're in the room, every single cell in my body—every nerve, every muscle, every breath—is lost in you."

My knees literally went weak, as in I felt like I was about to collapse.

A car honked, which made Charlie hiss out the word "Christ," and I looked away from him and saw my Uber. The guy gestured with his hands like he didn't have all night, so I dizzily—hazily, numbly—said, "That's my Uber."

"Can I call you later?" he asked, then muttered "shit" before his hands moved to the top of the jacket and his head jerked over onto his shoulder.

"What is wrong with you?" I asked, watching as his head rested on his shoulder like it was holding a phone in place and his hands were plastered against his own chest. "What are you doing?"

As if to answer, Puffball's tiny head popped out of the top of Charlie's jacket.

"Puffball?" I said, looking at that adorable fluffy gray face and stepping away from the car door.

"I don't want to be a dick," the Uber driver said, "but I'm going to take another rider if you're not going to get in."

"Oh."

"Let me drive you home," Charlie said, holding the cat against him with one hand over his coat while scratching the little guy's head with the other. "Please?"

The cat did it. I looked at that little furry baby, and then I leaned down and said to the driver, "I am so sorry."

"Forget it—bye."

I watched the Uber driver pull away before turning around toward Charlie. "Why do you have your cat?"

He looked down at his shoes, then just past my shoulder—anywhere but my face, it seemed—and then he said, "So how was the dance?"

I narrowed my eyes. "Why were you hiding Puffball under your jacket?"

He made a frustrated sound, like a groan and a growl, mixed together in the back of his throat, and he said, "I just, uh, had an idea, and then I realized it was stupid but it was too late to take the cat back to the car."

I don't know why, but his absolute discomfort in whatever was going on made warmth bloom inside me. This vulnerable side of him was my favorite, even after everything. "Tell me what your stupid idea was—the honest truth."

He held Puffball against his chest and petted his head for a second. Without looking at me he said, "I was going to give him to you."

"*What?* But you love that cat."

He sighed and finally summoned the courage to look at me, embarrassment in his eyes.

"Wait—did you think you could make me forgive you by giving me a cat?"

"No—it's worse than that," he said, looking back down at Puffball. "I wanted to show you that you can trust me to never disappear again. So I thought if I gave you my cat, it would be this big gesture because you know how much I love him. I figured it would prove that I'd be around because I'd want to see him every few days for, like, forever."

I looked into his eyes and didn't know what to say. My hands were shaking and there was a buzzing in my ears, because Charlie almost gave me his cat.

His cat that he adored. Was obsessed with.

"But on the way downtown, as I was practicing what I was going to say to you, I realized I couldn't do that to Mr. Squishy."

I nodded and my eyes felt a little scratchy, because that made sense.

Charlie *would* think of my cat's feelings.

Charlie was a cynical jerk, but he was a cynical jerk who did things like save animals from trees and make pasta for my mom and drive drunk girls home and—

"Why did you cancel your Friday-night party?" I stepped a little closer to him, suddenly remembering what Eli had said and desperate for Charlie to confirm it. I felt ready to burst as I breathlessly asked, "It was supposed to be Friday, but you kicked out your friends and moved it to Saturday. Why?"

His eyes traveled all over my face, and I swear to God I could feel his gaze like a physical touch. He set his free hand on my cheek and just said, "I had to."

I very nearly purred as I leaned into his palm. "Because . . . ?"

He swallowed. "Because you needed me."

Because you needed me.

"You actually canceled the party so you could come get me?"

It was too much, too wonderful, and I was hungry for him to say it.

"Nothing else mattered," he replied, setting his forehead on mine.

"I think we should kiss now," I said, emboldened by his actions, by his willingness to just dump everything when I'd needed to be rescued.

"So smart," he said, his voice a little growly as he lowered his mouth to mine. I felt breathless as Charlie kissed me, because this time, it felt absolutely real. Truly, madly, undeniably authentic. The shake in his breath, the tremble in my fingers, the thoroughness of his devouring kiss; it was perfection.

He pulled back and looked down at me, his eyes alight with that Charlie Sampson tease. "God, I love the Moldova."

"You remembered." I laughed, thinking back to Breckenridge.

"Of course I remembered," he said, an earnestness creeping into his voice as his thumb swept over my cheek. "When I'm a hundred years old, I'll still be able to picture you in that black dress with your bare feet and wild little smile."

"And I thought you were just using me for kissing practice," I teased, melting against him.

"So did I," Charlie admitted, lowering his head until his lips hovered just above mine. "Until your Moldova special made me never want to kiss anyone else ever again."

CHAPTER FIFTY-TWO

Charlie

As Bailey looked up at me with those gorgeous eyes that had the uncanny ability to see every single part of me, I felt fucking jittery. Like there was literally a damn tremble in my hands and I wanted to touch every inch of her, just to convince myself it was real.

That she was real.

It took losing her for me to realize that loving her wasn't even a risk.

At all.

She might not love me back, she might love me for a while and then stop, but every minute that I *had* her was worth the fall that might (or perhaps might not) eventually come.

I still thought happily ever after was sketch as fuck, but why not lean into the incredible, fucking lucky gift of Bailey's presence for as long as I could have it?

"What are you thinking?" she asked, her dark brows lowering. "Your face is weird right now."

I rubbed a hand over Puffball's head and felt happy. "I'm thinking that I'd like to take you out. Officially."

"Where?" she asked, gnawing on the inside of her cheek so I wouldn't know she was pleased.

I fucking loved her mind.

"Everywhere I've ever fantasized about kissing you," I said, then realized that was a fucking amazing idea. "The Jumpoline, my car, your car, the airport, Zio's—"

"You never thought about kissing me at the airport," she interrupted, grinning. "We *hated* each other at the airport."

"No, you hated *me*." I looked down at her freckles and couldn't believe it was still her. "I saw you at the baggage claim, after we landed."

"What?" she asked, a heavy dose of skepticism in her voice as she smiled. "Seriously?"

I nodded. "You didn't see me, but I watched you roll on lip gloss and then blot it onto a Kleenex."

She coughed out a laugh. "You're kidding with this, right?"

I shook my head, remembering. "There was something about your lips and the way I'd smelled that strawberry gloss for the entire flight that intrigued me."

Bailey reached out and petted Puffball, smiling at me in a way that made me feel like she didn't need anything else in the world to be happy. She said, "And then you fantasized about kissing me."

I nodded and lowered my mouth. "And then I fantasized about kissing you."

EPILOGUE

Bailey

"And do you take this man to be your lawfully wedded husband?"

"I do," she sighed, smiling up into his face.

"Do you think he'd hit me if I pretended to object?" Charlie whispered.

"Shh," I said, watching my mother beam up at Scott.

"What if I plopped down on the whoopie cushion that I secretly stuck in your purse?"

"Shhh," I whispered, shooting a look at Charlie, who I knew did not own a whoopie cushion.

He winked, which made me roll my eyes. And smile.

He'd been a huge pain in the ass all day, running amok with sarcasm and jokes and ridiculous wedding day games that were inappropriate and delightful. I'd beat him at the game where we'd each had to make up new words to "Here Comes the

Bride"—Nekesa and Aaron had been the judges—so as soon as we left the wedding, Charlie owed me a milkshake.

My entry, which was really lame:

> *Here comes the girl*
> *Who probably wants to hurl*
> *Everyone stares but she doesn't care*
> *Cuz she's getting hammered at the reception*

Charlie's entry, which didn't even rhyme and made mine look like a masterpiece:

> *Here comes the bride*
> *Doesn't she look nice*
> *Her dress has lace and she doesn't have lice*
> *Here comes the bride. Mic drop, bitches.*

So basically, Charlie had been doing his best—all day—to make sure I was distracted and okay as my mom got remarried.

Surprisingly, I was.

I still wasn't thrilled about the change, and I hadn't completely adjusted to living at Scott's house, but it wasn't as terrible as I'd imagined.

My stepsister, Lucy, was actually very sweet.

And she didn't get along with her mean cousin Kristy at *all*.

My phone buzzed and I looked down.

"You shouldn't be looking at your phone during a wedding," Charlie whispered, which made me *shh* him yet again as I clicked on the message.

Dad: You doing okay today, kid? Love you.

I swallowed, smiled, and put my phone back in my purse. I'd answer him when it was over. I sat back, beside Charlie, and watched as my mother married Scott. She looked blissfully happy, as did he, and as much as it pained me to admit it, they kind of seemed meant to be.

After the ceremony, the DJ started playing quiet music as the tiny crowd transitioned into reception mode. The event was happening in a banquet room at Planet Funnn, which the happy couple had selected because of my stellar employee discount, and everyone in the family was staying over so the group could enjoy the facilities all weekend long.

"You know," Charlie said as we slow-danced to an Ed Sheeran song, "this room is where we first met."

I looked at the stars on the ceiling and smiled, remembering our long days of training. "I think you're forgetting about the Fairbanks airport."

"Nope. This is the room where Charlie met Bailey," he said, his eyes moving over my face. "Before that, you were just Glasses and I was—"

"Mr. Nothing," I interrupted, laughing as I recalled Airport Charlie in that stupid shirt.

"I was Mr. Nothing," he finished. "Planet Funnn is where we first became friends."

I nodded, suffused with warm happiness. "And then we weren't."

"But now we are again," he said, lowering his head to murmur into my ear, "and now we're in love."

I giggled and quietly replied, "You *have* to stop saying that, Sampson."

"What?" He lifted his head and feigned frustrated innocence

with a tiny smile on his face. "I thought 'in love' was approved verbiage, but 'lovers' was not."

"'Lovers' *is* nausea-inducing." I leaned closer and inhaled, a little intoxicated by the close proximity of my face to his cologne—mmmmmm—and wondered how it was possible to be so happy. We'd been officially dating for only a few months, but it felt like so much longer because magically, nothing had changed. I mean, we kissed a lot more than before—duh—but he was still my best friend, still the person who was the most fun to spend time with.

I think we were both shocked that the boyfriend/girlfriend thing wasn't ruining the friendship. "But 'in love' is almost as bad. Maybe just say that you love me."

"Well, that seems one-sided and makes me sound desperate." He fake pouted, reaching out to toy with the strap on my dress.

"You know I'll say it back," I replied, lifting a hand so I could run a finger down the slope of his strong nose. "Come on."

"I love you, Glasses," he said, his voice rich with feeling as his dark eyes locked on mine.

"I love you, too, Mr. Nothing."

THE SOUNDTRACK OF
BAILEY AND CHARLIE

1 YOU'RE ON YOUR OWN, KID | Taylor Swift

2 ALL MY GHOSTS | Lizzy McAlpine

3 ALREADY OVER | Sabrina Carpenter

4 CRASH MY CAR | COIN

5 NOBODY KNOWS | THE DRIVER ERA

6 SMOKE SLOW | Joshua Bassett

7 ALL I WANT IS YOU | U2

8 I CAN'T BE YOUR FRIEND | Aidan Bissett

9 BEST FRIEND | Conan Gray

10 STRUCK BY LIGHTNING (FEAT. CAVETOWN) | Sara Kays, Cavetown

11 BREAK MY HEART AGAIN | FINNEAS

12 I COULD DO THIS ALL NIGHT | Ben Kessler

13 ALL THAT I'M CRAVING | Aidan Bissett

14 FRIEND | Gracie Abrams

15 KARMA | Taylor Swift

16 2AM | Landon Conrath

17 OVER TONIGHT | Stacey Ryan

18 ME MYSELF & I | 5 Seconds of Summer

19 KISS CAM | Zachary Knowles

20 OH SHIT . . . ARE WE IN LOVE? | Valley

21 FREQUENT FLYER | Devin Kennedy

22 LOWERCASE | Landon Conrath

https://open.spotify.com
/playlist/4hXl1LHn5oGNwgiXDDkl1D?si=5dee94e80c4e47c0

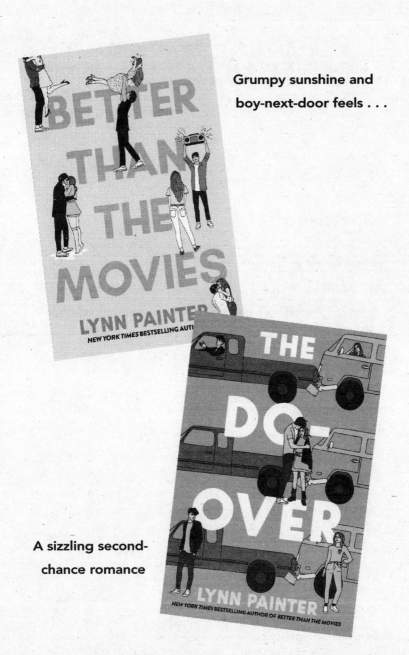

Grumpy sunshine and boy-next-door feels . . .

A sizzling second-chance romance

Wes had his dream girl but then he lost her.
The only way to get her back is to
scheme like a rom-com hero…

COMING OCTOBER 2024

ABOUT THE AUTHOR

Lynn Painter is the *New York Times* bestselling author of *Better Than the Movies*, *Mr. Wrong Number*, *The Do-Over*, and *The Love Wager*. She lives in Nebraska with her husband and pack of wild children, and when she isn't reading or writing, odds are good she's guzzling energy drinks and watching romcoms. You can find her at LynnPainter.com, on Instagram @LynnPainterBooks, on X @LAPainter, and on TikTok @ BookishlyPainter.